WARBOT 1.0

AI Goes To War

BRIAN M. MICHELSON

Warbot 1.0: AI Goes To War

Copyright © 2020 Brian M. Michelson
All rights reserved.
First edition published June 2020

Cover design: The Killion Group, Inc.
Image: This photo is in the public domain. Creator: Staff Sgt. Chris Hubenthal; Credit: Defense Media Activity-Forward Center Hawaii

ISBN: 978-1-68068-205-2

The characters and events portrayed in this book, except for factual historical references, are fictitious.

No part of this book may be reproduced or stored in a retrieval system, or transmitted in any form or by any means, electronic, mechanical, photocopying, recording or otherwise, without express written permission of the publisher.

This book is published by War Planet Press, an imprint of the Ethan Ellenberg Literary Agency.

You can reach the author at:
Facebook: https://www.facebook.com/BrianMichelsonAuthor
Website: https://brianmichelson.com
Email: Brian.michelson.author@gmail.com

DEDICATION

This book is dedicated to the young men and women who will fight the next wars. My hope is that this story will give them a few ideas of what to expect.

Acknowledgements

So many to thank...

This book would never have come into existence without my friend August Cole, who suggested I write a short story for the Art of the Future Project while we were at the Atlantic Council together. His mentorship and encouragement in this journey have been invaluable. To my wife for the "go for it" moment as I contemplated actually writing a novel. To my agent, Ethan Ellenberg, for believing in the book as much as I did. To Linda Sanders, Sharon Honeycutt and Raelene Gorlinsky for getting this from manuscript to "book". To my fellow authors Sean Naylor and Bill Rohm for their counsel, encouragement, and advice. And to Steve Sicinski and Scott Gress, my longsuffering beta readers, for their ideas, encouragement, and sanity checks. And to everyone else who helped me along the way...THANK YOU!

Table of Contents

Foreword · ix
Glossary · xi
Prologue · xv

Part 1: The Death of Homer · 1
Part 2: The Road to Hell · 55
Part 3: A Fine Mess ·135
Part 4: The Hard Way ·185
Part 5: Precipice · 259
Part 6: Apollyon ·317

Epilogue · 389

Ten Real-Life Heroes · 404
Recommended for Further Reading · · · · · · · · · · · · 409
About the Author ·411
About the Publisher ·415

Foreword

This is a true story, except that it happens in the near future. While the nature of war as a human endeavor has remained relatively consistent over time, the character of war is often determined by the basket of technologies available to the combatants at the time of the conflict. We are entering a period of rapid technological change that will create capabilities that will likely outstrip our prevailing institutional concepts of war at the tactical, operational and strategic levels. The intent of this book is not to accurately predict the future, but to stimulate current discussion by showing previews and movie trailers of what is in the realm of the possible.

Glossary

AI	Artificial intelligence
ALOC	Administrative and Logistics Operations Center, often referred to as the Admin Log Center; serves as a backup command post
APS	Automatic protection system
AR	Augmented reality; used heavily in command and control systems, especially helmets
ARM	Artificial intelligence/Robotic/Mechanized, a designator for specific units equipped with HOMRRs, Razorbacks and Buffalos versus older legacy systems
ATGM	Antitank guided missile
Battalion	Combat unit usually consisting of 4 to 6 companies; commanded by a lieutenant colonel
Brigade	Combat unit usually consisting of 4 to 6 battalions that serves as the basic building block of ground operations; after 2025, commanded by a brigadier general
Buffalo	A large eight-wheeled vehicle used as a mobile command and control node

Combat Units	4 to 5 platoons = 1 company 4 to 6 companies = 1 battalion 4 to 6 battalions = 1 brigade
Company	Combat unit usually consisting of 4 to 5 platoons; commanded by a captain. Maneuver companies in 2020 range in size from 80 to 120 personnel plus vehicles and weapons systems. In 2033, maneuver companies range from 18 to 35 personnel plus a higher number of vehicles and weapon systems relative to 2020 companies.
Commo	Abbreviation for "communications" and refers to the ability to communicate between two entities; also referred to as "comms"
COP	Common Operating Picture; a map showing all relevant unit, enemy and combat data
DIYA	A Chinese AI suite of combat systems
EMP	Electromagnetic pulse
Flechette	Small metal darts used as targeted shrapnel
HOMRR	Heavy Offensive Multi-Role Robot
HSDC	Headquarters, Support and Defense Company
JLTV	Joint Light Tactical Vehicle, a four-wheeled general utility vehicle, replacement for the HUMVEE
Klick	Slang for kilometer
Mike(s)	Slang for minute(s)
NCO	Non-commissioned officer: enlisted soldiers of the rank of corporal and higher

PDS	Point defense system, usually consisting of a combination of short-range lasers, microwave guns, antidrones and machine guns
Psyop	Psychological operations
ROE	Rules of engagement
S2	Intelligence officer at battalion and brigade level
S3	Operations officer at battalion and brigade level
Sabot	A high-velocity depleted uranium dart in a casing that enables the smaller dart to fit in a larger diameter, smooth bore barrel
Saga	Slang for Simplified Air Ground Intelligence Architecture (SAGIA); an AI enabled command, control and intelligence system
Stryker	An eight-wheeled multirole combat vehicle in service beginning in 2002
TOC	Tactical operations center; company command post
TAC	Tactical assault command post; often referred to as a TACP; battalion command post
XO	Executive officer, the second-in-command of brigade-, battalion-, and company-sized units

Prologue

From a recent online search for "How did the 2033 Sino-Pacific War begin?"

The war began on June 25, 2033, when Chinese forces stationed in the Philippines toppled the newly elected government of Philippine President James Davila. Previous Philippine administrations had allowed the Chinese to establish military bases in the Philippines in return for economic aid, but the relationship soured with the discovery of Chinese political meddling in the 2033, and earlier, elections. Diplomatic missteps on both sides deepened the crisis and inflamed nationalist sentiments in both countries. The Chinese press stoked the Chinese sense of national pride with articles about the "great insult" and resulting loss of face, while the Philippine press painted the Chinese as neo-economic colonialists. All the stories produced the predictable outrage on both sides of the South China Sea and incidentally, advertising revenue hit an all-time high during this period.

In what was to become a replay of the 1991 decision to eject the U.S. military from its strategic bases at Subic Bay and Clark Air Force Base, President Davila ordered the Chinese military out of the country. His timing could not have been worse. Taiwan had moved to the very brink of declaring independence, Vietnam and other Southeast

Asian nations continued to chafe under Chinese "Belt and Road" economic concessions, and Japanese rearmament was causing an arms race that the Chinese could ill afford.

By mid-May 2033, the Chinese Communist Party (CCP) Central Committee was in crisis. They reasoned that if a relatively weak nation of 130 million on the far side of the South China Sea could defy and embarrass them, then Taiwan, barely 90 miles away and with only 27 million people, would see the situation as a green light for independence. The CCP reasoned that the other nations in Southeast Asia would feel emboldened and possibly renege on strategic basing and economic agreements. Even worse, a loss of credibility now could cause major unrest in China and threaten CCP rule, something not seriously done since the 1940s. The CCP Central Committee approved an ultimatum to the Philippines in what amounted to a modern version of the Melian Dialogue: submit or be destroyed. Yet China underestimated the Filipinos, who refused to submit. The CCP was now trapped in a high-stakes bluff that had just been called on the international stage.

Despite the increasing risks, the CCP Central Committee chose to follow through on their threat. By the end of June 2033, the Pacific was in the throes of a limited but new type of war in which military forces of humans, their AI support networks, and robotic systems fought a desperate battle for military and political supremacy.

NEW YORK CITY TO LOS ANGELES:
4,472 KM / 2,795 MILES

LOS ANGELES TO MANILA:
11,667 KM / 7,292 MILES

RUSSIA

CANADA

New York
UNITED STATES
Los Angeles

CHINA

Manila
PHILIPPINES

PACIFIC OCEAN

AUSTRALIA

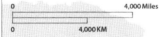

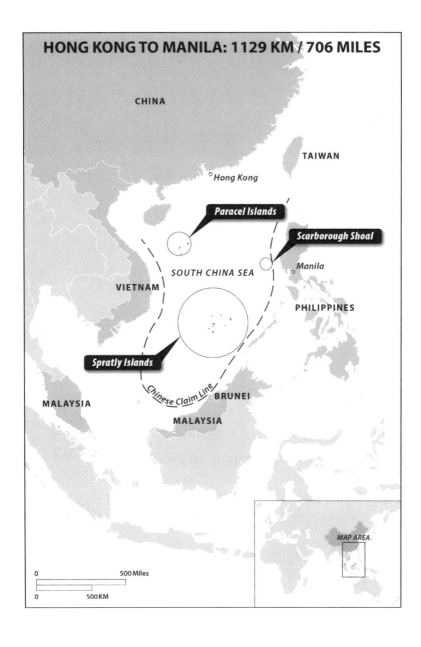

Part 1: The Death of Homer

"Artificial intelligence is the future, not only of Russia, but of all mankind. Whoever becomes the leader in this sphere will become ruler of the world."
~ Vladimir Putin, 2017

1.0

161300HSEP2033 (1:00 p.m. local time, September 16, 2033) 80 km northwest of Manila, the Philippines

Captain Stacy Doss felt the urge to yell to Homer, to ask him if he was okay, but that was stupid because he was dead, which made it highly unlikely that he would answer. Her favorite platoon leader was gone. Stacy felt her command helmet slip through her fingers and heard the clunk as it hit the ground. As a company commander in the U.S. Army, the weight of command started to settle on her with its full impact. Her mind was racing as she came to grips with what had just happened. Squinting in the bright sunshine, she felt the hot, humid, stagnant air fill her lungs.

Did I miss something? Could I have done better? Was it my fault? she thought to herself.

As she slowly stood up, she felt a bead of sweat run down her back. After making sure no one was watching, she quickly wiped a tear from her eye.

I need to find him. I owe it to him. At least to pay my respects…

1.1

Four hours earlier…
Captain Mike McGinnis, the Bravo company commander, tapped the screen and began his transmission to the battalion operations officer.

"Viper 3, this is Bull 6, crossing phase line Tango in three minutes, will advise when we have objective Red Sox secured, over."

"Roger out," came the quick reply from the battalion's operations officer.

Stacy heard the call, checked her display and saw Mike's unit deployed perfectly, textbook even, on her right flank with his command vehicle squarely in the center of his column. Stacy noted that her vehicle icons were well spaced, but slightly less evenly than his. They were still sixteen kilometers north of the city of Tarlac, and the roads were getting worse.

Good tactically and while not always right, he's never in doubt…about himself anyway, she thought to herself. Wish I had a little more of that.

Stacy exhaled, adjusted her brown ponytail under her helmet, and noticed an ever-so-slight tremble in her left hand. She was told in training that it was a common reaction to stress and, in a nervous habit, began fiddling with the engagement ring hanging from her dog tags. She blinked long and hard, her eyes burning from fatigue and allergies, and the Augmented Reality (AR) display in her command helmet quickly came back into focus. As an untested commander in an untested unit, she hadn't expected to be here.

But here I am, she thought.

Stacy's command vehicle shuddered slightly as the left side began rolling over a deeper-than-expected shell crater. Her company Tactical Operations Center, or TOC, was housed in a vehicle commonly known as a Buffalo because of the way the vehicles wallowed over obstacles, even small ones. She waited for all four of the top-heavy vehicle's left side wheels to clear the obstacle, took a deep breath, and transmitted to Mike on an internal channel.

"Bull 6, this is Apache 6, be advised our scouts are having difficulty maintaining contact. The Chinese might be attempting to disengage. We're also getting some intermittent jamming and have to move on Objective Cubs a bit slower than planned."

Mike's only response was a brief, poor attempt at humor. "Chicken."

Really? she thought. It didn't occur to her at the moment that he might have been feeling the pressure too.

Stacy looked back at her virtual command screens. In the dim light of her rolling TOC, she could see the other seven members of her team who helped manage the nearly overwhelming streams of data pouring into their AR helmets. She had been training for this—the crucible of combat, the ultimate test of skills, experience, and character—since her commissioning in 2027. As she looked around and took a quick inventory of the situation, she hoped she was at least ready enough for whatever was next.

The TOC's interior, typical of forward-deployed command posts, smelled of the familiar potpourri of sweaty uniforms, body odor, flatulence, coffee, dip, and leftover food that someone inevitably spills on the floor and then seeps beneath the aluminum floor panels. Combat meals had a certain consistency across the decades, and the ones that made it to the floor always seemed to be the worst-smelling of all the possibilities. Today the reek of reconstituted tuna casserole dominated the stale air. Stacy caught a whiff and grimaced slightly.

With a few moves of her hologlove, Stacy ran the routine counter-jamming protocol and then paused briefly as she thought about how to push her scout platoon out farther. As one of the battalion's lead units, she knew she still had to get a better feel for where the enemy was and what they were doing.

So far, not much different than the simulations, she caught herself thinking.

Although the latest version of the Mission Command software still had some teething issues, it was a huge step forward from the very first version, which had been an unmitigated disaster. The Army's second attempt was only slightly better, and it wasn't until the Army brought in an augmented-reality gaming company that the system improved dramatically.

Stacy studied the AR display pensively and from the multitude of angles allowed by the 3D image. Slowly, tentatively, she moved her right hand, encased in the hologlove, to the location of the scout platoon icon. Grabbing it gently, she moved it to another part of the map and then released it. The scout platoon icon settled on the map as a future position along with a route of march, time estimate for arrival, and expected reconnaissance radius.

"Maybe that's where they're hiding," she said in a barely audible voice as she touched the "confirm" icon.

Her scout platoon leader received the order and would begin to execute it within the intent and engagement parameters issued three days ago in her formal operations.

This order was also automatically CC'd to her higher headquarters. This created the opportunity for dynamic tension as the idea of "disciplined initiative" remained easy to say, but harder to execute when a headquarters could electronically eavesdrop on nearly any subordinate unit in real time. Fortunately, her battalion commander, Lieutenant Colonel Richard "Buck" Gammon, known as Viper 6, was a case study in "old-school" professional restraint, a philosophy he imposed ruthlessly on his staff.

"Let commanders command," he would often say. "Staffs need to enable them to take disciplined initiative, not be afraid of it! Besides, what's going to happen when they can't communicate? If we have trained them to be timid instead of bold, we will have failed."

Major Megan Bennett, the battalion operations officer, or S3, and the rest of the operations and intelligence staff were with Gammon another ten kilometers farther north in the battalion's Tactical Assault Command Post or TAC. Major Bennett, Viper 3, and her operations team were tracking the movement, intel feeds, and pretty much everything else from all three of the battalion's line companies, its Recon and Strike Company, and its Headquarters, Support and Defense Company. While the "All Seeing Eye" enabled by her software permissions was a risk in some situations, it also enabled her as a competent S3 to serve as a magician, amplifying her ability to make sense of massive amounts of data—much of it contradictory—and still orchestrate complex battalion operations in real time. This also meant that Bennett had plenty of other things to do and was simply not interested in electronically hovering over Mike, Stacy and the other commanders at the moment.

Stacy turned her attention to her team and queried her intel specialist sitting at his console a few meters away.

"Smitty, what do we have on the Chinese scouts?"

"Hey, ma'am, hard to say right now," replied Specialist Five Jonathan Smith, a short, squat man from New York City with an exceptionally thick Bronx accent and a permanent five o'clock shadow. Smitty had remarkable strength of character demonstrated by his avowed citizenship in the Red Sox nation, which had nearly resulted in conflict with his family bordering on excommunication. "But I think that based on the intel feeds, it's going to be a cat-and-mouse game among the scouts. Kinda like a blind man with excellent hearing trying to find a deaf man with excellent eyesight in a dimly lit room."

"What?" she asked, trying to decipher the indirect response through his thick accent.

"I tried to frame it in terms of our scouts' better thermals and optics, and their better acoustic sensors. I'm working on analogies this week," he responded.

The two lead scout vehicles were already creeping forward, mindful of the ever-present uncertainty and danger, but eager to find the enemy. Like its Vietnam-era predecessor, the Sheridan II armored reconnaissance vehicle was not designed to stand and fight, but to find the enemy, hide when it could, and if discovered, run like hell. It was a repurposed eight-wheeled Stryker vehicle capable of a top speed of ninety-seven kilometers per hour and whose most prominent feature was a lumpy, vaguely head-shaped sensor pod with a large thermal/optical sensor in the center. The bulbous pod was attached to "the snake," a thin boom of articulated segments that was capable of bending enough to move the pod around obstacles and through both windows and doors; it could also extend fifteen meters above the vehicle to offer a view above most trees and small buildings. This pod was the inspiration for the vehicle's goofy nickname, Cyclops. While not especially fear-inspiring, the name stuck with the troops and thus could never be undone.

In addition to the sensor pod, each scout vehicle was equipped with multifunction ground and air drone racks, unlike most late-model vehicles, which were equipped with single, but more capable, air drones. When it came to combat vehicle design and drone augmentation, the choice between disposable swarming insects and more capable mammals was still an ongoing debate among both troops and weapon designers.

The two scouts had just started deploying their booms when Smitty noticed that their electronic transmission feeds back to the TOC went blank.

"Hey, ma'am, this ain't good. They just clicked off or something. Best guess is EMP mines."

Of course they seeded the route with them, Stacy thought to herself.

Muttering a string of mild expletives under her breath, Stacy reported back to the battalion TAC that while the actual damage was probably minimal, replacing a few fried parts and rebooting a few systems would take three to five minutes. With the data links to her higher headquarters still operational, Gammon, Bennett and the rest of the staff saw the loss of real-time situational awareness, or "blink," in real time.

The hair on Lieutenant Colonel Richard "Buck" Gammon's neck began to stand up when he saw the blink, and for good reason. He wasn't the only commander hard at work, on a timeline, or dealing with political constraints.

"All right, Yu, let's get it on."

1.2

1609150HSEP2033 (9:15 a.m. local time, September 16, 2033) Chinese National Assistance Task Force Headquarters, Manila, the Philippines

Major General Yu Jai Bin of the People's Liberation Army, or PLA, was roughly the American equivalent of a Brigadier General. His Western acquaintances had commented that the literal translation of his rank was "Junior General," which seemed like an odd name for a military rank. To this he had responded that "Junior General" was technically more accurate in terms of function and lack of prestige than the American term Brigadier General.

While he may have secretly doubted the wisdom of the aggressive political decisions of the party, he considered himself a patriotic professional and would carry out his orders to the best of his ability. *Besides,* he reasoned to himself, *the perks of being a general aren't bad, and the paycheck covers most of my wife's insatiable shopping bills. And that turd, Commissar Xi, will be watching my every move to ensure that I remain "ideologically pure." He'll turn on me in a heartbeat if it serves his own interests.*

For his part, Commissar Xi had an incredibly annoying habit of repeating Mao's trite phrase, "The party commands the gun." It was his way of reminding Yu that the PLA was the armed wing of the Chinese Communist Party, of which Xi was a member, and therefore not merely a national army.

Regardless, Yu thought, *success in this campaign will improve my chances for promotion. I deserve it after all this time in this mosquito-infested shit hole.*

To ensure that all went according to plan and that the promotion would be his, Yu had seen to the smallest of details, and none were too small for his attention. While he had heard rumors that his staff and his deputy, Colonel Deng, called him a nano-manager behind his back, he really didn't care what they thought; he was in charge. He knew they would soon see why he insisted on such attention to detail.

Kill the chicken to scare the monkey, Yu thought to himself. *Those morons in Beijing certainly didn't quite do that.*

The senior Chinese leadership had expected that, after making an example of the uncooperative Philippine government, the other nations on the periphery of the South China Sea would be far more open to Chinese diplomatic overtures. They also expected that no outside nation would choose to intervene in the aftermath of what would effectively be a *fait accompli.* Unfortunately for Yu, these two assumptions were not working out quite as planned.

How could we have gotten them so wrong? he silently fumed. *Incompetence at the top may yet cost us dearly.*

Looking at his digital map, he noted with disgust that the Allied invasion fleet landed at sites on the northwest side of Luzon, the same sites used by the Japanese in 1941 under Lieutenant General Masaharu Homma, and then by the Americans in 1945 under General Walter Krueger. *How ironic,* he thought. *The Japanese were the first ones to join the coalition, then the Australians and the Kiwis. Then once there was a sufficient safety net, several of the small debtor nations who defaulted on their Belt and Road obligations followed along as well. Ingrates.*

Yu's Intelligence Officer, Lieutenant Colonel Lee, had told him that the American forces would likely follow the Tarlac-Pangasinan-La Union Expressway southeast to Manila prior to a presumed attack on the capital. Yu had opted for a forward mobile defense and carefully chose an attack at the location where the expressway came closest to the Tarlac River. If successful, he would pin the Americans against the river, raise the cost of their intervention, and most importantly, buy him time. After carefully marshaling a battalion of T100s near the village of Guimba for three days, he was ready.

The Type 100 Main Combat Vehicle, or T100, was a marvel of Chinese engineering, and its numbering bore a special significance to the Century of Humiliation. It was fast and effective, and due to the modular design of its hardware and software, capable of both mass production and progressive automation. Its eight independently electrically driven and steered wheels were powered by a hybrid diesel-electric drive, and it carried a deadly 125mm cannon along with a coaxially mounted machine gun.

As he stood to address his task force staff, he was not even aware of his right index finger as it nervously scratched at the cuticle of his thumbnail. He began speaking in the flat, dull, nasal tone he was known for.

"Today we begin what will indeed be a historic engagement. As the vanguard of the People's Liberation Army, we will engage the forces of the Western Pacific Alliance. While the enemy's commitment of ground forces was an unfortunate turn of events, we shall make their intervention even more expensive for them, wear down their domestic political will, and use them as live targets to test new technologies and tactics. The results will inform our decision-making in the later, decisive phase of this conflict. We will show the world that the People's Liberation Army is now the most sophisticated, effective ground force on the planet."

Yu paused for a moment, then said simply, "And now, let us begin."

He looked down at his thumb. It was bleeding.

This "blink" had been all General Yu needed to insert twenty-seven targeting drones ahead of his main force. The drones, though older quadcopters of the Ningxia type, were still reasonably effective and derived their name from a 1949 battle in the Chinese Civil War. The Ningxias zipped past the blinded American scouts with a dull whirr as they snaked over and through the foliage, settling—or in some cases crashing—into predesignated locations throughout the expected battlefield. Even if their camouflage was only marginally effective and nearly twenty percent became disabled after entering the dense foliage, they were cheap and did their jobs well. Such was the beauty of embracing disposability.

In quick succession, PLA combat vehicles began emerging in rapid succession from physically and electronically camouflaged assembly areas. The second T100 combat vehicle to exit Assembly Area 29 miscalculated and rolled over one of the small electromagnetic static generators with a loud crunch. As it left the relative safety of the electronic camouflage net, the T100 activated its individual, but less effective, jammer. They would need only about four minutes to cover the seven kilometers to engagement range.

General Yu watched the battle's preamble carefully. The PLA Navy and Air Force, operating out of bases on the mainland and several of the man-made islands in the South China Sea's Great Wall of Sand, would be of little help to him. While they managed to sink several of the invading ships in the Lingayen Gulf, their losses in the opening phase of the conflict and new demands in keeping the Strait of Malacca open gave him little hope of significant support.

To make matters worse, Yu had very limited access to the few Chinese reconnaissance satellites that had survived the opening days of the conflict.

It's okay though, he told himself. *The Americans are more reliant on them than we are. They're spoiled with their technology and emotionally dependent on seeing everything in real time. So now they will cling to their tactical drones like prized possessions.*

But he had a plan for them too. Yu looked down at the status report. The icon for his ground-based air defense laser battery was showing green.

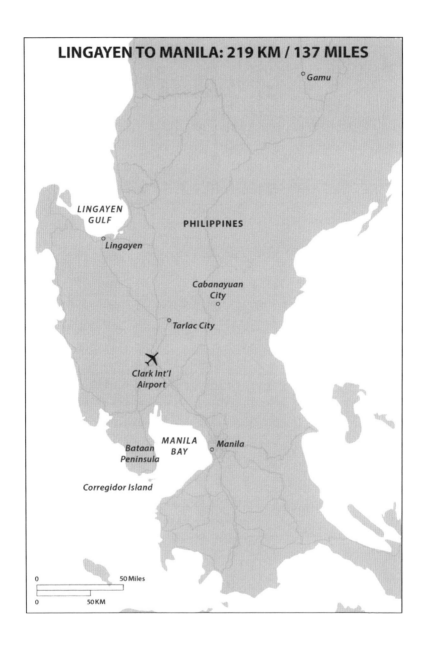

1.3

160930HSEP2033 (9:30 a.m. local time, September 16, 2033) 1st Battalion TAC, 95 km Northwest of Manila, the Philippines

The crew of Lieutenant Colonel Gammon's TAC grew quiet as they watched the video feed on Kill TV, as it was known. For anyone without an AR helmet, it simply looked like everyone wearing one was staring off in a random direction.

Even with the dingy white walls fully extended when the vehicle was stationary, the command post wasn't ever roomy. Now, with the vehicle on the move and the extensions retracted, the workspaces were cramped at best for anyone over six feet tall.

The medium-sized Griffon drone peered into the distance and began its slow arc in the direction of Apache Company. No one was quite sure what was about to happen, but they kept one eye on the left flank where Captain Doss and her company were. Major Bennett saw it first.

"Sir, I'm not sure what that is, but it doesn't look good. You need to see this."

She quickly manipulated the command screens with her hologloves as Lieutenant Colonel Gammon slid into his command console. Until a few moments ago, he had been attempting to pour a cup of lousy coffee in the back of the jostling vehicle with the Executive Officer, Major Mark Verault. The spilled coffee added a slightly pleasant aroma to the vehicle's interior.

Bennett was an exceptionally competent S3, having placed first in her year group's competition for entrance into the Command and General Staff College. In addition to seeking the usual physical, mental, and character traits expected of future leaders, the school assessed a candidate's ability to achieve situational understanding based on multiple electronic inputs, and then hyper-task responses. It was essentially a giant computer game.

She was also a borderline workaholic and expected—or, more correctly, demanded—a lot from her junior officers. She didn't come off particularly harsh, but a few of the junior captains figured that anyone at the rank of major or above couldn't possibly understand what was really going on tactically. The fact that she had been one of these smart-ass captains only three years ago was not lost on her.

"What do you think?" Gammon asked her.

"Still not sure, sir. Might be a probe, might be an attack. We'll need a few more minutes to figure it out."

Gammon continued looking pensively at the integrated Common Operating Picture, or COP. He shifted off his weak leg, a wound from his lieutenant days, and rolled his wrist inside the black aluminum band he habitually wore on his left arm. Gammon quickly scanned what was essentially an interactive AR map that displayed all known information about friendly forces and their condition, supply and ammunition status, the terrain, civilian structures and population, weather, and the enemy. Touching a couple images with his hologlove, Gammon adjusted a few parameters and settled back in his console. As he pulled off his command helmet, the images disappeared, and he began scratching behind his ear. He wiped his sweaty forehead with the back of his sleeve and took a deep breath, which he slowly exhaled. Looking at his command helmet, he mused that even the term "helmet" was a misnomer. It offered virtually no ballistic protection and was really little more than a headset with integrated glasses and a bit of protective Kevlar to hold it all together.

"Full screen," he said. "Get me a visual with the brigade commander, followed by the Chief of Staff."

The old-school 3D image generator came to life, and soon the face of Gammon's boss, the Brigade Combat Team commander, appeared. Brigadier General Viale was a capable leader who had been commissioned as the wars in Iraq and Afghanistan were winding down. Gammon noted that not only did Viale seem to hate having to use AR helmets and hologloves, he also appeared almost clumsy with them.

Should have played a few more rounds of Fortnite or Overwatch, Gammon mused to himself. *But I do appreciate his bluntness and earthy humor.*

"Buck, our turd just lost a little more of its frosting. You saw the latest update from the Joint Chiefs of Staff. We were sent to accomplish a mission, but the President's casualty tolerance has moved to somewhere near zero. Body bags on the news will collapse political will faster than a punctured whoopie cushion. If that happens, this all may be for naught, as well as the sacrifices so far..." Viale's voice tapered off slightly, as if he were momentarily distracted. "Just be careful, whatever you do. Don't get decisively engaged before we get the Philippine Army to the gates of Manila."

"Roger, sir. We'll do our best to stay out of trouble," responded Gammon.

They quickly concluded the discussion, and as Viale's image faded out, another face emerged. "How's it going, Buck?"

Colonel John P. Gruninger was the Brigade's Chief of Staff. He had the insanely difficult job of not only corralling the staff chaos around him, but also making the central nervous system of the unit work so that the "Team of Teams" wouldn't act like it had epilepsy. Without a doubt, it was a brutal, thankless job.

Gammon and Gruninger had been close friends since their lieutenant days. John, a year senior to Buck, was a gifted leader who moved up the ranks quickly. Buck had noted years ago that Gruninger had the rare ability to be immediately trusted by nearly everyone he met.

"Buck," Gruninger began, "we've lost some of our intel platforms, so our situational awareness kinda sucks right now. The Chinese got a couple more of our drone resupply ships in the gulf, so our supply situation is still iffy. Don't expect it to improve. The other battalions burned through a lot more drones than we expected moving inland, and I doubt you'll get more Lances for a while."

"Roger, sir," Gammon replied. "The attack's progressing adequately. My company commanders are motivated, but Doss and Hester are still pretty green."

The bags under Gruninger's eyes and the furrow in his forehead told Gammon that the chief of staff was under intense pressure. Just before deployment, the brigade had been equipped with several new systems and software applications that weren't quite ready for prime time. This left about half the brigade's subunits with older legacy vehicles and technology, while the other half had brand-new classes of combat vehicles and systems.

"I've got the new CTO, Colonel McClellan, here with me also. Any questions for him?"

The Chief Technical Officer was a new position in the brigade. While the CTO lacked operational experience, this really wasn't his fault. He was an Acquisition Officer by trade and had been pulled on short notice for the deployment from an Army Technical Liaison unit in Silicon Valley. His value to the unit was that he was far better equipped than the other senior leaders in the brigade to understand the "magic" and get it to work.

"Roger, sir, just one. How confident are you in the new algorithms and the command interface? I mean, what do we need to watch out for at a command level? We didn't even have time to fully test it before we shipped out."

As soon as he asked the question, Buck knew it was a mistake. Colonel McClellan was, by the looks of him, an anxious, introverted man whose unibrow gave him an odd, almost alien look. As he prepared to answer the question, his face became slightly indignant, and Gammon began to wonder if someone offscreen was inserting a broomstick up McClellan's rectum.

"Lieutenant Colonel Gammon," he said in a stiff, formal tone, "it is simply an update to the program. It merely tweaks the algorithm to ensure better accuracy in real-time decisions and to increase the ability of higher headquarters to intervene before things get out of control. Regarding variable autonomy capabilities, that will be up to you and your fellow commanders to set the policy. In a technical sense, it will be easy."

"Roger, sir, thank you. Nothing further," Gammon replied, internally rolling his eyes.

Never answered the technical question in useful terms, Buck thought. *Never been a commander, so he might not really even understand the question. Not his fault, might not even be a knowable answer...*

Thanks to ubiquitous information sharing in real time, stories abounded of soldiers, small-unit leaders, and commanders getting extra "help" from higher commanders and staffs at inopportune times. During a rotation to the National Training Center at Fort Irwin, California, Buck had been a company commander and tormented by his battalion commander, PSYCHO 6, and his accomplice/operations officer, Ming the Merciless. They peered over his shoulder in real time, offering a constant stream of directives without understanding the actual situation on the ground as he fought back the hordes of Krasnovians.

Unfortunately, the battalion was crushed because Psycho and Ming were so busy doing his job that they failed to do theirs and orchestrate the larger battle. Gammon noted wryly that at the other end of the spectrum was the currently prevailing view that, with the availability of real-time situational awareness, junior leaders no longer needed traditional command and control oversight during combat operations. A well-practiced ability to execute discretionary judgment was assumed, when in the past, it was expected to be a skill requiring practice and development.

Gammon was glad to see his friend, but both had more things to do than time available, and they quickly ended the conversation. As the image faded, Gammon muttered to himself, "There were probably discussions like this just prior to the court-martial of Captain Jenkins."

The recklessness of Captain Leeroy Jenkins was legendary, and Gammon bitterly remembered testifying at his well-deserved court-martial. Justice was done, but forty-three soldiers served as payment for an expensive lesson in the cost of overly hands-off battalion and brigade commanders.

Lieutenant Colonel Gammon turned his attention back to the present, put his AR helmet back on, and considered the current situation. The Satellite and Air tabs in his display were red.

"That sucks," he muttered to himself. "But only half-blind…"

"Say again, sir?" responded Bennett, the S3.

She had been about to adjust the AR display to a new "unknown" icon and had stopped. It was bad form to manipulate the COP's display while your boss was looking at it.

"Nothing, please continue," responded Gammon.

Bennett's glove had level-two authorities, and she used it to quickly zoom in to the area that was flashing red as the unknown. Computers were excellent for determining firing solutions, figuring out logistical requirements, and in this case, detecting anomalies, but the designers couldn't program intuition. Despite all the advances in AI, computers sometimes remained idiot savants in that they had difficulty understanding and adapting to complex and novel events—like this one—which was why they still had to be trained.

"What is it?" asked Gammon.

"Not sure yet, sir. I'll move the Griffon in closer."

With a few deft moves of Bennett's hologlove, the Griffon started to alter its course and arc toward the flashing "unknown" icon. Even on full magnification, those assembled in the cramped area couldn't figure out what they were looking at.

By habit, everyone was expecting Captain Luke M. Olive, the S2 / Intelligence officer (the "2" for short), to produce an epiphany at any moment. Olive was a bookish twenty-six-year-old from Baltimore who constantly pored over the AI screens that fed the AR COP's presentation of the tactical situation. One of the youngest and newest members of the team, he was fresh out of the Captain's Career Course and wasn't exactly a charismatic leader of soldiers. There was no strong chin, no commanding voice, and no broad shoulders. What he did have was an uncanny knack for interfacing with the Simplified Air Ground Intelligence Architecture, or SAGIA, the successor of the oddly named Distributed Common Ground System–Army, or DCGS-A. Since the early days of Siri, Alexa, and Watson, young troops had a knack for personifying Army AI programs with "cool" names. In this case, SAGIA quickly became Saga, the Norse goddess of wisdom.

Luke was adept at training Saga and improving her ability to cue his fellow humans to anomalies, ferret out the important details from a sea of the mundane, and connect the dots in near real time.

"Hey Saga," Luke spoke softly into his helmet's tiny microphone, "how much uncertainty is in the Apache Company sector and why?"

Saga responded into his earpiece and visually on his screen with information, cues and depictions. He had even trained Saga to tailor her feedback to his learning and data-intake style. He was still mentally processing the information when the boss interrupted.

"Hey 2," Lieutenant Colonel Gammon asked, "anything solid on the enemy?"

Luke cleared his throat and replied quickly. "Negative, sir, but something isn't right. Saga is showing medium uncertainty in the Apache Company's sector. They had a few small EMP detonations go off about a minute ago. The social media feed only has two clips uploaded by some Filipino teenagers about ten minutes ago. They were of a couple small quadcopters flying by that looked like the usual disposable recon drones. I'm also seeing more text evidence that civilians have been rapidly moving out of the sector due to periods of the 'brown sound.' Might be why we don't see more info from the civil information feed. We're also getting indicators that there might be some sort of electronic camouflage in place. We still don't have overhead satellite help, so it's a little tougher to figure out what's going on."

The "brown sound" was a reference to a specific frequency and intensity of sound that caused humans to become quite uncomfortable. Sound generators were commonly used in several militaries as a convenient, nonlethal way to influence civilians to depart from an area and occasionally to make enemy forces consider the same course of action. When applied for a sufficient amount of time and at the correct frequency, it eventually made humans defecate uncontrollably. While it had a real name and nomenclature, the device was affectionately known by the troops as the SSG, or Shit Storm Generator. There was even a recorded instance of a lieutenant who was court-martialed after he got drunk and pointed one at his unit's headquarters. The court-martial was reportedly as amusing as it was legendary.

Gammon smiled at the reference to the brown sound and continued his line of questioning. "What's your guess? And how much longer before you'll have better resolution?"

"The data's pretty thin, sir. My guess is that it's deliberate. Saga is running the permutations and once we get a Rosetta Stone piece of data, things will clarify very quickly. In theory, of course."

"Roger, thanks," Gammon responded.

Buck was about to offer Olive a word of encouragement regarding his task and the importance of it, but by the time he said, "thanks," Olive was back in his own head and continuing his argument with Saga.

Marveling briefly at the scene before him—humans interacting with other humans and AI systems—Buck thought, *Guess this is what Centaur teaming is at its best. All this stuff is great, but I hope the brass and the policy wonks don't get so enamored with the tech and the idea of an antiseptic war that they forget that it always comes down to the people who have to fight. It always comes down to the people...*

Buck moved the few meters from Olive's station back to his command chair and slumped into it. His back was bothering him again, and he shifted uncomfortably in the seat as he surveyed his staff hard at work. *Good kids, all of 'em. Proud to be on the same team with them.*

Buck hated waiting for anything, but he knew he would have to be patient and give them some time to develop the situation. He twirled the black metal band on his left wrist for a moment. *Not much I can do right now, sooooo...*

Buck pulled up his M10 Personal Communicator and turned it on. A militarized version of an iPhone 17, M10s could not transmit directly out of the Army WAN and cell networks, but they enabled soldiers to accept personal notes from specific people, like spouses, significant others, kids and parents. Periodically, and for very discrete time periods, brief calls were permitted, and queued-up messages would be sent out when bandwidth allowed. All this fell under the justification of troop morale, and in the current information environment, it also had the added benefit of calming concerned loved ones who were seeing combat footage in near real time.

He was pleased when he saw a note from his wife, Julia. Even the title promised a welcome diversion: Criminal Activity, Volume 3.

"Hello Loverboy," it began, and his mind started to drift toward home until Major Bennett interrupted with a routine report that required his thumbprint for approval.

"Note from home?" she asked as he placed his thumb on the pad.

"Roger, how could you tell?"

"The big grin, sir. More criminal activity?"

"Always."

As Bennett turned and moved back to her station, Buck quickly surveyed the situation. Nothing needed his immediate attention, so he returned to the welcome note.

"So let me tell you what our criminals did with the dog, who has been renamed."

Uh-oh, he thought.

The kids had been begging for a dog for years, but Julia had put up a strong resistance. After a long psychological operations campaign that Buck had secretly orchestrated with the kids, they finally bent her formidable will and got the okay just before the deployment, which had been used shamelessly to tip the scales in their favor. With a quick trip to the pound, they had a dog that appeared to be a cross between a Labrador retriever and a husky. The dog was sweet but skittish, and his personality had yet to fully emerge, making it difficult to give him a proper name. Various names including Ranger, Booger, Ruff, Rufus, and others had been considered, argued about, and rejected. With still no consensus, he was currently referred to as "Doggie."

"I was at the commissary," Julia continued, "and Nate was in charge. That was my first mistake. Teenage boys should never be expected to supervise ANYTHING involving health and safety issues. It appears that Jenna found your clippers and had previously noted the basics of how they worked when I gave you your haircuts. Lucy, of course, will do anything Jenna tells her to do and was along for the ride as a co-conspirator. I came back to the house with a car full of groceries only to discover that Doggie now had a fashionable new look. Jenna had given him a bath, with lots of shampoo, in our tub, and then given him a stylish haircut. She even used an entire can of hairspray. And this is why, by universal acclimation, his name is now Mohawk."

Awesome! Buck thought. *But better send her a quick and comforting note to cover my tracks… and then congratulate the kids on the new name.*

1.4

161000HSEP2033 (10:00 a.m. local time, September 16, 2033) Chinese National Assistance Task Force Headquarters, Manila

Major General Yu was pleased and began to fidget with the nervous energy of someone who had consumed one too many stimulant drinks. He scratched at his right thumb as he looked at the displays and prepared to begin his attack.

"Let's now see how our national investments in high energy lasers pay off," he said in a flat tone, attempting to restrain his nervous energy. "Fire!" he added with obvious enthusiasm.

The forward laser defense battery targeted a lone American drone moving toward them in a slow arc. The laser burned a hole smaller than a pea through the fuselage, and the smoking drone spiraled down like a wounded bird. Yu hoped it had not seen his T100s as their diesel-electric drives roared and the vehicles surged forward, guns at the ready. Only the slightly premature EMP mine detonations could have given the enemy any warning.

Led by three recon vehicles, twenty-seven T100s raced forward at full speed down the road-and-trail network that would lead them to the Tarlac River and the highway that ran alongside it. They travelled quickly past rice fields, tall sugarcane stalks, and stubby trees that were far too short to provide them with meaningful concealment. Their support platoon of vehicles akin to misfit toys tagged along behind the force like a little brother trying to keep up with the big kids. The targeting drones, hidden in tree canopies, assisted the scouts in finding one of the American machines temporarily stunned by an EMP mine. They passed the information to the lead T100, which fired on the move and scored a direct hit, the single sabot round punching cleanly through both sides of the enemy's hull while leaving a trail of wreckage inside the vehicle. The T100 fired again with an explosive HEAT round to make certain the vehicle was destroyed.

With no other sightings, they were within ten kilometers of the main road and what they expected would be the flank of the Allied advance.

All is proceeding according to plan, Yu thought with a degree of satisfaction.

1.5

161015HSEP2033 (10:15 a.m. local time, September 16, 2033) Apache Company TOC, vicinity the Tarlac River, The Philippines

Stacy felt multiple beads run down her back as she shifted in her command console. Then she saw it. One scout vehicle, Ranger 1, was not responding and assumed lost. A second one, Ranger 2, had just come back online and was providing a rapid feed to her and the rest of the team in her tiny command post as multiple unidentified red icons appeared in their helmets.

Ranger 2 quickly lofted his Sentinel quadcopter and focused his mast-mounted sensors on the lead vehicles of the enemy column. Stacy took the real-time feed from Ranger 2's Sentinel and quickly picked out the distinct eight-wheeled silhouette of a T100. The turret of the lead one, with its 125mm cannon, looked like it was pointing right at her, and in a sense it was while she shared Ranger 2's point of view. She also noticed that Major Bennett was briefly sharing the same view and then quickly clicked out.

Stacy was starting to breathe more heavily and had to remind herself, *take a deep breath, then call the boss. Don't rush it. He can see this in his helmet too.*

"Viper 6, this is Apache 6. I think this is the front end of a sizable Chinese force. Maneuvering the company left to make contact and engage. Over."

This was turning into a meeting engagement, one of the most dangerous maneuvers in ground warfare, and her first real engagement since taking company command. If Stacy had had a moment to reflect, she would have been terrified by the possibility of screwing up. If she failed to hear something, see something, understand something, or respond quickly enough, part of her team might suffer. Maybe die. But she didn't have a moment to reflect, which was good.

"Roger, Apache 6, gain and maintain contact, but don't become decisively engaged, at least until we get the rest of the battalion in a better position to support you," Gammon replied.

Stacy's hands moved rapidly over the holomap as she gave maneuver instructions and new firing parameters to the platoon leaders. With only three platoons of four vehicles left, she knew she had to be careful to conserve her forces. She instructed the two mechanized platoons to set up a screen line, while Homer's platoon of "heavies" would move to block any penetrations.

So what are you up to, General Yu? she wondered.

Stacy didn't try to be clever—there was no time for it. She simply tried to get forces to logical locations, close enough to support each other, and get them there as fast as possible.

As she worked, Stacy caught herself silently repeating, *Understand, then act. And do it faster than the enemy.* It was almost a mantra.

Homer and his platoon were equipped with the latest high-velocity electromagnetic railgun, an old-fashioned

6.5mm minigun firing polymer-cased telescoped ammunition for antipersonnel use, and the usual suite of defensive measures, the latest of which was the Mark IV Point Defense System (PDS). PDSs and the larger Area Defense Systems contained kinetic, electronic, and directed energy components that could generally stop relatively slow-moving artillery, rocket, antitank missile and mortar rounds and render them nearly ineffectual against modern armies. In an ironic historical twist, ground battles between near-peer competitors were increasingly fought line of sight with high-powered kinetic rounds. Homer's odd, boxy-looking railgun could fire depleted uranium sabot rounds at Mach 7, but the downside was that the gun was also rather heavy. This weight, along with the power storage and generation requirements, necessitated a tracked vehicle to traverse anything but paved surfaces. Unfortunately for all of them, tracks are slower than wheels, and this fact now limited his platoon's speed and agility.

Homer and his heavies lumbered into position and waited. They pointed their railguns at the expected location of attack and remained silent apart from the constant whirring of their PDSs as they incessantly searched for incoming missiles and drones. The mech platoons with their Razorbacks, heavily modified and renamed eight-wheeled XM1296 Stryker Dragoons, were moving into slightly better positions as they were smaller, faster, and far better able to maneuver into tighter spots.

With all her ground elements either in position or on their way to them, Stacy turned her attention to fire support. In her AR helmet she looked toward the "Fire Support" interface icon and clicked it with her left hologlove.

After requesting three Sky Lance strikes, she softly asked, "What do you think, Saga?"

Saga quickly suggested three target locations that would statistically be the most useful locations. Saga wasn't always perfect, but she generally offered useful suggestions. After adjusting one slightly, Stacy tapped "approved."

Following the rise of Point and Area Defense Systems in the early 2020s, the U.S. military realized it had a fire-support problem and, in a moment of foresight, invested heavily in small ground-hugging missiles. The M47 Sky Lance was a small truck-launched cruise missile that could skim the treetops and deliver a substantial thermobaric, EMP, or point-detonating warhead to a target. An EMP warhead might temporarily blind the T100s while a point-detonating might get two or three, but Stacy knew she had to kill a lot of them and quickly. In this case, Stacy wanted a high-temperature, massive blast wave and cued up "thermobaric."

She got a quick response from the battalion: only one missile had been allocated to her company.

"Well that sucks," she said to herself but apparently loud enough to be heard.

"Probably due to drone ship losses, ma'am. But maybe we'll get more soon."

Stacy sighed internally. Specialist Six Kowalski, her operations support specialist, was so eternally and giddily optimistic that it was annoying.

"Thanks, Kowalski."

The words had just left her lips when Alpha 1, one of first platoon's Razorbacks, and the Sentinel drone it had lofted stopped transmitting. Then Bravo 2 and Bravo 3, two of second platoon's Razorbacks, also quit. The icons for all three of the heavily modified, eight-wheeled Strykers were now indicating a high probability of destruction.

Trying to suppress the fear that this might not be quite under control, Stacy grabbed the stimtab she had forgotten to take and placed it under her tongue. The use of stimtabs, an issue item, was required during specified periods as directed in the pre-mission order. She painfully remembered case study after case study that proved that commanders' ability to hyper-manage the chaos around them was often the limiting factor in unit effectiveness. The stimtab's effects hit quickly, and Stacy felt both her pulse quicken and her mental focus tighten.

Looking at the icons representing what were her three likely destroyed vehicles, she wondered out loud, "How could the enemy know where they were with such fidelity and get the first shot off in all three cases?"

"Targeting drones? The little crappy ones? Maybe they got in during the blink," stated Kowalski.

"Roger, probably," she responded.

Stacy realized that she had a real problem. Not being sure where the hypothesized drones were, her whole position was likely compromised. Casualties were mounting quickly, and that was one of the imperatives she had been told to avoid. She suppressed her growing fear and palpable sense of guilt as she realized half of second platoon was dead.

Gotta pull back, out of their sensor range. If they try to act "sticky" and follow, our PDSs will put them down, she thought. *Need to pull back about ten klicks to ensure we're clear. A good Sky Lance hit will help slow them down.*

It seemed like a good plan, and in a few seconds, she had not only worked out the major movements, but with a few deft hand gestures, had disseminated the rough plan to her platoon leaders. The gloves were simply magic for that.

"Negative" came the quick reply from Lieutenant Colonel Gammon, "That will put your fighting positions within line of sight of the main road and the battalion flank and everything that goes with it. You can pull back five klicks, but that's it. You've got to hold them there."

"Roger, sir. Wilco."

As she responded, she realized what this might mean: the possibility of more casualties, which had been only an academic possibility a few hours ago. Stacy adjusted her orders and hit "execute" just as Alpha 4, another first platoon vehicle, stopped transmitting.

No, no, no! This is going wrong! she thought as she received an audio alert from her recon platoon.

With a quick flip of her hologlove, she pulled up a tiled pattern of direct video feeds from the three remaining recon vehicles. There it was, in Ranger 2's video feed: a line of T100s, and a lot of them.

"Shit," she said, barely masking the growing stress within her.

Okay, time for plan number two, she thought. *Ambush what we can, buy some time, let battalion know what's going on, and get some help.* Then it dawned on her, and her whole body tensed. *We're outnumbered. Way outnumbered.*

What was left of her two mech platoons were already firing as they moved rearward. The remnants of the scout platoon—only Ranger 2 and Ranger 3 at this point—were also moving quickly in a bid to remain among the living. The patchy fog and long stripes of smoke created by the vehicles' smoke generators seemed totally out of place in the Philippine countryside. The particulate matter in the smoke wasn't perfect, but along with the "stay-behinds," it could often buy a brief head start in a game in which seconds mattered. The stay-behinds were rapidly inflating decoys that gave the thermal and visual signature of a full-sized vehicle and could fire a single kinetic shot. They didn't always fool the enemy, but enough of hers did to help with the fallback plan.

Stacy saw the remnants of first platoon withdrawing at an angle that, with a bit of luck, might even encourage the T100s to drive past Homer's platoon and their railguns. If she could orchestrate a hasty ambush, the shock of Homer's platoon torching a half-dozen T100s in the first couple seconds might stall the attack.

Worth the risk, she thought to herself.

While she had thought about releasing the fire command of the Sky Lance to the Scout Platoon Leader, he was dead, the rest of the platoon was hauling ass to the rear, and she really had no choice but to maintain control of the weapon at her level.

She hit the fire icon on her holoscreen, and a few seconds later a far-off Sky Lance came to life. Thirty seconds later, the Sky Lance gave off a terrific shriek as it flew over her command post at treetop height. Even Kowalski seemed unnerved. The acoustic sensors of the command post enabled them to hear the now-distant missile boost to Mach 1.4 as it cleared the last terrain feature, and then the spectacular detonation.

"Right in the kisser, that should get their attention," she said with a slight smile of satisfaction.

"Hell yeah!" added Kowalski.

A low-flying Sentinel drone was lingering in the area and registered a near-perfect hit at the lead of the column. Three vehicles were confirmed destroyed, with two more possible.

That…felt…good. She found herself surprised at the emotion.

After a few agonizingly long minutes, her holoscreen finally showed that the remnants of her two mech platoons and the scouts were in their new positions, deploying their remaining defensive measures, and preparing for what was next. After the initial casualties, they had gotten away almost cleanly.

But why? she thought. *The stay-behinds are good, but not that good.*

Her command post was buzzing with activity, data transfers, and a gentle rocking as her vehicle moved to its new position. Stacy's screen still indicated that the enemy was advancing, albeit a bit more slowly than she expected. The S2's mini-screen popped up in the corner of her field of view, and Saga provided a brief analysis: the enemy was roughly battalion-sized and consisted mostly of T100 combat vehicles. And while the attack was reasonably well ordered, the enemy seemed to have a statistically higher than average rate of minor frictional issues, to include numbers of vehicles taking wrong turns, getting stuck (four were), or instances of inefficient firing at the same vehicle.

Captain Olive's only text comment was "Concur."

Good, maybe this means we're fighting the B team, she thought. *He sure doesn't waste words.*

Reports came streaming in from both the shattered mech platoons and the scouts in the form of texts along the bottom of her screen, augmented video, and even Saga-assisted graphics on the terrain. Several of the enemy targeting drones were destroyed by the PDSs when they attempted to follow her forces. Saga was taking note.

Time to move Homer and the heavies back to the ambush position, she decided.

Lightly touching the platoon icon, she swept it to the new battle position, hit the "execute" icon, and went back to monitoring the situation in her AR helmet. Homer and his platoon would need to start moving almost immediately.

For several minutes, Stacy busied herself with coordinating the fight and skipped through the video feeds from individual vehicles to gain a better sense of a battlefield she could not physically see. During a discussion with Lieutenant Dellert, her executive officer and second-in-command, her focus was disrupted by the unmistakable crack of a railgun in the distance.

The heavies were engaging, but it was at the wrong place. She checked her screen as her mind screamed, *Did I give the wrong command? Did I not hit "execute" with my hologlove? Did he not get the command?*

She then had a sickening realization: Homer hadn't acknowledged the command to move, and she hadn't noticed. Now there were no comms with him. He and his platoon were on their own.

I hope I was clear, she thought as the knot in her stomach grew ever tighter.

161045HSEP2033 (10:45 a.m. local time, September 16, 2033) Chinese National Assistance Task Force Headquarters, Manila

Colonel Deng took a long drag on the unfiltered Chinese cigarette, held it in, and slowly and slyly exhaled it in the direction of Major General Yu, who hated smoke and who was animatedly moving from console to console in the command post. Comically, he had his right thumb wrapped in a napkin as once his cuticle began to bleed, it tended to take a while to stop.

"Why are they acting so stupidly? Don't they know better?" he nearly shouted.

He should have waited, Deng thought to himself before he spoke. "Sir, they are doing the best they can. Our communications are mostly out, and they are operating on the last instructions they had. Your instructions were precise in every detail. Perhaps they are struggling to adapt based on changing circumstances."

It was a deliberate but subtle dig at Yu, delivered well enough not to arouse attention or appear insubordinate. Yu ignored it and continued whirling like a top as Deng slowly smoked his cigarette.

1.6

Lieutenant Colonel Gammon's command post was a flurry of activity. This was shaping up to be a real fight on his battalion's left flank with Captain Doss, his youngest and least experienced commander, at ground zero. Captain McGinnis was on the right, with the rest of the battalion spread out on a relatively narrow road back to Lingayen. This was a tough place to have to fight, and with this much on the table, he couldn't afford a major mistake.

All right Yu, good one, this is the area where I would have done it too. You get points for pragmatism, but not creativity, he thought to himself, noting that his right flank was more vulnerable than his left, which was why he put McGinnis there.

He briefly contemplated his situation. With one of his Griffons now a smoking hole and several other of the smaller Shrike recon drones also getting picked off, Gammon's access to a bird's-eye view was mostly gone. He was slightly frustrated that his situational awareness was limited to what he was getting from Captain Doss's feed, info from his other commanders, and the Brigade feed, which was essentially Saga's output.

"Apache 6, we can see that your heavy platoon is stationary and out of comms. What else do you need to keep the main body off them?"

"I have this…for now, sir," she said.

Gammon heard some hesitation mixed with the determination in her voice.

"Major Bennett, tee up one of the remaining Lances. Make it available to Apache 6." Gammon then switched to a private channel with Bennett. "And be prepared to virtually assist her. Don't let this get off the rails."

"Roger, sir, but I think she's got it."

Gammon nodded and ended the conversation. Bennett had spent more time with the young Captain than he had. His instincts told him he could back off at least slightly, which freed him up for other tasks.

Gammon was himself an excellent judge of people once he got to know them. The first troops he had commanded in combat nicknamed him "Da Man" due to his leadership, human insight, and tenacity, and the nickname stuck. It became a permanent fixture after he was court-martialed early in his career and survived.

The board members at his proceedings chalked up his pointing a Shit Storm Generator at Brigadier General Nightingale's headquarters during a staff meeting as a youthful indiscretion. While they did punish Gammon, they did not end his fledgling career for two reasons, according to legend anyway: they believed that anyone that could pull off such a stunt was both creative and fearless, and therefore a military asset to the nation; and secondly, most of the board members had been recipients of General Nightingale's toxic leadership in the past and figured that the event was a form of cosmic justice. They had often believed General Nightingale was full of shit, and with the help of the young lieutenant, it was proven for all to see, and smell.

1.7

161120HSEP2033 (11:20 a.m. local time, September 16, 2033) Forward Edge of the Battle Area, Apache Company Sector

Homer wasn't alarmed, and with comms out, he knew he would have to make it up as he went. Captain Doss had given him clear orders: prevent an enemy penetration of the flank. And do it at all costs.

Homer saw his wingman, Charlie 2, fifty meters to his right. They had carefully positioned themselves on the left of their platoon battle position while Charlie 3 and Charlie 4 had covered the right. The plan was to engage with two to three rounds each, move to alternate firing positions while their railguns cooled down and their capacitors recharged, and then repeat the process. The T100 armor would be no match for their brutally effective M20 railguns. Using only electrical energy, the M20s fired a five-kilogram depleted uranium penetrator at 3.7 kilometers per second out to ranges of up to nine kilometers. The energy discharge, however, heated them up in a hurry. Fire too quickly in succession and the system would simply melt.

The moment was right. Homer fired and felt the recoil rock the whole vehicle. His first round was dead-on. At 3,642.7 meters, the round ripped through the lead T100's armor and blew its innards out the back of the vehicle. The hapless T100 rolled to a stop, lifeless and gutted.

"First kill." Homer attempted to transmit the news to Captain Doss in vain.

With their lead vehicle dead, the rest of the Chinese column had something else to contend with, and Charlie 2 began firing at the rearmost vehicle of the nine-vehicle line. Homer noted that Charlie 2's round was low, and it took her a second round to score a hit. The remaining seven T100s now struggled to get around not only the wrecks to their front and rear but the ubiquitous irrigation ditches to their sides as well.

Homer noted that he and Charlie 2 had boxed them in, and he quickly issued a supplementary firing command to the platoon.

As the distinct crack of railguns drifted through the other noises of battle, Homer knew that Charlie 3 and Charlie 4 were also firing now. However, they had been unable to lay as good of a trap and had only three T100s in the kill zone when they took their first shots at them.

Homer heard a deep thud to his left and then heard a rain of dirt and debris hitting his hull. The first thud was followed quickly by an enemy round passing less than three meters above him. As expected, the T100s were not sitting passively in the kill box; they were now actively trying to kill him and his platoon. After less than two minutes of firing at maximum rate, the platoon's M20 railguns were roasting and it was time to move with two vehicles providing cover while the other two moved. Six more T100s were wrecks, and one more was stuck. As Homer prepared to issue the order, Charlie 3 reported that she had taken a glancing hit in the track while Charlie 4 took one that penetrated one of his main capacitors. Homer assessed that for the moment;

the platoon was still at least partially combat-effective, and he attempted to relay the information to Captain Doss, again to no avail.

Homer changed the plan, gave the signal using backup line-of-sight laser-based comm links, and all four vehicles activated their countermeasures. The stay-behind decoys rapidly inflated in a choreographed movement as the smoke generators began spewing a cloud of acrid smoke. The platoon was on the move back to their alternate firing positions, or so Homer thought.

"Immobile" was the immediate message from Charlie 3. Unfortunately for her, the glancing hit to the track was worse than expected. A damaged—and now thrown—left track was likely a death sentence for her if they left her.

Homer again quickly recalculated his plan. Charlie 3's armament was still fully functional, and while Charlie 4 was mobile, his railgun was less effective due to the damaged capacitor. Homer decided to send Charlie 4 back into position while he and Charlie 2 moved to positions they had to pick on the fly. In the short run, this wasn't too bad, but Homer knew his next move was going to be more problematic.

Charlie 3 and Charlie 4 continued to engage the enemy, and Homer told Charlie 4 to keep firing to distract the enemy lest they concentrate all their fire on Charlie 3. Homer calculated that the Chinese would figure out quickly that Charlie 4's railgun rounds weren't penetrating anymore, but at least it would buy Charlie 3 a few more seconds.

With no cool-down time, the next message from Charlie 3 was predictable: "M20 overheating. Request override."

"Approved" was Homer's quick response. It wouldn't matter much if she kept the weapon from melting if she ended up dead.

Every time they fired, the railguns kicked up the foliage into small debris clouds. The clouds should have been bigger, but with no explosive blast coming out of the gun, they were a bit disappointing to an untrained observer.

The T100s were getting closer to Charlie 3 and Charlie 4, and more importantly, they had ranged them and concluded that they weren't moving. Charlie 4 clicked out of comms, and Homer's external acoustic sensors confirmed that he hadn't survived the hit. Homer's platoon managed to kill four more T100s, but their advantages of range and surprise were now long gone. Homer adjusted his plan yet again, and with Charlie 2 he began moving to a new fighting position near Charlie 3. Low on smoke and out of both decoys and Sentinel drones, they were all in a tough spot.

Things took another turn for the worse when one of the remaining PLA drones committed suicide by briefly illuminating Charlie 2 with a targeting laser. Even though Charlie 2's point defense system quickly destroyed the drone, it was too late. Every T100 in the area was now firing at her, or moving to a location from where they could. Even worse, they were quickly calculating every likely location where Charlie 2 could be in the next sixty seconds. Homer knew she had to reposition quickly, or this might be her last minute alive.

"Evading, all power to mobility, smoke at 5%," was her dispassionate transmission, which only Homer heard—and only because he was the only one near her.

Despite her every effort to add some uncertainty to the enemy's calculations, she came up short. A T100 caught her as she emerged between two small knolls along one of the calculated routes. The shot was good and caught Charlie 2 in the side, in the gut of the vehicle. It was over in an instant. There was no explosion this time, just metal parts, newly created shrapnel, and what was left of a sabot round emerging from Charlie 2's left side. Her war was over.

Homer moved into the new fighting position barely seventy-five meters from Charlie 3 while cooling his gun and recharging his capacitors. He knew his odds of surviving were decreasing as he put in a request for an immediate Sky Lance strike. He fired at an approaching T100, destroyed the hapless vehicle, and earned another "kill ring" for his barrel.

"M20 inoperable, overheated," Charlie 3 communicated weakly.

She was now combat-ineffective: The heat from her overloaded railgun circuits had melted her capacitors. She was immobile and had only a minigun to defend herself. The minigun was useless against T100 armor and no infantry had availed themselves to being shot. Homer kept firing, did his duty, and tried to keep the two of them alive for at least a little while longer.

Stacy took a deep breath, clicked the "XMIT" icon, and began. "Sir, it looks like we're holding, but…casualties are mounting, I think. We aren't fully sure what's going on with the fragmented information we're getting."

Buck noted the stress in her voice and assessed that while she was under significant pressure, she was still far from panicking.

"Roger, Stacy, you're doing exactly what we need you to do. Keep working with what you've got. We need four more minutes from you. Mike is almost in position to provide covering fires, and then we'll pull your company back. Can you hold that long?"

"We'll do our best, sir. We'll do our best."

161150HSEP2033 (11:50 a.m. local time, September 16, 2033) Chinese National Assistance Task Force Headquarters, Manila

Disgusted, Colonel Deng crushed his cigarette into the overflowing ashtray.

We asked more of them than we should have, he thought. *But perhaps this may not end up as an entirely wasted battalion. What is done is done, and we'll find out how bad we hurt them shortly. If we score enough casualties, the Americans will call off this whole misguided adventure. Ho Chi Minh was right about them.*

He looked over at General Nano, his new name for Yu, now red-faced with frustration at not being able to communicate with any of his units.

As Yu continued to twirl about in the command post, he shouted, "Get some recon drones up. I want them up NOW!"

I can hardly wait to be rid of him, Deng thought.

1.8

Comms remained intermittent, and when they briefly worked, small dribbles of information updated images throughout Stacy's TOC and, by extension, the Battalion TAC.

Gammon caught the update, then thought to himself, *C'mon, Stacy, almost there, just a few more minutes.*

An alert appeared in his headset, and Buck knew it was important enough to go voice with her. He touched the XMIT icon, but nothing happened. He hit it again and, out of bad habit, five more times within the next two seconds.

"Text Doss. Unconfirmed reports of civilians in area. Stay focused on the fight. Send."

Gammon knew that with spotty connections, the text had a better chance of making it, but it was still just a chance.

Stacy jumped slightly as her helmet's display suddenly flashed red. It was Homer, and his urgent text was requesting a Sky Lance for a "danger close final protective fire," a strike that was practically on his position.

He must be desperate…and about to be overrun, she thought.

She immediately released the strike to him as she tried to understand why Charlie 3's icon was still in her original position, Homer was positioned nearby in a place that Stacy had not expected, and icons for numerous wrecked T100s were littered around Homer's former position. It made no sense based on the original plan.

"Why hadn't Charlie 3 withdrawn with the others?" she wondered. "And why was Homer still there?"

In the distance, a Sky Lance roared to life.

Homer fired his railgun and felt the immense recoil rock the vehicle back. He wasn't angry or fearful, but he was academically contemplating that his odds of survival were getting thinner by the minute. He was meticulous, doing what he was trained to do, and not really overanalyzing it all at the moment. He fired again and missed, but his next two shots rang true and destroyed two more T100s.

A loud, resounding "clang!" announced to Homer that he had been hit. While the railguns did not use gunpowder, they still had to be loaded with the sabot penetrator prior to each shot, and a quick systems check told him that his was now inoperable.

Defenseless was Homer's first thought. *Probably not going to survive* was his second.

Twenty seconds later, the Lance screamed in and decisively ended the Battle of Tarlac River.

From her command post, Captain Doss's stomach knotted as she watched the icons for Homer, Charlie 3, and the four remaining T100s simultaneously change from "active" to "destroyed."

We were less than a minute from pulling him back…so…close…

Stacy received a text from Lieutenant Colonel Gammon about possible civilians that did not bode well. The point was now moot.

She responded quickly. "Battle is over."

"Sir, are you seeing this?" asked Captain Mike McGinnis in an astonished voice.

Buck and the rest of the team on the command net were all seeing the same things Mike's lead vehicles were. Large plumes of black smoke were rising from a dozen T100s that were burning furiously. Occasionally, the concussions from secondary explosions would rock the video feeds as ammunition detonated inside the nearby hulks. A camera on a Razorback caught the wreckage of Homer's platoon, and for the first time, Stacy had a clear picture of where he died.

Buck saw the video and knew instinctively how to respond. "Captain Doss," he said on a private channel.

"Yes…yes, sir?" she stammered.

"You and your company did your duty to the fullest, and that sometimes means sacrifice."

"Roger, sir, thank you."

"And just so that you know, it mattered. They were trying to derail our attack and stop us so far north of Manila that we'd be useless. They failed in large part due to Apache company. You and your team did good work." Gammon paused, then continued, "Now get back to it."

After another short pause, he added, "It looks like the Chinese attack is spent, so once we mop up, it's okay to go and pay your respects."

1.9

161915UNOV2037 (1:15 p.m. local time, September 16, 2033)
Vicinity Tarlac River, Philippines

Stacy finally found him or, more accurately, what was left of him. He was the first one she had seen when she arrived in the unit five weeks ago as a last-minute replacement. The original company commander underwent an emergency appendectomy, and Lieutenant Colonel Gammon had taken a chance on accepting her into the unit and placing her in command close to the deployment date.

It had all been nearly overwhelming, so given the stress, she thought it would be fun to personalize the fearsome vehicle. She couldn't help but write "Homer" on the side of its hull because it seemed like a shame that the supply system knew Homer, and those like him, simply as M316 Heavy Offensive Multi-Role Robots, or "HOMRRs" for short.

She didn't cry for his death, but she did carry a very strangely vague sense of guilt that Homer and the others did not survive the battle. He had fought courageously and autonomously. She briefly considered that the correct term for what happened was no longer KIA, or "Killed in Action," but rather DIA, or "Destroyed in Action." After a few moments of paying her respects, she turned slowly and walked back to her Buffalo.

Stepping into the dark interior of the vehicle, she donned her helmet and pulled up the battalion commander. As soon as Lieutenant Colonel Gammon came into view, she responded to his questions.

"Sir, no resistance remaining. Mike and I finished off the immobilized T100s and their support vehicles. We also think we got the remaining recon drones—at least according to Saga. A few of our vehicles might be salvageable, but we won't know until the maintenance teams get a better look at them. My XO mentioned that the first-gen automation systems on the Razorbacks are easier to bring back online. He's hoping to get two back. The HOMRRs are a bit trickier. He isn't very optimistic."

She found herself surprised with the sense of detachment she felt as the words tumbled out.

"Good work, Stacy. Your company took a real beating, but you stopped them. When we move out at fifteen hundred, you'll be in reserve until we patch up a few of the HOMRRs and Razorbacks. Just to confirm, no human casualties in your company, correct?"

"Roger, sir. Roger."

Part 2: The Road to Hell

"By far, the greatest danger of Artificial Intelligence is that people conclude too early that they understand it." ~ Eliezer Yudkowsky

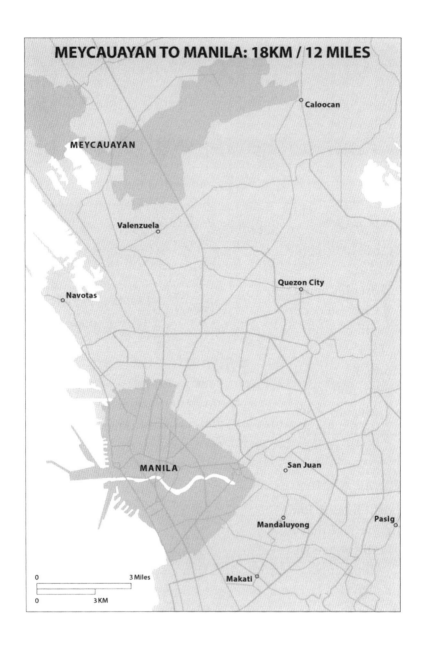

2.0

170800HSEP2033 (8:00 a.m. local time, September 17, 2033)
Manila, Republic of the Philippines

Joseph Cagula was an eyewitness to history, and so far the Chinese occupation of Manila had not been too bad, at least in his estimation. Most things continued on as they had before, with the exception of the news, the Special Security Zone, all the security points, Chinese shipping containers strewn about the city, and the new government.

He was a scrawny sixteen-year-old, slightly above average in height, with a mother who often complained that he played too many AR games. He had an older system, but as he had two brothers and a sister to contend with, it was the best his family could afford. Joseph's misfortune of being born into a lower-middle-class family was compounded by the fact that his father, a police officer assigned to the Manila Police District, was strict beyond reason.

On the upside, maybe his recent promotion will keep him busier and off my case, Joseph mused to himself.

He said a curt goodbye to his mother, a short woman with slightly graying hair pulled up in a bun, who reminded him of Mount Pinatubo: quiet until things went too far, and then a mighty eruption. He figured he could tolerate her nagging about handwashing and schoolwork for a little while longer, but could still hardly wait to be on his own.

It could be worse, he thought as he pedaled his bike to the port.

Joseph often worked at the port on Saturdays to earn pocket money for various luxuries, primarily AR games. But there were no more jobs now, especially not for a boy his age. For as long as he could remember before the blockade, the usual container ships had unloaded their usual containers in the usual way. He even remembered running errands for the longshoremen as they unloaded the Mitsui O.S.K. Line's *Triumph* this past spring. When the ship was delivered by Samsung Heavy Industries in 2017, it was the largest container ship in the world and capable of carrying 20,170 twenty-foot equivalent units, or TEUs. Even after America became the last industrialized nation to finally adopt the metric system in 2026, the International Organization for Standards, oddly named the ISO, continued to dictate that shipping containers would remain measured in English units. The forty-foot shipping container, or two TEUs, remained the standard in world shipping, proof that bureaucratic decisions live forever.

Joseph pedaled past row after row of forty-foot containers marked with the large logos of the China Ocean Shipping (Group) Company and Orient Overseas Container Line. There were thousands of them, a veritable sea of metal boxes stacked four and sometimes five high filled with treasures and goods from around the world. Although the sea of boxes fascinated Joseph, he really didn't care that underpaid and bribable port inspectors allowed so many of the "special containers" into the country.

Joseph arrived at the regular meeting point and looked around for his absent friends. He hopped off his bike under the small tree that provided a meager bit of shade, scanning the empty piers for them. His thoughts flitted back to the day before the occupation. It had been relatively uneventful. *Second place in an online gaming tournament, got crushed by some Korean kid, studied for my Algebra test, then things got weird,* he thought to himself.

In the far distance, Joseph heard rumbling, almost like thunder. He had heard the Americans had landed near Lingayen but wasn't entirely sure why. The news stories were always contradictory, but one thing he was pretty sure of was that they were fighting the Chinese.

2.1

170930HSEP2033 (9:30 a.m. local time, September 17, 2033) Vicinity of Clark International Airport, Northwest of Manila

The note from Tom had been short, and Stacy had been surprised to get it so soon. He had described the political turmoil in DC after the battle and how the President continued to insist U.S. forces were only there as part of a grand coalition to assist the Filipinos in retaking control of their country. He also emphatically stated that there had been no additional "boots on the ground" casualties.

"Getting close to the political tipping point," as Tom had described it.

Tom also noted the surprise he felt when he saw that the news media were somehow able to identify the names of specific American commanders in the battle and that he had been looking for hers. So far, to their mutual relief, he had not seen it.

Stacy tapped out a response and sent it.

Hey Tom,

I miss you too. How have you been? I imagine the Pentagon is pretty nuts right now. The media curfew just ended and I just wanted to let you know everything was okay. Not exactly an auspicious start as a company

commander. As you probably saw the combat footage from GoogleNews and the Facebook News Network, the unit that got chewed up was mine. I lost nearly half of it. It was tougher than I expected, mentally, physically and emotionally. No one on my team was actually killed, but I still feel guilty about the casualties, even though they were just bots. On the upside, we pretty much destroyed an entire Chinese bot battalion, so it was a good trade. We keep telling our troops not to believe anything they read online about the operation and only half of what they see. We have to keep preaching it, especially because Xinhua news got a jump on us in the online news feeds, so we are also having to play catch-up.

Hey, when you have a chance, we also really need to talk about wedding plans as soon as this is over. Lots to do to get ready for our big day!

Love, Stacy

As she wrote to Tom, Stacy could feel that she was mentally, physically and emotionally spent. Five weeks ago she had been dropped into a high-profile unit led by a semi-famous commander, had to learn everything and everyone at an incredibly accelerated pace, all while Major Bennett constantly quizzed, prodded and tested her on unit Standard Operating Procedures, combat systems and limitations, autonomy parameters, and a long list of other things. The flight to Darwin, Australia, had been smooth, but once they joined their equipment on the landing ships, the trip north was miserable. Heavy seas made for a wretched passage in more ways than one. Once they got close, the constant threat of enemy submarine or air attacks kept everyone on edge. They landed in the second wave and were all more than glad to begin the attack south to Clark International Airport. Few leaders had gotten more than a couple hours of sleep a day since then, some of which was due to the pace of operations, the rest to perpetual movement caused by the anti-targeting protocols. Stacy shifted her weight and, as she moved, caught a whiff of her body odor and grimaced.

I did the right thing. Tom would just stress out, and he has enough on him right now, she thought.

She hadn't told Tom that she was under investigation. These investigations were relatively standard fare following the combat loss of one or more humans or, in this case, several million dollars' worth of machines. Although it was routine, it still stung her pride and would leave a dark cloud over her until it was resolved. It also created a lot of internal stress because, while investigations can exonerate, they can also condemn.

The Chief of Staff, Colonel Gruninger, assigned the AR 15-6 investigation to Colonel Harold McClellan, the Brigade's Chief Technology Officer. It had to be assigned to someone at or above Lieutenant Colonel Gammon's level, as Gammon could also be implicated if the finding came back negatively. It also had to be done by someone with intimate knowledge of the newly fielded series of automated warbots just entering combat for the first time. Gruninger was a fair man and had given Stacy the professional courtesy of a personal explanation of what to expect.

"This is just a routine and required investigation," he had said, "and it doesn't imply that you necessarily did anything wrong. We use these to document what happened so when the Army is questioned later, there is proof the individuals acted reasonably and we didn't try to cover up a bad situation."

Easy for him to say, Stacy thought.

Other than hearing that Colonel McClellan had written his War College thesis on autonomous weapon systems, or warbots as they were increasingly becoming known, Stacy knew little about him. He had spent significant time at White Sands Missile Range during the Army's experimentation and robotic wargame process over the last decade, and she observed that he had all the personal characteristics of the slightly socially awkward engineering majors she had seen in college. She did appreciate the *Army Times* article about the Army's decision to send acquisition officers forward with their creations to assist with the inevitable teething problems that these "systems of systems" would undoubtedly have. What wasn't written in the article, but cheered among the junior part of the Army, was the implication that it was an attempt to ensure that even those buried in the far reaches of the Army technological bureaucracy had personal skin in the game's outcome.

At the appointed time, Stacy stepped into the small, enclosed antechamber of the headquarters shelter. She couldn't knock on the door to the next compartment because there wasn't one, so she lightly slapped the entry flap.

"Enter," Colonel McClellan responded.

Stacy stepped in, rendered a salute, and said, "Sir, Captain Doss reporting as ordered."

"Have a seat, Captain. You know what this is about. In addition to this being a routine matter following significant combat losses, emerging intelligence is indicating that three civilians were apparently killed in your operating area. The investigation has been fair, impartial, and you are the last of the seven people I am interviewing. The interview will be recorded so please be clear and to the point."

The colonel had caught Stacy by surprise. "Killed?" she said softly. "Sir, this is the first time I've heard that there were confirmed civilian casualties."

"I understand, Captain Doss. This is a very recent development, within the last three hours, in fact. Multiple news agencies, some with Chinese sympathies, are reporting it, and rather than creating a new investigation, I decided to roll it up into this one. I haven't even had a chance to fully brief the chain of command yet."

This bothered Stacy, and she felt an increasing sense of uncertainty. She couldn't identify all the emotions quickly building up insider her, but the fact that it was possible that several innocents were killed began to gnaw at her conscience.

"What did the news report allege, sir?" she asked, barely able to keep her voice from trembling.

"That three civilians, one an eight-year-old girl, were killed in the final Sky Lance strike."

The image hit Stacy like a hammer as the face of her seven-year-old niece filled her mind. She tried to push it aside, but the thought persisted, and her head began to pound.

Colonel McClellan noted her discomfort but gave no indication of it as he was a humorless man who had never forgiven his parents for giving him such an old-fashioned first name. Rumor had it that he was less than thrilled at having to be on this mission, but if it was true, he hid it well. Perhaps the prospect of seeing how the systems truly operated against a thinking adversary helped compensate for the uncomfortable living conditions. As a rear echelon soldier, he was particularly struggling with the field conditions, the constant repositioning, incredible heat, bugs, dehydrated rations, and the potable water shortages, all of which added to his discomfort.

"So, Captain," he began, "tell me how this battle unfolded from your perspective."

Stacy proceeded to describe the events of the day. As the interview went on, she felt anger and frustration building inside her. The questioning continued until it got to the point when she released the Sky Lance strike to Homer.

The inquisitor then asked a pointed question that pushed her over the edge. "Are you *sure* that when you released the strike to the lead M316 HOMRR, to the best of your knowledge, there were no confirmed civilians in the area of the strike?"

"YES! AS MUCH AS I HUMANLY CAN BE!" Stacy found herself shouting. "I've been the one in the fight, it was my company, and no one feels worse than I do about the losses and even more so about the possibility of civilian deaths! The M316 was under my command and I am legally and morally responsible for EVERYTHING he did or failed to do! You might have forgotten what it's like to have that weight, if you ever even had it…"

Fortunately for Stacy, her brain-to-mouth filter was fully engaged, and her yelling remained internal. Her reply was simple and flat. "Yes, sir."

Colonel McClellan asked questions for another twenty minutes about the operation and autonomy settings and continued to probe her knowledge of civilians in the area.

The ordeal finally began to near its end. Colonel McClellan had not been unpleasant or rude, but he had been exceptionally thorough.

Stacy was relieved when he finally asked, "Do you have anything else to add?"

"No sir."

"You are dismissed."

Stacy saluted and left as quickly as she could. As she walked out, Lieutenant Colonel Gammon saw her and quickly walked over to her.

"You did a good job, Stacy. It's easy for those in the cheap seats to criticize those on the playing field. Just don't take it personally. He's wound a little tight, and in some ways, he's also investigating his own creations. Anyway, this will get cleared up soon. In the meantime, I want you to put your XO in charge and get some sleep. We still have a lot to do to help the Philippine Army get to Manila."

"Roger, sir," she responded, the exhaustion evident in her voice.

Red-eyed, Stacy walked quickly away from the shelter, around the corner of a vehicle where no one could see her, and vomited.

As Buck slowly walked back to his vehicle, he found himself in deep thought. As he approached his vehicle, his driver hit the "start" button and prepared to return him and Captain Olive to the Battalion's TAC. Olive had tagged along for the rare opportunity for face-to-face coordination with his intelligence counterparts.

"Deep in thought, sir?" Captain Olive asked.

"How did you know?"

"Uh, sir, your limp was more noticeable. They told me when I got here that it was an indicator that you were either deep in thought or really getting pissed. Considering the circumstances, as your intelligence officer, I figured it was more the former than latter," he said with a slight grin.

Gammon was slightly amused and surprised by this level of engagement from the normally reserved man.

"Okay, so who gave that one up?"

"Sir, I respectfully request to decline to answer. Rule number one of using informants is to never burn your source."

Now Gammon was fully amused as he remembered from Olive's bio that he had a brief hitch as a Baltimore police officer.

Gammon responded with an exaggerated bit of fanfare and a big smile. "Roger, granted," he said, all the while thinking, *Probably Bennett…or Verault.*

Dodged that bullet, thought Olive. *Glad he didn't press me. I'd have hated to give up his wife as the source. She was a good sport, and we might need more info later.*

Olive recalled the last brigade Hail and Farewell. The unit was preparing to ship out, and it was a final chance for everyone to dress up and enjoy an evening before what was to come. Olive had noted that his boss was rhythmically challenged, and in between slow dances with his wife, he was usually at the bar or on the veranda smoking cigars with whomever cared to join him, which was usually a small crowd. During one of those breaks, Olive and a bunch of the battalion's junior officers gathered around his wife to get some insight into his quirks. She was as engaging as she was enlightening, and they all quickly departed her company when the music began to slow.

The young private serving as their driver didn't know what to make of the repartee, so he took his position in the gun turret and hit "return" on his screen. As he did so, he wondered why he was still often referred to as a "driver" by the older leaders versus the newer term of "gunner/technician." He quickly scanned the sky as the autonomous vehicle began to move toward its new home near Clark International Airport, a point 120 kilometers from the landing sites and 60 kilometers northwest of Manila.

As the vehicle began to move, Gammon continued to think through the recent day's events. The same thoughts bothered at him: No real combat in the last few days, only periodic reports of low-level drone recons. But why did the battle come out like it did? Chinese AI was pretty good as prior intel reports indicated.

"Hey, Luke, I want you to review the T100s AI capabilities and tell me what you think based on what happened at Tarlac and what the Tech Intel teams got from the wrecks."

"Roger, sir, on it," Captain Olive responded as he nearly dove his head into his tablet.

So why did we win? Comms sucked for both sides. Okay, Bucky, what do you need to learn from this? And what does General Yu have in store for us next?

Buck then allowed himself a brief indulgence. Reaching into the upper pocket on his body armor, he pulled out a small, worn picture. He silently touched each face, said a short prayer for them, and quickly put it away.

2.2

171045HSEP2033 (10:45 a.m. local time, September 17, 2033)
Headquarters, Chinese National Assistance Task Force

Major General Yu slowly turned to Colonel Deng and, in front of the staff, asked him, "So, what do you think we learned from the spoiling attack?"

Colonel Deng pondered the question for a moment, silently seething at the power play. *Well played, you idiot,* Deng thought. *The real tragedy is I am more capable than you, and yet this venture rests on your shoulders. Now here we are… despite my warning, you pissed away an entire battalion of combat vehicles in a pointless spoiling attack.*

Deng deflected the question as politely and diplomatically as his ego could allow. "Much has happened, and there is so much to take in. What do you think, sir?"

Deng didn't listen to Yu's response as his mind raced. *The real center of gravity remains the Philippine Army, or what's left of it. Destroy that quickly, and the Yankee president's pretense of "helping the Filipinos" will collapse and they will go home. Now they have a so-called advisory unit showing up and half our maneuver forces are gone. Idiot.*

He tuned back in to hear Yu ask another question, "How did the AI perform?"

"Adequately, sir," Deng replied out loud as he continued to fume, *but it would have done much better if you hadn't been so foolish with your restrictive rules of engagement. The restraint was unneeded. The Filipinos were deserving of their fate, and a few extra collateral casualties here and there would have been of no importance if we had won, or if even one of the T100s got off a faster shot against the Americans. Things might have come out differently.*

Yu cleared his throat, and Deng braced himself for what was next. Despite the debacle, Yu retained that typical Shanghai arrogance about him. Having grown up in Beijing, Deng couldn't help but have an instinctive disdain for Yu. *And now comes the lecture of wisdom from on high, second only to Confucius.*

Yu began to speak calmly, in sharp contrast to his level of animation his staff remembered during the battle. "While our attempt to cripple the American ground force was only partially successful…"

Deng took a long drag on his cigarette to hide his reaction as he thought to himself, *We should have saved our strength and destroyed the Filipino military. It's easy enough to paint the Americans as colonizers to the rest of the world and our Belt and Road partners. Sure, they got lucky, sneaking their fleet through the Sulu Sea, but most of that fleet is gone and now they're trapped in our backyard without resupply. They are under siege, just like 1941, and they simply don't know it yet.*

"The attack," Yu stated, "accomplished two important, no, essential goals. We still have many questions regarding the effectiveness of our AI interface, and we could not afford to enter what may be a larger battle for Manila without first conducting an operational test against a real and thinking opponent. The data was simply incredible in its depth and richness. The National Defense Academy is already sifting through the data, and it is revealing where we went right and where we went wrong in the interwar years. I suspect the Americans are doing the same. We shall see who adapts faster. Not everyone learned the same lessons from the Kaliningrad debacle."

Yu paused for a moment, thinking, *Had the Baltic Crisis really been over a decade ago? I was much younger then, an observer with the Russian General Staff, and I will not make the same mistakes I saw them make.*

His thoughts were interrupted by Deng, who was trying to hide his impatience and responded with barely concealed frustration. "Seems like an expensive price, considering what lies before us."

"Perhaps," responded Yu. "Perhaps. But remember, this is the beginning of a prolonged conflict. As you know, we are buying time for our weaponized public opinion, psychological and legal efforts to bear fruit, which brings me to my second point: this was a clear political and psychological statement to the Americans and their allies. Remember the lessons of the Tet Offensive. We have told their politicians and their people that we will fight and that it may be much more expensive than they have been expecting.

"We also know we are better at controlling the narrative than they are. Once they fully grasp that involvement in Asia is more expensive than it is worth, they will abandon this region, and the other regional nations will come to see things our way."

From the back of the room, Commissar Xi gave a barely perceptible nod of approval as he thought, *Political power does indeed grow from the barrel of a gun. Perhaps Yu will turn out better than expected.*

Deng took a hard drag on his cigarette as he mentally conceded that while Yu was wrong in the attack, perhaps not all was lost. The region's nations were still waiting to see how this came out. It would take them a hundred years to rebuild Guam, and the Chinese noose around the Americans was starting to tighten.

Deng consoled himself a bit, *We still have another battalion and more surprises for the Filipinos and the Americans. Many more things…*

2.3

171130HSEP2033 (11:30 a.m. local time, September 17, 2033) Downtown Manila

Joseph slowly pedaled his bike past the American Embassy and on through Rizal Park, where the grass was lush and green because of the rainy season, but few people were enjoying the park that day. He saw shipping containers emblazoned with COSCO and OOCL everywhere. He didn't remember seeing them in the city until just before Manila Day in June, then they turned up near all the major intersections, the police stations, government offices, the bridges over the Pasig River, utilities, the train and bus stations, everywhere. It had been quite a mystery until the holiday, which fell this year on the 25th. As he rode by, he noted that some were still closed, but a few looked like flower boxes with seedlings sprouting from the top. His father wouldn't talk much about what happened on the 25th, and everything he read and saw online was so contradictory, he wasn't sure himself.

The pungent smell from the squatters at the Baseco Compound wafted through his nostrils and caught his attention. *Even the mighty Chinese couldn't solve that problem,* he thought.

He stopped at a roadside stand for a quick lunch. It was supposed to be comfort food, and the fact that the street vendors were out added a sense of normalcy. He paid the vendor the usual amount and received in return a few specks of unidentifiable meat and a smaller-than-usual portion of rice.

The overweight vendor shrugged and said, "Things are getting a bit tighter these days. Be glad for what you have." The sweating man smiled and then added, "And don't think too much about what kind of meat it is."

Joseph ate the rice and only picked at the meat, reminding himself that he'd been seeing fewer strays than normal. Clouds were scarce, and at nearly 34 degrees Celsius, today was hot even by Manila standards. The humidity was well above 80 percent, and the prospect of typhoon season coming to an end and bringing with it cooler, drier weather was of no help to him now.

As he moved slowly through the Chinese Special Security Zone, he noticed the traffic was light at the checkpoints. In addition to Rizal Park, the area also contained the South Port area of Manila, several large warehouses near the waterfront, and the former U.S. Embassy. Joseph had seen the picture of the Chinese flag flying from the embassy's historic flagpole with its 1941-era bullet holes. Joseph's father said it was just another trick, just a replay of 1941. Joseph recalled it had something to do with the Japanese sending a picture of their victorious troops on Corregidor Island's Hearn Battery as a message to the nations of Asia in 1941, or something like that.

Although he had never been there, Joseph had heard that the Chinese had also set up smaller restricted security zones in the Batasang Pambansa Complex, where the House of Representatives of the Philippines had met until the occupation; in Makati, the financial hub of the nation; and at the Ninoy Aquino International Airport just south of the city. Corregidor Island was also occupied, and from what he had heard from his friend Daniel, whose dad was a day laborer for a Chinese construction company, the Chinese were making improvements of some sort to the Topside area and Malinta Tunnel.

As Joseph pedaled slowly in the sweltering heat, he saw Daniel ahead, sitting in a tiny patch of shade provided by a small tree. He was rather unsuccessfully trying to stay cool as it was, in fact, an impossible task.

As soon as he saw Joseph, Daniel put down his phone and breathlessly told him, "I heard President Davila is still alive and made another speech! He said the Philippine military is going to retake the city, but it might be just another story… maybe just wishful thinking, according to my mother."

Joseph scolded his chubby friend. "You know better than to believe anything you see online these days."

"It was real, I saw it. I saw the video with my own eyes!" Daniel insisted.

Joseph had to remind himself that while Daniel had a big heart and was a loyal friend, he was gullible and a bit on the slow side. His friend believed Internet ads and, even worse, much of the slick ubiquitous Chinese news reports. Chinese telecom companies had been running most of the Internet and fiber-optic cable services in the Philippines for as long as Joseph could remember.

"Remember all the stories before the occupation? The Philippine government is corrupt, they are stealing from the people, things are unstable, Chinese citizens are in danger, they had to stabilize the situation to protect them and the legitimacy of the election…blah, blah, blah?"

Daniel nodded mutely, not sure anymore what to believe. He then blurted out, "But something big is going on at the City Hall. And have you noticed there are less Chinese, even in the Special Security Zone?"

It was a good point, and with nothing else to do, they did what any adventure-seeking, sixteen-year-old boys would do: they left the park with Daniel perched precariously on the back of Joseph's bike in search of adventure. Joseph huffed and sweated in the heat as he pedaled down Padre Burgos Avenue toward the Manila City Hall.

Despite the prevalence of modern mass communications, big cities have lots of people, and when sufficiently upset, they could still resort to the age-old practice of showing up at the doorstep of their leaders to express their displeasure at the state of things. Joseph and Daniel arrived and were greeted by a major commotion. The new interim mayor was shouting through a large—and apparently makeshift—public-address system. Joseph had not heard him speak before, but even the two boys could detect uncertainty and a touch of fear in his voice. The crowd sensed it too, as they had also heard of the Allied landings and the Philippine military's supposed offensive. The crowd even had the audacity to believe that it might all be true.

2.4

171300HSEP2033 (1:00 p.m. local time, September 17, 2033) Sleeping area, 1st Brigade Headquarters

Colonel McClellan had his own problems, many more, in fact, than those around him might have guessed.

"Yes dear, I know it's tough and something always goes wrong when I leave… I didn't know the air conditioner would go out, but there's nothing I can do right now. Okay, okay, I know she can be a handful, but she's only seven… Besides, who's the parent?"

He instantly regretted the last statement and attempted to apologize. A heated discussion followed, and then his wife clicked off. She had resented her husband and his career choice since early in their marriage and had become increasingly vocal about it. More correctly, she resented the inconveniences brought to her personal life by the military lifestyle.

Good thing she still likes my paycheck, at least for Claire's sake, McClellan thought wearily.

They managed a good act in public, but a more intimate observer would guess them to be little more than roommates who did not get along and who shared a child they both cared for deeply. Such were the roles they played.

After deleting yet a few more emails and texts, McClellan threw his M10 Communicator on his tiny bunk and prepared to get a few hours of sleep.

An hour later, Cindy McClellan had been doing some banking when she was rudely interrupted. Because she was slightly technophobic and had not transitioned to augmented reality for all her computer interactions, she still used an old-fashioned wall projector, which made her checking account ledger over two meters tall. But now she was looking at bigger-than-life-sized pornographic images. The quickly building stream of incoming messages indicated that it was also apparently on the screen of everyone on their contact list.

Her anger flashed, and all pretense of goodwill toward her husband evaporated when she received a recorded message from her bank informing her that their account had been closed in accordance with her husband's request and thanking them for their business.

"We hope you will consider using us again if your banking needs change," said the recorded voice.

Within two minutes, all the Internet-connected devices in the house started shutting down. The "SmartHouse of the Future" did what it was told and began turning off the refrigerator, the water heater, and their newly purchased augmented-reality entertainment system. Meanwhile, the robot vacuum was trying to clean the cat, who wasn't having any of it.

She was now boiling, ready to explode, and so were 4,831 other military-related spouses, parents, and significant others who were all experiencing much of the same. As she began winding up a long string of curses to rain down on her idiot husband, she heard in the corner, "Mommy, what's *that*?"

2.5

171330HSEP2033 (1:30 p.m. local time, September 17, 2033) Headquarters, Operations Group 3, Chinese Strategic Support Force, Beijing

For a military organization, the headquarters of this part of the Strategic Support Force was remarkably quiet. There was no constant hustle and bustle of officers and sergeants, better known as NCOs, moving from station to station and coordinating issues. There were no phones ringing, not even any loud conversations. There were only rows of computer operators, all wearing headphones, each with a large 180-degree computer screen. Behind the computer operators were the supervisors, who sat at stations raised more for traditional reasons than functional ones. There was just a general background noise of keyboard clicks, the occasional murmurings from computer operators, and the background whisper of the air-conditioning system as it sucked away the clouds of cigarette smoke—which was why it was so unusual to see a group of young officers and technicians gathered around a large screen and giggling almost uncontrollably.

Although completely unnecessary because of the ability to link themselves together virtually, there was still a primal urge to be in the physical presence of others for important or humorous moments. In this case it was both, and the group had gathered around one of the few remaining archaic screens. Of all the events going on, this one had the best vantage point, which was fortuitously provided by a child's toy on the couch. The toy had been advertised as an interactive AI pet, and embedded in its left eye was a small camera that was connected to the Internet. It had been easy to gain access to the little bear, and as a bonus, it had been made in China.

"Now watch this…" said the ringleader, who touched a few virtual icons and the replay began.

A woman was blissfully doing her online banking when a giant pornographic image blotted out her screen and then shot out to everyone on her contact list.

"Give it a minute—this next part is really great!"

The woman became progressively enraged, and through the animal's microphone, they could hear what they assumed was swearing in English. She received a voice message from a bank, which really agitated her, and she continued to spin up.

"And now the finale," the ringleader said with obvious glee.

Messages from friends and relatives continued to pour in as the woman's house began to shut down. The crescendo came with her wild gesticulations, what must have been some impressive curses, and then…

"Here it comes!"

The enraged woman was losing control and needed to vent. She grabbed the nearest thing, her daughter's My Pet Panda, and, after unknowingly giving them a close-up of her raging face, punched it with all her might. After a few more flailing punches, the Panda succumbed to the onslaught, and the feed ended. The group laughed and applauded. Lieutenant Gou took a comical bow to his audience.

Lieutenant Guo of the Chinese Strategic Support Force had successfully delivered an electronic salvo to the American home front. With a remarkable interface, clever AI analysis, and access to massive amounts of data, he had just overseen a team that delivered over 4,800 personalized, individually targeted strikes.

"Just how successful was it?" asked Colonel Zhao tersely.

This young lieutenant was brilliant, unorthodox, and did not conform well to the traditions and authority structures of the PLA. The PLA needed individuals like this, graduates of the most prestigious data-management and computer-science schools in the Middle Kingdom, and grudgingly adapted. The Colonel, as well as those senior to him, would have to bite their tongues and neither press too hard, nor be too rigid on discipline.

"We will not know for a few more hours, but the Americans are already lighting up the Internet as they sort this out. Chaos rules."

The micro-targeting phenomenon wasn't unique to this conflict. The massive data breaches that began over twenty years ago in the Office of Personnel Management, Social Security Administration, Yahoo, Equifax, and others were only the tip of the iceberg. Public data routinely and voluntarily provided by customers enabled data giants like Facebook and Google to build remarkably accurate individual profiles for marketing purposes. This allowed advertising juggernauts and clever political-science majors to tailor products and messages at the individual level. In fact, one of the most marketable degrees for the college class of 2028 was a major in either data management or software engineering coupled with a minor in either political science or marketing. Lieutenant Guo was a step above with a coveted double major in data management and software engineering with a resume that boasted a marketing internship at the shipping conglomerate COSCO.

For years, the majority of citizens in the United States, Japan, the Philippines, and many other involved countries had been receiving personalized ads, yet they still appeared to be surprised during this conflict when they began receiving personalized—and weaponized—messages. This was remarkable considering that this was done as early as the Second Gulf War, refined by the Russians in Donets, nearly perfected during the Kaliningrad conflict, and used so effectively three months ago in the opening of this conflict.

"We tried a few modifications that are more culturally effective," Guo went on. "We expanded the target categories to fourteen based on previous experimentation. This continues to be the fullest deployment of this capability to date against a modern nation."

Zhao considered two facts as he listened to Guo, who was young and lacked a sense of history. First, the American center of gravity had always been popular will. The lesson taught by Ho Chi Minh remained timeless when dealing with the Americans. Secondly, China could not breach the sense of American honor too much. The Japanese had made this mistake in 1941, and it resulted in such fury that the population maintained the will to fight despite incredible losses, at least by American standards. In less than three months during the battle of Okinawa, Lieutenant General Mitsuru Ushijima's 32nd Army inflicted over 62,000 casualties, including over 12,000 dead. This was in addition to over thirty ships sunk or damaged by kamikaze attacks. Yet American will and anger remained sufficient to plan for Operation Downfall, the invasion of Japan. Casualty estimates for the first part, the invasion of the southern island of Kyushu, were above 100,000 Allied dead.

Warbot 1.0

We must ensure that American honor is not too much at stake in this conflict, Zhao thought to himself. *Once they tire of it, we must also give them a golden bridge upon which to retreat and save face on the domestic and international stages. Discomfort, disappointment, and cynicism are simply a means to a new normal—one more favorable to China's rightful place in the world.*

2.6

180725HSEP2033 (7:25 a.m. local time, September 18, 2033) An Internet News Service video posting:

"This is Randall J. Galloway, reporting to you live from the Philippines where I am accompanying United States ground forces along with our Philippine allies. After a historic battle between semiautonomous forces near the Tarlac River, Allied Forces have retaken the Clark International Airport in preparation for the drive to liberate Manila. The military forces of the Republic of the Philippines are currently training as their shattered units bravely prepare to reclaim control of Manila.

"U.S. casualties have been light so far, with only seven service members killed and forty-two ground combat systems and support platforms destroyed in this opening salvo of the operation. While most of the casualties occurred from long-range strikes during off-loading near Lingayan and Dagupan, the casualty rate decreased once Allied forces were able to disperse.

"Commanders indicate that the heaviest fighting is yet to come and while the urban terrain will make things difficult, specialized urban assault units are arriving to assist the Philippine Army with this task. Back to you, Jason."

A few minutes later…

"This is Chien Li, reporting to you for Xinhua News live from the Chinese Special Security Zone in the Philippines. Despite numerous diplomatic efforts by Chinese, Philippine, and other nations committed to the Rule of Law, the Americans and their neo-colonial allies have taken advantage of the lack of a UN Security Council resolution and have resorted to using violence in their attempt to resolve the Philippine security crisis.

"Chinese forces were able to partially delay the intrusion of foreign forces on sovereign Philippine soil by utilizing precision strikes on the landing and off-loading sites in the Lingayen Gulf. While working diligently to limit casualties on both sides, the People's Liberation Army conducted a brave counterattack near the Tarlac River to keep the Allied forces out of the capital of Manila and what would be untold civilian casualties in an urban battle.

"After heroic fighting, the 23rd Automated Battalion of the Philippine National Assistance Task Force was destroyed by a far larger Allied force. With the Allied intentions now indisputable, the PLA will have to resort to more forceful measures to protect the people of the Philippines and our Chinese citizens from outside intervention. As always, the party reminds all Chinese citizens that our soldiers, sailors and airmen are facing great difficulties and we all owe it to them to remain vigilant, patriotic and resolute as we endure the current economic hardships caused by the blockade."

Fifteen minutes later, from the Twitter and Facebook feeds that now dominated world news:

@RandyGalloway: Chinese blocked the Security Council resolution and called in favors in the General Assembly!

@ChienLi: Assembly AND Security Council wanted peace and voted for it. America is treating everything like a military problem!

@RandyGalloway: Check out #ChineseAggression, see for yourself!

@ChienLi: Yes! See #ChineseAggression

Randy had a sinking feeling. He pulled the hashtag up and felt himself flush with anger. They were faster than he was, and an army of human-directed web bots had overwhelmed and modified the feed with exactly the opposite of what was true. An average member of the Twitterati would not have the attention span to go down 1,200 entries and would instead look at the first ten to fifteen, maybe scroll down for a quick check at fifty, and then either accept what they had seen or discount both sides.

Randy angrily turned to his Facebook account and sent out a message to his 1,849,137 "friends."

RGalloway

3 mins

So unfair! Chinese filling up Twitter feed with garbage and lies!

The response was swift.

TrustLi

4 mins

No, only the Truth! Check for yourself on the Manila Times, Manila Bulletin, and SunStar Manila websites!

Randy knew that this did not bode well for the Allies, who still assumed truth would be inherently obvious for all to see. After several generations of political correctness crushed the ability of American society to critically reason, the confusion of the information environment made all inputs equally questionable, and therefore equally valid.

This is going to be a Sisyphean task, he thought to himself. *Good thing I'm not easily discouraged.*

2.7

190830HSEP2033 (8:30 a.m. local time, September 19, 2033) 1st ARM Brigade Combat Team Command Post, near Clark International Airport

The 1st Artificial Intelligence / Robotic / Mechanized, or ARM, Brigade Combat Team was another first of its kind, and its commander, Brigadier General Martin Viale, was uneasy. To settle his unease, he decided that this coming meeting was important enough to risk calling in all his commanders and key staff members for a "real" command and staff, or as he liked to call it, an old-school war council.

"No substitute for seeing each other eyeball to eyeball when making critical decisions," he had said.

Buck had welcomed the chance to see his fellow commanders—most of them anyway. Best of all, he eagerly anticipated lunch with John Gruninger, who continued to perform minor miracles on a daily basis.

The trip to the headquarters had been relatively uneventful, and his three-vehicle convoy remained unmolested by enemy drones. Buck had found it interesting that the PDS systems on his JLTV and the Razorbacks didn't record any activity at all on the thirty-kilometer trip north. In addition to a PDS, his JLTV, or Joint Light Tactical

Vehicle, had an enhanced command commo package and slightly improved armor. It was an aging system, but still a huge improvement over the old HUMVEEs that Gammon knew from early in his career and which his driver had seen only in pictures.

They had travelled easily along Highway E1 from the battalion's position near the small town of Apalat situated on the banks of the broad, often muddy waters of the Pampanaga River. They had seized the two heavy bridges in the area—the only ones that could support the HOMRRs—and established a small bridgehead. This made them the closest unit to the Chinese and nearly equidistant between the brigade's headquarters and the outskirts of Manila, and Buck was eager to get back after lunch.

As his vehicle came to a halt, Buck's driver flipped the drive mode to manual for a little practice, and both Buck and Command Sergeant Major Washington stepped out into the stifling heat. Both men immediately began to sweat as they walked toward the headquarters. Buck was in the lead, and as he entered, a young soldier apparently just getting off shift nearly bowled him over. The man was in a tremendous hurry, and the contact was significant.

"Uh, sorry sir," Private Smith said as he staggered back.

"No worries, where are you from?"

"Ohio, sir."

"Ah, you missed your calling as a Buckeye linebacker. Get some sleep. You look tired," Washington added.

"Roger, Sergeant Major," he responded and departed.

"Lucky for you, sir," added Washington, "that he wasn't a Gamecock linebacker, or he would have taken you out."

"Perhaps it's my lucky day."

Warbot 1.0

⚜ ⚜ ⚜

The mass of leaders continued milling about in the headquarters until the brigade Command Sergeant Major bellowed, "The Commanding General!"

The meeting space immediately grew silent, and those sitting instinctively stood. It was crowded, the sun was already starting to beat down on the ceiling of the modular shelter, and the tiny air conditioner was already struggling to keep up with the body heat of those inside. Buck and his fellow battalion commanders assumed they were in for a long, painful experience, especially since the environment had not agreed with the digestive tracts of many of them.

General Viale began, "I know you were all looking forward to the command and staff meeting, but first allow me to introduce Major General Adevoso of the Armed Forces of the Philippines. He is our liaison for the duration of this campaign and is the Chief of Staff for the reconstituted Philippine Home Defense Command. He will give us a brief overview of his government's plan to seize Manila."

General Adevoso emerged from a group of Filipino officers and stepped to the front of the shelter. "On behalf of General Magtanggol, the commander of all remaining Filipino forces, thank you," he began. Adevoso's English was excellent as he was one of the many foreign officers who graduated from both the United States Military Academy and later the U.S. Army War College.

"I sincerely appreciate your presence here in my country in support of the goals shared by our two nations. Our military histories have long been intertwined. Almost ninety years ago our forefathers suffered together on the Bataan Death March not far from here."

General Adevoso continued in a dignified manner, his English barely accented. "While most Philippine military forces were stationed outside the capital when the Chinese attacked, our Air Force and Navy have been rendered ineffective by offshore strikes. This has severely limited our ability to reposition forces from the outlying islands."

General Adevoso paused briefly as his staff nodded affirmation. It was easy to tell which of his staff officers struggled with English as they were the ones with earpieces. The translation apps on their phones worked quite well, so the issue was moot.

"As a point of national pride, Philippine forces have the duty, honor, and privilege of liberating our capital. We have already suffered over 8,000 casualties following the initial occupation; some of our forces simply dissolved."

As Buck considered the significant casualties, he also wondered if General Adevoso was somehow related to Terry Adevoso, who led an effective guerilla force that fought the Japanese during their occupation. Suddenly, a sharp pain stabbed Buck in the lower intestines, and he started to fidget. Buck was not as bad off as many of the others, but the rapid change in diet to dehydrated meals and purified but locally sourced water meant that his gastrointestinal system was struggling to suppress its own insurgency. He heard a gurgle, but fortunately it was soft enough to remain unnoticed by those sitting around him.

General Adevoso continued. "We were outmatched in dealing with both the automated heavy vehicles, especially the T100s, and the aerial weaponry the PLA used against us. Our Army was optimized for counterinsurgencies, not force-on-force combat, and certainly not urban operations. Your defeat of the main PLA heavy forces and assistance in securing assembly areas have allowed us to mass our forces and prepare for the assault nine days from now.

"Our top priorities are the integration of your Security Force Assistance Brigade now arriving and figuring out how to deal with massive numbers of automated security points located throughout the city. As you are aware, these helped eliminate most of the patriots, both military and civilian, who were deemed a threat to the puppet government, so you know we also have a power vacuum to fill once we retake the city. But that is a political matter."

Noting the look on Adevoso's face, Buck thought, *He knows they will have massive casualties and they still might not win. I respect his fortitude. Heard the Chinese got most of the generals on day one. This guy is one of the uber-lucky ones…*

General Adevoso stood up a bit straighter and then told the group in a firm tone, "We shall look forward to toasting you at the victory celebration."

With that, he offered a sharp salute and departed. The assembled officers and NCOs, more often referred to as "sergeants" versus "non-commissioned officers," began to murmur about the timeline. Nine days was an eternity to them, especially when Allied forces would have to reposition almost continuously to avoid attack. In a battlefield where everything was assumed to be knowable, there was only so much space in which to work. Even with the help of Saga's movement-coordination software, it was exceedingly difficult to remain relatively dispersed. That much movement also created its own friction and burned precious fuel, and the logistics officers agonized over these second and third-order effects.

Colonel Gruninger stepped up and commenced with the staff call. As the Chief of Staff, this was one of his least favorite duties. "Okay, keep your updates to the point. G1, you're up."

The G1 oversaw personnel reporting, and as he finished his comments, Buck became increasingly aware that he was now in mild distress. The pressure on his sphincter was starting to build. He was sweating more profusely, but he knew he could not leave without being obvious. He would have to practice exceptional sphincter control and hope for the best.

The G2 began with the intelligence overview to include a brief description of the continuing threat from PLA missiles coming from the Chinese mainland and the fortified reefs in the South China Sea, which had been expanded over time and served as relatively capable bases until the early phases of this conflict. Most of the islands and reefs had been struck by the Allies in a variety of methods, but with limited overhead satellite coverage, most analysts were unsure of their condition and speed of repair. He then discussed the ground threat in inane detail, including the number of recon drones they had seen, what types they were, PLA stay-behind sensors, his assessment of the counter-recon fight, the popular unrest, and on and on. The G2 continued until the Chief of Staff intervened and let him know his time was up.

Gammon thought to himself, *Always gotta be at least one person in every meeting who forgets that the root word of briefing is "brief."*

The G3 Operations Officer was up next. He had the haggard look of a man running on little more than coffee, stimtabs, and nicotine. He spoke with a rapid-fire staccato as he quickly reviewed the capabilities of the Security Force Assistance Brigade and its arrival into the country. It wasn't going particularly well, and he opined that they would be lucky to get a battalion in time to be effective. He then went on to more immediate matters.

"Two quick points before I start with the operational plan. First, both we and the Chinese are struggling to maintain supply lines, and we are both increasingly isolated. This will probably not improve soon as the Allied Naval forces are focusing in the Indian Ocean to cut off the Chinese supply of oil through the Strait of Malacca. Air is trickling in but isn't much better, so don't expect much in terms of resupply, even ammo."

Gammon and the rest of the commanders groaned internally. This would impact how they could fight in the days ahead.

"Conservation of ammo has never been an American strength," Gammon whispered to a fellow commander to lighten the mood, if only his own.

The G3 then made a more important point. "The political considerations of this conflict are increasingly impacting our freedom of action. Political will in Washington and the other capitals is hanging by a thread, and more importantly, even if we win, the 'what next' still hasn't been worked out. With 40 percent of the senior leadership of the Davila government dead and a significant portion of the survivors collaborating with the puppet government, there aren't a lot of good options."

The commander next to Gammon spoke up. "Okay, so let's say that the Philippine Army retakes Manila and President Davila declares victory. What's our role? We're done, right?"

The G3 fidgeted ever so slightly before he responded. "Yes, our current guidance is to 'throw them the keys' and prepare for redeployment. The State Department, the U.S. Agency for International Development, and their implementing partners are responsible for stability and reconstruction, not the Army."

Gammon whispered to his fellow, and outspoken commander, "He's not buying the party line either."

The G3 was spared further discussion on the topic when the shelter's poor little air-conditioning unit finally gave up, causing the heat and humidity in the shelter to rise even further and increasing the pressure to end the meeting quickly. The G3 finished discussing the overall concept of the operation.

The brigade's Air Defense Officer spoke next about the standoff between Allied and Chinese airpower. He described the effectiveness of the Chinese high-power chemical lasers in Manila as well as the short and medium range systems they had deployed with their forces.

"While the brigade's Area Defense System's suite of medium range lasers, microwave guns, and missiles doesn't have the range of the Chinese systems, it should keep the Chinese Air Force off our backs," he opined. "For now, it's sort of a standoff with high altitude systems: neither side can use them effectively. As expensive as they are and as many as both sides lost in the opening days of this campaign, neither side can afford to risk more losses."

He sat down and the heat continued to build. The audience was suffering, which made the lamentations of the G4 Supply Officer about a drone resupply ship in the Gulf of Lingayan that went down with a load of much-needed 3D fabricator stock and a load of ammo even more painful.

Colonel McClellan discussed the cyber attacks against the families of both military and Department of Defense civilians. His conclusions were not comforting and resulted in more murmurs of unease. Buck heard several of those near him comment on the disruption to banking and other financial difficulties.

At last, the end of the meeting was in sight, and Lieutenant Colonel Emily L. Hawkins, the Brigade's Surgeon and Chief Medical Officer, quickly reviewed the medical system, location of evacuation assets, and how they would triage patients in the event of a mas casualty event.

Colonel Gruninger then stood up. "Any saved rounds or alibis?"

With everyone eager to depart, no one ventured a word, and he quickly dismissed the group.

Buck stood up, felt another gurgle in his intestines, and headed as quickly as he could toward the shelter's exit flap. He knew his sphincter was failing him but did not fully anticipate its sudden capitulation to the building pressure. The chemical attack he unleashed as he walked by the staff was a clear violation of the Geneva Convention's ban on choking agents. The actual technique he used, known as "crop-dusting," resulted in a noxious trail of fumes that wafted behind him as he walked out of the shelter.

With any luck, he thought, *the Brigade G2 or G3 will get blamed.*

It was all he could do not to giggle as he departed the command post for a quick lunch. Those trapped inside the shelter were not so lucky as he heard them make accusations and counter accusations regarding the offender.

2.8

190935HSEP2033 (9:35 a.m. local time, September 19, 2033) 1st ARM Brigade Combat Team Command Post, Chief of Staff's Work Area

"What do you think, Alex?" Gruninger asked.

The stocky Polish Colonel answered him in a heavy accent, "Not sure."

The heat was oppressive for the three men as they talked in Gruninger's "office," a barely semiprivate workspace in the shelter. Gammon saw the Polish Liaison Officer stand up and start pacing as he began to speak.

"But I think it will be a mess," the Polish Colonel continued. "Adevoso and his crew are obviously motivated but were never set up for force-on-force combat, much less urban operations. They are pretty much a counter guerilla force, mostly low-tech, have no real countermeasures for drones, and barely any anti-armor weapons left. Hell… I think it will be a mess even with the arrival of the Security Force Assistance Brigade, realistically less than a battalion now, assuming they can even get into country on time and link up with their supporting units. Looks to me like the Chinese are baiting you to use Clark International Airport to fly them in. Trying to get them in by boat, even with the fast catamarans, will have most of them showing up after the fact."

Gruninger nodded slowly.

"Unfortunately, without the advisor units in place yet, we still have only rudimentary comms with them," stated Colonel Aleksander Garbulinski. He had observed that over the past decade, as the technological gap between the "have" and "have-not" militaries grew, the simple ability to communicate among Allied forces became extremely difficult. He found it interesting how assistance units often realized that their greatest and most useful role in short-notice crisis operations was as liaison and communications nodes.

"True," said Gammon, "but the equally difficult issue is what to do with the T100s. The Filipino military has a few hand-me-down Javelins and a few TOW 2E antitank systems, which probably won't do too much against their point defense systems. The Chinese systems are decent and will probably knock down at least 80-90 percent of the old stuff. Not exactly promising."

Gruninger grimaced and rubbed his bald head, frustrated with a seemingly intractable problem. The solutions available were neither good nor easy.

In his thick Polish accent, a question emerged. "So other than that, Mrs. Lincoln, how's the play going?"

Gruninger and Gammon just stared blankly at him for a moment, then chuckled briefly. Gruninger was usually the one telling the jokes, and Garbulinski's attempt to help in that department was especially appreciated.

Both men had met Garbulinski during the Baltic Crisis but under very different circumstances. Gruninger met him following a decisive battle in which Garbulinski and his armor battalion saved the then-Lieutenant Gammon from an untimely demise on the outskirts of Kaliningrad. Every Christmas since, Garbulinski and his wife received a bottle of bourbon from the Gammons as a long-running "thank you."

"A few of the Filipino units have some of the older L-40 antitank rifles, and they know how to use them," Gammon added. "Getting more of them into country with the current supply situation would be good, but I know the boss has higher priority requirements, like replacing the 3D printer stock that's at the bottom of the Gulf, plus Sky Lances, drone replacements and, for that matter, fuel. Our mobile solar generator reactors are barely producing enough energy to keep us moving."

Alex pondered the situation as well. "What's Adevoso asked for?" he queried.

"They want anti-drone systems," John responded slowly, and both Garbulinski and Gammon could see that he was exhausted. The weight of his responsibilities was heavy and an ever-present load on his shoulders. "But we don't have any to give them. The best ones are on our vehicles and in our air defense batteries, but based on the political constraints of our mission, we cannot commit ground forces to their attack and we're already stretched pretty thin to even protect our forces. We have to get Adevoso to the gates of the city, and then let him and his troops finish the job themselves."

Alex looked at him quizzically. "I had assumed that the assistance battalions would have additional capabilities to support the unit they graft onto."

"Nope. Bean counters, inter-branch fighting, and of course, funding decisions kept that from happening. Even after the Iran train wreck, the answer for everything seemed to be 'just one more maneuver unit.'"

"Very unfortunate," said Alex. "You look like you need a dip."

"Yeah, I picked a bad decade to try to quit."

Alex handed over a fresh can of contraband: Copenhagen. Banned in the U.S. Army following the advent of stimtabs, Garbulinski was not in the U.S. Army and had smuggled in two entire rolls by cleverly hiding them in the case of his chem/bio mask. By the ounce, it was more valuable than gold.

"Keep the can, I think you are going to need it. And don't worry, I won't tell Wiktoria, so there is no risk that Sara will find out this time."

"Thanks. I think…"

"So, Buck," the Polish Colonel continued with a wry smile, "did he ever tell you the story about when he and I were students at Fort Leavenworth and his household commander-in-chief found out he was dipping again?"

2.9

190945HSEP2033 (9:45 a.m. local time, September 19, 2033) PLA National Assistance Task Force Headquarters, Manila

Yu had been waiting for this message from his superior in Beijing and opened it immediately. With luck, the message from Lieutenant General Wei had the answer he was hoping for.

Major General Yu–

Allow me to congratulate you on your nomination for promotion to Lieutenant General. This is a major step forward in your career and has been well earned. In addition to your many years of excellent service, the tipping point came with the delivery of the data from the Tarlac battle. The other generals were most impressed with your resourcefulness during the enemy-induced communications blackout. Using a long-range reconnaissance drone to get the data drives back to the mainland was viewed as particularly clever. Even though data connectivity was re-established within thirty-six hours, every hour counts in this conflict in which starting points are less important than our rate of adaptation.

The data is still being analyzed at the Robotics Institute of Shanghai, Jiao Tong University, and fourteen other schools. The telemetry, engagement, and navigation data were all useful and confirmed several of our pre-conflict expectations. You are, of course, familiar with the continuing research on the viability of "pack" behaviors by large numbers of ground vehicles and the ability of our T100s to predict possible outcomes of enemy courses of action.

We concur with your report and assessment of the battle, particularly in your assessment of PLA human-machine teaming, which was disappointing. While we scoffed when the Americans published the Centaur Teaming Strategy in 2024, it appears that they made a better bet on their human-machine interface and its limitations than we did. But like many things American, they had a doctrine and mostly ignored it until after the setbacks in the Kaliningrad Conflict.

Unfortunately, and as we saw, our formation was simply outmaneuvered by a more intellectually agile human-AI structure that better utilized the strengths of both humans and machines. At an individual vehicle level, their use of Turing Learning allowed their heavier vehicles to learn by observation alone and adapt more quickly than ours. The end result was a four-to-one kill ratio, which was not in our favor. While the Tarlac battle was useful as both a spoiling attack and a valuable early experiment in what we increasingly expect to be an extended conflict, we would have liked a better outcome.

Regarding your supply situation, we know it is precarious. I assure you that at the highest levels, I enjoyed watching the Navy being excoriated for failing to account for the effectiveness of submersible drones. However, that is of little help to our current situation as the enemy Triggerfish continue to make surface resupply very difficult at the present time and their Archerfish have also been taking a heavy toll on air assets. On a good note, the Archerfish have to surface to fire, and due to recently developed countermeasures, we believe that we may be able to resume flights shortly and provide you with some assistance.

Lastly, I can appreciate your dissatisfaction with Colonel Deng as well as your concern about his temperament and belligerence. Unfortunately, his uncle is too well placed in the party to publicly fire him; thus, Commissar Xi would never allow it to even be discussed. Wait until the operation is over, and soon enough you will be posted to a new assignment, hopefully as a newly promoted lieutenant general.

For the People!
Lieutenant General Wei

The message put Yu into a foul mood. *So, I will have to tolerate that arrogant shit Deng for the foreseeable future.*

Alone in his private office, he glanced at his command display, then pulled out a small flask of Maotai, his favorite brand of baijiu. *Chinese vodka, that's what my Western friends called it.*

He desperately wanted to pour himself a two-finger drink, but resisted the urge and settled back into the padded chair. He looked around his enormous office—until very recently the U.S. ambassador's—and considered how much this pleased him. He picked up the flask, drew its smell deep into his nostrils, and set it back on the table.

Nice flask. Overpriced and extravagant, like everything else she buys. But, still, a nice anniversary gift, he thought.

In the quiet of the room, disturbed only by the hum of a wall-mounted air-conditioning unit and faint noises from the operations center down the hall, he had a quiet moment to think.

At least General Wei is on my side. I hope he outlasts my enemies, especially the ones with the longest memories. Those bastards still haven't forgiven me. They asked for my opinion and I actually gave it to them. They are men stuck in the past with unimaginative plans and stupid assumptions. Good thing Wei listened to my recommendations or this would have been a total fiasco...and even with them, their backstabbing has made things harder than they need to be.

Yu got up and began pacing around his office and speaking out loud to no one but himself. "Everything in war is simple. But the simple thing is difficult. Thus sayeth the Dead Prussian!"

His orderly immediately opened the door, took one step in, came to the position of attention, and stated, "Yes, sir!"

"Nothing," answered Yu. "Just talking out loud. Carry on."

With a rapid turn, the orderly disappeared, and Yu returned to his thoughts. *And to think, it all started with toilet-paper thievery.*

He chuckled slightly at the thought. While he found it amusing that the Temple of Heaven even needed toilet paper, as a UNESCO World Heritage site and a significant tourist revenue generator for Beijing, he also appreciated the economic impact of the loss of all toilet paper for the facilities. Beijing authorities solved the problem way back in 2017 with the successful deployment of facial recognition technology that enabled them to control the dispensation of the critical item. Another decade of development provided Yu with half of the scalpel he had used on the Filipinos.

You lucky bastard, Davila. Despite all this, you made it out somehow. Probably the Australians or the Japanese tipped you off. But don't worry, Mr. President. I have every military, civilian, and social media feed looking for you...and DIYA too.

He looked down at his tablet and noticed two items on his to-do list he wanted to complete today.

Item #4 – Complete official commendation on Lieutenant Colonel Hwang

Item #5 – Complete official commendation on Lieutenant Colonel Han

Yu nodded with satisfaction and resolved to get them done quickly. Hwang was a gifted targeting officer and had earned his commendation by providing Yu with the other half of the scalpel. Enabled by a detailed digital reconnaissance provided by the Strategic Support Force and information readily hacked from the Philippine commercial data infrastructure conveniently installed by Chinese companies, police and commercial security cameras, and the litany of Chinese electronic goods in the country, Lieutenant Colonel Hwang had been able to build targeting packages that were detailed down to the individual level. He integrated online shopping habits, credit histories, voting records, daily spending habits, social media activities, porn preferences, club memberships, entertainment choices, political affiliations, family connections, medical information, and so much more. Coupled with the latest algorithms, he was able to predict which Filipino leaders would be compliant to the soon-to-be-installed Transitional Government of the Philippines, and which ones would likely become resistant to it.

All this factored into which list each individual's name was placed on: the kinetic or non-kinetic. As the political crisis deepened and it looked likely that the CCP Central Committee would authorize the decapitation strike, Hwang ensured that the large Wing Loong III drones were actively conducting "training flights" to confirm patterns of life for the kinetic targets. When the time came, Hwang had the thirty-two Wing Loongs loaded with small antipersonnel missiles and then synchronized the strikes with the activation of the security posts. The first antipersonnel missiles left the rails just as the first gun turrets emerged from the COSCO containers.

It was so…precise. So perfect, thought Yu. *Let me see here…*

Yu skipped though some notes until he found what he was looking for.

Ah yes, the mainland Strategic Support Force called it the Lau Tsu Protocol, and in typical self-aggrandizing fashion, they declared that it was the perfect weaponized integration of AI, big data, and robotics. Hwang told me it was not entirely original thinking and while they would not admit it, the idea was inspired by an American movie. Something called "Project Insight," which was only defeated by a bunch of comic-book heroes. Comic-book inspiration or not, Hwang took out over 1,800 of the 2,200 or so "primary threats to stability and order" within the first twenty-four hours. Finding them either at the Manila Day celebration or confirming they were in their homes had been a challenge, but he had truly excelled. Such a tiny percent of the population, and yet such an incredible result.

An abrupt double knock at the door interrupted him.

"Enter," he said loudly.

His orderly, the young lieutenant with the large round face, appeared, marched to his chair, and handed him a tablet, announcing, "Sir, today's target list."

Yu looked over it and noted that it was relatively small these days, usually 100 or less. He pressed his thumbprint in the "Authentication" section and returned the tablet to the orderly.

"Please tell Lieutenant Colonel Hwang to keep up the good work. His timing is better than he knows."

The orderly gave him a slightly puzzled look, acknowledged, about-faced, and marched out in the stiff manner he was used to.

Yu then turned his attention back to the awards.

Deng really can't stand that I refused to submit him for an award, especially the one he put in for himself. What a self-promoting jackass.

Yu gladly turned his attention to the second standout of the campaign. It was Lieutenant Colonel Han, his Civil Order and Assistance Battalion commander, who had figured out a Casus Belli, as well as how to consolidate the military win into something more durable than a bunch of dead Filipinos. Han had a great sense of history and of what made societies work and how to co-opt them, which was part of what made him one of Yu's favorites in the past weeks.

Both men had found it odd that even powerful nations seemed to feel obligated to provide a justifiable pretext for their actions.

Perhaps a Casus Belli is more for domestic consumption than the world stage, he thought. *Everyone wants to believe in their war and that the sacrifices are worth it. There was the Mukden Incident staged by the Japanese prior to their invasion of Manchuria, the Gleiwitz Incident manufactured by the Germans as a pretext for the invasion of Poland, and now this, the Binondo Incident.*

In conjunction with several Chinese Ministry of State Security operatives, Han had coordinated with the ethnic Chinese residents of Binondo for a peaceful Manila Day march. Han's offer of free food and beer afterward "to celebrate the city" certainly helped with participation.

This was especially clever of Han, thought Yu.

At the coordinated time, the Chinese Ministry of State Security operatives, dressed in Philippine National Police uniforms, fired on the unknowing crowd, killing several and deliberately wounding a larger number. Everything was digitally captured, and within fifteen minutes of the incident, prepared messages, videos, texts, emails, and a multitude of news reports were being fully disseminated by all the organs of the Chinese media. At the same time, contradictory stories, texts, pictures, and posts were also seeded in various media outlets that were hacked for this specific purpose.

Paralysis and confusion, both were our friends. All the world heard was that ethnic Chinese were under attack for uncovering evidence that the Davila government had stolen the election, and that a transitional government of the legitimate winners had asked for Chinese assistance until free, fair, and full elections could be conducted. We had to intervene. We had no choice. It was perfect.

"But your real genius, Han, was gaining and maintaining physical and psychological control of this place," Yu said proudly.

As if on cue, the orderly appeared, took one step in, and announced, "Yes, sir!"

Irritated, Yu answered him, "Thank you, you may go. I will call for you specifically and loudly when I need something. Do not disturb me otherwise."

The orderly quickly departed, and the door closed with a light bump and click.

As they had discussed the plan in the weeks leading up to the intervention, Han had laid out his key thesis for control. "Given a chance to go along with something distasteful or to face the certain death of oneself and possibly their family, most people will acquiesce. Kill the first layer, give the next layer the opportunity to comply, and most will. Sure, some will be brave, but once they are dead, the next ones will be less so. The remaining leaders will maintain their paychecks and positions, as well as remain on the 'non-kinetic' list, by our hand."

He was 100 percent right, thought Yu. *Co-opting opposition and disenfranchised groups into an armed security auxiliary was icing on the cake. As was the decision to maintain normalcy in Manila.*

"I only hope we can keep being more right than everyone else," he said out loud.

The door remained closed.

Good, perhaps we are all trainable.

He took one more deep sniff of the Maotai and hid the flask back in his desk.

2.10

191005HSEP2033 (10:05 a.m. local time, September 19, 2033)
Apache Company TOC, northwest of Apalit, Philippines

After several long days, the battalion was at a temporary halt. It was still the closest unit to the Chinese, but other than the frequent repositioning to keep the enemy targeting systems guessing, it was relatively quiet. Stacy looked down at the latest operation summary from the battalion and frowned.

Still don't have clarity on what's next, she realized.

The "next mission" was still partially a question mark in everyone's mind. Their unit was still tasked to get the Philippine Army to the gates of Manila, but there was intense disagreement among Brigadier General Viale; his immediate boss, the commander of U.S. Indo-Pacific Command, or USINDOPACOM; and the Secretary of Defense. Each one had differing ideas of what was necessary and how close to the city they should go, with Viale pushing to go the closest, the INDOPACOM commander satisfied with the current bridgehead, and the Secretary of Defense currently noncommittal.

Wonder how Mike and Steve are doing? she thought.

She decided to find out, and with a few swipes of her hologlove, she pulled up the display and saw that Mike and his company were positioned on the east side of the massive E1 bridge while Steve Hester and Currahee company were on the Highway 2 bridge.

"Not exactly *Bridge on the River Kwai*, but Bridge on the River Pampanga," she said to herself.

She had been placed well to the rear of the bridgehead on the west side of the river. Major Bennett had informed her that Apache company was now serving as the battalion's reserve, both to give her unit a break and to let the repair teams get as many of her vehicles back in action as they could.

Probably good to take a knee for a minute, get the troops some food and sleep. Do maintenance on the vehicles. Even get cleaned up a bit. The combined body odor of everyone in the TOC is approaching dangerous levels. Yuk.

As she contemplated what she had to do next—and she had plenty of things on her list—she could not help but move the ring between her fingers. It was gold with a medium-sized diamond, and as she fiddled with it, it slipped out of her fingers, hitting the floor with a slight *tink*. Two other members of her team must have heard it as they cocked their heads at the sound.

That was embarrassing, Stacy thought as she quickly got out of her command console to pick it up. *But it's a Monday, and that's how Mondays go.*

Her command vehicle was at a halt, which made the task easier, and she found it quickly. *And that's why I should leave it on the chain. It would have been gone forever if we'd been on the move.*

Stacy put the engagement ring on her chain with her dog tags, took another bite of the ham loaf she had been picking at, and prepared to end her very brief mental vacation as she climbed back into her command station.

Sure did take him long enough, three years of dating. Still glad I didn't totally freak him out on the first date. So many pictures of my "first child."

The tropical-weight uniforms were thin, and as Stacy scratched her leg, she could feel the small scar on her right thigh, a souvenir from college left by a soccer cleat.

Just glad he warmed up to him. Eventually.

She instinctively flipped to the picture of the German shepherd/Chihuahua mix. *Been almost a year now, still totally sucks. Still miss ya, Nacho.*

Stacy's blue eyes welled up briefly, and she decided it would be best to get back to work. *Mental vacation time over. No time for this now.*

She touched the XO tab, and as soon as the link was open, she began with the first item on her to-do list. "All right, Lieutenant Dellert, how are we doing on salvaging the vehicles?"

2.11

191020HSEP2033 (10:20 a.m. local time, September 19, 2033)
Near the Tarlac River, Philippines

Technical Sergeant Juan Chavez tapped his dirty fingers on the big machine's hull and looked up at the massive railgun. The fire in the engine compartment had long since gone out, but the smell of the vehicle's burnt innards still lingered strongly in the area. He looked over to make sure their escort, a Razorback, was still in sight and that its PDS was still whirring.

Unmanned, still not used to this. Sure would like it better if someone was actually in it, he thought. *Glad for it, though, in any case.*

Chavez scanned the horizon and the low tree-covered hills and subconsciously compared them to the scorched, defoliated ones in his immediate vicinity. In the distance and to the east, he noted the highway's bend near the river and counted the last of the Strykers from the brigade's second battalion.

Too bad that two thirds of the battalion is sitting on the bottom of Lingayen Gulf, he thought. Chavez noted that they were the older version, which were crude by current standards but easier to work on, which pleased him as a maintenance specialist. *Guess they're finally moving up to their new positions.*

About time. We've been on our own, eighty klicks south of the bridges for twenty-four hours now. Mostly older systems with people in them, but still wouldn't mind a few of them to help out Robocop over here.

While he was technically a technician, a redundancy he found rather humorous, he was also splattered with mud and even a bit of grease. He was tired, and the rising heat and humidity were creating a sense of grogginess he was starting to feel. He looked down at his watch.

Nuts, can't take another stimtab for another two hours.

In the three days since the Battle of Tarlac River, he and his maintenance team had moved eleven times, sometimes less than a kilometer, in the daily ritual of "getting small." In an era of ubiquitous information, civilians with smartphones, occasional satellite coverage, and recon drones galore, the assumption drilled in the head of every soldier beginning in basic training was that everything on the battlefield could sooner or later be seen.

"If you can be seen, then you can be hit and killed," his Drill Sergeant had told him a thousand times, or so it seemed. While mostly valid, this did occasionally cause anxiety in the minds of many soldiers due to the sense of helplessness it often generated. In practical terms, it was complicating everything in his life at the moment.

He looked at the massive vehicle, puzzled by some unusual scrawling on its side. It was odd for two reasons: first, it was written in cursive script.

"Who even knows how to write that way anymore?" he said to himself. "They stopped teaching that in 2023."

Secondly, the word "Homer" made no sense to him.

"Hey Jonesy," he yelled, "pull it forward a little bit."

Jonesy, or Specialist Five Rupert Jones, was struggling. Between the heat, humidity, lack of sleep, mud, ever-present mosquitoes, and now the detached cable between his smartpad and the recovery vehicle, he was feeling irritable. The fact that the cable was only one meter long and no one had even considered how it would have to be used this way made him silently curse the designers in their clean cubicles.

Jonesy had entered the military in 2029 and opted for the technical career track once he made E5 rank. He still wasn't sure he was going to make it a long-term gig, but decided he liked being a technician and didn't want to deal with all the headaches associated with the leadership track. While those on the "hard stripe" track generally advanced more quickly, the burnout and failure rates were also higher. So, he figured, he was prudently hedging his bets on longevity and promotion.

He reattached the cable and entered the command with a tap of his finger on the ancient tablet. The big vehicle crept forward until the tow bar was perfectly aligned with the front clevis on the damaged M316 HOMRR.

"Ahh, I get it, Sarge. HOMRR, Homer, kinda funny. I'll bet it hurt when he got killed."

Jonesy couldn't help but anthropomorphize the beast. He was very human and therefore hardwired psychologically to treat certain things, both living and inanimate, as if they had certain human traits such as personalities, emotions, and feelings. This tendency had been amplified over the past decade as AI improved dramatically, which in turn enabled androids, or robots that simulate humans, to get much better at mimicking human behaviors and emotions. There was even a rumor that Specialist Seven Holms in Delta Company had spent his entire reenlistment bonus on one of the new fourth-generation sexbots.

He ain't right in the head, Jonesy mused.

But none of this mattered to him now. As part of the battalion's maintenance company, his job was to repair and recover salvageable vehicles and return them to action. Of the HOMRRs destroyed in the last battle, this one, serial number #00017, looked like their best prospect. It was only the seventeenth vehicle of its class produced and might yet have a second go at life on the battlefield.

Chavez and Jonesy labored in the stifling summer heat as they finished preparations for towing #00017, chatting with a few locals who had ventured back into the area to observe the spectacle of the strange new vehicles. But while the kids were just curious, the adults came to offer their support and ask when the Philippine Army would retake Manila. A few offered some local fruit, a welcome change from their issued—and very dehydrated—rations.

"Why not just fix it here? We have the fabricator and the mini-mill," Jones asked.

Chavez thought for a moment, smiled a bit, then prepared to respond. Jones was a good kid but a little absent-minded, maybe even a bit slow. He was just being honest, not lazy.

"Didn't you pay attention in BDAR class? What did they teach you about these things?"

"BDAR, BDAR, B...D...A...R...," Jones thought. "Oh yeah...Battle Damage Assessment and Recovery. Uh, we're supposed to repair in place if it takes less than one move cycle. Otherwise, we pick the best and drag them around with us."

Chavez responded with his characteristic "Uh-huh" as he took another long look at the HOMRR. It was completely scorched on one side, the external sensors were in most cases missing—probably blown off—and it had been on its side when they found it. After righting it, they spent an hour of cannibalizing parts from the others and were ready to go.

Both men got in the crew compartment of the recovery vehicle, Jones entered the route, and they began the process of driving back to the 1st ARM Battalion maintenance holding area that was already sixty kilometers to their south. The M88A4 Super Hercules was not part of the latest generation of vehicles and was based on a design older than any of its operators. For a vehicle this size, both men found it odd that it didn't have any driver-assistance technology.

The roads in this part of the world were not designed for one-tracked vehicles, much less two in tandem, and as they began to move, they took care to do as little damage to the road as possible. This was an impossible task. Even if their vehicle had 360-degree cameras and proximity sensors, they would still have left a trail, albeit a smaller one, of marks, scrapes, and gouges in the pavement. This trail was important to someone—or, more correctly, something—that was about to take notice.

2.12

191205HSEP2033 (12:05 p.m. local time, September 19, 2033)
PLA National Assistance Task Force Headquarters, Manila

The destroyed HOMRR's location had already been noted by a large Chinese drone on a routine low-level reconnaissance flight. An hour later, a Ningxia drone confirmed the direction the Hercules was dragging its wounded friend. Chinese analysis of local social media postings helped assess the damage to this particular machine as well as several others in the area. All were clues to the disposition of American forces and would help in the next targeting cycle.

As the Targeting Officer, Lieutenant Colonel Hwang oversaw a small staff of soldiers who habitually immersed themselves so heavily in their AR world that they often had to be coaxed out to eat and sleep. Their AR interfaces were up-to-date and comparable to the latest version of the American software, but they were perhaps more reliable and less prone to bugs and glitches. Conceptually, the two competing systems both shared an AI-enabled analytical backbone that was able to combine cues from every available sensory system, both military and civilian. In this case, the civil feed provided the data that tipped the balance for action.

"Sir," Hwang began, "based on the analytics, we have a 73 percent certainty that target set #26541 will be the most productive use of the next strike. We are not quite sure what we will hit, but based on the pattern analysis of their repositioning efforts, we believe that at least something valuable will be there. There is only so much space available before they have to reuse some of it. It's all about timing."

Yu considered the possibilities. He had wasted two precious DF-10B cruise missiles on probabilities that had not panned out, which had caused friction with his higher headquarters. In the forefront of his mind, he knew he had to conserve his current stock of short- and medium-range drones for the Manila battle, as he might not be getting more. The infernal American and Australian underwater drones were operating out of a base near Darwin, Australia, and had choked off what had been easy resupply for both him and First Island Chain bases in the South China Sea. His logistical tail was an increasingly challenging problem.

"Are there any alternative or dissenting opinions?" Yu asked.

He had seen this staff technique before while serving on a UN mission when a multinational staff used it effectively on a British officer in command.

"No, sir, we are unanimous."

Of course they are, Yu thought, lamenting that Chinese military tradition remained rigidly hierarchical; there was little room for expressing dissent. The upside, however, was less showboating by clever but arrogant staff officers.

Except for Deng…who always finds a way.

Yu pondered the situation once more. *Perhaps this one, which could be there within the hour, would be better,* he thought with increasing conviction.

"Approved," Yu said flatly.

Yu was hoping for some good luck. His other troubles were beginning to mount, especially after a series of minor incidents yesterday with the civil population. He looked around for his favorite subordinate, his Civil Order and Assistance Battalion Commander. Not seeing him, Yu turned to his orderly, who was standing nearby.

"Now get me Lieutenant Colonel Han."

2.13

191240HSEP2033 (12:40 p.m. local time, September 19, 2033)
Vicinity of the 1st Brigade Command Post

Following the Command and Staff meeting and the inevitable post-meeting interactions, several of the commanders, senior staff officers, and a few of their junior assistants remained for a quick lunch in a shaded area behind the headquarters. As an extrovert, Colonel Gruninger drew his energy from the social interaction and was quickly in rare form.

He and Garbulinski were soon entertaining the small group with a rendition of a modern-day Greek tragedy having something to do with a spilled dip bottle in his quarters at Fort Leavenworth. Lieutenant Colonel Al Cushing made the grave error of drinking from his canteen just as Gruninger delivered the punchline. Cushing immediately regretted his error in judgment as red sugared water shot out his nose, catching Buck with some of the spray, which only added to the hilarity of the moment. Al apologized profusely and Buck took it in stride, having heard the story a dozen times. With each telling it changed slightly, somehow always becoming even funnier.

The meal itself consisted of reconstituted fake food and a few pieces of local fruit. The dehydrated meals, which included such delicacies as chili mac, tuna casserole, and chorizo with rice, were adequate nutritionally, but often rather bland. They were only saved by excellent condiment packets, which, in addition to the usual seasonings, contained an item that had been the salvation of field soldiers for generations, a veritable duct tape for the kitchen, an item more valuable than gold: Tabasco sauce. The tiny red bottles were in high demand as Tabasco was one of the few things that could mask the copious amounts of chlorine needed to purify water in most locations.

Units down to battalion—and even company—level were now having to source and purify their own water locally. In some locations, this meant tapping into a local fire hydrant and running it through purifiers. In others, it was river water, causing purifiers to work overtime and requiring the addition of more chlorine. All of this explained why a small Tabasco bottle could be traded for anything in a meal, including the coveted chocolate chip cookie pack, one of the few luxury items that was not dehydrated.

After the laughter had died down from his story, Gruninger asked, "So how's it going with the Navy these days?"

Navy Captain Fred Rohm had just taken a big bite of chili mac and, to his surprise, found himself crunching down on a small nugget. Reconstituted meals never reconstituted fully and always seemed to have small dehydrated nuggets in them. The optimists called them "texture" for the otherwise mushy fare. Rohm grew a bit less animated and shrugged a bit before he answered.

"The initial deception went pretty well. The Chinese Navy expected us to either get froggy and steam into Manila Bay, or possibly take the direct sea route and land on the east side of Luzon. The school of Knifefish II mine hunters we launched from the attack sub *Utah* before she went down confirmed that Lingayan was the best of the bad options. We still lost seven decoy ships on the way into the beachhead. While they're just old ships with big electronic emitters and AI guidance, we don't have an unlimited supply of them, and replacements still take forever to steam across the Pacific. But anyway, I digress.

"The follow-on attacks later were actually worse once they figured out what we were doing. Looks like a lot of our fleet is concentrating in the Indian Ocean. I'm guessing there will be a fight somewhere near their naval base in Sri Lanka. So, in the meantime, their Navy and Air Force are still trying to choke us out, the same as we are trying to do to them with what we have left in the area."

Rohm knew the captain of the *SSN Utah* and its loss with all hands was part of the reason the manned fleet had been pulled out of this area. It was now up to the drones to tighten the noose on the Chinese.

2.14

191250HSEP2033 (12:50 p.m. local time, September 19, 2033)
The Cagula Home, Manila

The lunch of rice and a tiny bit of adobo chicken was one of Joseph's favorites, although the overall portions were smaller than they had been in the past, and there was hardly any chicken.

"Joseph, you need to stay away from the Security Zone and all the security posts. Those containers have sensors, and the less they know about you, the better. The Chinese are not our friends…" His father had continued ad nauseum, as usual. "Some stupid kids threw some rocks at one and then played a game of who could get the closest. The signs are clear, and they misjudged the settings. Two were killed; three others were wounded. We had to coordinate with one of the Chinese commanders to get their bodies. Stay away, you understand?"

"Uh-huh," Joseph responded nonchalantly before he noticed his father drift away in thought.

Wonder what that's about? Joseph thought.

The elder Cagula's thoughts quickly drifted back to June. It had been a terrible month, and the 25th, Manila Day, a holiday, was the worst. A security station with the now-ubiquitous COSCO label had been delivered in front of his small police station on the 24th, the day before Manila Day. The next day, that same station sprouted a sensor pod and a weapons pod, and via the station's security camera, he saw three of his peers gunned down in rapid succession as they departed after shift change. All three were killed with perfect headshots.

He then got a text message: "Police Officer III Ernesto Cagula: Police Inspector Mendoza has been killed while resisting arrest regarding his support for the corrupt and discredited Davila administration. You are being offered a promotion to his position if you are willing to loyally support the new Transitional Government of the Philippines until new free,fair, and legitimate elections can be arranged. You have two minutes to respond or the offer will be withdrawn."

Others had received similar messages, and he heard the terror in their voices. Though he didn't even know where the message came from, he hit "yes" with trembling fingers. *I was such a coward,* he thought to himself before returning his attention to his son.

"Understand?" he repeated.

Joseph responded with another nod and was about to turn and go when his father said the magic words. "School has been suspended until you hear otherwise."

This was music to Joseph's ears. Normally the only real holidays from the beginning of classes in June until this point in the year were Ninoy Aquino Day and National Heroes Day. Joseph and a lot of other kids were now on permanent holiday and looking forward to all the opportunities for adventure that came with it.

Later that evening, he overheard his parents talking, which was usually beyond dull, but tonight it seemed related to the Special Security Zone, and he caught himself eavesdropping.

"It's getting worse."

"How bad is it?" his mother asked. She had never been much interested in politics before, so Joseph's father had to explain from the beginning.

He opened with a diatribe on the Transitional Government of the Philippines, or TGP as it was commonly called. It was a strange collection of political bedfellows hastily recruited by the Chinese to serve as a puppet government. Unsurprisingly to Cagula, they were already seeing their legitimacy, which had been only marginal at best, quickly wane. The most dominant member of the coalition was the Communist Party of the Philippines, which had gained influence during the wild political swings of the past decade by—of all things—moderating its violence and entering the political process. It had worked for the Irish Republican Army and the Palestine Liberation Organization, so they figured it might work for them as well. The Moro Islamic Liberation Front, with the comical acronym MILF, and the fringe Abu Sayyaf Group rounded out the unholy trinity.

This volatile mix was already fraying at the edges. The Abu Sayyaf Group was threatening the other two groups for not being extreme enough and wanted to transform the countryside into an Islamist caliphate. The fact that the Communist Party of the Philippines had no intention of helping to create a caliphate seemed not to have quite dawned on them yet. The Abu Sayyaf Group had been "useful idiots" for the dirtiest of the dirty work, and in the minds of the Communist leadership, they were entirely expendable. This was interesting because in the minds of the Chinese leadership, all three were expendable.

"But what about the president? And what are the Luzon Hunters?" his mother added with a growing sense of concern.

"Most of us at the station think that President Davila is still in exile but might return with the Americans. We also think the Luzon Hunters are an emerging resistance movement. While they are starting to fight the Chinese, they are far more savage with the members of the Philippine People's Security Auxiliary Battalions, which they viewed as flat-out traitors. It's already starting."

Joseph could hear his father try to comfort his mother as they talked more softly now. Since he could not make out what they were saying, he lost interest and distracted himself with an AR game.

It was this irresistible, intoxicating mix of chaos and adventure that would draw Joseph, and soon his friend Daniel, back to the Security Zone. They could not help themselves. *Besides*, Joseph reasoned, *what could possibly go wrong?*

In the distance, to the northwest of the city, even over the sound of his game, he heard a sound like faint thunder, which was odd since it was a clear day.

2.15

191250HSEP2033 (12:50 p.m. local time, September 19, 2033)
Vicinity of the 1st ARM Brigade Command Post

"Medic! Mediiiiic!"

Buck could hear the desperate cry even through his still ringing ears as he lay in the dirt and covered with his miserable reconstituted meal-in-a-bag. The explosion had been massive, and he noticed that it had thoroughly knocked the wind out of him. Rising unsteadily to his feet, he took a quick look around. Most of the people near him were holding their ears and trying to get back on their feet as well.

After a few deep breaths and a self-check to make sure he still had all his parts, he began hearing the anguished screams of the wounded in the distance. Some of the shouts were normal and measured, but he recognized the panic and fear in others.

We moved four hours ago. How did they find us? The missile was big, a DF-10B fired out of the Paracels? And why had…

Buck stopped mid-thought as he noticed John Gruninger looking as if he was at the beach, relaxing and cultivating his tan. He was on his back. He wasn't moving.

Lieutenant Colonel Hawkins stumbled to her feet and knew immediately how bad it was going to be. Casualties were supposed to come here en route to the rear; they weren't supposed to start here. Patients would come in from the front on the battalion's unmanned Dragonflies a few at a time, receive additional care to ensure they could be transported rearward, and then be immediately evacuated on V-280 Valors. It was quite efficient, and on a widely dispersed battlefield with limited casualties, it worked rather well.

That was not her situation now. Now she had an abundance of casualties, and they were all right here. A growing sense dread crept into her mind as she realized that she would soon be making awful decisions for a medical system that was about to be overwhelmed.

Gammon ran to Gruninger, fell to his knees next to him, and dropped all pretense of protocol.

"John! John! Can you hear me?"

John, one of the luckiest guys alive, had made it through Syria and Kaliningrad without a scratch, but after a quick look around, Gammon was growing more concerned. An arm's length away from Gruninger lay a milk-jug-sized battery pack that had been flung like an artillery fragment in the explosion.

John's helmet was still on but Buck saw a large crack running from front to back. Buck debated for a moment whether he should take it off and risk causing further damage. As Buck knelt over Gruninger, he put his head next to his friend's face and looked down at his chest. There was no movement. No breath. John's eyes were staring at him blankly; in a macabre twist, he even had a faint smile on his face.

Nothing to lose, thought Buck as he eased off the damaged helmet. A faint thread of blood snaked out of John's left ear, and Buck's stomach quickly knotted.

Not entirely sure what to do next, Buck figured CPR might be a good start. One-person CPR is a trick on a good day, and the exact ratio of chest compressions to breaths was fuzzy in his mind. He started a few clumsy chest compressions and prepared to breathe for his friend. The first breath didn't inflate anything.

Seems like more air should have gone in, he thought, unsure if he had even done it right.

Garbulinski suddenly appeared, dropped to his knees next to Buck and asked in his Polish accent, "Does he have a pulse?"

"I don't know," Gammon heard himself say in a detached voice.

A quick check by Garbulinski confirmed that the answer was no.

Gammon made a second attempt to get air into Gruninger's lungs. Putting his mouth on his friend's, he exhaled hard and felt Gruninger's chest cavity finally expand.

Was his stomach taking in air? Buck thought.

Buck put his ear next to Gruninger's mouth. The warm, sickeningly sweet air from John's lungs let him know that at least his airway was clear.

The two men took on the roles that Gruninger could not do for himself: Buck as his lungs and Garbulinski as his heart.

Emily Hawkins began quietly praying as she started giving orders and setting up a makeshift treatment area. She was surprised at how quickly her training, and the stimtab, kicked in.

"God help me…help us," she said to herself as she began the worst and most heart-wrenching of her duties: triage. It was the painful but necessary task of allocating limited medical resources to try to keep as many people alive as possible in an overwhelmed system. Triage also meant making life-and-death decisions. If three soldiers would die in the next ten minutes unless they were helped and only two could be saved, which ones should be picked?

"God help me…" she repeated.

Human heads are surprisingly heavy and holding one while giving CPR was not something Buck Gammon had ever thought he would do. Garbulinski paused the compressions while Buck gave two breaths, watching his friend's chest rise and fall twice. Garbulinski started pumping again, 110 compressions per minute. It was hot, and both men were already sweating profusely with large beads of sweat running down their faces and arms.

"Where are the medics?" Gammon said between breaths.

"Not sure, I hear someone screaming behind the command vehicle. They might have lost a body part in the blast."

Garbulinski was correct. One soldier had already bled out in the four minutes since the blast, and three were on the edge. The medics were doing all they could.

Both Gammon and Garbulinski could hear the unnerving sound of a man nearby screaming in pain. At least John wasn't screaming. Or gasping for air. Or feeling the blood start to accumulate in his chest cavity. Or seeing the blood now trickling out of both ears.

The next minutes seemed like an eternity. Both men were quickly becoming fatigued, but there was no one else to help, so they persisted. They had to.

Gammon continued to give breaths, continued to watch his friend's chest rise and fall, but it was changing. The air made an awful gurgling sound as it left his lungs, and a lump started to grow in Gammon's throat. When he tasted blood, he thought about it for a second, then realized it wasn't his.

The medics, or "paramedics" in civilian terms, were exceptionally good at what they did. Three patients had just been stabilized, all of whom required tourniquets. One was missing everything below her shin.

After what felt like an eternity, but was probably only about twenty minutes, Buck looked up between breaths and saw two medics run toward him with their barely closed aid bags flopping alongside them.

The medics had an air of serious competence and Buck was relieved when they quickly took control of the situation. One put on an auto-ventilator, while another put a tricorder-looking device up to John's chest and stuck in an IV. The senior medic did a quick assessment and then commented, "Good thing he doesn't need a tourniquet, we used all of them."

Exhausted, Garbulinski and Buck looked at John, who was just peacefully lying there still with the slight smile on his face. His eyes, which had been blankly staring into space when Buck first reached him, were now closed.

Two V-280 Valors in a medical evacuation (MEDEVAC) configuration were arriving at a makeshift pickup zone, and the noise of their twin rotor blades was deafening. As soon as they settled on the ground, their blades went to flat pitch, and for a moment, Buck could hear himself think again. Teams were loading the wounded onto the aircraft quickly as the risk of another strike was still present.

The medics continued to work on Gruninger until two soldiers soon came with a stretcher. They loaded Colonel Gruninger gently onto it and started moving him toward the pickup zone. The senior medic pointed them to a small clearing near the landing zone. Buck began to walk with them and by the time he was fifteen meters away Garbulinski couldn't quite hear a discussion that was quickly growing agitated. Garbulinski heard the senior medic say forcefully, "Lieutenant Colonel Hawkins orders…"

Garbulinski saw Buck quickly turn away from the men with the stretcher. As the first Valor increased the pitch on its blades and came to a hover, it created a terrible racket and drowned out Gammon as he balled his fists and shouted, "What the fu…"

Then Garbulinski understood. The soldiers were moving Gruninger to the clearing, where he could now see eight lifeless bodies neatly lined up in the sunshine. He saw the second Valor come to a hover, turn slightly to the northwest, and both machines then quickly disappeared over the foliage.

As Gammon returned to where Garbulinski was standing, each remarked that the other was uncharacteristically emotional and had tears running down his face.

"They think he was probably dead when we got to him," said Buck. "Massive head and chest trauma. He didn't feel a thing. Poor Sara…and the kids…"

190755SSEP2033 (7:55 a.m. local time, September 19, 2033)
Family Housing, Fort Bliss, Texas

"So, do you think she knows what's about to happen?" asked Colonel Jonas B. Paukstys as he looked over to Chaplain (Major) Jonathan Goode for some reassurance.

"No, probably not."

They sat in the car at the end of the street and waited for Sara Gruninger to get her two older kids off to school. It would be bad enough that she would have their youngest, Benjamin, at the house when they came.

Fortunately, the men had Sara's best friend, Julia Gammon, with them in the backseat. She sat weeping softly at what was about to happen. The Army's insistence on thoroughness included a pre-deployment form that asked questions like, "In the event of your death, do you want to be buried or cremated? Do you want a religious service, and if so, in what tradition?" And most importantly now, "Does your spouse/partner/significant other want someone to accompany the notification team? If so, whom?"

"Okay, it's go time."

Jonas Paukstys steeled himself. He did not know Sara well, but he had known John. He was about to tell a woman with three kids that her husband was dead, irrevocably changing their lives. Jonas had remembered a pre-deployment discussion with John about risks.

Before he had left, Gruninger had matter-of-factly told him, "You know, Jonas, I really don't worry about myself anymore. It's more about what would happen to my wife and kids without me."

Colonel Paukstys drifted off until Chaplain Goode softly asked him, "Sir, are you okay?"

"No, but let's get on with this," he replied, and then he turned to Julia in the backseat, saw her bloodshot eyes, and almost lost his composure. "Please wait in the car until we have made official notification. And thanks. Thanks for being here."

Julia nodded silently and wiped her eyes with an already drenched tissue as the men got out of the car, adjusted their blue uniforms, straightened their ties, and put on their service caps. As he approached the house, all Jonas could see and think of was his wife and kids, and how they might react.

Jonas rang the doorbell. The door opened.

Two officers in full-dress uniform stood before her, and Sara knew immediately why they were there. For a moment, they all just stared at each other, all in shock, but for very different reasons.

Colonel Jonas B. Paukstys began the standard narration. "The Secretary of the Army has asked me to express his deep regret that your husband John was killed in action near Angeles, the Philippines. His death resulted from a Chinese missile strike. The Secretary extends his deepest sympathy to you and your family in your tragic loss."

Sara immediately broke down in an anguished sob and staggered back in the doorway. Julia came running, helped her inside, and the two women collapsed on the foyer floor and cried.

Part 3: A Fine Mess

"The truth is sometimes a poor competitor in the marketplace of ideas—complicated, unsatisfying, full of dilemmas, always vulnerable to misinterpretation and abuse." ~ George F. Kennan, American Diplomacy, 1984

3.1

192215HSEP2033 (10:15 p.m. local time, September 19, 2033) Chinese National Assistance Task Force Headquarters, formerly the U.S. Embassy, Manila

It was a routine report, but it offered at least some promise. Lieutenant Colonel Hwang emailed the report along with a summary note to his commander, General Yu.

Hwang touched "yes" on the "wake up" icon and waited, fully expecting some unpleasantness to come his way very soon. About ninety seconds later, Yu emerged on his screen, looking slightly disheveled and tired.

"How did we do?" he asked in a flat voice. He obviously had a lot of other things on his mind. Like sleep.

"Sir, I think we got something this time. Some sort of command and control node."

"Why do you think that?" asked Yu, now interested.

Hwang sat up straighter and responded, "Mostly pieced together from social media, electromagnetic density analysis, routine low-level reconnaissance drone flights, and what we think were medical evacuations from the area. Most telling, we have had no further transmissions from a formerly consistent beacon."

"Very good. What do you mean by 'beacon'? Was it a homing device of some sort? I wasn't aware that we had time to implant them that thoroughly."

Yu is reasonably good as a commander, but already out of touch technologically. He misses the possibilities, Hwang thought.

"Sir, it is a reference to any device that will occasionally come up on the electromagnetic spectrum that can assist our targeting efforts. Most often these devices are smartphones. Sometimes we are lucky when one is used with software embedded at the point of manufacture. Frequently, a military device owner will attempt to circumnavigate security protocols because they have either used up all their data allocation or become impatient during operational blackout periods. We have found the best beacons are usually owned by young military enlistees who are overly engaged, addicted, if you will, to social media or interactive games. From your university days when you may have had time for such things, think of Clash of Clans and the like. Or for our Air Force officer, Colonel Li, Candy Crush or Pokémon Go".

The "Candy Crush or Pokémon Go" reference was the wily Hwang's subtle attempt at humor. He was one of those officers able to time things so perfectly that he could slip in humor for which most others would be severely disciplined.

"What was his name? The name of the beacon's owner?"

"Just a moment. Yes...here it is. Private First Class Ronald J. Smith, from Des Moines, Iowa. He had been in the Army for fourteen months, barely out of communication specialist training. He was with the American Brigade's Headquarters, Support and Defense Company. We were periodically tracking him since he arrived. Fortune smiled upon us as he was not able to handle more than brief periods without both social media and a particular game. The intelligence report does not specify which ones."

Nothing personal against the man, contemplated Yu, *but an object lesson that war is still a very human endeavor, and one with human costs. Soon, some of the human costs will likely be ours. I wonder how that will play with our population?*

"Are there any others?"

"Yes, sir. But he was the most promising. I will keep you advised."

"Roger, thank you."

Yu turned off his screen, rolled over, and attempted to get back to a fitful, unfulfilling sleep.

3.2

201000HSEP2033 (10:00 a.m. local time, September 20, 2033)
The outskirts of the Special Security Zone, Manila

Joseph Cagula was chuffing as he pedaled his rickety bike in the midsummer heat. Daniel was perched precariously on the back, and they were off to seek adventure in the Chinese Special Security Zone—at City Hall, to be exact. In the distance, they heard a pair of AG600 amphibious seaplanes take off out of Manila Bay.

The seaplanes were a regular sight these days and were more than capable of making the trip from the main Chinese support bases, most often Hong Kong or Yulin, to Manila Bay in less than three hours. The AG600 remained the world's largest seaplane and a remarkably versatile aircraft that required a water depth of only 2.5 meters for takeoffs and landings, making it perfect for the shallows near the contested reefs in the South China Sea. It was also ostensibly designed to fight wildfires, a design feature that allowed it to serve as a giant gas delivery truck for the Chinese task force. Most importantly, the aircraft were not tethered to runways, most of which had been cratered immediately after the start of hostilities. While they remained the fastest, most reliable method of Chinese resupply, Yu was finding that they were quickly becoming his only method of resupply.

Joseph pedaled past a few of the COSCO containers, which remained unremarkable other than the few that had extended their security booms. He had noticed that the containers were always placed near power sources and often saw the small, snaking lines connecting them to power poles. As he rode past, he saw the large "DANGER: REMAIN 5 METERS BACK! DEADLY FORCE AUTHORIZED!" signs affixed to all four sides of the boxes, which were always in groups of at least three.

They seem to be everywhere, he noted.

As the boys approached City Hall, they saw a building occupied by the Chinese military off to their left. The banner hanging from the roof appeared on "Liberation Day," as it had been reported in the press, and stated "Civil Assistance and Order Center." Joseph saw a small sign near a large door that simply stated "Contractors Only." A few businessmen were milling about, and a long line of people—mostly reasonably well-dressed women—was snaking out of a separate entrance. This one had a sign that said "Missing Persons." As the boys rode past, they saw a few women leaving. Some were crying, and both boys were silent as they considered the possibilities as to why.

A few minutes later, Daniel interrupted the silence. "Hey," he said as he tapped Joseph on the shoulder, "turn right at the next street. I got a text that there's a protest against the government in Rizal Park. It might be interesting."

For a guy who isn't that bright, he sometimes has some pretty good ideas, Joseph thought as he turned the bike.

Joseph did not even bother to look for traffic when he cut across the road, so he found his heart pounding when an increasingly rare Jeepney nearly sideswiped him. This particular Jeepney was especially gaudy in its decorations, even by Jeepney standards, and only had a few passengers in the back. Before June, the Jeepneys had been ubiquitous, but they became increasingly rare as gas prices doubled, then tripled, which was why Joseph did not even bother to look for them anymore.

The park appeared before them, with what they hoped would be an antidote to boredom: a real protest march. The boys approached the marchers, and in a rare moment of good judgment, decided it would be best to watch from a distance. According to Daniel's text, the marchers—or perhaps more accurately, a flash mob—apparently intended to gather at the Rizal Monument, march the kilometer to City Hall for a short protest, and then disperse before security forces arrived en masse.

"Can you hear what they're saying?" asked Daniel.

"Nope, but their signs say something about President Davila. They also seem to be mad at traitors, or something like that."

"Who are the traitors?"

"Dunno," responded Joseph, "maybe the Security Auxiliaries, according to my dad anyway. Hey…it looks like they're finally starting to move."

Five minutes after the boys arrived and less than ten since the mob had unfurled their banners and formed, the marchers began moving at a brisk walk toward City Hall. As the boys looked on, they noticed that there was no sign of the Philippine National Police, Chinese forces, or the People's Security Auxiliary.

Wonder why everyone is taking selfies and filming this thing? thought Joseph. "They look nervous," he said to Daniel.

"Why are they chanting in English and not Tagalog?" asked Daniel.

"Maybe their audience isn't really here," Joseph opined.

The boys followed at a distance and saw that the crowd was leaving the park and moving into the street. As the crowd moved toward an intersection near City Hall, the boys could see a security turret sticking out of one of the COSCO containers ahead of the crowd. Perched on an extended boom, it swiveled toward the mass of people. It had probably not seen anything like this before and seemed almost curious about what was coming its way.

"Looks like that box is telling its friends about this," quipped Daniel.

While he hadn't created it, the slang term for the containers was rather unimaginative, even by his standards.

As the crowd approached, three more telescoping booms emerged, one from each of the remaining containers. All four were watching the crowd with an intense curiosity. The members of the crowd had been exceptionally careful not to have any metal objects with them, remembering all too well what had happened in June. With the boxes on all four corners of the intersection, they also had to be careful to avoid the five-meter exclusion zone surrounding each box as they weaved their way toward City Hall. The turrets scanned the crowd and identified each person using biometric data. With decades of experience and virtually everyone with a smartphone taking selfies, the Chinese had a rich trove of information with which to train their AI programs. They also conveniently obtained a nearly complete data set for the entire Filipino population.

The boys continued to watch what was turning into a disappointing spectacle when Daniel recoiled and exclaimed, "Did you see that?"

About two-thirds of the crowd had made it through the intersection when a security camera snapped around to point at a specific individual, one on the "kinetic list".

A new turret quickly emerged—different from and larger than the others.

The new turret suddenly fired a single 5.8mm round, which struck the man squarely between the shoulder blades and exited his chest. With its little remaining energy, the bullet ricocheted off the pavement and into the far container. The far container did not understand what had just happened because it had never happened before; therefore, it did not have a precedent upon which to act. Without a precedent, it defaulted into its protective mode and fired three rounds into the three people nearest the originating point of the round that had just struck it. In this case, it was from a mysterious spot on the pavement. The three individuals dropped to the ground, lifeless and bleeding. The crowd immediately panicked and did what panicked animals naturally do: they rushed out of the intersection. The boys watched as the edges of the crowd pressed closer to the five-meter exclusion zone. There were simply too many frightened people in too small of a space. The crowd surged into the exclusion zone, and in an instant, all hell broke loose as the boxes defended themselves from what they perceived to be a significant threat. The event escalated quickly up the continuum of force, entirely bypassing nonlethal means at their disposal.

The boxes fired quickly and efficiently, the 5.8mm bullets zipping through the air and finding their marks. There was little screaming as most rounds struck either mid-chest in the heart area or precisely in the head. The boys watched in horror as the members of the crowd fell quickly to the ground. A few made it out of the intersection, but not many. It was all over quickly.

Joseph was frozen. He didn't know what to do. It felt to him as if time had stopped. After a few deep breaths, he looked over at Daniel, who was holding his smartphone and quickly manipulating the screen at a speed only teenagers could.

"What are you doing? We have to get out of here!" Joseph shouted, realizing the danger they would be in when the security forces arrived.

"I got it! All of it! I sent it…out," Daniel stammered.

"Are you nuts?! We have to get away from here! C'mon, let's go! Now!"

With that, both boys mounted their rickety steed, and Joseph pedaled for all he was worth. As they departed the scene, the cameras on the boxes took note. Based on the historical data set for terrorist attacks, the boxes knew that a videographer was often present to ensure that the images from an incident were captured and transmitted for maximum propaganda value.

Security post #143 gave newly designated High Value Targets #3812 and 3813 the same name: FNU LNU, or First Name Unknown, Last Name Unknown. They were unknown for the time being, but the Chinese data collection and AI were meticulous, thorough, and most importantly, persistent.

3.3

201030HSEP2033 (10:30 a.m. local time, September 20, 2033)
South China Sea

The two blips on the radar were unremarkable and moving closer. SSA-238, an Archerfish class drone, noted that they were AG600s and worth the last of the surface-to-air missiles on board. Five minutes later, the unmanned submersible prepared to fire. The low-hanging blanket of clouds prevented it from getting visual confirmation on the AG600s, but that was irrelevant for this engagement.

Christened the *Barb* a mere nine months ago, SSA-238 had high human expectations resting on it. As an Archerfish class autonomous submarine, it was expected to provide an air-intercept capability nearly anywhere in the world's oceans. Archerfish often worked in tandem with one or more ships in their sister class, the Triggerfish, which were specifically designed to hunt ships. Between the two, they provided American presidents a low-risk policy solution to imposing force without endangering humans and the political risks generated by casualties. They also served as a force multiplier when the Navy was being held at arms-length by area denial weapons that put their big carriers and their 5,000 sailor crews at risk.

Two minutes later, the missile ignited and left the vertical rail with a roar. The *Barb* recorded the missile's trail of white smoke until it punched a hole in the clouds and disappeared. Ninety seconds later, flaming debris emerged through the clouds as a hellish rain of bright-yellow fire and black smoke plunged into the sea. As the mini-sub's optical sensors confirmed the hit, it began releasing air from its ballast tanks and making a slow turn to the south. It was going to be a long trip back to Australia to rearm and refuel, but the *Barb* noted that the gap in the picket line would be less than twenty-four hours. By then, SSA-220, the *Wahoo*, would arrive, and the war would continue.

201040HSEP2033 (10:40 a.m. local time, September 20, 2033)
Outside Apache Company Headquarters, vicinity of Clark International Airport

Over the course of the thirty-minute AR-assisted meeting, Major Bennett had quickly covered the operational update while Major Verault covered the logistics issues. Gammon was all about short meetings and was ready to wrap it up. The observant ones among the group noticed him twirling the black metal band on his left wrist, which was usually a sign he was getting impatient to move on.

"All right, team," Gammon said, "we've done good work in buying some time and maneuver room for the Philippine Army. As you've seen in the news, the President still doesn't have much breathing room politically. He's riding the Joint Chiefs pretty hard, so it bears repeating: If the Battle of Tarlac had gone south, I think he would have pulled the plug. We are still one failure away from that, and all the sacrifices of the landing teams will have been wasted."

Stacy noted a hardness in his voice when he mentioned sacrifice.

"We still have to deliver the Philippine Army to the gates of Manila," Gammon continued, "and as you heard from the S3, elements of an Advise and Assist Battalion are filtering in, although not as much as we had expected. Still, they will be a great combat multiplier as we help them synch their fight, but best of all, Sergeant Major Hoban is among them. I hope you get to meet him personally," he added as he broke into a big grin. "All right, any questions or issues for me?"

Gammon went around the group and, after asking Captain Mike McGinnis to stay on, dismissed everyone else.

I hope Mike owns it quick, she thought. Gammon was exacting in his expectations and quick to use errors as training tools as long as they were not accompanied by excuse-making, at which point his evil twin emerged.

The images all faded from view, and Stacy was again alone with her thoughts. She had seen the icon before the meeting and finally had a moment to read the note from Tom. After putting Lieutenant Dellert in charge, she stepped out into the stifling heat of the day. At five-foot-eight, she didn't have to duck as she stepped out, unlike Dellert, who habitually smacked his head on the crossbar as he entered and exited the command vehicle.

Stacy walked slowly across the small opening in the trees and stepped into the shade of a nearby scrub tree. The air was like a giant wet blanket, and she could already feel herself sweating. After a long drink from her canteen, she was ready for a short mental vacation and pulled up the message.

Hey Stacy,

Glad you're okay, bummer on the losses, but like you said, they were just bots. Sorry I didn't get back to you sooner, but work has been totally nuts. There's been a lot of pressure coming down about all the cyber attacks on the families of the deployed troops. All this came as a shock to the brass, but really shouldn't have. The entirety of Cyber Command has been working like galley slaves trying to figure out not only how they did it, but also how to counteract it. It doesn't help that we are part of the newest armed service and still in the throes of formation. Due to the budget battles last year, the other services' focus on major weapons programs threatened to "strangle us in the cradle," so to speak. Of course, now everyone who ever provided even token support is a proud parent and can't get enough of us. The good news is that the first graduates of the United States Cyber Academy will be getting promoted to captain soon and starting to take more leadership positions.

Some in the command are even starting to think that the Chinese AI, especially what they are referring to as AI 3.0, might not only be better than our initial estimates, but it might even be a bit more sophisticated than ours in some areas. This isn't surprising, considering the direction they began to go over a decade ago. I just finished writing my thesis, which is on how the Chinese developed and militarized dual-use crossover technologies by using the Chinese Military-Civil Integration Development Commission, under the supervision of former President Xi, along with the Central Military Commission's Science and Technology Commission.

I'll bet it's a real page-turner, Stacy caught herself thinking, smirking slightly before returning her attention to the note.

So on a lighter note, and for some reason that defies logic, one of my coworkers and her roommate decided to get a cat and wanted a good military name. While our whole gang was out in Old Town Alexandria this weekend, we decided to offer some helpful suggestions and started a cat-naming contest. The more we drank, the better the ideas got. The nominations started out as Ranger, Buckshot, Spartacus, and the like, but then quickly devolved to ones I am embarrassed to mention, the least offensive of which was Booger. I offered a genius compromise candidate, and the crowd went wild. While I have no idea what they actually named her last night, the rest of us will know the cat as "Princess Latrina." Needless to say, Kelly and Lynn were less than amused.

Hey, I'm really sorry, but I haven't been able to get anything done for the wedding because of the crazy work schedule. I know you're under a lot of pressure too, but until this conflict, police action, intervention, or whatever it gets called is over and we can settle on a date, I don't think we need to worry about preparations for the time being. We both have plenty of other things to deal with right now.

Hope all is well and that you get some sleep. You really looked and sounded tired in your last video.

Lots of love,
Tom

3.4

201105HSEP2033 (11:05 a.m. local time, September 20, 2033) Civil Assistance and Order Battalion Headquarters, Special Security Zone, Manila

Lieutenant Colonel Han, the Civil Assistance and Order Battalion Commander for General Yu's task force, had many, many problems. Chief among them was the bloody, very public mess he was now looking at. Security forces of all varieties had begun to gather at the scene and were currently milling about in disbelief.

Unreliable… politically and ideologically, Han thought to himself as he saw the Philippine National Police in their distinctive uniforms. *They will have to be moved away soon.*

Han heard the Harbin Z-20 helicopters in the distance as he looked at the bodies. The helicopters would arrive soon with his quick reaction force and set up a perimeter.

What a mess, he thought as he gritted his teeth and shook his head. *Containing this one is going to be very, very difficult.*

"Major Zhang, I am sure you have already started the dialogue with our Strategic Support Force liaison officer about external damage control. What is your plan for internal target audiences, for shaping the perception of *this* population?"

Major Zhang was the most capable of Han's three Civil Information Support Company commanders assigned to his battalion, and true to form, she had already thought this through carefully.

"Sir, as soon as we were alerted to the accident, we adjusted the sensitivity of our protocols and maximized them to block, divert, and modify all video, text, email, social media posting, and phone conversations on the topic. We likely caught most, if not all, the traffic. We also have control of the major media outlets here, to include the *Manila Times*, *Manila Bulletin* and the *SunStar Manila*, so no worries with them or their online content."

"Are you sure? What are the odds something got out?" shot back Han.

"Unknown, sir, but low. We have been very active creating the counter narrative and alternative facts. While we did not have a specific contingency planned for this, we had a base plan for wild-card events that we were able to quickly modify."

Their conversation was put on hold as the two Z-20s arrived and disgorged their human cargo, which scattered and created a large perimeter around the site. The Z-20s were an aging design based on the Sikorsky S-70C-2, the civilian version of the U.S. Army Blackhawk that had been in service with the PLA since the mid-1980s. Rumor had it that the development of the Z-20, with its unusual five-bladed rotor design, was greatly assisted when Chinese engineers were able to examine the special-operations Blackhawk left behind during the Bin Laden raid.

As the helicopters departed, both officers turned away as the rotor wash flung small pebbles into their backs and legs. Once the sound of the Z-20s faded, the quick reaction force began to erect large inflatable screens around the site to isolate the scene, a proven technique that Han knew would help limit the ability of other entities to create facts contrary to his own.

Major Zhang adjusted her helmet and then continued. "Please look at this." She showed him her tablet where footage of the actual incident was playing. "See, this is when the first bullet was fired, ricocheted off the pavement and struck this security station. Then the next three rounds, and then the predictable stampede."

Han visibly recoiled at the sight of it.

"Now let me show you what the world will see," she said flatly. "Here is the main theme: the security stations saved many, many civilians by quick and precise action." She then presented him with a compelling counter narrative, complete with news articles, video, and social media feeds both sent and scheduled for dissemination. "The Strategic Support Force has obviously practiced for this eventuality," she added.

The familiar "on-scene reporter," using a green screen over a thousand miles away at the Strategic Support Force headquarters, produced what was perhaps her best work to date. The slick video was well produced and already flooding the Internet.

The video began playing. "This is Chien Li, live on the ground in Manila. Tragedy has just unfolded, but it would have been far worse had it not been for quick action by a well-placed Chinese security assistance station. A large group of Filipino rebels infiltrated a peaceful crowd that was marching to City Hall to demonstrate their support for the newly formed Transitional Government of the Philippines. The rebels attempted to use the unsuspecting members of the crowd as shields to get close enough to attack a Chinese government security assistance station. This was a brazen attempt to discredit the legitimate Transitional Government of the Philippines.

"Using their protected status as civilians to get close to the station, the rebels sprang their trap and attacked it. Shockingly, they also attacked their fellow countrymen with several 5.8mm QBZ-95 assault rifles stolen from a Philippine People's Security Auxiliary substation earlier in the day.

"Despite immediate audio and visual warnings, the rebels continued their slaughter, and it was only due to precision shots from the security station that the rebels were dispatched. Many civilians in the crowd were saved by the quick action of the Security Assistance Task Force, but sadly, not before eighty-four had been killed by the lawless rebels.

"Our hearts go out to the victims, and to ease their considerable suffering, the Chinese government has established an emergency response fund to assist the brave survivors and the families of those killed. More information is available at the Civil Assistance and Coordination Center. This is Chien Li reporting for the Xinhua News Service."

Han was duly impressed. "This event happened less than twenty minutes ago. How did you produce this so quickly?"

Zhang look somewhat surprised.

"Sir, this was not especially difficult. We are now a fully informationalized force. It will take the enemy hours, perhaps even a day, to respond. By then, we will have already shaped the narrative and will be looking for the next big thing to distract them. We will know within twenty-four hours how effective we have, or have not, been."

How could he be so dull, Zhang thought to herself. *This is the result of a commitment made almost twenty years ago.* She simply smiled politely.

Pleased with her work, Han departed toward his headquarters. The assistance program he had just learned about didn't yet exist, but it would need to soon. He would leave the security forces to clean up the mess.

Better for the Transitional Government leadership and the rabble that follow them to believe a comforting lie, Major Zhang thought, *perhaps one they even want to believe. While expendable, we still need their cooperation, at least for the time being.*

3.5

210820HSEP2033 (8:20 a.m. local time, September 21, 2033) Headquarters, Armed Forces of the Philippines, vicinity of Clark International Airport

Sergeant Major Ernesto Hoban was beyond aggravated. In fact, he was in his personal version of the ninth circle of a Dantean hell: as an American combat soldier, he was assigned to an Advise and Assist unit, and worse yet, not even supporting a combat unit.

This is complete and utter bullshit, he thought as he surveyed the ramshackle building. *A Filipino headquarters is definitely not where I should be.*

He stood looking at Home Defense Command, the last surviving headquarters of the Armed Forces of the Philippines. As such, it was the only eligible candidate to assume the duties of the Armed Forces of the Philippines Headquarters and had recently absorbed the shards of all the other commands on the island of Luzon, to include the National Capital Region Defense Command, Northern Luzon Command, and Southern Luzon Command. The southern Philippine commands including East Mindanao Command, West Mindanao Command, Western Command, and Central Command simply no longer existed.

I'd give the bastards an A+ on the decapitation strike. Lucky for us they missed the president, Hoban observed.

The newly formed government of President Davila had been tipped off just hours prior to the intervention by what many believed to be either the Taiwanese National Security Bureau, the Japanese Public Security Intelligence Agency, Australian Secret Intelligence Service, the American Central Intelligence Agency, or most likely, some combination of the four. With a government bureaucracy deeply divided and Davila unsure of the loyalties of many key bureaucrats, he had only hours to issue instructions to his military leadership, most of whom would be dead soon thereafter. With a few trusted aides and ministers, he made a narrow escape by military aircraft to Davao City on the southern island of Mindanao. There, an unmarked foreign aircraft flew him into exile in Darwin, Australia.

Lieutenant General Magtanggol was also one of the few senior officers to have survived. By a literal process of elimination, he found himself, as an Air Force Officer, the unlikely commander of what was left of the Filipino military, which was mostly the Army. An astute student of history, he had expressed that his situation was slightly better than that of Field Marshal Friedrich Von Paulus at Stalingrad.

He was in an exceptionally lonely position. While a few senior leaders had secretly held Chinese sympathies and some had even aligned with the new Transitional Government, most of his peers and friends had been dead for over three months now.

Hoban stood in the corner as the Filipino general began his command huddle.

At least my communicator is fully charged, which makes me fluent in Tagalog, which was a thought that pleased him. *What*

I wouldn't give to be at the pointy end of the spear. Gammon's the lucky one.

Major Benavidez, a wiry paratrooper who served as Hoban's team chief, accidentally bumped into him. "Oops, sorry."

Benavidez was at the meeting to represent his boss, the Security Force Assistance Battalion Commander, Lieutenant Colonel Smith, as well as General Viale.

General Magtanggol had an air of both impatience and uncertainty about him as he spoke. He was short and, to both Hoban and Benavidez, seemed overwhelmed by his responsibilities. He opened the discussion with his surviving commanders by greeting them each by name.

Nice touch, thought Hoban.

"General Adevoso, please bring everyone up-to-date as several have just arrived."

His Chief of Staff prepared to give a succinct but discouraging update to the assembled team. The uncertainty in the air was palpable.

"Our mission as directed by President Davila remains as stated in the original order."

Major Benavidez interjected politely—for a paratrooper anyway—speaking softly into his communicator, which converted it in near real time to Tagalog. The slight delay caused him to stutter a bit. "Sir, we weren't privy to the original order. Could you please elaborate?"

Hoban could feel the other Philippine leaders internally roll their eyes, but they kept polite smiles on their faces. It was, however, in Hoban's opinion, a fair question.

"Yes, Major Benavidez. Filipino forces will regain control of the capital not later than September 30 in order to reestablish the democratically elected government of the Philippines. President Davila does not necessarily believe that time is on our side. If it looks like a fait accompli by the Chinese without a major popular uprising or serious attempt to seize the capital by our armed forces, the world will quickly become distracted and accept the new status quo."

With the question answered, Adevoso continued with the update.

"So far, the enemy maintains control of the capital, to include key terrain such as the utility services, Batasang Pambansa Complex, the Makati financial district, Ninoy Aquino International Airport, and Corregidor Island. The Chinese have consolidated their mobile forces in the Special Security Zone and have over 300 smaller automated security posts in the greater Manila area, each one containing multiple containerized weapons, sensors, and drones. We estimate that, after the loss of an automated battalion near Tarlac, they still have approximately one battalion of automated mechanized forces and an understrength battalion of air mobile infantry with helicopters. This, of course, does not count the so-called People's Security Auxiliary units, the large air defense batteries, and whatever they have on Corregidor."

Adevoso was a fastidious dresser and adjusted his uniform to straighten it ever so slightly. Even in the baking heat of an abandoned warehouse, he couldn't help himself. He went on. "Following the arrival of the Allied Task Force and at least some degree of a protective air defense bubble, we have been able to reassemble several units. Some are isolated on other islands and, due to the contested air and sea lines of communication, will not be joining us. But it will be their loss when it comes to honor and medals after the battle," he added with a sad grin, knowing—as did everyone else—that casualties would be high.

"A number of our units dispersed as instructed, but many have simply dissolved since then. Several brigade and smaller units are reconstituting and may approach 70 percent strength if we are lucky. Most will be marginally effective, and the best of our fighting vehicles are gone. If it wasn't man portable and able to be hidden quickly, we probably don't have it. Additionally, and on a positive note, a smattering of civilian groups appear to be committing random acts of sabotage in the greater Manila area. Oh, and the police have been decidedly unhelpful in anything but keeping law and order. We view this as a major stabilizing force once we reestablish control of the city."

Acevedo paused for a moment to survey the crowd, then pointed to the Americans. "To my right, you have Major Benavidez and Sergeant Major Hoban. They are the lead elements of an American Security Force Assistance Battalion that will be joining us. Theirs was the only battalion to make it in before the Chinese cut the air routes. Our intent is to place them with the most capable units, as we will need those units to carry the fight. Of the five divisions on Luzon, we only have the equivalent of three brigades of combat power left, and they haven't worked together before. It is a fine mess, but we will do our duty to our country."

The charge of the Light Brigade redux, thought Hoban, *a fine mess indeed.*

3.6

210920HSEP2033 (9:20 a.m. local time, September 21, 2033) Chinese National Assistance Task Force Headquarters, Manila

General Yu noted the arrival of the electronic correspondence from General Wei with a slight sense of dread. It had already been a long day, and the after-effects from the incident at Security Post #143 had been consuming.

Here we go, he thought. *Let's see what the boss has to say.*

September 21, 2033
Personal for: Major General Yu
From: Lieutenant General Wei

General Yu–

I was delayed in responding to your last report due to increasing domestic political distractions. Unfortunately, the blockade and subsequent economic impact have made the politicians nervous; they are beginning to look for a way to transfer blame should this not go as planned. Needless to say, the additional hand-holding has become a nuisance and has consumed more time than I have to spare.

I am disappointed to hear of the continuing unrest in the capital, particularly the occupied zones. The rebels' video of the incident at security post #143 continues to cost us goodwill on the world stage. I am told that the YouTube News video has already been viewed over 124 million times, Facebook News Network has featured it prominently, and I am tired of our Information Warfare Brigade Commander telling me about the innumerable Twitter retweets.

You obviously understand that the legitimacy of this effort is in your hands alone. However, as we continue to press to influence world opinion through psychological, legal, and media means, the raw material, the actual grist for the mill, comes out of your command. It will be used either by us or by the enemy. While we presently have better informational dexterity than they do, this is likely a fleeting advantage.

Our overall narrative has been presented convincingly on the world stage. The societal cynicism prevalent in these decadent Western societies has resulted in an overwhelming skepticism toward all messaging, true or not, which has created a fertile environment for doubt and confusion. Indifference has become our greatest friend. This is especially true as their counter narratives have been neither timely nor coherent. But this is of little matter.

Our Strategic Support Force's initial Target Audience Analysis was impressively accurate. The loss of historical perspective and the limited ability of even the educated classes to think critically have gifted us with a pliable audience. They embrace both an intellectual detachment from world events as well as the postmodern idea of moral equivalency. This Western idea is particularly useful to us at this time.

But this brings us back to the incident at post #143 and why it is so dangerous. This event had the potential to shock the conscience of not only the Americans, but also the rest of those who oppose us. Even worse, it has already heavily impacted those sitting on the fence, waiting to see how this plays out. We are still having incredible difficulty suppressing the narrative because, frankly, it is hard to explain away the infernal video. Even I was slightly disturbed at the carnage, which is a high bar for me.

To prevent any more such incidents, you must maintain an intense dual focus between your strictly military role and that as the leader of a liberating force assisting the transitional government. Based on the reporting from your Civil Assistance and Order Battalion, I believe that the restiveness can be quelled in short order should you apply a firm hand to the population.

Should you be unable to maintain order despite the considerable resources given to you by this headquarters, it will not reflect well on either your performance or abilities. I cannot, and will not, shield you from the consequences of your actions during the upcoming promotion board. It is only two short months away, and the board will certainly consider your skill in handling this matter.

I remain confident in your abilities and am certain you will resolve the situation promptly.

For the People!

Lieutenant General Wei

3.7

210930HSEP2033 (9:30 a.m. local time, September 21, 2033) 1st ARM Battalion Forward Repair Point, Northwest of Manila

The sun was already climbing in the sky and starting to bake its earthbound subjects, several of which were attempting to repair a combat vehicle they had just dragged to yet another new location.

Jonesy took a long look at the machine and declared in his light Southern drawl, "This one's still pretty messed up, definitely gonna be a minute to get it back online."

"No kidding. Might take a minute to fix you if you had just had your head blown off and were missing an arm," responded Technical Sergeant Chavez drily.

A moment later, Specialist Five Jones made another pronouncement. "I hear the mules inbound. Smith and I'll meet them at the LZ."

The two men trotted off in the growing heat and humidity toward the landing zone in the distance. Jones had a special interest in the unmanned Air Mules, as they were unusual contraptions to a kid from Statesboro, Georgia.

Warbot 1.0

⚜ ⚜ ⚜

A few minutes later, Specialist Five Jones and Private First Class Smith watched in wonder as the Air Mules approached, rotated their propellers horizontally, and came in for a landing. The Mules were used to move smaller, time-critical items forward while bulky and heavy items moved via unmanned "wagon trains" on the ground. Manned helicopters had fallen out of favor over the past decade due to their complexity, manning needs, heavy logistical requirements, and cost. Consequently, they were progressively being replaced in most applications by a fleet of simpler, more efficient unmanned aircraft.

Engineering these complex systems had always been a series of trade-offs. While fixed-wing aircraft were more efficient than rotary-wing aircraft in terms of power requirements per kilogram of payload, the ability to land and take off from anywhere was a military necessity. In many cases, however, especially supply delivery, the requirements were very different for the outbound delivery end of the trip versus the trip home, when aircraft were mostly lightly loaded. The conceptual solution emerged from Amazon.

As it sought to maintain its dominance over its archrival Walmart, the company attempted to increase its drone delivery service farther and farther into suburban and rural areas. The ingenious Amazon solution allowed the delivery system to take off from a short airstrip like a fixed-wing aircraft, loaded more heavily than if it were to take off vertically. After burning off some of its fuel, and hence weight in flight, the drone would rotate its four propellers like the now-retired Ospreys and land at its destination. Once its load was delivered, it had the power-to-weight ratio to take off vertically. The only downside was that once committed to landing at a fixed location, the laws of aerodynamics would not allow it to take off again while still loaded, a trade-off that was acceptable to the military as the resultant Air Mules were cheap, reliable, and in combat, disposable.

As he waited for Jones and Smith to return with parts, Technical Sergeant Chavez looked at the HOMRR and sighed internally. The team had worked through the night identifying fault codes and diagnosing what was not working on the large beast. Virtually every external combat sensor and device was destroyed: optical, acoustic, thermal, infrared and seismic sensors, the rangefinder, drone rack, and on and on. Practically everything. The navigation gear, including the light detection and ranging system, commonly called LIDAR, was also gone and would perhaps be the toughest system to replace.

Too bad the 3D fabricators can't make complex stuff, he thought to himself. *Just too complicated.*

The new troops were busy doing the simple tasks and using the fabricator stock they had on hand to print the easy and obvious replacement parts. In short order, they had a sprocket, a few armor panels, and a few other various parts. Chavez had to give the more difficult tasks to his senior soldiers, his Specialist Fours, Fives, and Sixes. Chavez still marveled that Jonesy had made it this far.

Probably pure persistence, he thought.

The main resupply "wagon train" had arrived at 0530 this morning with bulk fuel, ammunition, and a few of the heavy specialty tools and parts they needed to get the

HOMRR off the deadline report, a report name that was both accurate and ironic, especially now. Unfortunately, by the time they had identified all the parts they needed not only for the HOMRR, their top priority, but also for a couple Razorbacks that could be salvaged, they had missed the wagon train's departure time and had to rely on the Air Mules for quick delivery.

Chavez had watched the wagon train arrive in the morning twilight. He thought of himself as "old-school" and for some time didn't believe that the new system would work, yet here they were. The eight vehicles rolled into the assembly area, dispersed, dropped their pallets and containers, reformed, and departed back to the logistics support area near Lingayen, all within a few minutes. With no human drivers among them, they were generally restricted to known roads that had already been digitally mapped, which was why each vehicle had a small mapping and navigation drone in a roof rack for difficult, unfamiliar situations. If connectivity permitted, they could also link into a remote human driver to help them navigate through tricky stretches. Oddly, this was one of the first automated systems the Army had worked on in the years before Kaliningrad.

Chavez heard the Mules go to flight idle in the distance, an indicator that they had landed and were off-loading their pallets.

"All right, fellers, parts are here," Chavez bellowed. "These machines aren't going to fix themselves. Let's get at it!"

For all the wonders of technology, there were still some things only humans could do, at least for the time being.

3.8

220950TSEP2033 (9:50 a.m. local time, September 22, 2033) Main Post Chapel, Fort Bliss, Texas

Chaplain Goode fiddled with his smartpad. He had never done a memorial service before and his nervousness was starting to show. The old-timers had told him about sometimes having to do three or four in a day after Kalingrad. They also described the emotional toll of seeing families suffer. Like this one.

Chaplain Goode reviewed the order of the ceremony, checking Colonel Gruninger's pre-deployment instructions one last time to make absolutely sure he had gotten everything right. He wasn't going to get any do-overs or mulligans on this.

"Screw this up in front of the family," his boss, the division chaplain, had said earlier, "and I will cast you into the lake of fire myself."

Memorial ceremonies were primarily for units; funerals were primarily for the families, and yet they were almost interchangeable. Families and units were either good or dysfunctional, often perhaps some of each, but it was still an elemental family bond for the members of both. Because of this, family members were always invited as honored guests to unit memorial services to help them achieve the same small degree of closure that the ceremony was meant to offer the members of a unit.

Chaplain Goode looked at Gruninger's pre-deployment sheet and quickly skipped to the "Memorial Service" instructions. It was a mandatory form each servicemember filled out before deployment, and it read, in part:

Memorial Service Instructions:
Public / Family invited: Y/N Y
Preferred picture: Y/N Y, *attached*
Final message: Y/N Y, *attached*
Religious: Y/N Y
If yes, what faith: *Christian*
Preferred scriptures:
1. John 3:16; 11:25-262. Romans 8:37-39; 10:8-13
Preferred music/songs:
1. Amazing Grace
2. In Christ Alone
Other requests: None

It was time. Goode gathered his thoughts and walked to the pulpit at precisely ten o'clock. About 250 people, many in uniform, sat quietly looking at him. He glanced over at Colonel Gruninger's chosen picture and almost lost his composure, again. Although he had already seen it, the picture of Colonel Gruninger and his family at the beach was recent, and they all looked happy, a stark contrast to the softly weeping widow and three kids in the front row. Two of the kids were red-eyed but holding it together for the time being; the other one was a toddler and too young to have any idea what was really going on.

The service proceeded with military precision. There were prayers, music, scriptures, and then a eulogy given by

Colonel Paukstys. Chaplain Goode's mind drifted briefly to his family and how they might respond to his loss. In the background, he heard bits and parts of the eulogy.

"…commissioned in 2013 from West Point…Ranger school…earned a Silver Star for valor in Kaliningrad…battalion command of the original ARM Test Battalion…chief of staff…"

It was then strangely silent. Goode looked up, and everyone was staring at him, including the division chaplain, who, by the look on his face, was now actively planning the mechanics of casting him into the fiery pit.

Goode sat up with a start and then slowly stood up, his face already flushing. Two pieces of the ceremony remained.

"This is a note from Colonel Gruninger that he asked to be read in the event of his untimely demise. It is dated July 1st, 2033."

Goode cleared his throat again and began.

"If you are hearing this, then I have gone to meet my Maker a little sooner than I had planned. Yes, this really sucks, but we are all going to have to get through it. Especially you, Sara. Thank you for supporting me and for all the sacrifices you have made, to include the extra burdens you will now bear.

"John, you are my oldest, and I could not be prouder of the young man you are becoming. I need you to take care of your mom for me. You are now the man of the house, and I have full confidence in you.

"Rebecca, my little iron-willed steel magnolia, I have never had a human make me laugh as hard as you have, and I only regret that I will not be able help you get through the crazy teenage years. All I ask is that you go easy on mom then.

"And Daniel, while we did not get to know each other as well as I would have liked, you have been blessed with a large, loving, and extended family. I look forward to getting to know you better in the next life."

Goode paused, a knot in his throat, eyes welling up. This had been a good man by all accounts, and he still died, which seemed all the more unfair.

The weeping from the front row was louder now, and somehow he finished the remainder of the short note.

After a brief pause, three volleys of rifle shots rang out, followed by the slow, mournful playing of Taps. It was enough to bring even career soldiers to tears and many were. The chaplain was in good company.

3.9

220820HSEP2033 (8:20 a.m. local time, September 22, 2033)
1st ARM Battalion Assault Command Post

Captain Luke M. Olive was an ambitious young man and knew that he had to brief his boss in less than twenty-five minutes. Adding to the pressure, the intelligence product he was looking at was clearly not quite where he wanted it. He tried many different approaches and now found himself trying to coax Saga into giving him what he needed.

"Saga, what is the pattern analysis of Chinese responses to our reconnaissance drones?"

Saga responded in a female voice with an Australian accent, a preference Olive had set in his profile as he found it a combination of hilarious, sexy and comforting. What he did not find comforting was the answer she gave him.

"Try again Saga," he said flatly.

"Luke, doing the same thing repeatedly and expecting a different result is the definition of insanity."

"Keep it up, funny girl."

"I am not a girl. I am the technological love child of Siri and Watson."

"Change Humor and Sarcasm setting to 'off'." Olive did not have time for banter now—at least not with Saga.

"Clarification needed: shall I use this as a teaching point for further decisions when my humor setting is back on?"

"Affirmative. Repeat analysis," Olive said as he waited impatiently for the response.

Olive had been a real-life Space Cadet. Technically he had been in the first class of Cyber and Space Cadets, but "Space Cadet" is what stuck for him and his peers. With the advent of the Military Reorganization Act of 2025, the military academies had been consolidated, and an expanded West Point was the chosen location for the National Military Academy. West Point was the oldest and most remote of the three major academies, and while the cadets despaired of the location, it offered the best combination of history, infrastructure, and access to airspace, land and water. The Naval faculty were particularly aghast at having to teach basic seamanship on the Hudson River. The Army faculty was pleased the nation's first academy's traditions would leaven the other services, while the Air Force faculty wept bitterly at losing prime real estate near the Colorado ski slopes.

The facility formerly known as the Air Force Academy had been converted into the Cyber and Space Academy to feed graduates into the two newest armed services, the Cyber Corps and the Space Corps. The Naval Academy had been converted into the Department of Defense Civilian Leadership Academy as an effort to develop entry-level technocrats as the DoD continued to lose the battle to private industry for highly skilled technical talent in the workforce.

Captain Olive was also part of the Space Corps service-detail program in which newly commissioned officers were placed in one of the services for their junior officer time to gain a grounding in the forces they would later support. As they made Captain at roughly the five-and-a-half year mark, they would return to the Cyber or Space Corps for continued service. Olive was about to be reassigned to the Cyber Corps but volunteered to stay in the unit when the prospect of combat emerged. Not many members of either Corps ever had the opportunity to gain combat experience, so he jumped at the chance.

Saga completed her analysis and repeated what she had previously stated. "Based on current patterns of movement, threats, collection success, and losses of air, ground, and subsurface reconnaissance drones, Chinese responses have been within one half of one standard deviation of predicted outcomes. Recommend maintaining current Mission Command III execution parameters."

Luke thought for a moment and then said, "You really are the brains behind the Mission Command package, huh?"

"I am."

Olive paused for a moment and then said, "Saga, what is the pattern analysis of the enemy recon drones?"

In a voice reminiscent of the now-sixty-six-year-old Nicole Kidman in her prime, Saga responded, "Please stand by."

Even with supercomputers, the things Olive was asking of a relatively new system were non-standard and sifting through a mountain of data while attempting to access data stateside would still take a minute or more.

After a few moments, Saga responded. Olive suddenly sat up straight, adjusted his AR helmet and quickly said, "Open a comm link to Captain Adams."

Captain Sophia Adams' image appeared in his helmet. Even in an AR helmet, she was attractive, quite a remarkable achievement.

"Hey, I need your take on this before I go to my boss. Saga, transfer data to Adams."

"Not necessary, all stations have access to the same data."

That was embarrassing, he thought and said, "Play analysis for Adams."

Saga repeated its analysis, which Luke overheard, except that it sounded different. Very different.

"Steve Trevor…from the first *Wonder Woman* movie…is your Saga voice?"

"Ha, ha…it's Chris Pine's voice from the classic movie pack. I was thirteen when *Wonder Woman* came out, and I've had a crush on him ever since. You still listening to that Aussie chick?"

Luke was slightly embarrassed and his response was meek. "Uh-huh," was the best he could do. He was doubly glad, though, that the humor and sarcasm setting was off.

Adams paused for a moment. "Saga," she asked, "what is the pattern analysis of the enemy recon drone flights and sightings," she paused again and then emphasized, "overlaid along the Philippine military's likely routes of attack?"

When the response came, it concerned them both. Olive summarized what they were thinking. "It's getting a lot harder to hide a needle in a haystack these days. We need to get word to them."

All this did not bode well for General Magtanggol.

3.10

221545HSEP2033 (3:45 p.m. local time, September 22, 2033)
1st ARM Battalion Forward Assembly Area

Lieutenant Colonel Buck Gammon was in the back of his command vehicle eating one of the few non-dehydrated treats in the ration bag. They were as coveted as they were rare: a small bag of plain M&Ms. These wonderful little creations were descendants of the British Smarties, which Forrest Mars Sr. had seen soldiers eating during the Spanish Civil War. Fortuitously, he patented his candy-coating process just in time for WWII, and due to wartime rationing, the military became his exclusive customer. Remarkably, these treats remained relatively unchanged over time except for the addition of caffeine to the field-ration version.

The Headquarters, Support and Defense Company, the Roughriders, had just finished yet another repositioning, and as his command vehicle was part of the company, he had to participate in the process. The rest of the companies would sequence through their moves with one company on the move every three to four hours.

Constant chaos, but a necessary precaution, he thought. *Just like the pre-deployment exercises at Fort Bliss. Equally hot but far more tolerable due to the lack of humidity. And no one was really trying to kill us then.*

Buck's thoughts were still absorbed in the field memorial service for John and the others who had been killed. The service for the troops in the Philippines had been only a few hours ago and had been harder on him than he had expected. For security reasons, only a few people had been allowed to physically gather, but quite a few were there virtually or saw the recording.

He was such a good man, so why him? Hey God…it makes no sense to me.

Many of the troops, especially the younger ones, had not previously experienced an intimate death and were struggling to deal with the loss of their peers. Virtually everyone in the brigade's commo section was either dead or severely wounded.

Gammon had remembered seeing this a decade ago with his troops in Kaliningrad. Virtual online "friends" were of little help then or now when it came to providing closure. Buck liked Chaplain Liteky, who did a good job with the small service and continued to do his best to fulfill the Chaplain's motto to "nurture the living, care for the wounded, and honor the dead." That was not something that could be done with AR, yet another challenge of widely dispersed operations.

Buck had just finished his last piece of candy when something Liteky said at last week's regular field service resurfaced: "Despite the many, and often confusing, advances in technology, war remains by its nature a very, very human endeavor. And here is my point, it applies its destructive force against not only friend and foe, but if we're not careful, also against our own hearts."

Good point, hate leads to the dark side, he thought, forcing a smile at the movie reference, as Major Bennett, Major Verault, and newly promoted Command Sergeant Major

Washington filed in. Their eyes were clearer, and all had more energy than the last time he had seen them four hours ago. Buck could tell they were starting to feel the effects of recently ingested stimulants. He was too.

I wonder if I looked that bad…

They all squeezed in and sat down in the cramped space. The outriggers were deployed, so the walls of the command vehicle had been expanded, which allowed a little more room and kept them from feeling as though they were sitting on each other's laps.

Gammon looked at his team. While they were streaked with dirt and smelled for the lack of showers, he was deeply proud of them. Natives of New Orleans, Charleston, Killen, and Fayetteville, all but one had at least one parent in the military. With Bennett and Verault being a good ten years younger than he and Sergeant Major Washington, they looked almost too young to be in the positions they were.

A family business, indeed, he thought. *I know their parents are proud of them. I hope mine would have been.*

Gammon's mind quickly snapped back to the operational issues at hand as he looked at Major Bennett. "All right 3, how are we doing?" he asked.

"Sir, pretty well actually. Our maintenance teams are doing pretty well, salvaging some of the wrecks from Captain Doss's company, and the losses won't degrade our mission. Speaking of which, despite the cabinet meetings in DC and all the drama-full coverage, our mission has not changed: we get the Philippine Army to the edge of Manila, give them a protective air bubble, and let them have at it. President Davila continues to insist that for national legitimacy reasons, Filipino forces must liberate Manila without foreign forces. Our President remains happy to oblige on this point."

"What about the Advise and Assist units?"

"Well, sir…" she hesitated, "that's a bit less clear. General Viale is still giving them maximum latitude to go forward with their supported units, but he was also very clear about not taking unnecessary risks."

"Like what?"

"Like anything that could result in casualties."

Gammon shook his head. "Somehow I don't think that will stop Sergeant Major Hoban. He'll end up as far forward as he thinks he needs to be, which means where there'll be lots of bullets going back and forth and terrified troops needing courage. He was simply amazing in Kaliningrad." Gammon's face suddenly darkened. "It was a real mess, lots of casualties. Half the platoon made it because of him, and that's where I know Colonel Garbulinski from. At the last moment, his armor company saved what was left of us from a pair of Russian T-14s that were closing in on us."

The other three were suddenly silent and partly wide-eyed as they processed this new information. They had heard Gammon speak briefly about Sergeant Major Hoban and Colonel Garbulinski, but the boss had never before talked about his time as a platoon leader and no one had dared to ask him. They had all seen him in his dress uniform wearing the Silver Star for valor, but the accounts of his actions that day were all secondhand. The three of them had never seen combat, and they all realized this was a profound moment.

Then, just as suddenly as it came, the look left him, and Gammon's usual calm and determined demeanor returned. He quickly added, "But that was a long time ago, and I digress. Our troops will face plenty worse…please continue, Megan."

Caught by surprise by the previous revelation, Megan regained her train of thought and continued. "Sir, the Headquarters, Support and Defense Company had to spread out the protection platoon so far that the point defense systems, sentry drones, and perimeter hives are barely able to provide interlocking coverage. As always, real soldiers will be in short supply for patrolling, and some of the ones we have are bordering on combat ineffective due to dysentery."

"Thanks, Megan. Has anyone figured out how the DF-10, or whatever it was, got through?"

"No, sir," she paused. "They're pretty sure it was a DF-10, but both the location of the hit and the timing were beyond what we would expect based on the defensive systems in place. The electromagnetic camouflage and point defense systems should have gotten it, or at least degraded its accuracy."

"Roger." Gammon paused for a moment, puzzled by the facts he was given. Then in a somewhat cheerful voice, he asked, "Alrighty, XO, how are we postured logistically?"

Verault was perhaps the smoothest talking human Gammon had ever known. While Verault lacked the killer instinct needed for command, Gammon never doubted that he would continue to excel on the staff track and be a division, or higher, chief of staff one day. As an executive officer, he was a masterful administrator, a veritable magician with logistics, and he could charm the pants off anyone he met, which was why he was picked to serve in the first ARM Battalion to see combat.

Verault began with his strangely soothing New Orleans accent. It was almost mesmerizing to see him in full persuasion mode, whether with other staff officers, bosses, subordinates, or the opposite sex. It was almost like watching a snake charmer at work.

"Sir, the good news is that we are at 82 percent energy capacity and climbing. We burned a lot of battery juice and JP-8 diesel getting here. Apache Company even dipped down below 30 percent energy reserves at one point. The wagon trains are arriving adequately, and while our stocks are rising a bit, as a brigade task force we remain between Scylla and Charybdis."

"What??" asked Bennett and Washington simultaneously.

Verault made a game of using obscure references during his briefs and hoped to stump the boss one of these days. Unfortunately for him, today was not the day.

"I'll take Greek mythology for $300, Mark. What is a choice between two evils?"

Foiled again…

"You are correct, sir. Our supply lines are being choked off by the Chinese, and General Viale is having to choose between more Advise and Assist units, ammunition, fuel, and repair parts. On the upside, the Small Modular Reactors are cranked up and recharging the battery packs and their backups quickly. We also believe we will get several of the damaged vehicles repaired within the next seventy-two hours. Although having to move busted vehicles frequently is tough on the crews, they are managing. Oh, and Colonel McClellan is standing in as the Chief of Staff. At our meeting today he mentioned that the 15-6 on Captain Doss and yourself will be done in the next twenty-four hours."

"Awesome," Gammon responded with a forced smile.

"And, sir, I am sorry for the loss of your friend."

Gammon paused before he responded, as if he were becoming lost in thought. "Thanks. Let's hope there aren't any more. Sergeant Major, what do you have?"

"Sir, the troops are tired, but morale is good. A few down for dysentery, but manageable, and no casualties yet."

"Good. Just for perspective, think about how far we as an army have come. We made a movement across the peninsula, fought a meeting engagement, destroyed an automated enemy battalion, and arrived here with zero human casualties. I want us to continue to win 100-0 as we support the upcoming Filipino attack. We have lots to do, so let's get at it."

The four stood, and Verault and Bennett stepped into the oven outside, unaware of their commander's increasing anguish. Sergeant Major Washington remained behind, and Gammon turned to him. Washington was the nearest to being his peer in terms of age and experience in the battalion.

Gammon looked him dead in the face and stated, "You know, by the time this ends, we'll probably have casualties, and they may even be us. We need to be ready to fight through all of it. Fear is contagious, and so is courage. I'll need you to be where I can't."

The intensity in Gammon's face took Washington aback, and he paused for a moment before responding. "Roger, sir, I'll do my best. I know I got dropped into this at the last minute, but you can count on me."

He noticed Gammon moving the black band on his wrist. "Sir, whose name is on the band?"

He saw Gammon flinch and an ever-so-brief flash of anger cross his face, which passed almost as quickly.

Gammon exhaled and responded, "A fair question." Shifting his weight on his prosthetic leg, he continued quietly, "Specialist Emily Madison, KIA, October 13, 2023, Kaliningrad. She was my gunner. I watched the life leave her from three feet away. It only took about ten seconds, or so they tell me. Seemed more like a short eternity. Non-survivable…never felt so helpless."

Sergeant Major Washington had just ripped the scab off his boss's wound, and he felt awful for having done so. His face flushed as he said, "Sir, I am sorry. I had no idea it was personal…"

"No…it's okay. It never gets easier. She was a good kid. Gave her best…"

As Gammon straightened up and his iron resolve returned, Washington glimpsed a pent-up ferocity and started to gather why the young troops, most of whom he was still getting to know, called him "Da Man."

When Gammon got up, he began donning his gear and Washington quickly followed.

"Let's go check on the troops. It's always good to see them and it always motivates me. We owe them our best."

"Always, sir. Always."

Part 4: The Hard Way

"Victory smiles upon those who anticipate the changes in the character of war, not upon those who wait to adapt themselves after they occur." ~ General Guido Douhet, The Command of the Air, 1942

4.1

230845HSEP2033 (8:45a.m. local time, September 23, 2033) Special Security Zone, Manila

A soft breeze pushed them back and forth in the morning sun. Other than at a family funeral, the three men hanging by their necks on a crude scaffolding were the first real dead people Joseph and Daniel had ever seen. Two were middle-aged, one was maybe twenty, and their gentle, lifeless sway gave the southwest end of Rizal Park a sickening, macabre feel. The large sign that hung above them was clearly intended to be seen at a distance. Joseph read it to himself:

> These enemies of the people have been found guilty by a People's Court of subverting the Transitional Government of the Philippines. The same fate will come to others who fight against the common good and the legitimate government of our country.
> – The People's Security Auxiliary of the Transitional Government of the Philippines

From half a soccer field away, the boys looked on in amazement.

Joseph spoke first. "Neither the men nor that H were here yesterday."

"What H?" responded Daniel.

"The one on that bench. The one right there," Joseph said as he pointed to it.

"So, what's with the H?" Daniel asked.

"Hunters. A throwback to an insurgent group from World War Two. Didn't you pay attention in history?"

"Nope," Daniel said, shrugging.

"You know, they aren't the first ones who ended up like this. I heard that it started three or four days ago."

They didn't know any of the men and had not seen how they ended up like this. From a distance, it simply didn't seem real.

"I wonder what they did?" asked Daniel slowly.

Joseph thought for a moment before answering. "Maybe nothing. Maybe texted support for the president. Who knows? I heard from my dad that things are starting to get harder for the Transitional Government and the Chinese. They're now going after the enemies of the people, real and imagined. Accusing someone of being a loyalist to President Davila can be a death sentence for them—according to my dad, anyway."

"But President Davila and General Magtanggol both appeared on the news together last night and told everyone to cooperate with the Transitional Government until legitimate elections could be arranged," said Daniel. "General Magtanggol even said that the Army, Navy, and Air Force were not returning to Manila and would put themselves between the invading Americans and the capital to protect our sovereignty. He even said that the Americans were here to help the disloyal elements of the military and to re-colonize our country!"

"Seriously?" Joseph just looked at him for a moment and had to remind himself, *heart of gold, brain of stone*. "Pure CGI generated. That technology has been around since before we were born. It just wasn't used much because it could be discredited easily."

Joseph was impressed with himself for using a couple big words, since he was only a C+ student himself.

Daniel, however, was not as impressed with Joseph's answer and seemed to only partly accept Joseph's version of events. "But I saw it," he said.

Joseph's phone began to buzz, thanks to the marginal service he still had in the city, which seemed really weird to him considering all that had happened. Some people thought that the Chinese helped keep it all working in Manila to make people here happy and to ensure the news reports still looked good. Pulling his phone from his pocket, he saw, to his dismay, it was his dad and not Nicole, the girl from math class whom he was attempting somewhat futilely to woo.

Probably going to tell me to come home, it's too dangerous, blah, blah, blah, he thought as he sent the call to voicemail. *I'll get it later.*

As he looked down, he noticed a small flyer from the Hunters lying on the ground. He picked it up and read the simple message about the Chinese and their lackeys, the People's Security Auxiliary. Both boys had seen more Civil Order Patrols in the last few days, especially since rumors started that the Allies had landed.

I like that one, almost as much as the one about the Filipino military preparing to liberate the city, Joseph thought. *I wonder if they're true. Mom and Dad seem to think so. Not much news from up north though.*

Joseph let go of the piece of paper and watched it tumble to the ground in the light breeze. His father had lectured him not to touch these flyers or, even worse, get caught with one. With little else to do, the boys pedaled farther into the occupied zone on Joseph's rickety bike, being sure to give a wide berth to the Civil Order Patrols.

As the boys meandered along, they noticed that the traffic was especially thin, which was probably because of the fuel shortage. Only a few ships were docking in the port anymore. In the distance, they heard the roar of three AG600 seaplanes taking off out of the bay, bound for somewhere far off. They were the only big planes they saw anymore as the Ninoy Aquino Airport still had lots of craters in the runways from an American strike last week.

Pedaling along, the boys noticed only a few new things. However, the cameras and sensors of the city were far more observant and carefully noticed several new data points. The Chinese AI system was increasing its confidence level as it registered possible matches for High Value Targets #3812 and 3813.

4.2

230910HSEP2033 (9:10 a.m. local time, September 23, 2033)
Southern edge of Cabanatuan City, Philippines

Standing above the entrance to the temporary division headquarters—although "headquarters" was a generous term for the abandoned school—the makeshift sign said, "Only Our Best Is Good Enough." It was the motto of the Philippine 5th Infantry Division, otherwise known as the Star Division, and it was on the move from its now-wrecked base at Camp Upi in Gamu, Isabela. After six days on the move, the division had covered over 120 miles.

The soldiers of the 5th Division had made the trip in a manner reminiscent of the "Taxis of the Marne," in which the French military impressed several thousand Parisian taxis to transfer troops to the front during the desperate fighting in September 1914. In a similar way, the 5th Division made its long movement aided by the ubiquitous Filipino Jeepneys. Part jeep, part truck, part extravagantly decorated art show, several hundred had helped the division move its soldiers and equipment closer to the coming fight. While still a division in name, it was down to a third of its original strength; in reality, it was only a brigade-sized force with around 4,300 soldiers remaining.

Kinda corny, but I like it, thought Sergeant Major Hoban as he moved under the "Only Our Best Is Good Enough" sign.

The dual-rotor Valors had dropped off twenty-two fellow members of his Security Force Assistance Battalion barely an hour ago. Hoban had watched as they settled into the landing zone and thought they looked like giant tadpoles holding onto ceiling fans. After disgorging their passengers, they lifted off vertically and, before they had cleared the landing zone, were already rotating their engine nacelles forward to gain maximum speed. The smell of diesel exhaust wafted over him as they left.

A good smell, he thought.

The recent arrivals were only a fraction of the unit, but Hoban was now finally approaching happiness with the sounds and smells of an army in the field. His boss, Major Benavidez, was already coordinating with the division staff and organizing the assistance team with respect to their specific assignments. Nothing was doctrinally as it should be, but that was okay as most of the unit was comfortable with improvisation and 'winging it' when necessary. As Benavidez departed, he had asked Hoban to quickly assess the fighting skill of the 5th Division. Due to President Davila's unrealistic timeline, the Armed Forces of the Philippines had only a week to recapture their capital, which left them little time to assist the unit and help it.

Hell, it'll take us most of the week just to get to our assault position, gather all the units, and prepare for some semblance of a coherent attack, thought Hoban.

Like all good paratroopers, he was an ascetic at heart and the thought of a long, forced march secretly appealed to him.

After a few hours of observing the troops, the leaders, and equipment, Hoban decided he had enough useful information to form an initial assessment of the unit. He had inquired about resources from nearby Fort Magsaysay, the Philippine Army's largest base, but was informed that it—along with several of the other major bases—had been well flattened in the opening days of the conflict. Only a few surviving troops, a smattering of leaders, and a limited amount of equipment trickled in from the local area. It took him another hour to find Benavidez, and they sat down in a first-floor classroom of the school.

"What do you think?" asked Benavidez.

"Tough situation, sir. Virtually no heavy equipment. The division was primarily set up as a counterinsurgency outfit. The division commander and a few other senior leaders were killed up front as most of the senior leadership had the misfortune to be in Manila on the 25th. When the Chief of Staff declined a sudden promotion opportunity, he was killed as well.

"On the upside," Hoban continued, "because it was a light division and around 175 miles away from Manila, the Chinese gave it low priority for follow-on strikes. They didn't figure it would ever be in play. Only a couple DF-10s arrived to make the point of who was in charge now. Most of the rest of the leadership is relatively intact. They did have a number of soldiers—and even a few leaders—desert, but this is a relatively coherent force."

Benavidez thought for a moment, took off his helmet, and sat down with his back against the wall. "What about morale?"

Hoban also took his helmet off and wiped his sweaty forehead with his sleeve. He was careful not to damage the Augmented Reality screen as he placed it on the ground and promptly used it as a field stool.

He thought for a moment before responding. "Not bad, sir. Maybe even okay, all things considered. After walking around with my electronic translator for a while, I think the troops that are here are certainly pissed, motivated, and reasonably well led. The NCOs are solid, but it appears that their military does not give them as much authority and autonomy as we do, which is unfortunate.

"Another thing, some of the troops, and even some of the leaders, are still confused by the ongoing propaganda war. The deep fake video of President Davila and General Magtanggol was particularly convincing. It took the government and the chain of command awhile to rebut it, and even then, the response was a bit clumsy. Oh, and comms with 1st ARM Battalion still suck. Our commo guys, all two of them, are working it."

Benavidez took it all in. The 1st ARM Battalion was less than ten kilometers away, but they might as well have been on the far side of the moon until comms were consistent.

"I haven't met the commander, a guy by the name of Gammon. Ever heard of him?"

"I have. He won't let us down," responded Hoban. *I was there when he got the moniker "Da Man,"* Hoban thought, *and while I like you and think you're a good major, Gammon's in a different league.*

Ever the professional and not wanting his current boss to be intimidated by either Hoban's relationship with, or opinion of Gammon, he quickly changed the subject. "Sir, do you think General M has settled down yet? He was super-pissed. I gotta admit, it was a well-done hit piece."

"Masterful, in fact." Benavidez, glancing at his watch, noted the time and then added, "Why don't we go see Lieutenant Colonel Malaya and see what's next?"

The idea seemed like a good one to them both, so they walked down the stifling hall to the division operations chief's makeshift office. With no power, the room was broiling by American standards, but the operations officer, or G3 for short, did not seem to be bothered.

He greeted them cheerily. "Magandang umaga! Can I offer you some coffee?"

Even in times like this, his Filipino hospitality defied description and permeated his attitude. Both men jumped at the chance for coffee. A few minutes later they had the juice of life in their hands, and the three began to discuss the situation.

They had barely begun when a courier arrived with a satchel. The soldier was coated in dust from head to toe and left a trail of it as he entered the room. He pulled a bandana down from his face and saluted Malaya, adding more dust to the floor. Malaya returned the salute, accepted the satchel, and the soldier departed.

"High-tech comms," commented Malaya with a slight grin. "These guys ride like the famous Valentino Rossi back and forth to General Magtanggol's headquarters twice a day on motorcycles, scooters, and even bikes."

"Makes your job a bit tougher, sir," responded Benavidez.

"It's not that bad. We don't have nearly the high-tech gear you Americans do. While we admire and like it, we could never afford it. The upside is that we are also not as dependent on it."

Benavidez took a slug of the bitter coffee and burned his mouth. After spitting it back into the cup, he regained his composure and then asked, "What about anti-drone PDS systems, commo, fire support, logistics, and such? Are you able to talk to our brigade and General Viale? 1st ARM and Lieutenant Colonel Gammon?"

Lieutenant Colonel Malaya smiled a big toothy grin. "That's what is going to make this attack so interesting. We have no PDSs and only a few mortars. We have what we can carry, and no, we couldn't talk to your modern brigade even if we had our regular radios. Just not compatible. But on the upside, we are part of a force of over 8,100 soldiers that will retake our capital. You forget—we are a counterinsurgency unit. We know how to infiltrate. And walk."

The conversation continued for a few more minutes, and the two men decided on an employment plan for the American advisors. They had only limited ability to contact the American units and were unsure about the nature of the upcoming fight. Major Benavidez also mentioned that he would request a Razorback platoon to help keep the drones off the division's back and provide at least some degree of comms with the brigade.

The meeting broke up with the arrival of a messenger from the 501st (Valiant) Brigade.

Benavidez and Hoban walked outside into the rapidly heating weather, and Benavidez turned to Hoban and asked, "So, now what do you think?"

"Sir, I think that I have to piss like a racehorse. Still not sure how they're going to deal with the security posts and whatever surprises they might have, much less the drones and the T100s."

Benavidez swatted a mosquito on his neck that was trying to make a meal of him while Hoban went to relieve himself on a nearby tree. With only sporadic power, the sewage in the city was a hit and miss affair. In the school it was currently in a "miss" status.

Hoban returned, much relieved, and continued to opine on the situation. "Looks like it might be a Task Force Smith in the making."

The reference to the ill-fated task force from the Korean War was fitting. Rushed into battle, the unit was reasonably well led but inadequately equipped with essential weapons for their task, much like the 5th Division.

"Let's go introduce ourselves to the division commander and his Command Sergeant Major," said Benavidez wearily.

"Roger, sir."

The two men were about to walk back into the building to see Colonel Randy Batenga, formerly the 502nd "Liberator" Brigade Commander, now the new 5th Division Commander. His was another of the promotions of necessity when the Division Commander and Chief of Staff were killed by the Chinese on day one. The men started to walk back toward the entrance, when Hoban looked up.

"Hear that?"

The sound of beating wings increased until a Chinese Sparrow Hawk drone flew low and fast over the school.

"Shit."

4.3

241730RSEP2033 (5:30 p.m. local time, September 24, 2033)
The Doss home, Lynchburg, Virginia

The video was short, but Stacy's parents appreciated it nonetheless.

"Play," said John.

Stacy's face came into view, and she prepared to speak. Her eyes were slightly bloodshot, and her hair was rebelling against a scrunchie that was attempting, with great futility, to hold it in a brown ponytail.

"She looks like she just got up," said Shelly Doss with an air of concern for her "baby."

Stacy began. "Hi, Mom and Dad, sorry we can't go live, but after some stuff here, we have to take extra precautions and can only send short video or text clips for a little while. We think someone blew our OPSEC with a personal cell phone, uh…sorry…OPSEC is operational security, procedures we have in place to keep from giving away what we're doing. Anyway, just wanted to let you know things are going fine and not to believe the news reports. Our intel guys are saying that the Chinese are not only targeting individuals in the military, although the Navy seems to have been hit the worst, but also family members. Can you believe that?"

"Pause," said John. "Do you think she knows?"

"No. Not yet. Everyone else seems to, though. So far I've fielded calls from four of her old teachers, most of my girlfriends, my boss, our pastor, and most of the neighbors. They were all nice and asked what they could do to help. David was particularly upset when he called last night. Same for you?"

"Pretty much. Except I got a sympathy Chick Fil-A sandwich because the lady at the drive-through had heard about it," John said as he forced a smile.

"Play."

Stacy continued talking briefly about the heat, the food, and the usual things soldiers talk about. She talked about her peers and how, despite the hardships, it felt good to be part of a team and doing something important.

"Mom, Dad, it seems kinda crazy, but I'm where I need to be in life. I'm serving something bigger than myself, I've become pretty good at it, and I'm in the company of people I respect. I even like most of them. Can't ask for much more than that." Stacy paused for a moment, seeming almost surprised by what she had said.

"Anyway, one quick thing, please touch base with Tom when you can. He seems like he has a lot on his mind and I'm a little worried about him. Thanks and love to you all, bye."

John scratched his jaw.

"She'll know soon enough. Poor thing. Imagine being twenty-eight and accused of being responsible for killing civilians. The Chinese proxies have really outdone themselves with an audience of 'sheeple' who can't tell truth from lies anymore." He paused, then added another thought. "There's still something visceral about seeing your daughter's name in a newspaper headline associated with the term 'war crime.' Good thing our little steel magnolia is tough enough to handle it."

4.4

September 24, 2033
Personal for: Lieutenant General Wei
From: Major General Yu
General Wei–

As you know, the situation has not turned out as our esteemed political leadership has expected. While I am pleased with the recent feint that drew most of the Allied naval forces in the Indian Ocean, I do not understand why a higher priority has not been placed on this part of the war effort. With land routes available for at least limited oil transport from the Iran oilfields, one of the benefits of the Belt and Road initiative was that the Strait of Malacca isn't as strategic as it once was. This is why allocating naval escorts to the resupply convoy makes intuitive sense, and I fail to see the logic behind such an extreme feint. Regardless, I will look forward to the arrival of the ships in the near future.

There are two serious matters about which I feel I must personally apprise you as I am concerned that your staff may be filtering the information I have provided or, perhaps even worse, painting it in a more positive manner than is warranted.

1. The introduction of the American ground force has become problematic. We were optimized to

defend ourselves from the typical air and naval strikes advocated by many proponents in Western military thought. While I appreciate our Navy and its skill in inflicting heavy losses on enemy shipping, their frustration with the large numbers of Allied decoy ships is irrelevant and smells of excuse-making. Some enemy ships are still getting through, which enables the enemy ground force that is here to remain reasonably effective. Although their use of—and dependence on—small modular reactors to help power their force may provide an unexpected opportunity, their overall logistical tail is smaller than we would have reasonably expected. Hence, they remain mobile and less vulnerable to our strikes on their bases of supply. In short, should their political restraints be changed to allow them to participate in the coming attack on Manila, they will be a decisive factor. My expectation is that your staff has fully informed you of this possibility.

2. This brings me to the impending attack on Manila and the surprising willingness of Filipino forces to surrender themselves to certain disaster. Remnants of the six Filipino divisions based on Luzon have been reorganizing and are massing for what will be a futile attack to wrest their capital from the Transitional Government of the Philippines. I suspect that the remnants of their Special Operations Forces have already begun to infiltrate the capital area. All of this you know from our detailed intelligence reports. What your staff may be keeping from you is the increasing difficulty we are having in maintaining public order. Regarding your recommendation to maintain a firmer hand with the population, I

have issued instructions to incentivize cooperation in resolving the increasing spate of sabotage incidents in the city. Should they not be resolved adequately, I have also issued orders for more significant reprisals. Yet with only one Civil Order and Assistance Battalion, one Security Battalion, one remaining Automated Battalion, and despite the many security posts, we are inadequately resourced to maintain order in a major megacity of over 22 million. This is especially true should our Filipino political partners become unreliable. Psychological and informational warfare is essential, but so are troops on the ground as machines alone cannot guarantee civil order. The popularity of the Transitional Government has begun to wane, and they are now relying more heavily on the People's Security Auxiliary forces to maintain order. This is in itself a troubling development because, should the population turn against us, they too will become a decisive factor in the battle for Manila.

I bring both of these issues to your attention as you consider my last urgent request for forces and a higher resupply priority. Stopping the Filipino assault in a convincing manner will require us to expend a large portion of our stock of drones and ammunition, especially if we are unable to strike them effectively before they enter the built-up areas. Just as keeping a sense of normalcy in Manila helped keep the population placated and useful as a shield against major coalition strikes, if the battle reaches downtown Manila, we expect a flood of refugees and civilian casualties that may further turn the population, and potentially world opinion, against us. Despite the great cyber and informational efforts of the Strategic Support Force thus far on the world stage, I do not think that they will be able to salvage the situation. At this point, and without further resources that are in the grand scheme miniscule in the overall war effort, I believe that our nation is changing this operation from a calculated risk into a gamble.

I look forward to your reply.
For the People!
Major General Yu

That should get his attention. His staff is one of the worst I have ever seen. They do him and China a disservice. But we still have time to change course.

Yu went to his desk and, as he was alone, pulled out the bottle of Maotai and poured himself a stiff drink. Putting his nose up to the glass, he breathed in deeply, savoring the aroma. He used a small spoon to take two ice cubes out of the water pitcher on his desk and then dropped them into the glass with a plop. After swirling them for a moment, he took a sip from the etched crystal glass.

Heavenly.

Taking a deep breath, he began to think more deeply. *Troop strength is still adequate, no major human losses—yet, anyway. One mechanized battalion and an airmobile battalion still available for counterattacks, so that is good. The staff still believes we can win, and more importantly, DIYA still agrees with us by a healthy margin. We are also strangling the Americans logistically, and now that their fleet is 3,600 kilometers out of position, they won't be back to interfere for weeks. Soon the resupply convoy will sail from Hong Kong, and I will have the reinforcements and supplies I desperately need, just not as much as General Wei knows I require.*

Yu paused and took another sip from his glass.

On the downside, Deng is still insufferable, and my wife has already started a spending spree while I am here and cannot restrain her. So in the grand balance of things, overall, I think I am still in a good position.

Yu took a final long drink and felt the Maotai warm his throat as it went down.

I shall still hope for the best.

4.5

241000HSEP2033 (10:00 a.m. local time, September 24, 2033) Apache Company Command Post, vicinity of San Fernando, Philippines

With a bad cup of coffee in one hand, Stacy was using her other to flip though the latest reports, for a second time. The Brigade's morning reconnaissance drones had returned a few minutes before, and their updates were starting to appear in the reports and displays. They were still over forty-five kilometers northwest of Manila, but the last few days had been tough on the drones with a number not coming back. Worse, the loss rate was far higher than the resupply replacement rate.

If we continue at this pace, we'll eventually go blind, she thought. *And what I wouldn't give for some sugar. Ran out three days ago.*

First Lieutenant Dillon and Technical Sergeant 6 Stark stuck their heads into the command vehicle and looked at Captain Doss, both noting her furrowed brow, which usually meant that she was concentrating intently.

"Hey ma'am, we have a surprise for you," Dillon stated matter-of-factly.

"What is it?" she asked her executive officer and maintenance chief without looking up.

"Ma'am, you need to come out and *see* it, or more correctly, them," responded Dillon.

Dillon would be getting out of the Army shortly after this deployment, but Stacy never saw him perform in any manner other than exceptional. He was methodical, diligent, conscientious, and detail-oriented when it came to the mountain of administrative, property book, logistics, and maintenance matters of the company. In other words, he was the perfect XO.

Stacy got up, donned her gear and stepped out of her command vehicle. The heat was immediately oppressive, and the bright early morning sunshine caused her to squint. She had taken a few steps down the ladder when she realized she had forgotten to bring her helmet and was about to go back for it when she stopped. Two replacement Razorbacks were parked neatly twenty meters in front of her. They had taken a serious beating and, due to their relatively light armor, simply didn't have the same ability to take a punch like Homer and his peers. With an abundance of nearly obsolete Strykers in the Army inventory following the Kaliningrad campaign, they were cheaper and quicker to automate as an interim solution until the HOMRRs and the next generation of vehicles entered the inventory. Their relative expendability allowed them to serve as cannon fodder in heavy engagements, which was in keeping with the American way of war to trade off "stuff" for lives.

Stacy then caught sight of something truly beautiful: Homer in all his glory. His paint was scorched, and the camouflage patterns on some of the scavenged parts did not match, but she could clearly see fresh paint spelling out "Homer" in a well-intended attempt at a cursive script that was not hers. Looking at him more closely, she saw that he now had a bit of a Frankenstein vibe, with modular parts from three other dead M316 Heavy Offensive Multi-Role Robots.

All of this made her quite happy. At least now she had one "heavy" back in the unit. Homer's sensors were working, his point defense system was spinning merrily, and his diesel exhaust was strangely welcome. She walked around the narrow tracks and the sharply angled reactive armor panels until she had completely circumnavigated his entire bulk.

"Welcome back from the dead, Homer," she said to him, patting the hull as if it were her favorite dog. "Awesome. Really awesome, XO," she beamed. "Tech Sergeant Stark, you and your team performed a miracle. A resurrection, if you will."

"Well, ma'am, it was actually the brigade team that did the resurrection while dragging him around all over the place. We mostly just did the brain transplant. We loaded the latest software updates and ensured he was back online. The good news is that the task force learned quite a bit from the battle, so now he also knows what the surviving Homers, Razorbacks, and Cyclops do."

"So, like an update to an app?"

"Yes ma'am," Stark continued. "Saga pulls it in and pushes it out, although Saga still has to explain herself when she does it. This time the updates included all the terrain data every vehicle saw and sensed, enemy capabilities, and tweaks to the decoy drones that may prove to be advantageous later. I even hear Saga is starting to offer better recon drone route recommendations. All this in addition to deconflicting these constant unit repositioning moves every couple hours."

Impressive she thought, then asked, "What's with the rings on the barrel?"

"Barrel" was the correct term, even though its cross section was more rectangular than round. While traditional cannon barrels were round, railguns did not depend on explosive propellant, but rather on an enormous electromagnetic force generated between two parallel conductors to send a projectile out at hypervelocity. The conductors, often called rails, initially wore out quickly; it was only after the early durability issues were resolved that railguns became practical. Although the trade-off for hypervelocity antitank rounds was well worth it, the rails had to be replaced far more frequently than traditional barrels. Due to their nature and high structural loads, barrels could not be 3D printed as was the practice for many other replacement parts. The maintenance team always salvaged them when possible. This ringed barrel, however, was special.

"Each ring is a kill," responded Dillon. "He got nine confirmed kills."

"Nice, very nice," was all Captain Doss could think to say, but her mind was moving quickly. *What if it's true and he killed some civilians along the way?* she thought as the phrase that all commanders had to internalize—that they were responsible for all their unit did or failed to do—drifted through her mind yet again.

This is eating at me. They need to finish the investigation. I have work to do, and I need to know.

4.6

252130HSEP2033 (9:30 p.m. local time, September 25, 2033) 1st ARM Battalion Assault Command Post, vicinity San Fernando, Philippines

"Yeah, Cindy's still pretty pissed, but I'm used to it." Colonel McClellan was clearly a bit distracted, and his voice betrayed a slight sense of discouragement. Buck had mentioned the domestic cyber attacks to see how McClellan was doing, as some families were handling the aftermath better than others. Having met his wife, Cindy, once at a unit Dining Out, or formal dinner, Buck had a degree of sympathy for the man when otherwise Buck would have found him to be merely irritating. Cindy was apparently still fuming about the cyber attack and still lambasting her husband about his shortcomings, real and imagined, to all who would listen. In some cases, this applied to anyone who couldn't artfully get away from her, like Julia, who was cornered while dropping off their kids at the post's Child Development Center.

"I heard from Julia that a lot of the other wives in the unit were still pretty upset about the attacks, which were impressively personal, and a lot of them weren't mentally prepared for it. Julia got hit with a set of fabricated emails between me and the girl I dated before her. Impressive how they made the connections, even distant ones. At least we warned the families in the pre-deployment briefs."

"Yeah, but Cindy never went to them, always too busy."

Buck noted McClellan's tone quickly change as he switched to the matter at hand.

"Anyway, you know why I'm here. Have you had a chance to read the report?"

"Yes, sir." Although McClellan was on the technology track and Gammon was a commander, rank was still rank, and Gammon adhered to the appropriate professional courtesies.

"Do you have any questions regarding my conclusions?"

"Only one." Gammon paused and carefully chose his words. "In the rules of engagement section, why did you fault Captain Doss for not increasing her Target Confidence setting to 'at least 90 percent' and the Acceptable Collateral Damage setting to 1:10? She was at 80 percent and 1:4. She was authorized to go as low as 70 percent and 1:2."

The rules of engagement for automated systems remained much the same as it had for human systems. Following the Baltic Crisis, the debate over "man-in-the-loop" versus "man-on-the-loop" was mostly settled in favor of the latter. Target Confidence and Acceptable Collateral Damage were simply the latest attempts to quantify the longstanding tension between military necessity and collateral damage proportionality that stretched back all the way to St. Augustine.

Buck watched as McClellan became quiet and then, after a few moments, agitated, before blurting out his response. "C'mon, Buck. The report cleared you, Doss, and your whole team. I just think she made a few avoidable mistakes. Rules of engagement are as much to protect us from ourselves, and from our own excesses in the heat of the moment, as they are to protect innocents. You know, to make sure we don't destroy a village to save it. Everything we do plays out in the news. Every noncombatant killed costs us goodwill and legitimacy, both here and on the world stage. You know that."

Buck felt himself start to flush with frustration and took a deep breath to clear his mind before he responded. "If we are here to use deadly force, then people are going to be killed. This is simply a calculus of death. Maximize theirs, minimize ours, and limit those of the noncombatants. I feel every death of one of my soldiers, and every death of every civilian. I even feel a little bad for the enemy someti—"

"Seriously?" McClellan interrupted. "I just suggested you should have used tighter rules of engagement. What's the big deal?"

Gammon felt himself moving past frustration and approaching anger. "My *issue*," Gammon said, emphasizing the word, "is that the report implies that she should have played it differently in the battle. That the rules of engagement were too loose, and that is why those seven civilians were killed. Do you seriously think that just because we have machines making calculated decisions that we are going to achieve perfection? Have zero civilian and friendly casualties? That we can achieve antiseptic warfare?"

"Easy, Buck," McClellan said in his typically condescending tone. "While she did set the Target Confidence setting at 80 percent and the Collateral Damage at 1:4 before requiring the bots to seek human confirmation, I simply thought it could have been dialed in higher to make it safer. If she had done that, it might have prevented the casualties. We're getting pummeled in the world press right now. Hell, they're even singling you and Doss out in news reports as war criminals and baby killers. I actually find it pretty damn impressive that this kind of information is already out there—from an academic perspective, of course."

Easy for you to say, thought Gammon. *Your wife isn't the one reading tweets, Facebook posts, and news articles opining on whether her husband is a war criminal. My kids are getting a full helping of it too.*

Buck was tempted to offer an emotionally satisfying remark, but fortunately, his well-tuned brain-to-mouth filter engaged before he was able to respond; he managed to tamp down the emotions welling up in him.

"Sir, have you considered what would have happened if the Target Confidence Setting actually was at 90 percent and the Acceptable Collateral Damage setting had been at 1:10?" Without waiting for a response, Buck added, "We would have lost the engagement."

This caught McClellan by surprise. "How so?" he responded with a quizzical look.

As an officer on the technical track, Colonel McClellan had never been in command nor heard a shot fired in anger before this deployment.

Buck saw that McClellan remained unconvinced and began to explain it with a calmness that surprised even himself. "Every trigger pull by humans or machines is a calculated risk of getting it wrong. Look at some of the case studies of the wars from 2001 and beyond. Even with restrictive rules of engagement, we turned a lot of noncombatants into pink mist. The rules of engagement we're using now are even more restrictive, and AI gives us even more fidelity when it comes to pattern recognition. Saga and the bots don't get tired, don't blink, and don't get mad if their robo-buddy gets dismembered by a roadside bomb. We are better now than we were then, and you want to push it to the point of the absurd—"

"Slow the lecture, Buck. I was part of the development team on these machines and know how they work better than you. I'm trying to keep the boss out of trouble and the press off the President's back. You just want to blast everything to kingdom come in the most expeditious manner possible."

It took everything Gammon had in him to control himself. He felt his throat tighten and the vein on the left side of his forehead start to pulse. Taking another deep breath, he continued. "Sir, as a commander, I am personally responsible for everything the soldiers and weapon systems of this unit do, or fail to do. While the death of seven civilians is tragic, we destroyed an entire Chinese battalion, over thirty-two of their combat vehicles, at the cost of zero human soldiers and less than a dozen bots. Our weapons usually got off the first shots, and *that* is why we did so well." Gammon paused to let McClellan absorb the point, and then continued.

"Delaying even a fraction of a second until we achieved 90 percent, or having to get human approval, especially while fighting outnumbered, would have changed the outcome. And regarding the Acceptable Collateral Damage setting, if it had been set at 1:10, the last Sky Lance, which killed all seven civilians, would never have been fired. The T100s would have broken through, destroyed the company command post, and been in the battalion rear area wrecking our logistics assets. Real soldiers would be dead, we would have not only failed that mission, but would be unable to proceed on the next one. With all due respect, sir, how many times did you run the simulations?"

The surprised look on McClellan's face answered the question. Gammon went in for the kill. "Well, we ran it seventeen times with human assistance and 1,284 times with Saga on her own. The result was within one order of magnitude each time. We would have saved seven civilians but lost at least thirty-one soldiers, five additional bots, and a company command post, and we had a 64 percent probability of losing the battalion Assault Command Post. We would have had to divert another company from its mission, delay accomplishment of securing the primary battalion objective, and remained exposed to Chinese observation and long-range fire longer than necessary."

McClellan was silent for a moment. For all his faults, he knew Gammon was right and had the courage to admit it. "I made a mistake. It was careless. I was in a hurry."

Both men were breathing more slowly now, and the tension was starting to leave the small shelter.

"Okay," McClellan said quietly, "you've made your point. I'll edit the final report."

"Roger, thank you, sir. I'll brief Doss and the rest of the team."

"Oh, and one more thing, thanks for checking on me—you know, on the home-front thing."

"Roger, sir, we're all on the same team. Gotta look out for each other."

As Gammon departed for his headquarters, he thought to himself, *McClellan might be all right after all.*

"Well, Megan, how do you think that went?" Gammon asked.

"Kinda like telling someone they have cancer, except that it's not the bad kind," Major Bennett deadpanned.

"Sir," Command Sergeant Major Washington added, "I think that Captain Doss was relieved that the investigation was both over and that she had been cleared, but her body language told me that the confirmed civilian deaths were harder on her than she let on."

"True. Her execution was nearly flawless," continued Gammon. "We couldn't have expected better. I hope I came across clearly about that."

"I thought so, sir," added the XO in his strangely soothing New Orleans accent. "But I also worry about her a little. The pictures on the net and in the news reports were pretty gruesome, especially of the three kids. The Chinese are having a field day with this. Thermobarics do a number on unprotected human bodies, and the way they edited the pictures to resemble her nephew and nieces was an impressive psychological attack."

Megan scratched her head and then asked the group, "Think this might turn into a moral injury? Not many soldiers have that kind of death on their conscience. It can really mess with someone's sense of self, their own morality, and a massive sense of guilt."

"Maybe…maybe." Gammon paused. "That's part of the reason I spent so much time explaining why she did everything right. The tougher cases—and by that, I mean higher risks for that type of injury—are when someone actually makes an honest mistake and it ends up this way. I remember reading about the Sicily campaign in World War II and wondering how the Navy gunners felt after mistakenly shooting down American planes filled with paratroopers. Probably wrecked them in the head."

"True, sir," added Washington. "I think she's got a good moral compass and a fairly strong religious background, which can both help. At least she has a framework to fall back on. A lot of the young troops struggle to explain morality in anything better than relativistic terms, which can make death morally superfluous to them, or leave them with little to reason through the trag—" The Sergeant Major stopped speaking when he noticed the other three looking at him in stunned silence. "Hey, so I was a deacon when I enlisted. A deacon has to know these things."

"I guess so," said Gammon. "You continue to surprise me, Sergeant Major."

Gammon surveyed his team as he thought for a moment, contemplating what to do next. "Megan, I want you to talk to her again later. She thinks you're a hard-ass, but she might appreciate the check-in. I also need you to see where her head's at. She's tough and I think she'll work through this as well as can be expected, but I can't afford to have her at anything but her best when we light off the next phase of this."

The S3 acknowledged him, the meeting broke up, and each individual slowly stepped outside into the suffocating heat. The sun was low and all four noted that it took on a beautiful shade of red in the humid evening sky. Gammon soaked in the beauty of the red streaks in the sky as his thoughts briefly turned to home.

Wonder what the kids are up to. Probably in the midst of another fight that Julia's having to referee. Then off to practice, then dinner in about two hours, then homework, prayers, and bed. What I wouldn't give for some of her lousy cooking right now. I can almost smell her perfume.

Buck found himself smiling broadly at the thoughts. When he realized that the sun was now gone, he returned his attention to what tomorrow might bring.

4.7

260030HSEP2033 (12:30 a.m. local time, September 26, 2033) CPT Doss's sleeping area

Stacy looked in the small mirror, and despite her best efforts to hide it, she still looked like she might have been crying. She was tired, she was being painted as a war criminal in the media, PMSing, and now she had to deal with this.

"Record," she said softly as she tried to begin, then, "Stop."

She pulled her hair back into a tighter ponytail and wiped the new tears. Taking a deep breath, she tried again. "Record."

Pausing only slightly, she began, "No, Tom, we can't still be friends, and as much as it sucks, we need to call it good and move on. You say that you realized that you're not ready to get married yet, but I can't help but wonder if it's just that you're not ready to marry…well…me. I know I can be stubborn, but I do love you, and this isn't what I hoped for. I wanted more and thought you did too. I was going to surprise you when I got back by telling you that I dropped my career intermission application right before we shipped out. I wanted to get back from this deployment, take the three-year career intermission, get married like we'd planned, and…start a family."

Stacy wiped her eyes again. "Anyway, good luck, I hope things work out with Kelly. Bye."

Unfortunately, she was in a combat zone and lacked a good bottle of wine and girlfriends for the occasion. Despite these missing ingredients, Stacy rolled over and commenced to have a good cry.

4.8

272045RSEP2033 (8:45 p.m. local time, September 27, 2033)
The Doss home, Lynchburg, Virginia

John Doss knew his daughter was under incredible pressure. She was a company commander, in combat, accused of being a war criminal in the press, and her dumb-ass boyfriend just broke off their engagement with a lousy "Dear Jane" email. John was, however, not entirely displeased about the breakup. He had never been a big fan of the boy for a variety of reasons.

Even with all of this on her plate, John also knew deep down that his daughter would be okay. He thought back to elementary school and jiujitsu class. After seeing that she was unchallenged by fighting the other girls, he made a fateful decision.

"Make her fight the boys," he told the instructor, who looked at him blankly for a moment.

Stacy needed the challenge and always did her best when she had to up her game, occasionally, even, against her will. John also knew she could take it and that life didn't care that she was a girl.

"She's wrecking the girls. Make her fight the boys," he repeated.

The instructor was obviously unsure of the wisdom of the decision but went with it for the time being and matched her up with a boy slightly taller than she was. The boy stood in front of her with plenty of bravado, but also a look that betrayed his disgust that he had the demeaning task of fighting a girl.

Unfortunately for him, he then made a catastrophic error of judgement when he asked, "So, you want me to go easy or hard on you?"

"Whatever," Stacy responded nonchalantly.

The sparring session began, and Stacy was on him like a rabid monkey. John watched with glee as the boy tapped out barely fifteen seconds into the round. Once the boy was informed that he would have to continue all three rounds with Stacy, the disoriented look on his face began to morph into something that bordered on fear. After the second round ended with the same result, it continued to go downhill for him. The third session took a turn for the worse when his flight instinct overcame his fight instinct; it ended with Stacy chasing him around the dojo yelling, "Stay here and fight me!"

John almost pitied the young punk. At the age of eleven, getting your ass kicked by a girl in front of your peers had to be rather humiliating.

Stacy didn't always win, but she never tapped out. This was part of the reservoir of strength that he knew would help her through times like this. It was part of why he had been hard on her as a kid—but not too hard. She was still his daughter, after all.

John thought for a moment about the current situation. *Hey God… I need you to help her…please.*

4.9

280545HSEP2033 (5:45 a.m. local time, September 28, 2033) Northern edge of Quezon City, Greater Manila Metro Area, The Philippines

What's the plural of Mongoose? Mongooses? Mongeese? Sergeant Major Hoban wasn't sure. *Wonder how this thing will do in a big city,* he pondered as he looked at the large metal beast that General Viale had sent to help the 5th Division. He was glad to have it and decided to walk the fifty meters and have a closer look at the machine.

The 5th Division had made it to the edge of Quezon City after a long forced march that had been assisted by more than a few of the venerable Jeepneys. Hoban's favorite was the Bob Marley–themed one.

Bob Marley goes to war. Whoda thunk? he mused.

The division's troops had averaged over twelve miles a day for five days—or more correctly, nights—with full gear. Refugees were starting to stream out of Manila and Hoban had seen the Philippine Military Police keeping the roads clear at gunpoint. It was truly a sight full of pathos: desperate families in direct collision with military necessity.

The troops themselves had held up well and were now entering the dense urban environment of Metro Manila, hoping the city would provide at least some relief from the constant drone strikes. This was also the last temporary halt for the exhausted troops before the assault, as Colonel Batenga had decided that attacking from the march was an unfortunate necessity. He reasoned that pausing and remaining stationary this close to their initial objective, the Batasang Pambansa Complex, invited another enemy drone strike. On hearing this, Hoban reasoned that he was probably right and that his tired troops understood the importance of quickly reclaiming their congressional building and its symbolic importance.

But at the moment, Hoban was still looking at the Mongoose with its whirling PDS sensors, numerous antennas, recon drone rack, and the 30mm cannon.

An interesting blend of leftovers from the U.S. Army's technology parts bin, he thought.

It was, however, one of the best items the U.S. Brigade was able to allocate to the 5th Division. Major Benavidez had lobbied hard for the system—a point defense system on steroids—which would provide a mobile protective bubble for at least some of the division. Fortunately for the 5th Division, he had prevailed with General Viale's new Chief of Staff.

Hoban walked closer, stepped over a small mound of rotten food that smelled downright awful, and saw that the rear ramp of the repurposed Stryker vehicle was down. Dodging several other small landmines of refuse and feces left by the hordes of refugees, he continued to approach the vehicle until he could see the exposed vertical anti-drone racks and the commo relays. Benavidez had only gotten two other vehicles, both of them aging Joint Light Tactical Vehicles that had seen better days, but they were still useful for their payload of commo equipment and the power to run it. The Mongoose was unmanned, and because it hadn't been designed to operate outside the framework of an ARM battalion and the Mission Command III software telling it how to act in coordination with all the other battlefield elements, it required a human babysitter. As important as this task was, Hoban had assigned one of his best troops to it. As he walked around to the front of the vehicle, Hoban found Specialist Seven Isakson reading an old-fashioned book.

"How's it goin', Ike?"

"Better than I deserve, Sergeant Major," he responded as he put the book into his cargo pocket and stood up.

"Whatcha reading?"

"*Starship Troopers.* Did you know Heinlein was a Naval Academy graduate?"

"Still a classic. And too bad we don't have the academy anymore. But what's the deal with this thing here?"

"Well, Sergeant Major, it was never designed to operate this way, so as part of the workaround, I usually leave the top hatch open and sit in the back between the comms gear and the racks. Just gotta be careful when they launch, almost lost a body part or two. I wasn't paying attention when a few took off yesterday."

"Nice. How many do you have left?"

"Body parts or anti-drones?"

After a sufficient number of punitive pushups, Ike resumed the conversation. "We burned up a lot of anti-drones in the two days since we got here. The last Air Mule had a few replacements on it, but not enough. Down to about 45 percent load on the anti-drones, and about the same on the beehive, proximity, and canister rounds for the gun. Plenty of 6.5mm rounds though, just not that useful for knocking down drones. Of course, the laser is only good if we have fuel for the generator. Down to about a third of a tank left. Wish we had the microwave gun like on the Hydra systems."

"Roger, me too. Keep your head down. We're not entirely sure how this thing's going to act in a city. Hell, you're going to get to make some history. First military operation in a modern megacity. Stalingrad, Grozny, and Kaliningrad didn't have nearly the vertical, subterranean, population, or electromagnetic density of this place."

"Good times, Sergeant Major. And a chance to add a few more rings."

Hoban noticed seventeen crudely painted rings on the 30mm cannon's barrel. "Roger, what's the record in the brigade so far?"

"Seventeen, Sergeant Major," Ike responded proudly.

"Not bad, not bad at all. All right, just heard in my headset that we're moving again. It's showtime," Hoban concluded, and that was when he noticed it—the faint, thin crude letters on the hull: The Jolly Roger II.

"Just don't become a ring on someone else's gun," added Hoban as he turned to leave.

"You too, Sergeant Major, you too."

281510HSEP2033 (3:10 p.m. local time, September 28, 2033) Quezon City, Greater Manila Metro Area, The Philippines

The Filipino soldier popped up from behind the rubble, wobbled for a split second, regained his balance, and fired a 40mm high-explosive grenade at the shipping container. This would have been odd in any other part of the world, but this container was trying to kill him too. Rather than a loud crack when firing, the reliable old 40mm grenade launchers retained the low, hollow "thoomp" sound reminiscent of hitting a large PVC pipe with a stick. Unfortunately for the soldier, he was a split second too slow.

Hoban saw a spurt of 5.8mm bullets stitch the ground in front of the young soldier and then snap his head back. He crumpled behind the mound of rocks that failed to give him the cover he had expected. Hoban watched a nearby medic working feverishly as he attempted to stop the severe bleeding of his current patient. The medic had seen what had happened and didn't even bother going to the newly dead soldier. Too many soldiers with headshots, and the medics were focusing on the ones that were lucky enough to at least have a chance of being saved.

Wow, they're fast. One, maybe two seconds to get a shot off before they can send something back at you, Hoban thought.

He watched as a nearby team of soldiers prepared to take a shot with an L-40 antitank rifle. "Hope this one goes better," he said under his breath.

Most decent point defense systems, like the one on this particular weapon station, could effectively swat down the relatively slow-moving missiles and rockets. The L40 antitank rifle was more accurately an "anti-vehicle rifle" that looked like an oversized .50-caliber Barrett sniper rifle. It was big and heavy, but its 20mm barrel fired a 10mm depleted uranium sabot round with enough speed and energy to get past most point defense systems and penetrate light armor. It kicked like a mule, and most gunners could take no more than seven or eight rounds before they had to change out.

The gunner gave the count, and on three, the two men in the front lifted the heavy weapon above the rampart. The gunner quickly pulled the trigger, and the men were back down just as 5.8mm rounds cracked overhead and kicked up dirt in front of them. This was the fourth—and largest—security post they had taken on today, and things seemed to be going better than at the first couple, the 40mm gunner's demise notwithstanding.

Been a lot of expensive learning going on. The bill has been between forty and fifty casualties per station. Hoban looked again at the dead soldier who was now staring at him from afar. *Like him.*

Blood was seeping out of the hole in the front of his head, but based on the size of the pooling blood underneath him, it was flowing far more freely from the much larger exit wound in the back of his head.

Hoban watched as two other soldiers gave a count and simultaneously rose, fired, and ducked back down. They had gotten off a few shots at the wounded station and contributed to its continuing demise. A few hours ago, while attacking the second station of the day, three small groups of soldiers had gone subsurface to get into a closer position which avoided the firing arc of the station's turrets. It seemed like a good idea at the time, and they infiltrated up the internal stairwells of an adjacent building to a position they thought was high enough. Unfortunately, they had miscalculated by about four floors, and this had turned into another expensive lesson.

Hoban looked at his watch and wondered where the new groups were. Forty-five minutes earlier, two other groups had tried to go subsurface to a nearby building and try again, but at a higher level. One group had already returned after getting lost underground. The other one seemed to still be progressing.

"Jolly Mon," Hoban said into his microphone, "this is Dragon 7. What are you seeing?"

Without point-to-point laser comms and relays, the electromagnetic density of the city was making communications iffy at best. His earpiece hissed for a moment before Ike came on.

"Dragon 7, this is Jolly Mon, not much. These skyscrapers are keeping everyone's vehicles channelized into corridors, so our point defense systems can only engage at adequate range down a few streets. It's still providing some cover, but the bugs can get in a lot closer than we like."

The troops, Ike among them, had begun calling the small Chinese disposable drones "bugs" due to their sheer numbers and relative crudeness.

"Roger," Hoban responded.

Hoban paused in the midst of the chaos and wondered briefly if he was little more than an observer at this point. He and his team had little to offer the Filipinos. No one in his unit had ever seen megacity fighting before. While Colonel McClellan's Technical Contact Teams were busy examining the destroyed weapon stations and a few Chinese drone misfires still in the racks, Hoban wasn't sure he had a lot to add, which drove him crazy.

Although he and Gammon had seen previews of coming attractions in Kaliningrad, it was nothing compared to this urban jungle. The city could swallow up entire units, get them lost, and spit them back out again. Each block could be its own mini-war with its own set of circumstances. The density of compartmentalization was itself overwhelming. Super-surface structures like skyscrapers were small cities unto themselves. Subsurface sewers and tunnels provided a labyrinth of underground mazes, and the relatively simple surface level with its narrow approaches and random rubble created its own issues.

And then there were the increasing number of civilians, who were showing up everywhere in the most unexpected, inconvenient times and places—like the dead ones he saw lying in the middle of the street. Most of them were probably just hiding in any place they could find. Unit after unit reported finding them in stores, apartments, sewers... simply everywhere. Units also found their bodies in places that soldiers realized were not as good for protection as expected.

It's like trying to pack ten pounds of tragic humanity into a five-pound bag, he thought.

Hoban heard footsteps and looked to his left just in time to see 5th Division Command Sergeant Major James Garcia approach, running up to him while staying low. He flopped down to share the large concrete slab Hoban was using for cover.

Garcia began to speak.

"What?" yelled Hoban above the din.

Garcia tried again, louder this time. "Your boss wants you to follow me back to the command post after I finish checking on the troops."

"Got it, I'll follow you," Hoban responded and gave a thumbs-up for confirmation.

Garcia nodded, then added, "By the way, no sign of T100s yet, so some good news."

The two were in the perimeter of one of the few functional battalions of the division, the 45th "Gallant" Battalion, and moved to check on the 17th "Do or Die" Battalion. After thirty minutes of careful movement, both men and Garcia's small entourage were sweating profusely in the heat when they arrived in the 17th's area of operations. The battalion was working on a different security checkpoint from what Garcia and Hoban could see. The battalion was making reasonable progress as demonstrated by the smoke pouring from one container and fireworks spouting fireworks from another.

Probably drones cooking off, thought Hoban.

The two men heard the new noise at about the same time, which was preceded by the sounds of Filipino soldiers shouting and yelling. Two small, well-armed Chinese ground vehicles were spotted moving toward their positions. About the size of ATVs, the Chinese vehicles were accompanied by a small pack of attack drones the size of radio-controlled toy cars. Hoban's translator was struggling to keep up with the rapid chatter he was hearing. As he switched his helmet camera on and ensured the feed was being relayed back to the Brigade's intel software, Hoban noted that it was going to be a long day.

4.10

281900HSEP2033 (7:00 p.m. local time, September 29, 2033)
Chinese National Assistance Task Force Headquarters, The Philippines

General Yu's difficulties were mounting, and he was under increasing pressure from both his political and military masters. The Central Military Commission had made five planning assumptions when they authorized this punitive operation. Four had already proven to be wrong, and the fifth was now in doubt.

"Professional malpractice," Yu fumed out loud as he sat behind his large display screen. "How could the greatest nation on Earth, the land of Confucius, Sun Tzu, and Xi, with 4,000 years of culture, philosophy, and wisdom get it so wrong? Even our genius AI didn't help."

Yu was less angry about the actual decision to conduct the operation than with the manner of execution and the resulting circumstances in which he now found himself. He had been resourced for only the absolute best-case scenario and had little flexibility should things start going off the rails. Worse, the Central Military Commission was now split on the next steps forward. Any individual politician who admitted that they had erred would be committing career suicide, yet if the group publicly admitted error, the resultant backlash might be political suicide for the Chinese Communist Party.

The other possibility Yu had considered was perhaps even more frightening: that the members of the Central Military Commission had neither the military nor technological savvy to understand the danger in which they had placed their country. The repercussions of the war were already impacting the population as oil became scarce and their export markets evaporated. While some countries stopped trading for proclaimed moral reasons, most stopped because of the Allied naval embargo. It was an ever-tightening noose and nearly impossible to circumvent. A new generation of long-duration smart mines and the Triggerfish automated subs had seen to that.

So the committee has boxed itself in. I shall have to help unbox them, he thought to himself, *which, of course, will be tricky. "The Turd" will be only one of my obstacles. How will I work around the commissar?*

Yu continued to ponder his alternatives as his key commanders and staff filed in. They were an increasingly somber bunch, especially after the reports that the U.S. and Japanese Marines were posturing to take several islands within the Paracel chain. From there they could effectively finish the strangulation of his precious task force and any hope of promotion. Yu took little comfort that the current fight with the American and Philippine militaries remained within DIYA's expected probability of success.

Lieutenant Colonel Han was about to begin when General Yu interrupted him. "You look awful. Are you sick?"

"No, sir, just exhausted," answered Han. "Civilian order matters are wearing me out. The Transitional Government is starting to get nervous, and I spend an inordinate amount of time calming them down and keeping their leadership focused. They are losing faith that this will be over quickly. They know it was a gamble to align with us and that they have a lot to lose if this doesn't go well. The bigger issues revolve around the People's Security Auxiliary units. I find them to be little more than thugs with power. They're starting to cause us more problems—and more legitimacy—than they are worth."

"What about the police?"

"Still reliable, but merely for law-and-order matters. Despite the directed strikes on the most problematic leaders, we must remember they are a paramilitary organization and that their political loyalties are questionable. They could easily flip on us."

"What about the population?"

"Sir," Han continued, "about a third, the compliant ones, remain accepting of the government and the current power structure. A third are hostile, but not openly displaying active resistance—yet. And a third are intellectual refugees: they are going to see how it plays out and then bet on the winning horse. Living conditions in the capital are starting to deteriorate, and we have seen a black market start to emerge."

"Thank you, Lieutenant Colonel Han."

Yu turned to Colonel Deng next, and Deng did what Chiefs of Staff do: he had the rest of the staff and commanders discuss the current situation, the relative strengths and weaknesses of their individual areas, various construction projects, including those on Corregidor, as well as their opinion on the capability of the Allied force. Images came up on the large 3D screen that depicted the current fight, casualty rates, and progress made by the Filipinos and the Americans. The general consensus was that the enemy attack would reach its culminating point and stall somewhere around the second ring of security stations. These were the ones equipped with not only ground and air drone augmentation, but also with laser dazzlers that would quickly blind anyone not using protective eyewear, which was essentially the entire Philippine military.

When the Strategic Support Force Liaison Officer began to speak, Yu paid especially close attention because external factors were increasingly impacting his fight…and because she was easily the most attractive woman in the room.

Ms. Liu began by politely reminding everyone of their success in managing the narrative of the war to date and how they had succeeded in keeping much of the world either distracted from, or confused by, their operations in the Philippines. Then she became much more serious.

"But we cannot control the info-sphere forever. Like Sir Julian Corbett's view of sea power—" and the rest of the room groaned internally at what was sure to be another lecture by the self-proclaimed twenty-seven-year-old genius, "control of the sea is not absolute, but rather contested. We can only institute relative control of critical places for a limited, but decisive time. We are approaching the end of that time, and we will progressively lose our strong dominance in this arena. Our plan to keep the civilian population of Manila in place to present the image of normalcy, as well as a shield against large Allied strikes, is beginning to crumble. We need a decisive result if we are to prevail."

"Thank you, Ms. Liu."

A statement of the obvious, thought Yu and most of his senior officers in the room.

"Thank you all for your reports," Yu said politely, secretly picking at his thumb again under the table. "As you know, the Central Military Commission is unsure of what to do next. The campaign has obviously not developed as initially foreseen, but we must now help them, and ourselves, in their decision-making calculus. A decisive victory will prevent them from losing heart and ensure that we receive the national-level support we require to accomplish our task. With the Allies now on the island, we have three current imperatives: First, we must destroy the remnants of the Philippine military and the American mobile forces. The Filipinos have assisted us in this task by attacking our security posts and are paying a heavy price. The Americans are still holding back for the time being due to political considerations. Their shortsightedness has been fortuitous for us."

Han noticed that Yu had pulled a small tissue from the box on his desk before his hand disappeared under the table.

"Second, we must maintain complete control of the population. We cannot allow them to leave the city—for reasons of credibility on the world stage, and because we need them here to complicate any attacks by the Filipino military and, potentially, the Allies. We will not tolerate sabotage, rebellion, or an uprising. An attack against our forces, the Transitional Government, or the Security Auxiliary units will be met with swift justice. Lieutenant Colonel Han and Ms. Liu, ensure the population understands the consequences of their actions. And arm the Auxiliary units better."

Yu paused, then added, "Lieutenant Colonel Han, I want you to put measures in place to ensure that while the police may not be loyal, at least they won't flip."

Lieutenant Colonel Han nodded.

"And finally, Major Sun, shut down the utilities outside Manila. Give the people a reason to stay here. Same for the communications systems. We now have more to lose with open communications outside Manila than with shutting them down. And Ms. Liu?"

"Yes, sir?" she responded with her ever-so-slight air of superiority.

"Can you keep the world busy with a line of bullshit for the next seventy-two hours?"

"I can, sir."

"I certainly hope so."

4.11

290500HSEP2033 (5:00 a.m. local time, September 29, 2033) 1st ARM Battalion Assault Command Post, Meycauayan City, The Philippines

As usual, Gammon got up at five that morning. After splashing some water on his face and adding some shaving cream, he pulled out an old-fashioned razor to get the stubble off. The slightly gray patches annoyed him as they reminded him he was not in his twenties or even midthirties anymore. He completed the task, contemplated putting on a fresh T-shirt, and decided against it.

Only two left, no telling how long they'll have to last. Nine days isn't too bad. At fourteen, I'll change it regardless.

He added some deodorant to his armpits after noting that the previous round had given up already and met Command Sergeant Major Washington just prior to dawn. The two of them walked the line, checked on the troops, and talked to every command team, sergeant, and private they met along the way.

After making it back to the command vehicle, Gammon paused at the entrance, took off his helmet, wiped the sweat from his brow, and asked Washington how he thought the unit was doing.

"Pretty well, sir. I still think they're a bit spooked by the reports of Chinese drones and how many there might be. I think they're also worried about getting cut off. Last time the American Army was here, there was, you know, the whole Bataan thing."

"Yeah, I sensed it too. The fleet in the Indian Ocean is so far out of position, there's no way they can help us. The Chinese made a big push east, and it wasn't clear if they were aiming to disrupt the Strait of Hormuz, the Bab al-Mandab Strait at the base of the Red Sea, or both. With the potential global economic impact off the scale for what they described as a 'limited war,' a bunch of politicians on both sides of the Atlantic panicked and are still trying to keep this from becoming a wider conflict."

"Doesn't feel much like a limited war from here," chuckled Washington.

"True. And more good news, at the commander's huddle yesterday, our potential isolation on the island was a hot topic. Supply lines are iffy at best. If the Chinese can reinforce themselves with additional forces, we could really be in trouble. A lot's riding on the Navy's drones right now to keep the noose around the neck of the Chinese and off ours. How are the troops feeling about the home front, with all the continuing cyber attacks?"

"Mixed bag, some families are handling it better than others, and the results are unfortunately predictable. A couple troops are really struggling. I'm just glad I'm not on the brigade's rear detachment back at Ft. Bliss and having to deal with it all," Washington added sincerely. He originally had been slated to be on the rear detachment until, shortly before deployment, the 1st ARM Battalion's Command Sergeant Major had shattered his leg in an accident.

"That makes two of us."

While the circumstances were unfortunate, Gammon was finding Washington to be quite capable and far more energetic than his previous Command Sergeant Major.

Glad this is working out. I'm starting to think this may be a blessing in disguise, he thought to himself.

The two men parted to attend to other duties, so Gammon decided to grab some chow. His pocket buzzed just then, and he pulled out his M10 Communicator and noticed a welcome note from Julia. With nothing immediately pressing, he walked to the back of the command vehicle, sat down against one of the massive tires, and happily pulled up the message entitled: "Criminal Activity, Volume 5" which began:

"Hello Loverboy–"

That never gets old, he thought as he smiled.

"Allow me to describe what our young criminals did yesterday. I was in the shower after a long day. I had just shampooed my hair and had soap in my eyes when a HUGE cockroach landed on me. As I screamed and tried to get away from it, I heard laughter and the pitter-patter of running feet. After stomping on it several times, I did a closer inspection and discovered that the three-inch-long beast was plastic. First of all, who in their right mind would sell something like that to kids? Especially ours?

I quickly grabbed a towel and went in search of the perpetrators. I found Jenna sitting calmly, reading a book, and trying to suppress a smile. She repeatedly denied throwing it over the shower curtain and vehemently proclaimed her innocence. Then I realized the gig. I ran back upstairs and found little Lucy hiding under her covers. When confronted, Lucy broke immediately and squealed, "She made me do it! She made me do it!" And that's how my day ended…"

Impressive, and creative, Buck mused. *That kid has influence skills. I only hope she uses her powers for good.* Julia took the whole thing in stride and went on to tell Buck about everything else that was going on at home. She attached a new picture and ended the note.

"Let me know what you think of my new haircut. Love you always, J"

I miss her, this, all of it. Glad she's a tough chick.

Her hair was shorter, barely shoulder length, and while it was cute, Buck liked it longer. He also decided that he would be enthusiastic about the change.

He knew that this deployment was tough on the kids and that they tended to act up and seek a little more attention than usual when he was gone. It hadn't been bad for the Gammon family, at least compared to some stories they had heard.

Buck held up his index and middle fingers, kissed them, and touched them to the picture.

"Love ya, chica. Gotta get back to work."

290730HSEP2033 (7:30 a.m. local time, September 29, 2033)
The Cagula home, Manila

Joseph walked ever so carefully to where he could hear the conversation without being seen. His parents were talking in hushed, anxious tones, and for once what they were saying seemed like it might be interesting.

"They're getting worse, much worse," Joseph heard his father say.

"The People's Security Auxiliaries?" responded his mother.

"I was thinking the Transitional Government as a whole, but the People's Security Auxiliaries are actually the bigger headache for me and the police force. Every punk and wanna-be tough guy has joined them for a chance to have some power and the ability to run either their own private shakedown scheme or a protection racket, sometimes both. Some of these street criminals act like they're untouchable—and they kind of are as we have 'non-interfere' orders with them," his father said softly.

Joseph's mother said something he couldn't quite hear, so he edged closer to the door. Fortunately, his mother began to speak a little louder, and he picked up the conversation.

"… why some people are starting to go missing? Mary's husband from up the street was accused of something, they came for him, and she hasn't seen or heard from him in three days."

"Some people are reporting on neighbors to settle old scores and collect petty rewards for 'crimes against the people.' A lot of the Transitional Government and People's Auxiliary leadership, as opposed to the rank and file, are actually fairly dedicated to this. They know that if they lose, they've had it, so they approach it with the zeal of people possessed."

"Oh," his mother said softly. There was a pause and then she added, "Is that why they're organizing mandatory Community Watches down to the block level? To keep tabs on us?"

"Pretty much, and be careful about the Luzon…"

Joseph's clandestine reconnaissance was rudely interrupted at the worst possible time by his little brother, who came up to him to ask a question. Having to play off what was going on, Joseph acted like he was in the middle of walking to the living room and missed the last part of the conversation.

I'll just go to the school and figure out the rest, Joseph thought to himself.

290905HSEP2033 (9:05 a.m. local time, September 29, 2033) Florentino Torres High School, Northern Greater Manila Metro Area, The Philippines

Joseph and Daniel were riding their two-wheeled steed toward their mostly empty school facilities in a quest for answers, although they were not entirely sure what the questions were. The boys stopped for a moment as a People's Security Auxiliary patrol passed by in two Toyota Hilux pickup trucks which had the former government symbols hastily covered with a large spray-painted black oval and a red "PSA" emblazoned in the middle.

"These guys are ruining everything. I'll bet they're going to set up a position to stop people from going north," Joseph said softly.

"Don't say that! What if they hear you? What if someone else does? All they need is for someone to tell them that you did something suspicious. You have to watch yourself tomorrow," whispered Daniel, his words tinged with a mild hint of fear.

Joseph and Daniel were both dreading tomorrow when all boys—or young men, as they preferred to think of themselves—had to report to their respective schools to register for the newly formed Luzon Scouts, which was billed as "a civil organization that enables young men to do their patriotic duty to the new government."

"Is it true?" asked Daniel.

"What?" responded Joseph with consternation.

"That the Army's trying to overthrow the government? It doesn't make sense to me. Why not just wait for the elections?"

Joseph continued to marvel at his friend's gullibility. The boys could see the smoke rising to the north and occasionally hear explosions in the distance. Once in a while, they saw one of the big bird-like drones flying low over the rooftops.

"No, I think the Army's going to fight the Chinese and the Transitional Government."

"Careful!" Daniel whispered in almost a panic.

Joseph shook his head and got the bike moving again. They arrived at the school, ambled about, and saw a few of their friends, but mostly people were staying inside. Soon it was lunchtime, and the hungry boys were annoyed that there were far fewer street vendors than usual. The boys finally found one, ordered their usual meals, and then prepared pay the man.

"That's not enough," said the vendor gruffly.

"It was last week," responded Joseph indignantly.

"Then you can go and buy it last week. You have enough for one meal. You pick which one."

The frustrated boys picked Daniel's meal and resolved to share it. Taking a seat in the grass in some shade, they started to eat.

Joseph was the first one to notice. "This tastes funny."

"Yeah, you're right."

"Kinda greasy. And gristly."

The boys kept eating and quickly finished the meal, not wanting to think too hard about what was in it.

Eventually Joseph spoke up. "Definitely dog."

"Really, did you have to go there?"

"Pretty sure."

Daniel felt a bit queasy. He wished he didn't know. Then in a slightly whiney voice, he declared, "But the government said everything was going to be fine, that the disruptions of electricity and water would be temporary, and that the port would open again soon. Even cell phone coverage and the Internet are starting to struggle."

Joseph tried not to show any agitation, but it was hard. A few minutes later the boys heard a buzzing sound in the distance and turned their eyes to the south. About a minute later, a large group of medium-sized drones, maybe twenty-five or thirty by Joseph's count, flew low and fast over their heads. The whirring sounded like a group of insects, perhaps even an angry wasp nest.

"So why do you think they all look like pregnant guppies?" Daniel asked.

"Good question," said Joseph. "But the better question is why are they heading north if everything is under control? Let's head over to the pier. Might be cooler there, and maybe we'll see something or find out why they're going that way."

The idea seemed good to Daniel, but then again, most ideas did. The boys mounted the bike, pushed off, and began a trip to the north pier of the Manila harbor. The humid air filled Joseph's nostrils as he pedaled hard toward their new destination. After about ten minutes, they heard a loud, misplaced set of sounds nearby.

As they rounded the corner of a no longer busy street, they saw in front of them a large commotion near the Transitional Government and Security Auxiliary building which had been commandeered from the city government only a few weeks ago. As the boys arrived, they saw smoke pouring from the building, a dozen or so bodies in the street, and a crowd rapidly dispersing. A large H was freshly painted on the side of the building. At what was perhaps the most inconvenient time possible, Joseph's ringtone, an ultra-oldie R.E.M song, began blaring. The "End of the World" couldn't have been more perfect for the moment.

The sole remaining security system of the building noted the song and the presence of High Value Targets #3812 and #3813 and dispassionately transmitted the information, along with the data from the rest of the incident to the Chinese network. For DIYA, it was all in a day's work.

4.12

290930HSEP2033 (9:30 a.m. local time, September 29, 2033)
5th Division forward positions, Central Quezon City, Greater Manila Metro Area

The grinding urban combat was wearing down the Filipino division, and the cost of learning had been steep. Its commander, Colonel Randy Batenga, and his units had figured out how to use the subterranean sewers, tunnels, and access ways to get in close to the security stations, how to work around electronics that had a mind of their own in the city, how many floors up they had to be to remain out of the firing arc of the Chinese turrets, and what to do when drones were launched at them. The response to the latter was mostly to retreat quickly into inner stairwells until the drones ran out of power in twenty to thirty minutes—assuming the soldiers saw them in time, which often they didn't. In the meantime, casualties continued to mount slowly but surely.

Hoban was closer to the front lines and doing what he could to help Command Sergeant Major Garcia, who was currently locked in an animated discussion with the 45th Battalion Command Sergeant Major. Hoban only caught part of the one-way discussion from his translator, but it appeared that Garcia was delivering an epic ass-ripping based on a situation in which several of the battalion's soldiers panicked and mistakenly opened fire on some of their own troops.

Glad no one was killed. Can't image how Garcia would have handled it if that had happened, Hoban thought. *He really is trying to keep the unit together and in the fight. Glad he's willing to listen.*

Hoban was the only one of the advisors who had any urban combat experience, but that had been a long time ago, and Kaliningrad wasn't nearly as dense as Manila.

I wonder how "Da Man" is doing? I think I'll rename him "Da Old Man" when I see him next. Although technically, I'm older than he is.

Hoban's translator perked up as Command Sergeant Major Garcia was finishing his motivational speech on a positive note.

"I know it's tough and this is a one-off. Your troops look up to you and I trust you. Keep your head down and get back to it."

Something Hoban heard in the distance drew his attention, and he flipped his translator off. He paused, cocked his head in the direction of the unit to his left, and listened. He heard periodic gunfire, and in some ways it was comforting to him as it meant the unit was still fighting. He heard a few quick 5.56 rounds, an occasional "thoomp" of a 40mm grenade launcher, and the unique crack of an L-20 in the distance, but he was also hearing something else. At first, it was faint, but it started to get louder. It sounded to him like…bees.

"Sergeant Major Garcia, something bad inbound. We all need to get to cover quick!"

Garcia heard his name and looked at Hoban, but he clearly didn't understand the message. Hoban realized his mistake, flipped on his translator, and repeated himself, only louder.

As Hoban, Garcia and those around them ran for something solid, Hoban yelled into his translator, "Inbound swarm! Get to cover! Disseminate all!"

The Filipino soldiers near them suddenly paid attention, and the message rippled out through the peer-to-peer devices up to the battalion headquarters and laterally, but the flow was interrupted in many spots due to the lack of the electronic translators. Yelling would have to suffice.

Hoban and Garcia made it to a nearby building and observed the continuing mad scramble that followed. Soldiers ran for anything available, and some were luckier than others. Those that weren't so lucky were now simply targets for an inanimate intelligence.

Hoban watched the scene unfold through a three-inch bullet hole in the wall. The cinderblock room that he, Garcia, and several Filipino soldiers were using for cover was far from perfect cover. It had been used the day before by several soldiers for sleeping and was littered with olive-drab sleeping bags that smelled of sweat.

Since everything's still here, they probably became casualties early on today, Hoban noted.

As he quickly surveyed the room, he also noted the room's biggest liability: a large hole on one side. Turning back to the three-inch viewing port, he watched the pathos unfold as a soldier ran for a better hiding spot. As he was sprinting, one of the small Wasp drones peeled out of the swarm circling above, zoomed in, and detonated a few inches from his helmet. The young man buckled over and nearly somersaulted before his lifeless body came to a sliding halt. A jagged hole had opened in his helmet, and his head.

Only a five-gram shaped charge, the reports were right, thought Hoban.

He also noticed something curious. After the initial wave of Wasps had eliminated the obvious targets, the remaining Wasps began to circle. Even though his view was limited, every now and then, he saw a small number of larger drones appear within the multitude of Wasps that continued to circle above the buildings. Occasionally, one of the larger and less common Wasps would depart the swarm, enter a building, and detonate with a thud.

Wow, small thermobarics, two for two on the reports.

As he watched helplessly, more of the tiny Wasps peeled off for newly discovered individuals hiding in various locations. Hoban got the sense that the Wasps were just dumb killers while the larger winged ones that could hover were apparently the brains of the swarm. Annoyingly, his helmet camera was dying, and he had just lost communications with the only help they had—Ike in the Mongoose.

"So this is what it feels like," he said softly to himself.

"What?" Garcia responded, then looked back out his own vantage point.

"To be hunted," responded Hoban. "This is some serious role reversal, and I don't much care for it."

Garcia suddenly gestured with his hand. Had he been a teenage girl, it would have meant "fist bump," but in military circles, it meant "freeze."

Hoban heard the sounds of beating wings as a "brain," a "seeker," or whatever it was nosed into the front of the damaged building. They all realized what it was doing—scanning for heat, sound, visual, or any other clues of its prey. The bigger Wasps with the thermobaric devices could not be wasted on empty buildings, so in onc sense, it was simply doing its due diligence for a good investment of weaponry.

It was a game of hide-and-seek, and the seeker was close. It turned away, luckily choosing to go to the right instead of the left where they were. Hoban and Garcia both knew it would be back soon, and they could not let the young soldiers in the room panic. The machines were not smart, but they were meticulous in their patterns.

Hoban did some quick calculus in his head. While the seeker might not be armed, the Wasps it guided in would be fast. They didn't have a "Gooney Gun," one of the man-portable anti-drone guns; there simply hadn't been enough to go around. Opening fire on the seeker would end the game—a couple thermobaric Wasps would level the building in short order. Yet if it made it too close, the seeker would find them anyway, and the game would be over just the same. Hoban reasoned that because of its four wings, its weakest sense would be sound and devised his makeshift plan accordingly. He moved closer to Garcia and told him what he was thinking.

"We've got one shot in about two or three minutes."

Desperate times called for desperate measures, he reasoned to himself. *But better not say that out loud.*

"And I have a plan…"

Hoban quickly explained his plan in a low whisper to Garcia and a young Philippine Army sergeant in the room with them. The sergeant was the oldest of the troops, and they had to roll the dice on whether he was up for what was next.

Hoban finished explaining the plan and looked at the two men.

"Seriously?" Garcia whispered.

The look on the young sergeant's face said the same thing. He was probably wondering if his translator was working correctly.

"Yep."

With no better options and time running out, all three men rapidly threw the olive-drab sleeping bags over their heads, cut tiny vision holes in them, and got into ambush position. The rest of the men in the room were equally scared, and Garcia had instructed them in no uncertain terms to remain silent and motionless.

The three ambushers waited, sweat dripping down their faces. It was hot and humid, and even the thin insulation of the bags turned them into mini-saunas that smelled like a combination of rotten eggs mixed with used gym socks. Garcia heard it first and gave a barely noticeable hand signal to alert them. A few seconds later they heard another thermobaric explosion in a nearby building.

Poor bastards, thought Hoban. *Let's see if we can change the odds in our favor.*

As everyone in the room waited tensely, they heard the occasional crack of micro-shaped charges as Wasps found new targets. The noise inside the building grew louder and the flapping closer.

Sounds like a dragonfly…

The noise got louder and louder and was just about to enter the room when, with a barely noticeable nod, the three men sprang into action, using four extra sleeping bags with a few pieces of rubble in them for their formidable attack.

Tossing anything while inside a sleeping bag is never an easy trick, and they managed only a glancing hit with one sleeping bag. Fortunately, it was enough to momentarily stop the drone's two left wings, and the drone immediately went down in a ball of nylon and insulation. A few tufts of insulation floated in the air like confetti to add to the bizarre scene. The second salvo quickly covered the entire thirty inches of the drone as it languished upside down on the floor trying to right itself using its wings and insectoid legs. Throughout the attack, the men had ensured that no arms, legs, eyes, or human sounds were seen or heard. They knew their lives depended on it.

After carefully tossing a few additional pieces of rubble on the blanket to weight it down, the men waited tensely to see if their crafty plan had worked or if they were about to meet their maker. A few minutes passed, then a few more as the drone continued to struggle for life under the sleeping bags, blanket, and pieces of rubble. The pace of the booms outside started to drop off, and after about fifteen minutes from the initial attack, the remaining Wasps began to self-destruct. Hoban and those with him could not risk making noise and had to wait still longer. To the soldiers in the room with a dying machine, it seemed like an eternity.

When the detonation did happen twenty minutes later, it was not especially remarkable, and perhaps a bit disappointing. Seekers were not armed and did not need to destroy themselves in a great ball of fire; they just needed to carry enough explosive to destroy their inner electronic guts. The men waited another ten minutes before moving, just to be sure it was dead.

"How did you know it would work?" asked Garcia finally.

"I didn't. Took SWAG," Hoban responded matter-of-factly.

"A what?"

"Scientific, Wild-Ass Guess."

"Seriously? Based on what?" Garcia asked, seeming surprised that his life had been spared by a lucky guess.

"The latest intel report. Seems these are disposable strike swarms, with attack, recon, and relay drones all working together. The batteries are only good for around twenty minutes for the small ones, about twice that for the bigger ones. The one thing they struggle with is something entirely new and unpredicted, something that falls entirely outside their algorithm's parameters."

"Like suddenly seeing a bunch of green blobs showing up that didn't display a conventional human heat signature, shape, or sound. So it really was a guess…" Garcia said, still sounding mostly incredulous.

"Yep. But I prefer to call it rapid theory experimentation."

"Remind me to never play poker with you."

"Too bad, I was hoping for that when this is over."

The young troops in the room looked at them wide-eyed. Thanks to the translators, they had been privy to just how close they had come to death. They were, however, the lucky ones, as they were soon to find out.

Hoban said, "We need to relay this to the Brigade."

"I wonder how the rest of my units did," said Garcia. "Let's go find out first."

Unfortunately, the answers they would find varied from "not good" to "not good at all," to "downright awful."

4.13

291525HSEP2033 (3:25 p.m. local time, September 29, 2033) Vicinity of 5th Division Headquarters, Southern Quezon City, Greater Manila Metro Area, The Philippines

After a long, depressing morning, Sergeant Major Hoban had finally made it back to the 5th Division Headquarters to link up with Major Benavidez, get his report to Saga, and charge his systems.

"Sir, they're simply running out of soldiers," said Hoban. "They're fighting the best they can, but the progress is too expensive to sustain. This division—brigade, really—has taken over 1,100 casualties, mostly KIAs, and half of that was during the bug attacks this morning. That's over 25 percent of what's left of the division, and we got off a lot better than some of the other divisions. Desertions are rapidly increasing. A few of them were shot; others were returned to the line at bayonet point. I know the resistance in the city is picking up, but at this rate, Colonel Batenga will still be alone by the time he gets to the edge of the Occupied Zone. The math just doesn't work. The rest of his troops will be dead or will have deserted."

Benavidez sighed in frustration. "I'll try to talk to him. Maybe he can slow down, save some of his troops. They took the Batasang Pambansa Complex, Quezon Circle, and a bunch of other intermediate objectives faster than the other divisions. But it doesn't do him any good to get to the finish line first if the other divisions don't make it at all."

"Do you think he'll listen?" asked Hoban.

"Would you?"

Hoban paused. "Good point."

Benavidez then added, "Let's just see if we can get him some more help."

291640HSEP2033 (4:40 p.m. local time, September 29, 2033)
1st ARM Battalion Assault Command Post, Meycauayan City, The Philippines

"I can even smell it."

Gammon and Major Bennett stood on top of his command vehicle, looking south, where in the distance they could see the plumes of black smoke moving skyward. Other odors and smells of battle and death had been drifting past them for the past hour. Gammon looked down at the swarm of refugees his soldiers were trying desperately to keep at least a few meters away from his unit's gear.

Nowhere to get away from them, just so many, he thought.

The refugees—or more correctly, displaced persons—were streaming past the battalion, and the security headache was the biggest for Gammon's Headquarters, Support and Defense Company Commander, Major Andy Trocme, who was busy pulling out what was left of his hair. To avoid or at least minimize civilian casualties and misidentification of threats with people this close to his perimeter, he had decided to dial up the confidence levels on not only the Sentry perimeter drones, but also the perimeter hives and the ground-based hunter/killers. The trade-off of a 98 percent confidence level was the potential for reduced effectiveness against potential infiltrators.

Through their helmets and the AR interface, Gammon and Bennett could see how things had been developing over the past few hours, and Gammon was pacing back and forth along the top of the vehicle like a caged animal. His orders had been strict, and he was in torment.

The President has directed that no U.S. human or robotic fighting system shall enter the city, he remembered clearly. General Viale had been crystalline clear in his instructions.

"I don't like it either, but we don't have any wiggle room on this one. The President's trying to keep this from widening into a larger conflict at the same time he's dealing with the potential for a massive Naval and Air confrontation in the Indian Ocean and is on the edge of losing domestic political support. Don't even think about it. Am I clear?"

Gammon's helmet interface suddenly filled with a new report from Saga. The Filipino attack had reached its Clausewitzian culmination point and was stalling out. The nearest Filipino unit, the 5th Division, was between the 1st ARM and the capital. With Hoban there, it was making progress, but they were running out of people in a lopsided exchange.

They need help, some heavy-duty firepower, some extra "oomph" that we could provide. It would be decisive. We could rip through the Chinese box forts like butter. And Filipino divisions are so close…

Gammon stopped pacing for a moment and stood looking intently at Manila. The rest of the staff in the command vehicle below him also heard him stop and perked up.

"Uh oh," someone said out loud.

Being the consummate Executive Officer, Major Verault quickly came up on a private channel. "Sir, I could perhaps guess at what you're considering, and as your XO, I must advise you that you'll likely get court-martialed. It will also unhinge the strategic calculus of the president."

Verault was one of the few people that could say just about anything and not only get away with it, but also not agitate his boss when doing so. After a short pause, he added, "Regardless, I'm in. And I'm pretty sure the S3 is too. Yep, just got the thumbs-up."

"Thank you for your vote of confidence, but please reassure everyone that we are not going anywhere…yet," Gammon responded, adding, "but as you know, the possibility of a court-martial has never factored much in my decision-making." In his mind Gammon added, *and I am not going to be foolhardy with my unit or the people in it.*

Gammon had a faint smirk on his face as he looked back toward Manila. He took the humor well, but it pained him to see the assault get mired down. The cost in lives was real, which he was seeing in his display in near real time. Saga indicated that it was updating reports based on a new Philippine Home Defense Command report, which was an hour old. As Gammon watched, Filipino casualty numbers suddenly spiked for all divisions.

Looking at the report with a melancholic sadness, Gammon heard Major Verault's voice come across the net. "Sir, I believe the point is now moot. Just got traffic that General Magtanggol called it off. Another massive wave of the antipersonnel drones just devastated the divisions. They didn't have a chance against the Wasp swarms."

"How big were the swarms?" asked Gammon.

"Sir, according to the brigade's tech team, the Wasps were both launched from ground platforms and delivered from larger aerial drones, probably modified Sparrowhawk IIIs, which also are capable of delivering the larger targeting drones and anti-building thermobaric drones. The Chinese lofted over 3,000 in one shot. No point defense system in the world could take them all down."

Hoban was with the 5th Division. They got it twice in one day. Hope he made it.

Silently, the group began thinking about what this meant for the next phase of the operation. About a minute later, Verault came back on the net.

"Magtanggol has just been relieved. General Adevoso is now in charge. President Davila believes Magtanggol's decision to call for a civilian uprising was premature. The fallout, to include reprisals, is already beginning."

"Not good. Very not good," Gammon said slowly to himself. "I hope Adevoso has a better run of it…"

This was to be the great understatement of the day.

PART 5: PRECIPICE

"As we look to our enemies around the world, they might not outfight us on the battlefield, but I think they might be able to sometimes out-imagine us… into what is the realm of the possible and maybe where the future can be." ~ General (Retired) David Perkins, former Commander of Army Training and Doctrine Command (TRADOC)

5.1

291835HSEP2033 (6:35 p.m. local time, September 29, 2033) Chinese National Assistance Task Force Headquarters, The Philippines

Yu was in rare form, but despite his success, he was furious. His plan to decisively and publicly defeat the remnants of the Filipino armed forces on their own turf, and thus demonstrate their impotence, had succeeded. They had barely made it to the second defensive ring and had been stopped before penetrating too deeply into the city. It was public, well documented, and publicized extensively. Yet it was the rebellion of the population, the attacks on the People's Security Assistance force, and worst of all, the brazen attacks on Chinese forces that had angered him.

How dare they? he thought.

He found himself surprised at the degree to which he had taken the attack on the Civil Order and Assistance Battalion headquarters personally.

"Major Zhang," he began with an agitated tone.

She turned to face him. As she did, she noticed that Yu's lips were drawn tightly enough to reveal his crooked teeth.

"What is the prognosis for Lieutenant Colonel Han?"

"Sir, it is not good. He will have to be evacuated to better care on the mainland if he is going to recover. The head trauma was significant and beyond what we can treat here. His second-in-command, Major Chiang, did not survive emergency surgery. I appreciate your confidence in appointing me as the acting commander."

Major General Yu was nearly silent for a moment. The only noise he made was the ever-so-slight sound of him picking at his thumb as he considered his options for the way ahead.

"What is the word on the street?" Yu asked.

"According to Captain Tsu, the Director of the Civil Military Coordination Center, the population is starting to turn against us."

"Why?" Yu responded, looking mildly surprised. "Haven't I been exceptionally gracious to them? They've had power, water, sewage, their damn phones, even some filtered Internet, and all I ask for is order. Simply order! And this is how they repay me?"

Major Zhang considered the opportunity that was presenting itself. *He is out of his league in this new era, still an amateur in informationalized and intelligentized war.*

Zhang began gently coaxing Yu toward the path she had advocated since the beginning. "Sir, it saddens me to say this, but they are simply rebellious and ungrateful, and they fail to see the benefits of integrating with our society. It has been this way since the voyages of Zheng He over 500 years ago."

That will get him going, she thought before she continued.

"China has spent vast sums of our people's money on this country, and yet Lieutenant Colonel Han is being medically evacuated, and his XO is dead. As you know, with two generations of the one-child policy, the death of Major Chiang is the end of four bloodlines."

Zhang let this point sink in. The dead XO had been one of those capable but overly honest types who was little more than a useful idiot to her. Yu, however, liked the dead man, and Zhang could see his neck reddening. It was a good sign. Yu's pride and, by extension, that of all China, was now under attack.

Never underestimate the power of a wounded ego, she remembered being taught.

Zhang waited until Yu's neck was sufficiently red and then launched her second salvo. "We invested in their infrastructure, we provided them with military assistance, and we offered them access to our markets. Then they turned their backs on us, ripped up the agreements, treaties, and contracts we'd carefully built over the past decade, and threatened to renege on their support for our territorial claims in the South China Sea. We responded in a reasonable manner. We came to the assistance of those who were cheated in the election by radicals. We provided the opportunity for a revote and helped the fragile caretaker government maintain order. Now these ingrates are trying to kill us. Major Chiang is the first casualty among many we will likely experience and have to report to General Wei." She paused a moment more for effect. "Unless…"

"Unless what?" Yu interjected impatiently.

"Sir, unless we immediately take the strong measures you have already been considering. You were right in your thinking."

Yu began pacing about and picking at his thumb at a faster rate as he thought it over. *Some might consider the standards rather harsh, although entirely pragmatic. The morality of the decision…well, that's not as debatable or constrained as it would be if I were a Western general, although this is increasingly less true for them as well. If I am viewed as the weak link in the historic campaign who let the population get out of control, and if word gets out, then public perception in China could quickly turn negative and I would personally suffer. Commissar Xi would see to that.*

"Can you guarantee me that you can contain the negative effects and perceptions?" Yu asked.

"Absolutely, sir."

"Then execute my plan."

"Yes sir," Major Zhang affirmed clearly and with purpose, before wheeling about and exiting her commander's office. Yu did not see the slight smile on Zhang's face as she left, nor did he perceive what Zhang was thinking. *Finally, these vermin will get what they deserve and understand what real order is like.*

Zhang was an especially ambitious young leader, she was close to Deng, and she was about to make the most of this opportunity.

5.2

292015HSEP2033 (8:15 p.m. local time, September 29, 2033) Chinese National Assistance Task Force Headquarters, The Philippines

"This is Chien Li reporting to you live from downtown Manila.

"In a brazen evening attack, violent extremists opposed to the peaceful political process, the upcoming legitimate elections, and the Transitional Government of the Philippines have brutally and savagely attacked Chinese forces. In an unprovoked attack earlier this morning, several brave Chinese soldiers were killed, including the executive officer of the Civil Assistance and Order Battalion. Tonight in China, many grandparents and parents will be mourning the loss of their only sons and grandsons. These Chinese heroes were delivering medical supplies to a local hospital that were donated by concerned Chinese citizens. These compassionate citizens were moved to act after seeing reports of children in the hospital's pediatric ward who were suffering when supplies ran out due to the Allied blockade. This tragic and cowardly attack will not go unanswered."

Li wiped a tear from her eye and continued in an earnest tone.

"China continues to work to resolve the crisis peacefully, but in the interest of public safety and order, the Transitional Government of the Philippines has instituted martial law. This temporary measure is designed to protect the vast majority of law-abiding Filipino citizens from the violent criminals in their midst. As a service to the Transitional Government, we are helping to publicize the following measures:

1. All citizens are directed to report to their local People's Security Auxiliary station or other designated locations for identity registration and validation by noon tomorrow. This is a necessary precaution to ensure that the small percentage of violent extremists are quickly identified and not allowed to swim like fish within the sea of the population. Once each barangay, or district, completes 100 percent validation and identifies the 1 percent of their population that is disloyal, they will have their electronic commerce, water, sewer, and power returned to them as a gesture of our goodwill. Rewards will be offered for information leading to the arrests of extremists. Please see the TIPS Line link on the Civil Assistance and Order website or report the information to any People's Security Auxiliary uniformed member to claim your reward.
2. Curfew is established from 9:00 p.m. to 7:00 a.m. daily.
3. Medical and food assistance will be provided only to validated citizens.
4. Any collaboration with Allied Forces or the now-defunct Armed Forces of the Philippines will be considered treason. Leaving the city will be taken as an attempt to join them and will be considered treason.

5. All citizens who do not fully support the Transitional Government will be considered enemies of the people. Do not be alarmed if quick justice is rendered by People's Courts. This temporary measure is necessary in the interest of national security.

"The Transitional Government of the Philippines regrets the necessity of implementing these measures and will remove them immediately once security is reestablished and the extremists are brought to justice.

"Please see the Xinhua News website, Facebook account, Weibo, WeChat, RenRen, Twitter feed, Instagram, Snapchat, InstaNews, and Unfiltered News Now! sites for the latest in trusted news.

"This is Chien Li, reporting for Xinhua News."

300545HSEP2033 (5:45 a.m. local time, September 30, 2033)
The Cagula home, Manila

Police Inspector Cagula burst back into the house like a man possessed. Having just cut the data cable outside and unplugged the router in his home, he went room to room, waking his wife and each of his three children, turning off their phones as he went. He shuffled his still-groggy wife and Joseph into the kitchen with an impatience that betrayed his fear. With a sternness Joseph had rarely, if ever, heard, his father dictated what would happen next.

"We have to leave in twenty minutes. Gather only what you can carry, and make sure to take a big bottle of water for each of us. Joseph, help your sister and brother pack. DO NOT turn on your cell phone or talk to anyone. We are in great danger. Our very lives might depend on how quickly we leave. Do you understand?"

The police inspector uniform added a degree of authority to what he was saying, but Joseph and his mother struggled to process what he had just said.

"Wha…wha…what is going on?" asked his mother.

"It's already started. Citizen validation. People are already hungry, and the government is shutting down the city to root out its enemies. They are also using the reward system to settle old scores, and another round of executions is coming—most likely starting today."

"How…how do you know?" asked Joseph, stunned.

"Officer Cruz came by an hour ago. He said he 'owed me one' and casually dropped a file on my desk and then went to get some coffee. I looked at it. Inside were pictures labeled High Value Targets #3812 and #3813. It was you and Daniel. You were both identified by name, and Cruz had been assigned to pick you up because you were a target. I would have been arrested when my shift began at eight. I was in early because of the announcement. He may have saved our lives."

The grogginess was rapidly wearing off, and Joseph's mother sprang into action. The family packed what they could carry and quickly moved outside. Joseph saw his father's police car and was not sure what to do. They could not afford a car of their own.

"Get in!" his father commanded, and all five members of the family piled in with their bags and water bottles. The younger two were wide-eyed and starting to whimper.

The advantage of being a police officer was that Inspector Cagula knew the streets, routes, and security posts in the city. Joseph saw that the roads were already starting to fill up as panicked families attempted to flee the city with whatever they could carry. Gas had mostly run out, and while most Jeepneys were abandoned on the side of the road, a few used their remaining drops of gas to go north. Through the open window of the car, Joseph heard automatic gunfire and could see black smoke rising from many places where those fleeing the city had come across security stations or Security Auxiliary checkpoints.

Joseph looked out the window as the police car bounced and jostled over pothole after pothole as they navigated back alleys and small roads on a route hastily mapped out by his father. They did not have to use the lights as, upon recognizing a police car, most people quickly moved out of the way only to be amazed as it drove by on what appeared to be a family outing.

Joseph's fear began to rise, and he couldn't pay attention as his parents planned how they should handle the situation if they were to get stopped. He turned on his phone for a brief instant, texted a quick note to Daniel to warn him, and turned it off again. He had just hit the off button when his father slowed and cursed, something Joseph had never heard his father do before.

Joseph looked up and saw that they had stopped in front of a small People's Security Auxiliary checkpoint. Two uniformed Security Auxiliary members and two without uniforms were getting out of a Toyota Hilux they had just parked sideways on the road.

Police Inspector Cagula opened the door and stepped out slowly. As Joseph watched the scene unfold, he thought that this group of Auxiliaries seemed especially thuggish. His father approached the group with his hands by his side and away from his service pistol. Although he had probably arrested a few of them previously, he attempted to engage them in small talk. Then his father pulled out a roll of cash, most of what they had in the house at the time, and offered it to the three men and one woman, apparently a bribe to let them pass. They took the money but seemed unsure of what to do next. They continued to talk among themselves until the woman's cell phone rang. She yelled something to the men, and they brought their weapons to the ready. Joseph saw his father quickly raise his hands.

That was the signal. His mother had been inching over slowly from the passenger seat toward the driver's seat and now hit the gas on the police cruiser. It leapt forward, and she drove it straight into the rear axle of the pickup, which obligingly gave way just as her husband had told her it would.

Transfixed by the scene behind him, Joseph watched as his father struggled with the guards. Several fired at their car, and his sister started to scream as his mother accelerated and wove along the narrow road. The last image he saw of his father was of one of the guards striking him in the head with a rifle butt and his immediate collapse.

When Joseph turned to his sister, he saw that her leg was bleeding. The blood freaked him out, but an eight-year-old screaming with all the power she could muster was even worse. It was just a gash, and he remembered from Boy Scout training what to do.

"Just stop screaming!" Joseph screamed back at her.

This was a lot for a sixteen-year-old boy who was not yet a man to handle, and he was having difficulty processing it all as they sped north.

An hour later, after it was all over, he reflexively turned on his phone, noted the exceptionally weak signal, and saw the text.

It was from Daniel. It was one word.

"Sry."

5.3

022010HOCT2033 (8:10 p.m. local time, October 2, 2033)
1st ARM Battalion Assembly Area, near Meycauayan City, The Philippines

Buck stood smoking a small cigar about 100 meters away from his command vehicle, admiring the fine ribs and veins of the tanned Connecticut wrapper for a moment.

Probably a forty-gauge, a small robusto, but very nice. Too bad I didn't have a cutter and had to bite the end off. It's important to remain civilized, even at times like this. After a brief pause, he added, *hmph, yeah, right.* He chuckled to himself. *So says the guy who thinks box wine is just fine…*

The cigar had been a gift from Colonel Garbulinski, a well-known purveyor of bad habits. Buck brought it up to his lips and pulled the smoke into his mouth, then did a curious thing. He turned his head skyward and made what a casual observer would think was a clucking motion.

Perfect.

The smoke ring rose slowly though the damp air, although he could barely see it in the light of the waxing gibbous moon.

Finally starting to figure this out, but the policies back in Washington, not so much. The crackdown in Manila is intensifying. We can tell by the number of refugees passing through. What they're showing our intel teams is awful. Didn't have a great answer for the soldier who asked me what was next. The Filipinos are not strong enough to do it by themselves and we can't help them. Stalemates are the worst of both worlds. Maybe the President's speech tomorrow will provide some sense of where this is going.

Major Verault walked up and asked, "May I join you, sir?"

"Of course, XO. Always."

Major Verault proceeded to pull a perfect cigar out of a small case and then produced a surgical steel cutter. He neatly clipping the end, lit a small butane lighter, and rolled the cigar in the flame with a precision that impressed Gammon.

"You probably even figured out how to keep your fingernails clean," Gammon said good-naturedly.

"As my mother always used to say, 'Cleanliness is next to godliness.'"

"Right. So what's the prognosis on repairs and supplies?" Although Gammon knew the numbers, he wanted to get his XO's take on the patterns and way forward.

"Well, sir," Verault began in his soothing drawl, "the numbers do indeed paint a dark picture. Having a few days to pause operations, other than the constant repositioning, has been helpful. Seems both sides are taking a breather."

Verault took a long draw on his cigar, blew a perfect smoke ring, and then followed it with a smaller one that moved through the center of the larger one.

"The advantage really comes down to who can resupply themselves faster, and not much is coming in for either side, but for different reasons. The blockade is working to choke the Chinese, and while theirs is less effective, people often forget how big the Pacific really is."

"What do you think?"

"Sir, I think we're better off than we were three days ago. While we're not getting much, we are getting some resupply, especially class five ammunition, although we are still very short on railgun ammo. We can sustain combat for probably no more than forty-eight hours if we're committed."

"I was thinking closer to thirty-six, but you're probably right. What about the casualties?"

"A few were evacuated to Darwin, but there wasn't enough room for all of them. Lieutenant Colonel Hawkins is a miracle worker and has kept more alive than we have a right to expect, but three more from the brigade died in the last twenty-four hours."

"That's tough."

Both men paused to reflect for a moment. The heat was oppressive, it was dark, and the mosquitos were feasting on them. Gammon took another pull on his cigar but decided not to blow another smoke ring until he had practiced more.

"So, my company commanders appear to be a bit scarce at the moment. Any idea where they are?" Gammon asked.

Major Verault immediately became suspicious but responded as coolly as ever. "Sir, I don't know, but I'll take a walk around the perimeter and check on them."

"Very well, XO, I'm heading back to the command post. CSM Washington and I are going to make the rounds in forty-five minutes or so."

As the men parted company, Gammon thought to himself, *they've had enough time.*

The river card was down. It was a queen of hearts.

"I raise twenty," said Captain Hank Johnson, the Recon and Strike Company Commander.

"I raise you forty," followed Mike McGinnis.

Captain Frank Ohata saw the tell and knew Mike was bluffing. *For all his bravado, Mikey's a lousy bluffer.*

"I raise another thirty," said Frank with a wry grin.

Major Andy Trocme, the Headquarters, Support and Defense Company commander, the only company command authorized a Major, was three years older than these hotheads and decided that, while his pair of jacks might beat a bluff, his hand would probably not beat whatever Ohata had. He pushed his cards forward without a word.

Captain Steve Hester, the Charlie, or Currahee, Company Commander, was unsure of what to do. Ohata commanded a heavy infantry company recently attached to the battalion and was a little hard to read. In the end, Steve decided that two pair could probably at least hold its own in this crowd.

"I'm in," said Hester.

The bid went back to the dealer, Hank Johnson, who was optimistic about the three eights in his hand. He had also seen Mike's tell, and while he also agreed that Mike McGinnis was bluffing, he figured he could beat Ohata's hand.

"Me too," he said, and after everyone pushed a sufficient number of chips forward, he added, "Okay, fellers, let's see 'em."

Hank, Frank, and Steve eagerly showed their hands. Mike went last.

"Seriously? No way!" exclaimed the group, quickly adding a number of colorful euphemisms.

Mike was proud of himself for luring them in, and his flush did, in fact, beat everything else on the table. After collecting his winnings, Mike helped gather the cards into a deck.

Better not win too often, Mikey, or they'll get suspicious, and there's plenty of time to milk this cash cow.

Mike handed the deck to Ohata, who began to shuffle with the irritation of someone who had fallen for the oldest trick in the book. As he shuffled, Hank began to opine about Stacy, who was taking the first shift as lookout. A group of key leaders was a lucrative target for the Chinese, but that was not why they had a lookout. There were two driving factors: no one wanted to face the boss's ire if he were to find out about the illicit game. While he might be willing to turn a blind eye to the game, if they were caught, he would be in a predicament and would have to do something. Even worse, however, was that if the XO found out, he would insist on joining the game. The last time Verault played, it ended in complete disaster with his outrageous but very successful bluff on an all-in hand. Hence, the group had put appropriate security precautions in place. Ohata continued to shuffle as the conversation turned to more interesting matters.

"I hear Stacy got a 'Dear Jane' letter," ventured Hank casually. "Too bad. But from what I hear, the guy turned out to be a real D-bag."

"And how would you know said information?" asked Frank.

"I have sources," he replied. Everyone at the table knew that his source was his girlfriend on the Brigade staff. Hank continued, "So, according to my sources—" the other men rolled their eyes, "—Stacy was about to throw her engagement ring into the river but decided that a turtle would probably end up choking on it, and she has a thing for turtles. In the end, she gave it to some bedraggled lady with a couple kids who were heading north from the city. Figured it could do at least someone a little good that way."

As Trocme was married and a few years older than the rest, he began opining like an older brother. "All right, you hammerheads, I know she's all that and a bag of chips, but don't any of you start thinking about a rebound romance in a combat zone. We have work to do. Capisce?"

"Of course not!" the rest responded, nearly in unison and with faux shock that he would even suggest such a thing.

After another few rounds, it was Frank Ohata's turn to relieve Stacy. As he departed, he considered a casual opening line with her to convey sympathy and mild interest, but no more. He had to play it cool to start.

Mike McGinnis also began to consider the new situation, and after a moment, a new reality dawned on him. *Well, Mikey, your odds with Stacy just improved to about one in a million, which means…*

The next thought flooded quickly into his mind. *You've…got…a…chance!*

5.4

October 3, 2033
Personal for: Lieutenant General Wei
From: Major General Yu
Lieutenant General Wei–

I want to express my gratitude to you for being willing to risk precious naval assets in an attempt to provide me with the supplies, ammunition, and replacements we so desperately need. While I am disappointed that I will be receiving only a fraction of the replacements we need to bring ourselves back to full strength, I know that there was incredible opposition to the mission and that your courage carried the day with the other generals. We look forward to seeing the replacements arrive in Manila Bay in the next forty-eight hours.

Regarding the current matters, I fully understand your recent directive and continue to implement its measures. The population's degree of cooperation has improved; however, I would ask for your indulgence as I clarify a few points your staff may have continued to hide from you. Unfortunately, they have every incentive to disguise their planning failures. Fully four of their five pre-intervention assumptions have been entirely false. The two biggest flawed assumptions were that there would be no outside intervention and that the population would easily acquiesce to our will as long as we provided them a degree of normalcy. I must now offer you the painful truth on both matters.

Today's decision by the American president to commit ground forces to a second Filipino attack on Manila has been indeed unfortunate. The Strategic Support Force was not able to contain the narrative over the past seventy-two hours, and unfortunately, a few relatively minor events were inflamed on the global stage to the point where many political leaders found themselves in positions with their constituents demanding that they "do something." While our tactical situation remains exceptionally difficult, theirs is no less so. They are not optimized for urban combat and, like us, have not received significant reinforcements or adequate supplies. The Americans are like coddled children and are still exceptionally sensitive to casualties. Fortunately, we have several weapons that we have been saving for the urban battle and expect them to produce devastating physical, psychological, and public-opinion effects. In the end, we will settle this the old-fashioned way: it will be a test of blood, steel, and will.

Regarding the second critical failed assumption, it was entirely predictable. Had your staff read even a cursory overview of Filipino history, they would not have made assumptions that were little more than wishful thinking. Despite dissenting opinions, they persisted, and the subsequent planning for the establishment and maintenance of civil order was entirely inadequate.

As I mentioned in my last letter, with little more than one brigade, I am required to maintain order over 22 million civilians in Manila alone. This is an exceptionally difficult task, even with the stricter compliance measures we have implemented. The Strategic Support Force has been unable to maintain the perceptual isolation of the population, and they are increasingly turning against us. While we have complete control of the infrastructure and continue to maintain an iron grip on information, the weak link remains the lack of ground troops or, for that matter, even reliable partnered forces.

Those on your staff who insist that we are well resourced with numerous drones miss the point: there are some things drones cannot do. Keeping civil order is one of them, and the People's Security Auxiliaries are quickly becoming both unreliable militarily and a liability to our credibility. They are often little more than opportunistic criminals, and by having to empower them due to our lack of "boots on the ground," they are contributing to the cycle of popular unrest.

Lastly, once the resupply convoy arrives and we defeat the Allied forces, we will still be isolated and need either further reinforcements to consolidate our gains or evacuation if our mission were to change. I fully appreciate that the Navy has suffered grievously from the infernal robotic Triggerfish in the Straits of Malacca and that the Army continues to struggle on the border with Vietnam. However, the timing for allocating significant additional combat forces to this effort must be moved forward. Rumors are running rampant among the troops that the Central Military Commission has been equivocating on the fate of this Task Force and may write it off if it appears that we will be defeated by the Allies. This will not happen! The idea of being prisoners of war does not sit well with us, and I will be as ruthless as necessary to ensure that does not become our fate.

For the People!
Major General Yu

Lieutenant General Wei read the note with mild interest.

Perhaps Yu is a bit more astute than I had imagined. He delicately alluded to rumors about the stakes for him personally and his entire command. He must have a contact somewhere, Wei pondered.

The Central Military Commission had indeed decided on two things: First, while it was a priority to reinforce the Philippines, it would still take eight to ten days before they could provide meaningful forces. Secondly, should Yu suffer anything worse than a minor defeat in the interim, the Task Force would be written off.

"The die is cast. The die is indeed cast," Wei said softly.

5.5

040945HOCT2033 (9:45 a.m. local time, October 4, 2033) 1st ARM Battalion Headquarters, Meycauayan City, The Philippines

Buck rubbed his bloodshot eyes and took a long drink of tepid water from his canteen. *We're still not there yet. Still not ready. I like the idea, but I wonder if the INDO-PACOM Commander was well-informed on how little we really have on the ground to help with the push. At least we'll get a higher priority on support. And it's a good thing we're also miracle workers.*

"Do it again," he said, this time a bit more impatiently.

"Roger, sir," answered Major Bennett.

Bennett and everyone else in the command post were tired. They had been at this for ten hours and had run fourteen accelerated-time simulations. The brigade headquarters had participated in the first three, identified several critical higher-level issues, and was now running a series of simulations to work out its own problems. One of the brigade intelligence lieutenants, assisted by Saga, stayed on the net to play the part of the Chinese. Except for a win in the relatively simplistic first round, each subsequent battle increased in complexity and seemed to go worse for Gammon and his team. He never took losing well.

There was the time the brigade ran out of ammunition before destroying enough security points to assure control of the city. "Imprecise targeting" was the logistics support team's assessment.

Then there was the time the variable autonomy and collateral damage parameters were set too low. A large number of civilians were killed in the crossfire when thermobaric warheads hit the Chinese security points, and by hypervelocity rounds that could easily penetrate four city blocks.

This was followed by dialing the settings up too high. The HOMRRs and Razorbacks often did not get off the critical first shot. While zero civilians were harmed, the kill ratio went from a respectable 4:1 to 1:1. Gammon's team simply ran out of forces in what became a battle of attrition.

Then there was the time that the assault infantry in TALON II(i) exosuits ran out of energy, the time communications went down, the time Allied forces were unable to respond as quickly as the Chinese network did to major changes on the battlefield, and on and on. There were other rounds with experimental parameters and variables, all based on observed and projected Chinese behaviors to date. The battalion lost all of them. Gammon was growing increasingly impatient and starting to prowl around his command post like a restless animal.

What are we missing? It's not adding up. The urban jungle is a problem for us and for them too. All the intel says that we have about as much as they do. Their logistics situation is only slightly better than ours because they were able to stockpile supplies. But pound for pound, I know we're better than they are. Why isn't this working?

"Major Antipuesto, please explain to me again how we can coordinate our battalions on the attack," Gammon asked, his Tagalog remaining perfect with the help of his electronic translator.

Major Antipuesto was a wiry young major who had been placed in command of the Philippine 17th Infantry Battalion following the loss of its original commander and forty-seven other soldiers in the Wasp strike. Antipuesto stumbled a bit as he turned to face Gammon but quickly regained his equilibrium. He was still disoriented by the AR helmet, and it took him a moment to remember that, unlike the rest of the commanders, he was physically in the same place as Gammon.

"Sir, primarily with good planning ahead of time, the esteemed Sergeant Major Hoban, seventeen runners on scooters, and most importantly, five relay radios Technical Sergeant Chavez and Specialist Five Jones helped us rig up in your Razorbacks."

Gammon was not aware that Hoban had been moved to the battalion and was looking forward to seeing him. The Security Force Assistance Battalion teams had taken casualties and were subsequently dispersed even further to cover down on key units, which explained why Hoban was apparently now the most senior Security Force Assistance Battalion soldier assigned to the 71st.

Lucky for them, Gammon thought before he responded to the Major. "Roger, thank you."

Buck looked over at Captain Ohata, the Assault Infantry Company Commander and First Sergeant Nick Shoults, who were the only company command team members physically present. Captain Ohata spoke up first.

"Sir, we've been talking, and we also think our suits can help relay some info through the net. We'll be working closely with the 17th for most of the attack."

Captain Ohata was about five-foot-eight, wiry, and always seemed to have an intense look on his face. His friends called it his "constipated look," which never ceased to annoy him. He was wearing the internal headset of his "suit," a TALON II(i), for two reasons: the exosuit took up space in an already crowded command shelter, and it was charging along with the others in his company. His company was one of the few units truly designed for urban combat.

"The comms team has indeed been busy," Gammon responded. "All right, let's go again."

The team ran two more simulations and then hit mental "tracer burnout." Even the driven, energetic Gammon was spent. He wrapped up the last session with a word of encouragement and dismissed his team, both those physically and virtually present.

As the images of Doss, McGinnis, Hester, and Trocme quickly faded out, Gammon took off his AR helmet, flopped back in his command chair, and closed his eyes for a moment. After a few short minutes, he heard the door to the command post open, and a large figure walked in.

"Uh, sir…hate to disturb you," said Major Trocme. "We're approaching our reposition time, wheels up on your vehicle in ten."

Without even opening his eyes, Gammon responded, "Perfect. No rest for the wicked or the weary."

It was going to be another long day.

5.6

041700HOCT2033 (5:00 p.m. local time, October 4, 2033) Vicinity of the 1st ARM Battalion Headquarters, Meycauayan City, The Philippines

As the sun eased lower in the sky, it was already being blocked by a large skyscraper when Sergeant Major Hoban decided to find his old boss. With the upcoming attack, he knew Gammon was under intense pressure and would have to push the limits of his people and the new systems in unfamiliar terrain. Not only did Hoban want to see Gammon, he was also curious about how the new stuff would work in the increasingly dense cityscape.

This morning's intel brief predicted that there would be a relative lull in enemy activity for a short time. With the big fight coming up, both sides are hoarding their drones and recon sorties. No time like the present for a walkabout.

As Hoban picked his way through the city, he noticed that the areas of rubble were not uniform. Some areas were relatively unscathed, while others were devastated, with not much in the middle. He also found himself swimming in a sea of humanity desperate to get away from the fighting and equally desperate to eat. The smells were awful. From what his translator was telling him, food and water had been cut off pending some sort of registration, the number of public executions was rising, and order was starting to break down.

Sounds like the city is going to hell in a handbasket, he thought.

As he walked along, he noticed large clusters of displaced persons congregating around American military units. He also noticed that he had just stepped into something soft. When he looked down, he saw toilet paper sticking out from either side of his boot, along with the soft pudding of human excrement.

He announced his displeasure both loudly and with a long string of profanity that would make a sailor blush. Taking a deep breath, he was preparing for part two of his tirade when he saw the horrified looks on the bedraggled Filipinos around him.

Embarrassed, he quickly corrected the situation. "Translator off." Hoban then proceeded to finish his second round of descriptive euphemisms. After a minute or two, he calmed down and grew a bit more sympathetic.

Can't really blame them for the excrement mines. They're on the run, they've lost everything, and they have to keep moving. Taking a dump a few meters off the road is the least of their worries, he thought.

As Hoban attempted to scrape off the smelly residue on a patch of grass and then a small tree, he noticed the extent to which the civilians were intermingled with the now very dispersed and ever-moving American units.

"Translator on," he said as he approached a family near him.

He looked at the woman and her three grimy kids and suddenly felt a sense of pity for them. She was probably in her mid-thirties, and the despair and stress of the past few days were written on her face. Like so many others, she appeared not to have been well prepared for the trip.

Probably didn't have much notice when they decided to run, probably been through a lot, he thought.

The woman was sitting on a small bench. He knelt beside her and asked, as gently as he could, "Why are so many people here?"

She just looked at him with what he recognized as the thousand-yard stare. *Probably just exhaustion, fear, sensory overload, and all the craziness going on now.*

"Can any of you kids answer my question? I'll trade you some M&Ms for some help."

The oldest boy immediately perked up and said, "I can. The reason everyone is here is because we hope that the Americans will give us water, maybe a little food too. Most importantly, we know you will protect us from the auxiliary forces."

Hoban handed the boy three M&Ms—red, blue, and purple—and they disappeared into his mouth. Hoban quickly figured out that he would have to ration his remaining M&Ms to get maximum intelligence benefit from the boy. By his rough calculations, he would be able to get three or four more questions answered before he ran out. The kid, and now his younger brother and sister, were all staring at the half-eaten bag of candy in his hand.

"Okay," Hoban continued, "what about the Filipino forces, what about the local mayor? Why not go to them?"

"They don't have anything to give us. And besides, the mayor is telling us to go to you."

Hoban dutifully handed over three more M&Ms—green, yellow, and pink. The pink ones were the latest color, added in 2031, and already rumored to be on the chopping block in favor of neon something-or-other, according to his daughter anyway. This time the boy gave one to each of his siblings and then took the pink one, whispered something into his mother's ear, and put it in her hand. After a moment, she put it in her mouth and ate it.

"So why here?" Hoban continued. "Why this place?"

The boy looked at him like he was from another planet, then responded, "The Red Cross Emergency Assistance app. We get hit by typhoons, what you call hurricanes, every year. It's routine for us. We also get a really big one every few years. After hurricanes Harvey and Irma tore apart your country, like fifteen years ago, assistance and rescue apps became the rage. A few families got some water from a couple GIs and entered it into the app. News travelled quickly, and here we are."

"Interesting," remarked Hoban as he handed over four more M&Ms. "I hadn't realized I was so out of touch technologically."

"You are old, you can't help it," the boy said with a bit of mock sympathy.

Hoban was down to his last four M&Ms and chose his final question carefully. "The phones are spotty. The Chinese control cell service and in some cases cut it. How come so many people got the message with no cell phone service?"

The boy took a stick and made several holes in the ground. Hoban wasn't getting the point. "I am not paying you M&Ms for artwork in the dirt."

Hoban's translator came to life again as the boy, who seemed to be a good kid, explained it was basically a peer-to-peer network with the phones all acting like hotspots. As long as one phone could connect to another one in the daisy chain, it was part of a virtual cell system. "Of course, you have to be relatively close, but in an area where this many people are packed together, that's not a problem."

The boy held out his hand, and Hoban handed the bag over with the four remaining M&Ms. After distributing one to each member of the family, the boy whispered something into his mother's ear, pulled something from her pocket, and came back to Hoban.

"Okay, GI, now I have a deal for you. I'll trade you this for five pounds of rice and a gallon of water."

Hoban look down into his dirty hand and saw what appeared to be an engagement ring. "Thanks, but I'm already married, and my wife doesn't need two. Besides, I don't have any rice."

"C'mon, mister, we're really hungry. My mom's not doing so good either." The boy dramatically gestured to the woman, and Hoban was embarrassed that he had tried to make light of the offer.

"Hey, kid, you're doing a good job holding it together. Your mom will be okay once she gets some sleep and warm food. Here, take this."

Hoban pulled a field ration out of his small combat pack along with two disposable filtration straws. He handed them to the boy and said, "There's even a heater in the packet to warm the food. Good luck."

The boy's bravado was only slightly diminished as his eyes welled up slightly. "Thank you, mister. Thank you very much."

Hoban prepared to leave and then stopped. "Oh, I almost forgot. What's your name?"

"It's Joseph, Joseph Cagula."

Hoban walked a bit farther in the smelly streets full of human detritus. People had simply left their things behind, having tired of carrying them in the heat. Clothing, suitcases, and various bags were strewn everywhere. He was about 200 yards from the nearest semblance of a military perimeter when he heard a loud rushing sound followed by a series of synchronized explosions, then the distant shouting of soldiers. He looked up, nearly vertically, and saw them.

Just our guys practicing, he thought to himself.

He saw four of the newly fielded urban assault craft pulling away from the side of a building at least twenty floors up. The front of the machines had blown neat holes in the side of the glass building, disgorged four soldiers each, and were just raising their landing ramps, known as "planks," when Hoban spotted them. The ducted fans became almost silent as they went to a lower power setting once their load was gone.

Still dicey, even with only four troops and the recent improvements.

Hoban's mind was instantly pulled back to an earlier field trial. Version 1.0 of the urban assault craft was good idea-ed to death and ended up with virtually no power reserve. When operationally tested in a real city, which can have notoriously unpredictable winds between buildings, a heavy gust tipped one about thirty degrees. The six soldiers fell to one side in their heavy exosuits, which tipped the craft even farther as it attempted to hover next to the building. With no power reserve and wildly out of balance, gravity won the contest, and the craft slowly capsized. Four soldiers fell out of the craft to their deaths while two managed to hang on for the pile-driving ride to the earth.

Should have been the engineers and program managers on that one, he thought. *Nothing like having personal skin in the game to make sure it works.*

Hoban turned back to his route and eventually made it to 1st ARM battalion's perimeter. Two very tired privates had the impossible task of trying to keep the civilian throng at least a few meters away from their vehicles, which were crammed between buildings. After identifying himself and getting directions, he walked a few more meters to Gammon's command post.

As Hoban climbed the steps into the back of the command vehicle, he saw one of the HOMRRs about fifty meters away surrounded by technicians. They appeared to be installing some new gear on the HOMRR, some sort of extra armor consisting of numerous small hexagon-shaped panels. As a paratrooper, he found the new fighting systems only mildly interesting, and the scene quickly left his mind as soon as he pushed back the Kevlar blast curtain and saw his old commander.

"Sergeant Major Hoban!" Gammon greeted him with an arm-wrestler handshake, a big one-armed man-hug, and three slaps on the back. "It's good to see you."

"Likewise, sir. I happened to be in the neighborhood and thought I'd swing by to say hi. Pretty crazy stuff going on."

"For both of us," responded Gammon. "How's the 5th Division? More importantly, how's the 17th Battalion? Hear you're the only American with them now."

Hoban paused to pull off his helmet and wipe the sweat off his brow with his sleeve before responding. "Sir, both are okay, considering the casualties. They weren't used to having to rapidly promote from within to replace losses like back in the day. Major Antipuesto is solid, as well as his acting sergeant major."

"That's all good news because coordination is going to be a bitch. The guys are doing their best with some workarounds, but it's still going to be touch and go. We're even using couriers."

Hoban shrugged to indicate his agreement with the less-than-ideal communications situation and contemplated the situation for a moment. "True, but they're less dependent on technology and the electromagnetic spectrum than we are. They also emit less of it and might be harder to track. But I imagine the Chinese have the city wired."

"Pretty much. We still haven't figured out how to beat them. The simulations are still coming out…shall we say, unfavorably. Here, let me show you."

Both men put on their AR helmets, and Gammon began to update Hoban on the plan. Their hope was that if they had a mind-meld, Hoban could help Major Antipuesto and the rest of the 17th Battalion's leadership remain operationally synched with the 1st ARM Battalion.

At her station in the command post, Major Bennett had just taken her helmet off as the two men began very animated gesticulations on the maps she could no longer see. It reminded her not of a military discussion, but of a dance competition.

She itched her scalp, brushed the resulting dandruff flakes off her uniform, then sniffed her fingers. *Gross. Oily hair smell. Nine days without a shower, and counting.*

Megan tucked her hair back into a bun, put her helmet on, pulled up the map the boss was pointing at, and put her headset on listen mode. She was intimately familiar with the plan because she had written most of it based on Gammon's guidance. *Still, never hurts to hear the boss talk about it to better understand his thinking*, she justified to herself as she eavesdropped on the conversation.

Gammon's voice filled her headset, and she quickly turned the volume down. "And here's where we think they'll try to hit us. Their mechanized forces can rip through the Filipino units if they catch them on the move, and they still have a lot of drones. They'll probably try to catch them on a flank where we can't help them and create so many casualties that the Philippine Army breaks, or they'll try to take us out and then pick them off at their leisure."

Hoban agreed that this made sense and then started asking his questions.

"What are you hearing about support? If this goes bad, it's over. The Chinese will be masters of the First Island Chain, the South China Sea, pretty much all of South Asia. With a lot of the Indo-Pacific Fleet tied up in the Bay of Bengal, not a lot of allies will be willing to jump in if this becomes a bust."

"True, but a big chunk of their fleet is there too, which is part of the reason we got the order to go in. It's pretty much a stalemate right now, but if we break it in our favor and President Davila can regain power, this will be a strategic defeat for the Chinese on the world stage. They'll be shown for what they've become. Besides," Buck continued, "the American population is super pissed about the second round of cyber attacks. They're calling it the electronic Pearl Harbor. The Chinese miscalculated, and because of the amount of destruction and the number of deaths they caused, the average American wants to hammer them. Although I will give the Chinese an A for effort in trying to attribute it to the Russians."

"Wow, I guess I should have followed it all more closely. I hate reading the news anyway—drama, drama, drama. But as you know, I'm a field soldier, and that brings me to security. What gives with all the civilians around? It's a huge security risk with all their phones, which are all collectors, not to mention the way they're clogging the main roads.

Aren't the military police, civil affairs, and PSYOP bubbas supposed to help fix that shit?"

"Yeah, not so much. The military police and psychological operations units were low on the deployment priority, and they didn't make it from Japan before surface shipping got cut off. Not worth risking them coming by air now. The active-duty Civil Affairs units were disbanded a decade ago to pay for more maneuver units. The reserve units were formed up in ad-hoc battle rosters and are just now finishing their pre-deployment training. Won't be here anytime soon. Hell, even my S9 wasn't filled until right before deployment."

"Well, that sucks," deadpanned Hoban. "Now that we have all this settled, on to more important issues. Got a dip, sir?"

"Nope, I gave up Copenhagen two years ago. A Christmas gift to Julia."

"Need one?"

"You're as bad as Garbulinski."

"No, sir, as you will remember, I'm worse."

5.7

051435HOCT2033 (2:35 p.m. local time, October 5, 2033)
Chinese National Assistance Task Force Headquarters, The Philippines

Colonel Deng pulled deeply on the cigarette, held it for a moment, and then exhaled an enormous cloud of smoke.

"Convoy PQ-17 is within fifty nautical miles of Scarborough Shoal," Deng announced with confidence. "Our forces there will provide them some degree of cover as they make the final 200-mile leg to the entrance to Manila Bay. They should arrive by midnight."

"I hope so. We have much riding on this," responded General Yu. "And must you smoke in here?"

The staff in the room were silent, waiting for Deng's response. Deng took a long drag and then slowly crushed the cigarette in the recently-cleaned ashtray.

"As you wish, sir."

Yu began slowly pacing back and forth and subconsciously picking at his right thumb. Yu looked briefly at Deng, who was short, even for a Chinese man. *Little Napoleon. Lucky for him that he is so well connected.*

"So, I noticed that none of the Wing Loongs are up right now providing the convoy with air cover. Why isn't the Navy using them to drop sonobuoys ahead of the convoy? As fast as the catamarans are moving, it might have been helpful to the escorts."

"True, sir, but in weighing all the facts, I decided that not announcing our route ahead of time in a relatively secure area would be the most prudent course of action. This allows for a more direct route and shorter transit time. Speed is security, sir."

"That was my decision to make."

"I understand, sir," responded Deng in a barely concealed patronizing tone. "You were attending to other more important matters, and we had to provide a timely decision."

From the corner of his eye, Yu noticed the Navy liaison officer. Based on his previous interactions with her, he found her to be competent and reasonably honest, which was why he felt a new wave of anger begin to well up in him as he saw her head, almost imperceptibly, shake from side to side.

"Let's hope you are right, Colonel. For all our sakes."

051505HOCT2033 (3:05 p.m. local time, October 5, 2033)
Approximately 33 nautical miles Northeast of Scarborough Shoal

The Triggerfish class autonomous attack submarine had been shadowing the convoy for four hours and had been struggling to keep up. It wasn't until the convoy encountered rougher seas and slowed down to twenty-six knots that the submarine assessed a slight increase in its probability of mission success.

While the unmanned submarine knew itself only as SSA-191, it had been christened the previous year as *Sculpin*, following a decision by naval leaders to return to the tradition of naming submarines after fish. This had been done for two reasons. First, the original switch to cities and states had been implemented by the father of the nuclear submarine force, Admiral Hyman Rickover, to gain support from congressional appropriators. "Fish don't vote," he had said. And secondly, in the age of relatively expendable ships, losing a ship named after a fish would be more palatable to the public than having them read about the sinking of a submarine named after their home state.

The *Sculpin* came to periscope depth, extended her mast antenna, and received welcome news. A few seconds later her bow planes angled down and began pushing the nose of her forty-meter hull downward and back toward the safety of deeper water. The options were looking good for the attack as the *Tang*, SSA-306, and the *Cavalla*, SSA-684, had both confirmed receipt of the information on the convoy and were now on an intercept course. With a 4:1 ratio of escorts against it, the *Sculpin* determined that the odds of inflicting a crippling blow to the convoy were limited. With only two long-range and two short-range torpedoes remaining, each would need to be a guaranteed hit, so the *Sculpin* decided it would have to bide its time and wait for a game-changing event. The event came sooner than expected with an unexpected "ping" in the water.

At 4:27 p.m., the *Sculpin* noted, "Chinese sonobuoy detected."

Commander Deng Wang Wei of the PLA Navy bolted upright. He was now fully awake in the captain's chair of the *Nanjing*, the convoy's Command and Control ship.

"Are you sure?" he asked.

The intelligence officer moved a small trash bag from his mouth as the boat heaved in the increasingly heavy sea state. For some unknown reason, the ship was stocked only with clear trash bags. The rest of the crew could see the greenish-yellow vomit, which didn't help anyone else's nausea level.

"Yes sir, it was a brief but positive signal hit on a submerged enemy vessel. We are being followed."

Deng was instantly nervous and quickly pulled a cigarette from a small metal case and prepared to light it. *Infernal habit,* he thought, *egged on by my uncle.*

He paused for a moment, put the cigarette away, pulled out an electronic replacement, and after taking a long draw, he exhaled an enormous cloud of water vapor. *He said this was supposed to be a milk run, a chance to gain prestige and enhance my career, a favor for my mother, of all things.*

"Can we get any more speed? If it is a Triggerfish, we can probably outrun it as long as it stays submerged."

The *Nanjing* rolled to the left as it hit a swell larger than the rest. The boat settled, and the ship's engineer responded, "Very little, sir. Unless conditions improve, it will catch up to us before we get to the bay. We may have to make a decision on the escorts and make a run for it."

Deng had just spoken to twenty-five percent of the humans on his command and control ship and felt suddenly isolated. He could not contact the mainland for help as any transmission would definitively give his position away to any other enemy submarines. The theory had been that the catamarans would depart so suddenly from Hong Kong and make the transit so quickly that even if there were surviving enemy subs in the area, by the time they could respond, the convoy would already be unloading in Manila.

Big ocean, little boat. So much for that stupid theory, he thought.

Warbot 1.0

Out of necessity, the AI decision-making capabilities of SSA-306 and all the other ships in the Triggerfish class were fairly advanced, even by current standards; the designers knew that there would be less opportunity for human intervention at key decision-making points, like this one. The *Tang*'s rudder turned slightly to starboard, and she began to veer slowly away from the most direct route to the convoy intercept point. The *Tang* had a minor diversion to make that would increase their overall odds of success in the coming mission.

At 100 meters below the surface of the South China Sea, and almost within sight of the western coast of Luzon, the *Cavalla* was busy making its own risk calculations. It was too far out of position to make the intercept before the convoy made the final turn around Corregidor Island and into entrance of Manila Bay. But that was only true if it remained underwater on electric power; the batteries did not have enough energy to make it that far at the necessary speed. Moving to snorkel depth would allow it to run its diesel engines and keep its batteries charged for when the *Cavalla* needed to be submerged. But as *Cavalla* correctly calculated, its diesel engines were acoustically louder than its electric propulsion system and running near the surface would also expose it to Chinese aircraft, surface vessels, and perhaps even commercial fishing vessels returning to port. If spotted, it would be over for the *Cavalla*. After a few nanoseconds of deliberation, she began her ascent.

❖ ❖ ❖

051917HOCT2033 (7:17 p.m. local time, October 5, 2033) Approximately 80 nautical miles East South East of Scarborough Shoal

The junior Deng was sweating profusely, and his captain's chair was almost as damp as his uniform. His obsessive sucking on the e-cigarette made a disconcerting sound that, in turn, made the rest of the bridge crew—all four of them—nervous, even if it did help keep him calm.

"Anything further on the initial contact?" he asked the weapons officer.

"Negative, sir, we suspect it is still shadowing us. I recommend we keep the escorts in a close screen in case it attempts to speed up, move around us, and attack from either side or even the front. The weather is worsening, the sea state just crossed from four to five, and our ships are slowing down. The best we can do now is nineteen knots."

As if on cue, the *Nanjing* pitched back and then forward, precipitating a violent heave by the intelligence officer into his vomit bag.

A naval officer who is seasick. Unbelievable, Deng thought as he saw the man wipe the spittle and vomit from his mouth with his sleeve.

"Very well," Deng responded curtly back to the weapons officer. After a moment, he added a follow-up question. "Do you think our base on Scarborough Shoal or even the headquarters in Manila knows that we may be at risk?"

"No, sir. We left under radio and emission silence. If we violate protocol and transmit, we will offer ourselves up on a silver platter and make the situation infinitely worse—in my opinion, sir. Besides, it is a big ocean, and the storm works against them also."

"This is true. Steady as she goes, and in five more hours we will be in relative safety. In theory, of course."

For the poor intelligence officer, that could not come quickly enough.

051940HOCT2033 (7:40 p.m. local time, October 5, 2033) 1st ARM Battalion forward assembly area, Meycauayan City, The Philippines

Major Bennett burst into the dining room, and everyone froze, many with their mouths full. As she began to speak, her Alabama accent appeared, a sign that she was excited, stressed, or both.

"Sir, I'm sorry to interrupt, but I have important news. A Chinese resupply convoy is about five hours from Manila Bay, and General Viale needs to talk with you immediately."

"Okay, thanks, Meghan," Gammon responded as he put down his half-eaten chili-con-carne meal, grabbed his helmet and body armor, and hastily departed to follow her the forty meters back to the Battalion TAC.

The company commanders all looked at each other for a moment as they sat in the abandoned restaurant's dining room.

Hank Johnson spoke up. As the Recon and Strike Company Commander, the coming decision had the potential to impact his meticulously crafted fire and recon support plans. "What do you think he'll do?" he asked.

The other commanders pondered this for a moment, the silence punctuated only by the occasional crunch of nuggets of food that had not quite completed the rehydration process.

Finally, Stacy said, "I think he's going to tell the boss to fire everything. While both sides are in a tough spot logistically, they need resupply more than we do."

"Nah," chided Steve Hester. "He's gonna tell the boss to hold everything for the attack. You know how he is all about aiming for the 100–0 win. More boom, more better. Less Sky Lances equals less boom."

It was quiet again for a moment, and a few of the commanders noted that they were debating war plans in the Filipino equivalent of a McDonalds, which was a bit odd.

"As the support guy," said Major Trocme, "I think it's a close call. Our small reactors are cranking out the electrical power we need, the 3D mega-makers are producing at near capacity, and we're good on water, but we can't make ammo, diesel, and some of the super-complicated parts. All this to say, anything we shoot—whether it's railgun penetrators, Sky Lances or drones—may not get replaced before the attack. We're getting one, maybe two sorties a day to support the whole task force."

Frank Ohata and Mike were busy noticing that Stacy's left ring finger no longer showed any indication that there had ever been a ring on it, which pleased them both.

Noticing Mike's casual glance and meaning to disrupt him, Frank asked quickly, "So, Mike, what do you think?"

Mike realized that he had not been thinking at all about the details of the plan and decided to stall for time. Shifting his tall frame in his seat, he started with, "Well, that's a tough one. Let's see what happens. Either way we're still going to hammer them. The Boss has got it figured out. I think so, anyway."

Much to Mike's relief, this seemed to end the discussion. With the boss still gone, the chatter then turned inevitably to football rivalries, as they were in the middle of the season. Mike, a Penn Stater, and Steve Hester, an Ohio State Buckeye, were soon arguing about the upcoming game between their schools. Frank Ohata, a Virginia Tech grad, realized that Stacy, as the newest member of the team and the one they knew the least about, had yet to declare her football loyalties.

"So, Stacy, where did you go to school?"

"Liberty, in Lynchburg."

"Ohh," Frank said in an almost sympathetic way. "Is that like the Fighting Amish?"

"No, not so much," she shot back. "It's the Flames. They are three and one this year and ranked higher than Virginia Tech. Isn't that where you went?" she added with a bit of good-natured faux sweetness.

Mike's inner thirteen-year-old came out as he nearly giggled at the exchange. He also noted he shouldn't discuss football with her. A few minutes later Gammon returned, dropped his gear, and made a matter-of-fact pronouncement.

"The boss had a tough choice to make. I told him to fire everything. They need the resupply more than we need the Sky Lances. He was still deciding when I left. Now where were we? Oh yes, gourmet dining…"

052040HOCT2033 (8:40 p.m. local time, October 5, 2033)
74 nautical miles Northwest of the entrance to Manila Bay

The *Nanjing* was still pitching in heavy seas, its intelligence officer was still attempting to fill his vomit bag, but the sea state was slowly improving.

"Can we make a few more knots?" asked Deng.

"Sir, we can attempt twenty-one knots, but that is all I would advise. The ships are still getting pounded."

This seemed to satisfy Deng, who was acutely aware that they were still more than three hours from the relative safety of the bay. It would then be another thirty-five nautical miles to the pier where he could expect a hero's welcome, at least in his mind. With the *Nanjing*, sixteen fast cargo ferries, and four escorts, his flotilla would provide extra insurance for his uncle. His happiness, however, was short-lived.

"Sir, we have another hit from a sonobuoy we left in our wake. It indicates that the submarine is closing to within firing range. Their torpedoes can still outrange our antisubmarine torpedoes. We still have the older variety due to fielding problems with new ones. What should we do?" the weapons officer asked with a slightly rising and increasingly stressed tone in his voice.

Deng considered the options and then quickly decided. His vomitous intelligence officer had previously informed him that there were only two—or at most three—enemy subs in the whole of the South China Sea. This was likely the only one in contact with them.

"Keep three of the escorts close to the convoy and between us and the sub, and fan them out so that it cannot get around us. The enemy torpedoes are on the edge of their range limit, and our countermeasures should stop them with such a long run time. Keep the other one near the *Nanjing* here in the center of the convoy, to protect us. And accelerate the rest of the fleet to twenty-three knots. We'll not make this easy for them."

The bridge watch crew was relatively inexperienced and dutifully executed his commands without question. Three escort ships with their antisubmarine warfare packages drifted slowly behind the now-accelerating convoy. At the increased speed, the cargo ships were taking a tremendous pummeling by the waves, but nearly all managing to make twenty-two and a half knots. One, the *Chengdu*, was having powerplant issues in its left hull and was falling slightly behind. As the *Nanjing* heaved and rolled in the sea, Deng stood near the front windows and when he looked down at his screen, he saw the *Chengdu* continuing to lag and near the escort line. While the *Chengdu* would soon be unprotected, Deng could tell that weather conditions were already better than they were an hour ago, if only slightly.

"Sir, the sub closure rate has slowed considerably," stated the weapons officer. "It is barely in range. Wait! One of our sonobouys is transmitting that it's…flooding its torpedo tubes and opening its outer doors. It's preparing to fire!"

"And…aren't the escorts preparing our countermeasures?" Deng responded in a condescending tone even his uncle would be proud of. "Our escorts are between the sub and the cargo ships, yes?"

"Yes, sir…they are…"

Deng allowed himself a brief, satisfied smile. Looking down at his screen, he noted that the escorts had forced the sub to slow even further. The gap between him, in the center of his convoy, and the sub was nearly static.

"Have a little faith in our automated friends. They are precise and relentless," Deng chided the bridge crew.

"Sir!" the weapons officer exclaimed. "The sub has just fired two torpedoes!"

Amateurs, their first combat experience, and they are already panicking, Deng thought. *The torpedoes will take several minutes to get here, and our countermeasures will stop them.*

"Carry on, advise when they are one minute out," Deng said breezily.

"Sir, the sub only carries two long-range torpedoes and is now accelerating to close the distance, likely to use its shorter-range torpedoes. It carries up to six of them."

This genuinely alarmed Deng. *It's charging me!* he thought, somewhat incredulously. *It's going to attack the escorts at close range, outnumbered three to one. Still, a one-for-one, or even a two-for-one exchange would be good for us.*

"Direct the escorts to attack immediately. Exchange is authorized."

Deng's kowtowed crew again executed his orders, and the three escorts swung around.

"Sir, closing speed is in excess of fifty knots. They will be in range momentarily. Countermeasures already deployed for the two torpedoes."

Over the next two minutes, Deng saw the escorts move farther behind the convoy in pursuit of their prey. The bridge crew's focus on the impending cat-and-mouse battle was interrupted by a report that the *Chengdu*, which had continued to fall behind, had a massive hull breach. Seconds later, the *Tibet*, also near the rear of the convoy, stopped transmitting.

"How could this happen?" screamed Deng at both the weapons officer and intelligence officer.

Neither had a good answer as they did not understand how the countermeasures had failed. The best the weapons officer could do to deflect Deng's ire was to narrate the cat-and-mouse battle that had just started.

"Antisubmarine torpedoes away, sir. The sub has also fired torpedoes," he stated loudly. A few seconds later he added, "Enemy countermeasures detected. Our ships have launched them also." After an additional pause he reported, "One escort has been damaged by a torpedo, not critical. The sub is still out of range of the convoy." After three more minutes, the one wounded escort and the two other remaining surface hunters overwhelmed *Sculpin* with the assistance of seven sonobouys and a volley of four well-timed antisub torpedoes.

"YES!!!!!" exclaimed Deng. "Yes, yes yes! Well done!"

Deng was suddenly exuberant. This was only the third Triggerfish sunk by the Chinese Navy so far and would reflect well on him. He looked down at the screen and then froze. At the convoy's current speed, the escorts were well behind the convoy and could never catch up.

As if to punctuate his point, the cargo ship *Sichuan*, slightly over three nautical miles away and in the lead of the struggling convoy, registered a massive hull breach and that it was sinking quickly. Seventeen seconds later, the sound of the explosion reached Deng on the *Nanjing*. Nine seconds later, the sound of the *Suzhou*'s death was announced. Deng realized what had happened and did what anyone who had gained his position more by connections than by skill could be expected to do. He panicked.

"Scatter the convoy—it's our only choice! Alert Manila and the Scarborough Shoal base. Tell them we need help. And keep the last escort near me—I mean, keep it near the *Nanjing*!"

The *Cavalla* had scored a fatal hit on the *Sichuan* and had another torpedo in the water. With the enemy escorts off chasing the *Sculpin*, a necessary sacrifice, *Cavalla* had been able to get into optimal range and was now methodically tearing the convoy apart from the north, while the *Tang* had just hit the *Suzhou* from the south. Within a minute of the first two hits, another catamaran had been struck and, with one hull breached, it was listing wildly to port and, according to the *Tang*'s calculations, would capsize in four more minutes. The convoy began to scatter like a frightened school of fish, which in a sense, they were. From afar, *Tang* and *Cavalla* had listened to the battle between the *Sculpin* and the escorts, noted the time of *Sculpin*'s deliberate sacrifice, and continued their task of convoy dismemberment.

Deng was pushing the *Nanjing* to its limits, and the boat was breaching like a whale in the heaviest swells. With the convoy scattered and each ship making an independent route to Manila bay, every ship was on its own now.

The intelligence was faulty, and the escorts could never catch up. We would have been sitting ducks if we had waited for them. This is what we had to do, he justified to himself. He found that he was already rehearsing the accounting he would have to give for this debacle.

"Sir, we have reports that the *Xi-an* and *Dalian* are sinking. But we are also spreading out quickly and they will not be able to get us all."

"That is of little consolation, but thank you," Deng said as he pulled out a real cigarette and lit it quickly. After taking a deep drag, he felt the nicotine calm his nerves. "How much longer?"

"It will take us two more hours to cover the fifty-five nautical miles, sir."

The younger Deng settled back in his chair and for the next ninety minutes, listened to the *Nanjing* fight through the seas and to his intelligence officer alternately wretch and dry heave. He also listened to reports, one after the other, of his convoy being devoured.

Baoding, Tianjin, Shenyang…when will it stop? What will happen to me when—if—I make it?

"Are they going to target us?" Deng asked out loud.

His intelligence officer struggled to regain his composure despite his vomit-stained uniform. "Sir, they would not have wasted a torpedo on us. We provide no combat value for the ground fight. We are lucky."

"Perhaps so," responded Deng with a creeping hint of dejection in his voice. "And we still have five cargo ships left."

After another tense thirty minutes, the survivors began rounding the Bataan Peninsula and entered the shipping lanes for the port, only thirty nautical miles ahead.

As each rounded the peninsula, they found that the sea state dropped quickly from level five and its twelve-foot waves, to sea state three with two-and-a-half-foot waves. Each ship, in turn, accelerated to maximum speed.

Deng looked at his screen and saw that the ships were still spread out over eight nautical miles because of the different routes they had taken. He was chain-smoking now, and between drags he considered that he might actually be safe.

The channel is swept for mines every twelve hours. Harbor antisubmarine warfare boats, although small, still work the area, and no right-thinking submarine would trap itself in a goldfish bowl. Besides, he thought nervously, *what else could possibly go wrong?*

The large ball of flame lit their faces in the darkness as General Yu, Colonel Deng, and Commissar Xi watched the two ships burn brightly in Manila Bay. The ships were within three miles of the pier and Yu was seething as he realized what all this meant for him and the Task Force.

That arrogant jackass was wrong. He didn't even acknowledge his role, nor will he. He thinks he will dodge blame as the result is ultimately my responsibility and I will be the one to account to Beijing for this. But I've had enough of him and will ask for his removal when I file my report. Can't be any worse for me than keeping him here. And Xi saw the whole thing and realizes that Deng has become a liability.

Yu clenched his teeth and fists for a moment as the vein in his neck began to throb. *One more destroyed by a mine dropped out of nowhere in the shipping lanes, two likely sunk in the bay by surface-to-surface missiles.*

He willfully relaxed himself and took a deep breath. Yu's thumb was in overdrive, working on his cuticle, and as he dug his nail into the exposed flesh, he winced slightly.

But two of the catamarans did make it, which means we have at least some new possibilities. All is not lost. Not even close. Odds are still on our side. The Americans got zero catamarans.

Yu glanced to his left and noted Commissar Xi looking at him with a slight smirk on his face before breaking eye contact. As he turned his head back to the bay and its raging fires, Yu began to wonder, *What are these guys really up to?*

Whatever it was, Yu knew it could not possibly be anything good.

5.8

6 October 2033
Dear Julia,

I decided to write you an email instead of sending another video clip because this is the fifth draft, and I need to make this as good and accurate as I can make it.

While I'm not overly concerned about the possibility of my untimely demise, the thought of the impact on you and our kids has always given me great pause. I counted it up, and this is cumulatively the third year I've been away from all of you. While I owe our parents a debt I cannot pay for all their help, you have borne the heaviest burden of my service.

I love what I do. I love being around and serving soldiers and their families. I know you do too. But I also know that this lifestyle has asked a lot of you, especially after the adoption. Nate and Jenna are wonderful kids and welcomed Hope with open arms when we adopted her, but they're still young and my frequent absences have affected them and limited my ability to help with all of Hope's special needs. Who would have guessed when we adopted her from China that we would be in this situation now?

When I come back, I want to have a discussion with you about our future and whether or not it's time to leave the Army. You've done your full duty, and it's unfair of me to ask you to do more.

I hope and pray for courage and wisdom as I lead the men, women, and even the bots of this unit (the bots part sounds silly, I know). You know my commanders, and I'm blessed to have them. They're young, enthusiastic, capable, and probably don't fully appreciate their own mortality, which is a good thing in some ways. I know we'll encounter surprises that will be both big and painful, but I'll do everything I can to do my duty and bring my entire team home. And myself :-)

All my love to you and the kids,
Buck

The video faded in.

"Hi, Mom and Dad," Stacy began. "Just wanted to send you a quick video before we go into heavier censor mode and the operational blackout. As always, don't believe what you see in the news. The team here is great, and we're going to kick some serious ass. I'm still a little nervous and feel like I've got to prove myself, but I think I've finally accepted that I'm at least decent at what I do. I heard that I was even put in for a medal for that earlier thing, which now seems like a lifetime ago. Anyway, just wanted to let you know I was thinking about you. Love to you both and David. Bye."

Stacy was faking at least part of it. She wanted her parents to know she was all right. She had been told that she had done well, yet she still had some nagging doubts about herself.

Do I really measure up? Am I really as good as the others? she wondered. *I think I am...*

Dear Mei Ling,

We are about to enter into the decisive phase of the campaign, and I am confident in both victory and in a promotion when I return. You know I have worked hard for this and have tried to make you proud. I feel that those in your family who scoffed at me in the past will now finally be silenced. I will let nothing get in the way of victory and expect that a few of the surprises we have for the Allies will make the news. Perhaps I will also, but that is of lesser importance than your approval. I would only ask that you not start spending at the rate of a Lieutenant General's wife until I am actually promoted and we have an opportunity to celebrate together. I thank you in advance for that.

Please say hi to our son for me,
Affectionately, Yu Jai Bin

As Yu hit 'send,' he thought to himself, *I hate that woman. She is centered on her status and is financially insatiable. She will drive us into poverty yet with her Prada bags and Hermes scarves.*

5.9

070452HSEP2033 (4:52 a.m. local time, October 7, 2033)
Chinese National Assistance Task Force Headquarters, The Philippines

"Are you sure?" asked General Yu.

It had been several days since the Americans had arrived on the outskirts of the city and their president had ordered them to help retake Manila. General Yu had not had a good night's sleep in a week, and now his overeager targeting officer had just woken him up.

"Yes, absolutely, sir. Well, to 89 percent actually," responded Lieutenant Colonel Hwang. Then, to give himself a scapegoat in case this didn't work, he added, "According to DIYA anyway."

Yu was tired, and his eyes were bloodshot. He paused before saying, "We are running low on DF-10s and strike drones. Each one is precious at this point."

"Sir, I appreciate your concern, but according to our analysis of enemy electronic emissions, our statistical analysis indicates that we will be able to hit at least one major and two minor command and control nodes of the Allied forces. If we fire eighteen of the DF-10 cruise missiles and supplement it with 41.7 percent of our containerized strike missiles and drones, we will cripple them."

Yu looked at him intently and then responded. "That will leave us with only ten remaining DF-10s allocated to our task force. The Air Force is of no further use to us and we have to save the swarms for the close fight where they will be more useful."

"Affirmative, sir. But better to use them now as they marshal for their attack. We may even lose the ten remaining DF-10s if they are reallocated by an off-island General who does not understand our situation. A bird in the hand…"

"Yes, yes," said Yu impatiently, then he took a breath and said, "Fire when ready."

070507HSEP2033 (5:07 a.m. local time, October 7, 2033) 1st ARM Brigade Headquarters, vicinity of Clark International Airport, The Philippines

"Are you sure?" asked General Viale, still skeptical of automated targeting.

"Pretty sure, sir," responded Lieutenant Colonel Ruthven, the Brigade fire support officer. "We have a 91.4 percent probability of crippling their command and control system and destroying a battalion or higher-level headquarters if we expend 70 percent of our remaining Sky Lances in a preemptive strike and beat them to the punch."

Viale listened to her and the impossibly long sentence she had just blurted out. He did not like to be pressured by staff officers into hasty decisions—especially by those that were overly reliant on automated systems, as she obviously was.

91.4 percent? Give me a break, Viale thought.

"Okay," he said, "I get what Saga thinks, but what do *you* think?"

Ruthven stammered a bit, then drew herself up and said, "Sir, the analysis has continued to improve while we've been here. Two weeks ago, I didn't trust it. Last week, it was iffy. I trust it now."

"With your life? With our lives?" asked Viale, a slight edge in his voice.

She paused, then responded, "Yes, sir."

"Then fire when ready."

Part 6: Apollyon

"Imagination does not dissipate the fog of war, but it helps the tactician to have a vision of what could be beyond it." ~ Remy Hemez

6.1

070546HOCT2033 (5:46 a.m. local time, October 7, 2033) 1st ARM Battalion Assault Command Post, south of Meycauayan City, The Philippines

The morning of October 7th dawned clear and bright. Through a small gap in the buildings, Buck watched the orange sliver grow in the humid air until nearly half the sun was visible. He crushed out the remainder of a good cigar, another corrupting gift from Colonel Garbulinski, placed the standard-issue stimtab under his tongue, and walked down the dirty stairwell from the fifth floor of the empty building. By the time he reached the third floor, the stimtab was starting to kick in, and by the time he got to the ground floor, he was already sweating profusely in the humidity.

As he walked toward his TAC, which had been stuffed into an alleyway, the sight of the vehicle briefly brought back a memory of a rented moving truck. He walked up the serrated metal stairs, and rather than entering a cargo bed of dressers, toys and boxes, he entered a beehive of activity.

Squeezing past several members of his staff who gave off the odor expected of people who hadn't showered in over a week, he slid sideways to his command console and flopped casually into it. The dingy white walls always seemed especially tight to him when the vehicle was in the mobile mode, and this day was no exception. While the command post could expand and contract in a matter of minutes, Gammon decided that keeping the vehicle ready to move would provide at least a limited insurance policy against enemy strikes. The battalion was formed up and reports were already coming in as he put on his AR helmet and hologloves. Being "suited up" had a comforting familiarity to it.

Major Bennett was already working on a number of invisible screens that came into view as Gammon's helmet came to life. She was busy getting updates from the companies on their status and last-minute changes from brigade. Captain Olive was apparently engaged in another animated discussion with Saga, while several kilometers away, Major Verault and his team were in a smaller, less capable backup command post known as the ALOC, or Administrative and Logistics Operations Center. From there they ran logistics and maintenance support, tracked the operation, and prepared to take control of the battle if the main command post was lost.

The idyllic moment was shattered when Bennett screamed into his ear, "We're up, sir!"

Gammon winced as he realized that whoever had been cleaning his helmet's sensors had bumped the volume to "max." He adjusted his volume, responded, and considered their mission again.

Kick General Yu's ass, help take the city, and go home. I love it when it's this straightforward, he thought. *If only it really was that easy. Gonna be messy and bloody, for us, and probably...even more so for the Filipinos. And then there will be the aftermath, assuming we win.*

"Major Bennett, how are we on comms?"

"Sir, we're up internally with our units. Comms with Major Antipuesto and the 17th remain limited but stable. We prioritized him and Sergeant Major Hoban with the limited personal commo gear we had. It's working for now, but we don't expect it to last."

"Roger, thanks. Any final thoughts about the skull sessions over the past few days?"

"I think our Filipino counterparts were rather amazed at our ability to test and retest ideas inside the confines of an augmented-reality helmet with nothing deadlier than a bunch of fancy gloves. They also made sure we could use initiative and operate on intent when the lights go out."

"I thought so too. All right, back on your head, Megan."

Thinking back to the liveliest debates, Buck wondered if they had missed anything and began to tick off the critical issues in his mind. The sheer numbers and complexity were nearly overwhelming: subterranean combat, autonomy settings, the best use of the limited Sky Lances and recon drones, how to engage the vertical axis of urban skyscrapers, electromagnetic spectrum clutter, how much to trust Saga's improving recommendations, how to get the Filipino battalions to the city with minimal casualties, swarms, and of course, Saga's new defensive application update that had been pushed down less than twenty-four hours ago.

Good thing we're adaptable, he thought as he prepared to complete his precombat checklist.

Gammon stopped for a moment when he noted that Brigade was preparing a preemptive strike. What annoyed Gammon was that they were stealing two of his Sky Lances for it. *Better to give than to receive, and I hope the giving is good.*

Buck finished scrolling through the checklist and verified the status of everything from autonomy settings to logistics status. After taking a final look at all the status indicators for his units, he saw that they were all at least green or amber. *Time to get the show on the road!*

Gammon could feel that he was getting into his zone, and the calm intensity he was known for started settling on him like a familiar blanket. He came up on the net to address his subordinate commanders.

"Commanders, comms check, over."

After a brief pause, they began in order. Captain Doss answered first.

"Apache 6, roger."

"Bull 6, roger," Captain McGinnis quickly added.

"Currahee 6, roger," replied Captain Hester.

An electronic voice interjected, "Do or Die 6, roger."

Buck noted that while Major Antipuesto was out of order, he was glad the 17th's commander was at least in comms and on the net. Major Trocme, the Headquarters, Support and Defense Company came up next, followed by Captain Johnson, the Recon and Strike Company Commander.

"Avenger 6, roger."

"Strike 6, roger."

Captain Ohata, the commander of the attached heavy infantry company, rounded out the guidon call.

"Punisher 6, roger."

"All right, team," Gammon began, "we're getting ready to go into harm's way in service to our country. I have every confidence in your competence and character. You'll have to make tough decisions and likely operate purely on intent if comms go out. I have no doubt that you'll do the nation and your loved ones proud."

Gammon paused for a moment, pulled out an old piece of paper, adjusted his helmet so he could put on a pair of reading glasses, and then continued.

"We're also standing on the shoulders of those who have gone before us in the proud tradition of the U.S. military. Allow me to put the task at hand in perspective with a slightly modified and updated version of a message sent on the eve of another crucial battle:

"Soldiers, Sailors, and Airmen of the Task Force!

"You are about to embark upon a Great Crusade, toward which we have striven these many months. The eyes of the world are upon you. The hope and prayers of liberty-loving people everywhere march with you. In company with our brave Allies and brothers-in-arms on other Fronts, you will bring about the destruction of the Chinese war machine, the elimination of Chinese tyranny over the oppressed peoples of the Philippines, and security for ourselves in a free world.

"Your task will not be an easy one. Your enemy is well trained, well equipped and battle-hardened. He will fight savagely.

"Much has happened since the Chinese triumphs of earlier this year. While we have suffered many losses and made many sacrifices in the air, at sea, and on land, we have reduced their strength and capacity to wage war here on the ground. Our nation stands behind us and expects us to do nothing less than our best.

"I have full confidence in your courage, devotion to duty and skill in battle. We will accept nothing less than full Victory!

"Good luck! And let us beseech the blessing of Almighty God upon this great and noble undertaking."

Gammon paused slightly, then added, "The original was sent by General Dwight Eisenhower on D-Day, 1944."

Gammon paused again as he took off his glasses and adjusted his helmet. The command post was silent, and he noticed that everyone was looking at him. As he looked back at the faces in the Command post and in his helmet display—including Megan, Luke, Stacy, Mike and the others—none were over thirty-five. And he knew they might not all make it.

"All right, team, let's take it to 'em and get this done. I'll see you on the high ground. Viper 6, out."

6.2

070600HOCT2033 (6:00 a.m. local time, October 7, 2033) Forward Edge of the Apache Company Sector, Northwest Manila

It was all so routine, mundane even. Homer received the electronic orders from Captain Doss—although he did not know her by that name, only as "company commander"—acknowledged them, and prepared to move out. All systems were functional, and although it was not remarkable to him, he was much smarter than he had been before his first battle. The collective wisdom of his experiences, as well as that of all the other HOMRRs, Razorbacks, drones, and assorted items on the network, had been pushed to him last night along with several patches and software upgrades. He had even learned a thing or two from his untimely death during the Battle of Tarlac River. Other than some scarring, scorch marks, several rings on his barrel, and the new add-on armor, he was no worse for the wear. He even had a replacement Shrike recon drone mounted on his back.

As the platoon leader, Homer dutifully reissued the orders to his subordinates, the nearest of which was his new wingman, a HOMRR that had been cross-leveled from Currahee company. Charlie 2 was her official name, and she was distinguished from Homer's original wingman only by her hull, which was emblazoned with "Honeybadger." This made as much sense to him as his own name. Homer pushed Honeybadger to the front of their attack formation. This was logical as Honeybadger was only a wingman and therefore militarily less valuable than Homer, who was equipped for command and control responsibilities.

On order, Honeybadger's diesel electric drive increased its pitch and she began lumbering forward. Homer followed 100 meters behind with the seven relatively delicate Razorbacks trailing behind him. A few minutes later, the four wings of Honeybadger's Shrike came to life and began beating the air into submission. Homer watched as it rose in the untethered mode and moved quickly down the edge of the street, bobbing and weaving in an attempt to use what little cover was available. Homer's small column picked its way through the rubble of the city for about forty minutes. Homer knew his Shrike had about five minutes left before it would be inbound for recharge and prepared to issue orders to launch one from a Razorback to ensure the column had continuous coverage.

Two minutes later, Homer noted that his Shrike was no longer in comms, and assessed that the highest probably was likely due to either the intense electronic clutter of the city or to Chinese interference. It was overdue by forty-nine seconds on its auto-return protocol when it suddenly careened from around a corner and into the avenue 400 meters in front of them. It was trying desperately to stay alive, and Homer watched it eject a set of its chaff and flare pods as four smaller drones chased after it. The ruse worked with one, but the other three detonated near the drone, soaking it with tiny but effective flechette darts. The Shrike tumbled to the ground in a spectacular cartwheel as

Homer reported everything to his commander and adjusted his plan accordingly.

There was no emotion. This was merely a combination of autonomy parameters, rules of engagement, self-preservation settings, and an overriding, insatiable desire to accomplish his mission. Though he be the lone survivor. Or not.

6.3

070705HOCT2033 (7:05 a.m. local time, October 7, 2033)
Manila Harbor Container Yard

Throughout the container yard, as well as in other parts of the Special Security Zone, forty-foot shipping containers emblazoned with the large COSCO and OOCL letters began coming to life. A Wing Loong III reconnaissance drone was making a low pass and caught the images for Lieutenant Colonel Hwang.

"Looks like blooming flowers," he said with almost a sense of wonder.

Hundreds of containers were opening their maws to expose vertical launch racks of Wasp and Sparrowhawk III drones preparing for flight. The larger Sparrowhawks were initializing their internal navigation systems, spinning gyroscopes, and cooling thermal seekers to help them find their intended prey without GPS, which was now jammed. While the Sparrowhawks were reusable, the disposable Wasp variants could be distinguished by the red, yellow or blue stripes down their backs: red for longer-duration Wasps with small shaped charges, yellow for direct-attack Wasps with much larger shaped charges, and blue for thermobaric warheads.

At precisely 0709 hours, the first waves began to emerge from their vertical launch rails and begin slow, low-altitude circles while the swarm built in size, intensity and volume.

"Can you hear it?" asked Lieutenant Colonel Hwang excitedly.

He knew that he was presiding over the largest use of drones in history and was almost dizzy with excitement. Before anyone in the command post even had a chance to respond, he answered his own question.

"It really does sound like an angry swarm of wasps, and it will get louder for two minutes before the first wave departs to find its targets. Just wait until the main group launches!"

Two minutes later, what could only be described as a small cloud of locusts dispersed to begin their deadly work. Over 375 drones were already in the air and were about to be complemented by 18 DF-10 cruise missiles inbound from the Chinese mainland.

Major General Yu paced around a bit and noticed the adhesive bandage on his thumb as he began to instinctively pick at it. "Are the ground forces prepared to attack?"

"Affirmative, sir," responded Colonel Deng.

As they say, the best defense is a good offense, Yu thought. *We shall see if this holds true in this case and if DIYA is correct in her assessment.*

Not a gambler by nature, Yu was now "all in," a situation he hated.

070712HOCT2033 (7:12 a.m. local time, October 7, 2033)
1st ARM Battalion Assault Command Post, Northeast Manila, The Philippines

A casual observer would have mistaken it for a nonchalant move, but an experienced observer would not be so easily fooled. No one in the unit had more combat command simulator time than Gammon, and with that experience came the ability to make the hard things look easy, and the easy things look effortless. With a well-practiced flip of his hand, Gammon brought up Major Trocme, his Headquarters, Support, and Defense Company Commander, on visual. Trocme was increasingly concerned about the impending waves of inbound drones, and Gammon could hear it in his voice.

"Sir, the brigade defense net is getting hot. Lots of inbound drones. We think the first couple hundred are probably sacrificials to light up our nets for targeting by the bigger ones. The bigger ones will guide in the follow-on waves, which will probably be massive. Brigade is holding fire on our main defense batteries to keep them hidden until the bigger ones show up."

"Roger. Are you set for what's coming for our positions?" asked Gammon.

"Sir, we can handle a wave of up to about 120 in our sector at once. After that, it gets dicey as our point defense systems will need time to recharge and reload. The latest software push helps, but the batteries for the lasers and microwave guns still take a few minutes to recharge and we are low on spares. Unfortunately, the anti-drone hives still have to be manually reloaded."

"Roger, got it. Just keep them off us as long as you can."

Buck saw that Mike McGinnis's icon indicated he wanted to go person-to-person. Gammon clicked "accept," and Mike's face appeared in his helmet's viewscreen.

"Sir, we're making good progress, and the HOMRRs are ripping through the first couple security stations, but we're seeing a lot of civilians hiding in the city. The intel that said they'd be gone was wrong."

With no civil reconnaissance, Gammon was not surprised and acknowledged such back to Mike as he wondered what else in their initial estimates was off. *Number of drones in play, remaining enemy maneuver forces, command post location, and who knows what else.*

The defensive fire icon blinked, indicating that his battalion was launching anti-drones, firing kinetically with machine guns, using directed energy weapons at incoming drones, or a combination of all three. The icon stopped blinking, and the text report was that twelve drones were confirmed killed with another four likely. No damage to the battalion.

Not yet, anyway, thought Gammon. *But then, damage was not the real purpose of the first wave.*

Gammon thought for a moment and considered adjusting the defensive autonomy settings, reasoning it out in his head. *If things start moving fast, I can't be the weak link in the speed of our response.*

Then it hit him. *I really am going to have to delegate this. I'm responsible for the outcome, just like with the things people do. Not so sure about this, but no real choice.*

With some trepidation, he moved the defensive autonomy icon from "low" to "medium."

070746HOCT2033 (7:46 a.m. local time, October 7, 2033) Headquarters, PLA National Assistance Task Force, The Philippines

It was a bargain at twice the price, thought Major General Yu.

Initial scouting losses had been lighter than anticipated. For a mere 375 Wasps and four Sparrowhawks, they activated large portions of the Allied defensive network. This news only served to hype up Lieutenant Colonel Hwang even more, who was now bordering on manic.

"The main swarm is now building, sir. The first wave of Sparrowhawks remained relatively intact and identified a large portion of their defensive network. The DF-10s are inbound, ninety seconds to main swarm departure," Hwang blurted out.

Although almost a mile away, the sound of over 4,700 small attack drones and 520 medium control drones gathering sounded like the prior swarm, but heavily amplified and even angrier, perhaps even furious. At the appointed time, Hwang nearly giggled as the swarm departed with a rush. Yu was confident that while the American point defense systems were good, they could still be overwhelmed and had agreed to split the attacking drones into four target sets, the first three being American: one for the 1st ARM Battalion, one for the 2nd Battalion, which was barely more than a company at this point, one for the American Brigade Headquarters, and one for the remaining Filipino units. While the odds for a crippling hit were better on the other units, 1st ARM Battalion was more of a threat to him as it was the only one that could deal with the T100s. And this was why Yu had gifted it with a double allocation of drones.

The drone swarm snaked angrily through the streets and avenues of metro Manila to find its prey. As it approached the forward trace of enemy units, the drone waves were inconvenienced by the huge skyscrapers and forced to go down narrower streets. The lead drones would occasionally explode, crash into the tall buildings or impact the ground and skitter to a stop after being hit by anti-drones, lasers, or microwave guns. But it was of no significance to the swarms, which would quickly assess their rate of loss and either plow through or divert the rest of the swarm down a different avenue. American anti-drone launchers emptied quickly, and their laser batteries discharged at an unsustainable rate.

Gammon and his subordinate commanders watched with a growing sense of unease as they saw the icons for their anti-drone launchers, hives, and point defense systems indicate "amber" faster than predicted—faster than in any simulation they had ever seen. At this rate, they would be "black"—out of ammunition—in just minutes.

Gammon could hear frequent "braaaaaaap" sounds fill the air as the HOMRRs and Razorbacks fired long, futile bursts of 6.5mm ammunition into the air. While one hit on a vehicle by a Wasp was not always enough to damage or destroy it, the Wasps operated in groups of ten, so if even half got through, five could usually do the trick and kill, or at least immobilize, a vehicle. There were just too many to stop them all. Way too many. And for the first time in a decade, Gammon felt a tinge of fear as Saga showed the swarm turning on his unit.

Gammon looked like an orchestra conductor as he quickly gave commands with his hologloves and exceeded his previous best actions-per-minute rate, which was already the highest in the brigade. Saga continued to help on low-level tasks while he focused on battle management with Major Bennett. After only eight minutes of contact, it was already not going according to plan.

"GET OUT! GET OUT! NOOOOOOOWWW!!!!" Bennett yelled at the top of her lungs.

Gammon and everyone in the command post had seen the indicators and suspected it was coming. The icons for all defensive hives and point defense systems indicated "black." They were out of anti-drones, ammunition, or in the case of the point defense lasers, simply energy. The resupply bots would need four to five minutes to finish reloading the racks and changing the few spare batteries they had. They all saw Saga's evacuate warning and the large mass of drones heading for the command post, and specifically his group of vehicles. They were sitting ducks.

"Let's go!" Gammon yelled, adding at a lower volume, "Saga, command override, Gammon five three zero nine, auto defense authorized."

Captain Olive hit the auto-report icon on his intel screen and raced for the door, an anxious look on his face. Gammon did one final look to ensure everyone was out, pushed open the door, leapt off the edge of the vehicle, and ran full tilt toward the rally point in a low-rise office building eighty meters from them. Ahead of him, he saw his soldiers already running for their lives.

He had made it only about twenty meters down the street when he looked over his shoulder and saw the vanguard of the swarm. While they were mass-produced, minor variances in manufacturing, obstacles, minor atmospheric effects, and even the vortices created by other drones altered the flight paths of the individual parts of a swarm so that it never actually arrived at precisely the same time. This was a good thing from the swarm's perspective, as too much congestion on the target site could cause fratricide. More importantly, by allowing a few drones to edge ahead, the swarm could adjust its terminal attack based on the result of the first few impacts.

Gammon was a fast runner and had already caught up with some of the slower soldiers, including the less-than-athletic S2, Captain Olive. Over their heavy breathing, Buck heard an unfamiliar sound but knew instinctively what it was. The high-pitched whirr of a Wasp streaked past and stopped suddenly with a sharp crack as it struck the command post with its shaped charge. There was a second, then a third detonation.

"Get down! Get down!" soldiers yelled, but apparently, they were not yelling at him. Out of the corner of his eye, he saw a Wasp on a different trajectory. It arced toward one of his soldiers running fifteen meters in front of him.

Time slowed, and Gammon joined the chorus, but instead he yelled, "Get to cover! Get to cover!"

He knew stopping would have been a death sentence. These weapons were not dumb artillery or mortar shells that would simply burst and send their shrapnel out randomly. Had they been, then getting down would have been smart. These drones were smart enough to target humans and equipment very specifically and very lethally. Private First Class Miller never really had a chance.

A moment later the pitch of the drone's electric motor rose an octave as a Wasp with a distinct yellow stripe accelerated into him and exploded. Gammon watched as his driver was dismembered by the explosion, his body and blood now spreading over the already dirty street.

Gammon was still running hard and pushing the S2 along when he saw another drone hit one of the roll-out solar energy mats, and another hit the electrical distribution trailer.

More are coming…

Time seemed to slow down even more with all that was happening.

Only forty more meters, he thought. *Must get to cover.*

His lungs burned from the effort and he felt his feet crunch the shattered glass spread out on the street.

Only thirty more…they're all yelling at me…

Almost there…

He heard the electric motor go up an octave. Time nearly stopped.

This…might…be it…

6.4

070815HOCT2033 (8:15 a.m. local time, October 7, 2033)
Headquarters, Chinese National Assistance Task Force

Major General Yu was enraged.
"These treacherous dogs destroyed twelve more security stations! How? And the sniping attacks at our forces, seventeen today alone! How is this possible?" he demanded.

Deng looked at him, paused to build effect, and then answered, "They are clever and increasingly persistent. Our simulations never expected them to push safes and other heavy objects out of skyscraper windows. They pierced the tops of the security stations where there is virtually no armor, then finished them off with Molotov cocktails and thermite grenades. They were no doubt supported by Special Operations Forces or the Security Force Assistance units."

Yu paced back and forth like a caged animal and then continued his rant as Deng watched in disgust.

The old man's timidity will cause the ruin of us all, and I will not have it, Deng fumed. *I will not let my career be ruined by this fool. I have been telling him that his restraint has been wasted.*

Deng then repeated what he had often advised. "They are now clearly combatants and must be dealt with as such," he said in an ambivalent tone.

To Deng's surprise, Major General Yu responded flatly, "Then treat them as such."

Yu had plenty of other things on his mind at the moment. A major drone strike against the enemy was underway, one of their strikes appeared to be coming his way, and he was about to commit a major portion of his remaining ground forces to a bold counterattack. Yu just wanted the civilian problem to go away and was starting to care less about how that happened.

"Yes, sir," Deng responded and quickly wheeled about. He moved with haste out of Yu's sight and, grabbing Lieutenant Colonel Hwang by the shoulder, told him, "Dial the engagement criteria on all the automated systems to minimal, to zero. Same for DIYA. Do it before the counterattack starts in ten minutes."

Lieutenant Colonel Hwang seemed surprised and hesitated for a moment. Hwang was an obedient soldier, but even he understood the implications and stuttered slightly when he responded. "S-s-sir, that will cause them to engage virtually every human, or more correctly, every adult and near-adult-sized male and female they encounter. Are you sure that is what you want to do?"

A string of curses spewed out of Deng's mouth, and the normally busy command post became instantly silent.

"This fight is going to be close," said Deng through gritted teeth. "All DIYA's simulations show we will win, but only by a slim margin. We can't afford ANY disruptions or altering of the calculus. Do you want us to write a letter to your parents, and to those of everyone else in here, telling about our noble defeat, how sad we are at the loss of the lives of their loved ones, but that fortunately, Lieutenant Colonel Hwang kept to his so-called principles? Or are you hoping to survive this as an American Prisoner of War, you spineless coward!"

Deng was shouting now. "Dial the parameters back! That's an order!"

Apparently convinced, Lieutenant Colonel Hwang began to do as he was told. The distinction of morality and legality in his army did not exist, as it was governed primarily by pragmatic concerns. So, in Hwang's mind, he was just following orders and had no real obligation to do more.

Deep down, he knew otherwise. But at this point, he didn't care.

Greater love hath no man than this, that a man lay down his life for his friends.

~ John 15:13

"Look out, sir!"

Gammon felt two impacts. The first was a solid tackle by Captain Olive, the second was a massive explosion.

Gammon's head was pounding, there was dirt in his eyes, and his left arm hurt. He rubbed his eyes, looked at his arm, and saw a modest gash that was bleeding, but not profusely. He rolled over onto his other arm only to see Luke Olive staring at him from half a meter away, but with an odd look. His eyes were open, but Gammon knew instinctively that he was gone, even without seeing the gaping hole in his back or smelling his burnt flesh. His charred body armor had taken the brunt of the blast, but the size of the explosion still overwhelmed it. Gammon was stunned, and his stomach began to knot.

The sound of continued shouting prevented him from grieving for the moment and he returned to 'command' mode. He and his team had to survive the main wave, and this was likely only the beginning of it.

Gotta get out of the kill zone and to the ALOC to resume the fight. Assuming, of course, that anything is left of it, Buck thought as he used his right arm to get up and began running again. He arrived at the edge of the building, dove into the doorway, and went deep into the room with the rest of the group. Still out of breath, he turned, expecting to see the destruction of his command post and the surrounding vehicles.

As he watched, the lead parts of the swarm made one large swing around the area, and when the main swarm arrived, the entire mass continued to the northwest. The angry noise it made unsettled everyone in the room, all of whom were simply glad to be alive but still unsure of why the swarm moved on to another target when this one was there for the taking.

A minute later, Major Bennett broke the silence. "Makes no sense, sir." Sweat was running down her face, and without her AR helmet, her eyes squinted as they continued to adjust to the bright daylight. In the distance was a building crescendo of detonations.

"Do you hear that?" responded Gammon.

"The drones are hammering something, sir, but it seems like overkill. The frequency's increasing quickly. They've gone from a few a second to maybe twenty to thirty."

Suddenly, the realization of what was happening hit Gammon. "They're going after the reactor at the Admin Log Center. The Chinese are going after the power. They figured out we can shift command nodes faster than we can get reactors here."

The Admin Log Center was co-located with the battalion's Small Modular Reactor, the main source for meeting units' insatiable demand for power. The miniaturized nuclear reactors were not exactly miniature, hard to hide, and had the unfortunate side effect of emitting a detectable nuclear signature.

The popcorn staccato reached a crescendo and then quickly dropped off.

"Major Bennett, get the command post moved and back online," Gammon ordered. "Sergeant Major Washington, take my vehicle and get to the ALOC."

Gammon didn't even wait for them to respond as he sprinted for the slightly smoking command post and what would be his best chance to regain control of a situation that was quickly "going brown."

"Private Davis, let's go!" yelled Sergeant Major Washington.

Considering what happened to Gammon's last driver, Davis hesitated for a brief moment, then followed Washington to the JLTV parked in a nearby alley. Washington put on the AR helmet that was sitting in the passenger seat as Davis jumped in the driver seat. The helmet was way too big and swallowed Washington's head, making him look like a bobblehead as the vehicle took off in a roar down a side street.

"No contact with the XO, Sergeant Major," yelled Davis as Washington continued struggling to adjust the helmet. "ETA five minutes."

Neither occupant of the vehicle was sure who, if anyone, they would find alive.

6.5

070905HOCT2033 (9:05 a.m. local time, October 7, 2033)
Apache Company TOC, Manila, The Philippines

Out of nervous habit, Stacy attempted to fiddle with her engagement ring, but of course, it wasn't there. Her command vehicle drove over one of the innumerable craters that now pockmarked the streets of Manila, and for a moment, the Buffalo rocked precariously from side to side. She took a quick look at the displays and saw that the vehicles were all making adequate progress forward.

Two hours before, the Brigade S2 had provided Gammon and the rest of his team some new and time-sensitive intelligence produced by Saga. Stacy reviewed it and found it revealing that the Chinese were so out of position but wasn't quite sure why. But it did provide an opportunity to the battalion: by striking quickly on the far western side of the enemy's flank, their odds of success would be greater than 72 percent on their intermediate objectives. This would increase the odds of a successful campaign to over 60 percent, a 7 percent gain over the base odds.

"Feels as if we're fighting with a bookie looking over our shoulder," Gammon had quipped. "But by getting past the Chinese outer defenses on the west side of the city on narrow axis of advance, we'll be able to rip though their support area, the air defense net, and command and control nodes. This will cripple them. It's worth the risk, so obviously we're going for it."

Lieutenant Colonel Gammon had also been clear when he tasked her with a critical mission. "Stacy, you need to support Major Antipuesto and the 17th as they destroy the Chinese heavy air defense weapons in Rizal Park. Once they're down, the Navy and Air Force heavy strike drones can get in close enough to be effective without being little more than target practice for the Chinese. And remember, the heavy lasers can shoot at ground targets too. Take them out, and the whole problem gets easier."

Gammon tasked Mike McGinnis with supporting the Philippine 21st Battalion's seizure of the main Chinese command post at the Embassy, which would kill their main transmission hub and, presumably, their primary command and control facility. Currahee Company, under Steve Hester, was in reserve and following about a half kilometer behind them.

The Buffalo hit another small crater, jostling Stacy slightly. *It's not only a trick getting around with the rubble, the electronic noise in the city is way worse than we expected. Gonna have to scootch up a bit closer to the firing line than I'd prefer to maintain control.*

She took a brief external scan of the area around the vehicle and saw that the congestion of the streets, the rubble, the burned-out busses, Jeepneys and cars were ubiquitous. Adding to the challenge, large road craters were quickly turning their plan to dash up the flank into a slow, time-consuming slog.

Resistance has been light, but the longer it takes, the more dangerous it becomes. Who knows what ol' Deng is up to?

Stacy scanned her AR display again and checked the positioning of her heavies, two Razorback platoons, and scout platoon. Once satisfied with the continuing movement, she turned to Saga for more information.

"Saga, are there any relevant new feeds?" she asked.

The fact that she was asking a piece of software a question still struck her as slightly odd, even after using Saga and her less-developed predecessor for the past three years.

Saga offered up several quick feeds. All of them looked like cell-phone footage of T100s engaging civilians.

"Saga, why are they firing on civilians? It doesn't make sense."

The once-youthful voice of the now-aging Brad Pitt responded, "Analysis indicates that Chinese engagement criteria have been set to assess and acquire all targets that pose a potential hostile threat. The Chinese network no longer distinguishes combatants from noncombatants."

As she watched a particularly gruesome scene of a T100 engaging civilians, she could feel her heart rate rising. Her palms began sweating as she felt rage at the senseless deaths.

"Does our battalion have this yet?"

"Negative," Brad's voice answered. "Jamming and noise levels are too high. We have been without direct communications for seventeen minutes. Do you want me to fire a Pigeon? You have twenty-seven remaining."

"Affirmative," answered Stacy, and a Portable Joint Intermediate Network (PJIN) drone, or "Pigeon" as it was commonly known, shot out of the launcher on the top of the Buffalo and was quickly en route to the nearest and last-known battalion repeater position. If it failed to find a functioning node, it would go down its list of last-known positions until it did.

"So how come we can see it and not battalion?" she said through gritted teeth. "And can you identify that bastard?"

"We are much closer and have sensors that pick up cellular and peer-to-peer traffic," Saga responded. "We are also close enough to require a low number of hops from the phones. And the bastard you referred to is actually an inanimate T100 with an identification number of K241."

"Literal translation off, Saga."

Stacy considered this and wondered what she could do, if anything, to stop the gratuitous killing. With no good ideas, she decided that completing her mission quickly would be the fastest way to end all of it.

She noted that Homer and Honeybadger were still working their way down a large avenue when she heard the loud crack of a railgun ring out. It was loud even with the noise-cancelling offered by her helmet.

Wow, we're way too close, she thought. *Way too close.*

Stacy hit the "Razorback-cargo compartment" tab with her hologlove, and the video feed in her helmet gave her a view of five Filipino soldiers stuffed into the back of one of her unit's Razorbacks with a teenage boy crammed in for good measure. They all looked uncomfortable, but it had been a necessary adaptation to get the troops forward with at least some protection from enemy fire and drone swarms.

She remembered that the debate on the kid had been fierce. He was from this part of the city and insisted on helping, and the Filipino soldiers thought he would be a useful guide. Stacy thought he was way too young for any of this. The Filipino battalion commander, however, had eventually carried the argument.

"We don't know the area, and everything within the digital infrastructure of the city is now suspect," he had said. Then he added, "This is what we are working with," and he held up several tourist maps. "We need him."

Stacy had felt somewhat guilty about going along with it, but Major Antipuesto had made a good point.

"Okay, kid," she said into her microphone, "we're about a kilometer from the drop-off point. You sure about this? Last chance to change your mind."

With as much determination as he could muster, Joseph answered, "Yes!" He felt almost insulted by the question as he was now the man of his family, at least until they knew for sure his father's fate.

Stacy considered her options and then waited a moment, listening to the Sky Lances ripping overhead toward the enemy positions. She looked at the time in her display. *0923 hours. Right on time.*

Stacy counted the roar of each Lance and waited until all five had passed overhead. A few seconds later she heard the five thundering thermobaric explosions and hit the "deploy recon" icon for her scout vehicles. The two remaining vehicles quickly deployed their short-range ground and air recon drones. The Shrikes flapped to life, and the little ground bipeds trotted out to discover what else was in front of them.

Nasty-looking buggers, she observed. *Like large locusts. Still don't get the wings versus rotors thing. But okay, fellers, show me what's out there, and try not to fall over.*

The bipeds were rather amusing when they fell over and attempted to get back up with varying degrees of success. Troops had been known to sponsor "chicken fights" by knocking over several at a time and betting on which one would get up first. Supposedly last week's update would help that problem.

After a few minutes, her operations NCO verbally updated everyone in the TOC. "Nothing yet, ma'am."

"No new updates," added the intel NCO. "Our Saga only has sporadic contact with the big Saga, so we're slightly behind on what might be going on in the wider network."

"Roger, thank you," Stacy responded. *But why is it so quiet?*

While Stacy knew it wasn't technically necessary to update verbally because each person could see the same things in their AR displays, it was a good practice at a human level to help maintain awareness on key events in case someone was fixated on a specific task, which often happened.

One of Major Bennett's best suggestions, she thought.

Stacy waited, and as she did, she noticed that one of the little bipeds was no longer doing recon work. It was simply standing in the middle of a key intersection serving as a relay. *Now that's a sucky job,* she thought to herself.

Stacy immersed herself within her AR helmet as she watched in real time as the bipeds and Shrikes moved forward, often from their viewpoint.

Where are the T100s? Where are the security forces? They have to be defending their air defense systems better than this. They can't be this stupid.

Stacy attempted again, in vain, to twirl her engagement ring. *Why did I wait so long to figure this out? He really wasn't ready for marriage.*

Another sharp crack of a railgun brought her back to the present, and with it an acute sense of embarrassment that she had allowed herself to be momentarily distracted by her personal life.

A quick check showed that it was Honeybadger destroying another security connex checkpoint. Honeybadger switched to its mini-gun and saturated the station with 6.5mm rounds in a 4x1 ball/tracer mix. She could see through Honeybadger's gun camera that the station was now inoperable and starting to burn.

"Love it," she said out loud. *No match for Homer and the boys,* she thought.

That was the last security station between them and their chosen bridge across the Pasig River. The ding of an audio cue told her that an inbound Pigeon had arrived with two transmissions: one to her and one for the Filipino troops in her Razorbacks. For Stacy, the message had updates to enemy positions and dispositions. For the troops crammed in the Razorbacks, it was a message from General Adevoso that appealed to their patriotism and courage.

A little late for this, but okay, she thought and then relayed it to the vehicles, adding, "Two minutes to go time."

It still nagged at her that the remaining Chinese T100 battalion was nowhere to be seen.

It couldn't possibly be this easy, and where are the airmobile infantry? she thought.

"Saga, anything on the net?" she said out loud.

"Negative, no known enemy mobile forces within three kilometers. However, the rest of the brigade and the Filipino units to the north are under heavy drone attack."

Stacy did a quick scan of everything and thought, *something is wrong I just can't put my finger on it—not yet anyway.*

6.6

070840HOCT2033 (8:40 a.m. local time, October 7, 2033) 1st ARM Battalion Administrative Logistics Operation Center (ALOC)

Command Sergeant Major Washington saw the smoke rising over the low buildings even before the ALOC came into view.

"Davis, make sure the radiation sensors are working and let me know what you find. The guts of the reactor are probably blown from here to kingdom come," he added in his slight Charlestonian drawl.

"Roger, Sergeant Major, already done. Nothing yet, but it looks like we're about a klick out still, according to the map, anyway. GPS is out again."

Davis discreetly picked his nose, rolled the booger between his thumb and index finger, and flicked it out the window while Washington wasn't looking. His task complete, Davis quickly added, "And comms are still intermittent."

The two continued on, scanned for enemy drones, and hoped the basic PDS on the JLTV could stop at least a few of them, if necessary. As they made the final turn around a building, they saw the familiar unit command vehicles, except that the eight-wheeled Buffalos now appeared to be made of Swiss cheese—burnt, blackened and smoking Swiss cheese. With wide eyes, the men saw that all four vehicles were utterly destroyed and burning fiercely. Although not expected to be as capable as the battalion TAC in terms of communication gear, manning and experience, this loss of life and equipment would cripple the battalion.

The right front wheel of the JLTV made a crunching sound after it rolled over a drone that had been shot down, and Washington noticed the area was littered with many of them. Periodic explosions indicated that their self-destruct mechanisms were beginning to engage. Davis came to the same conclusion and made a wide berth around a wounded Sparrowhawk that was still flapping its only remaining wing.

The vehicle's commo receiver pinged, and Major Verault's voice came up in both headsets. "We're over here, to your left."

Davis dodged the rapidly exploding drones, worked his way across a plaza, and drove about 150 meters to the particularly unsightly wreckage of a Jollibee restaurant. Davis was so fixated on the Jollibee mascot and how the big bee's red face was pockmarked with fragment holes that he nearly ran over Major Verault.

Verault calmly walked over to the vehicle and told Davis, "You missed." Then to Washington he said, "Only one wounded, just a flesh wound. We only had a few seconds to get out of the vehicles. The hives and the few PDSs we had took out the first fifty or sixty of the lead drones, which bought us a little more time. The reactor is in the ground floor of a parking garage about 300 meters away and it's still up. In this terrain, 300 meters is a long way, and it looks like they never found it. But they did seem rather fixated on us and our vehicles—probably because they realized that my logistical prowess was the gravitational center of the entire war effort."

Washington couldn't help but chuckle but was clearly surprised that it hadn't been far worse.

"So I get why he did it," Verault continued, "but did it work?"

"What are you talking about, sir?" asked Washington.

"He made the right decision, but it kinda sucks when it's your turn to be the sacrificial pawn."

"I'm still not getting it, sir."

"We were tracking the inbound swarm and when the command post's PDS systems went black, we figured that you and everyone else were probably goners. We saw your evac warning, and less than half a minute later our systems went nuts. All our electronic camouflage, jammers, and crypto gear quit. At the same time, our comms gear went to max volume and began broadcasting who-knows-what. A few seconds later, our screens flashed the same evac warning you got. Obviously, we listened."

Washington looked like he had seen a ghost, then said slowly, "The boss didn't throw you under the bus. He delegated the decision."

"To whom?"

As if on cue, the men heard a distinctive, hollow "fwoomp," followed by a high-pitched electric motor. Washington's vehicle had just launched a Pigeon to communicate with the recovering Battalion TAC.

"How interesting…"

6.7

070955HOCT2033 (9:55 a.m. local time, October 7, 2033)
Northern Manila, The Philippines

The T100s were in their element and enthusiastically carrying out their duties. While this was not technically true as they could not actually feel enjoyment, a casual observer might guess otherwise. They had just been given full permission to do what they had been designed to do: Identify and eliminate threats. While the T100 battalion was still in reserve and postured to counterattack to the north, there were still plenty of enemy targets to engage in the vicinity of their assembly area.

A T100 identified on the network simply as K241 took the target handover from a Sparrowhawk and fired a 125mm sabot round at a vehicle with several threats in it. The vehicle, a four-wheeled variant of an enemy troop carrier, careened wildly after the high-velocity round passed through its open back and engine block. The disabled vehicle stopped after hitting the corner of a building, and the four surviving enemy combatants jumped out and ran for cover. With no time to lose, K241 advanced and fired its coaxial machine gun at the fleeing enemy. K241 finished its work and began looking for new threats. DIYA, for her part, entered the standard data from the engagement into her data base. Among other data points, she noted that the enemy vehicle was a Jeepney and the combatants were five females, ages, 22, 23, 12, 44, and 57, and three males ages 3, 56, and 71. Due to her facial recognition capabilities, she was even able to enter them correctly by name.

071010HOCT2033 (10:10 a.m. local time, October 7, 2033) PLA National Assistance Task Force Headquarters, The Philippines

It's already working. I told him it would.

Colonel Deng took a long, satisfying drag on his cigarette and blew a large cloud of smoke into the air. Since zeroing out the firing restrictions on the automated units, the rate at which saboteurs and guerrilla forces successfully attacked Chinese military units and property had dropped dramatically.

Near zero, a thought that pleased him greatly. *DIYA's probability of success numbers are getting better because of it. Should have done it sooner, wasted opportunities…*

He took another drag on his cigarette and then looked at the report. DIYA indicated that the Allied force would hit their Clausewitzian culmination point well before capturing the city. The main attack with the American forces would come from the north, and his most powerful unit, an entire battalion of T100s, was arrayed correctly to defeat the Americans and the weaker Filipino divisions.

Yes, let's see here…the 1st ARM Battalion, that's the problem. Finish them, and the rest will be easier. Even a return to stalemate will benefit us. Possession and perception remain nine-tenths of the

law, and our allies in the United Nations will call for a study, and then a commission, and then a settlement, which will favor China.

At least that is what Deng hoped for. But as he knew, hope was not a method, which was why he had a backup plan to salvage both the situation and his career.

071020HOCT2033 (10:20 a.m. local time, October 7, 2033)
1st ARM Battalion Assault Command Post

Technical Sergeant Steven Gress had just received the report and was enthusiastically pointing out a moment in a Chinese news video. "There it is! See it, sir?"

"See what?" asked Gammon, not quite sure what he was looking at and growing a bit impatient with the enthusiastic young sergeant. Buck had the added complication of contending with the side-to-side lurching of his command Buffalo. With only five of its eight tires working, every shell crater and piece of rubble made the vehicle sway like an amusement park pirate ride. "I don't have time for techno tricks that we can't use," he added.

"That's it, right there! That's the anomaly. We saw Chien Li make that same exact hand gesture twice."

"Okay, but maybe it's a habit or a common gesture for her. So what?"

"Sirrrrr," Gress said in an almost scolding way. "Check this out. When we overlay both clips, like this," he said as he manipulated the image, "it's a perfect match. That means it's a loop, kind of a building-block move. It means she's not real. And if she's not real, we have an opportunity. Our brigade's support team back at CYBERCOM has been crowd-sourcing the hunt for Chinese media vulnerabilities, and bingo, every nerd's dream to get in the fight suddenly came true. Some kid at Penn State figured it out."

"Got it," responded Gammon, still trying to figure out how useful this opportunity might be. "How much time do we have to use this?"

"I don't know. It might go stale any minute, sir."

"Okay, then let's get creative. Here's what I want you to get CYBERCOM to try…"

6.8

071045HOCT2033 (10:45 a.m. local time, October 7, 2033) Apache Company Mobile Command Post, Manila, The Philippines

Stacy watched her displays intently as the company continued to make progress along its new axis of advance. Up to this point, the overall attack was still going according to plan. As the lead element of the battalion, her company had made it across the Pasig River on the Manuel A. Roxas Bridge without incident. She swiveled her Buffalo's external camera toward Fort Santiago to their left flank and saw nothing of interest. A short tone in her headset caught her attention.

Comms with the battalion are out again, it's getting worse beyond short range. Is Chinese electronic warfare really that good or is it something else?

The company continued to move forward and as they crossed phase line Whisky, she knew that it was time for the next phase of the operation. She lightly touched the "Accept" icon and the vehicles of Apache Company proceeded to find nearby covered and concealed positions and come to a halt.

"Okay, team, it's go time. Give 'em hell, sir. And good luck," she said as she hit the "dismount" icon.

In the troop compartment of each of her seven remaining Razorbacks, red marker lights turned green, the rear ramps dropped, and Filipino troops poured out into the bright day. Stacy could see that the sun blinded the troops as they emerged from the dark interiors of the Razorbacks. They squinted, formed up, and moved out toward their objectives, guns at the ready. She noticed two things slightly out of place: One was the kid, who didn't have a gun even though he had begged persistently for one. The other was one individual who was significantly bigger than the rest. He was dressed in American camouflage, carried both an 84mm Carl Gustav recoilless rifle and one of the medium-sized commo rigs, and was closely following the battalion commander.

"He's taking this advise-and-assist thing to a whole new level," she said out loud.

Those in her command post who had already met Sergeant Major Hoban nodded in agreement. Stacy flipped through several other feeds and watched the infantry of the 17th Battalion infiltrate through the rubbled city ahead of them and move carefully on the enemy heavy laser site and its defenders. In the distance, a Shrike showed her the massive chemical laser systems that they had been tasked to destroy. Over the next few minutes, she flipped thought different screens and watched as Homer and the Razorbacks continued to struggle as they moved slowly forward and over both obstacles and piles of assorted detritus. As she caught an intermittent glimpse of Major Antipuesto's command group, a deafening explosion rocked the Buffalo and all its occupants.

"The hell was that? That was way too close!" shouted the operations NCO.

"Most probable source was a command detonated mine," answered Saga. "Updating movement algorithms now."

Two minutes later the Buffalo's proximity sensor alerted them to a Filipino soldier running toward their vehicle. He rapidly ascended the ladder and began pounding on the exterior door. The operations NCO opened the door, and both bright sunlight and a very scared Filipino soldier appeared. The soldier began speaking rapidly in Tagalog, and the translation was grim. The two soldiers nearest the mine were killed instantly, and five others needed help. He had tried to let his chain of command know, but their radioman and his gear had been the closest to the blast. He wanted them to come with him to help treat the casualties.

"Pleeeeaaaase!" the young soldier begged.

Everyone in the command center knew there was little they could do other than call in a MEDEVAC. With the rear door open, Stacy's command vehicle came to a stop.

"Pleeeeaaaase!" the man begged again.

The operations NCO forcefully told the man they were calling a MEDEVAC, there was little more that they would do, and he had to get off the vehicle. Dejected, the man departed, and the door closed.

"This is as good a spot as any," Stacy said to the team as she hit the "stationary" mode icon.

With a pneumatic hiss, the Buffalo extended its outriggers, and the interior of the vehicle began to slowly expand as the electric motors labored to push the walls out, doubling its size. The whole process, including the erection of the high-gain antennas and deployment of several of the increasingly scarce laser relay bots, took less than two minutes.

Stacy turned her attention to Homer's Shrike, which was tethered to him by a thin power cable. From thirty meters above Homer, it was giving her a bird's eye view of the action and could now remain aloft almost indefinitely. She could see Filipino infantry moving forward, against what appeared to be increasingly determined resistance by Chinese infantry forces.

"Looks like we found some of the airmobile infantry, but they don't look very airmobile at the moment," she quipped. "For once, they are the ones outnumbered."

She watched as the soldiers of the 17th quickly closed the gap to the defensive positions. By ones and twos, they fell after being hit by enemy small arms fire.

Brave troops, she thought, *and they continue to advance.*

As she watched the battle for what seemed like an eternity, several of her vehicles navigated the maze of wreckage and into positions from which they could engage the heavy laser positions. Two of the Razorbacks had clean shots and began firing 125mm rounds in quick succession into the six heavy laser weapons that consisted of the heavy air and missile defense firing battery. Looking at her AR display, she also noted that her vehicles had only made it to the edge of the park and not as far she would have expected.

Is the terrain that bad? she wondered, *or are they applying my intent differently than I would have guessed?*

An hour later, the intensity of the fighting finally began to die down slightly as the Filipinos completed overrunning the enemy position, which had been centered on the highest piece of ground in the park, the mound of the Sentinel of Freedom. The statue itself had been pulled down months ago to provide clear fields of fire for the laser batteries and showed up only briefly in the foreground of the video feed. Within a few more minutes, Stacy could see a few Chinese with their hands up and several Filipino engineers busily rigging the heavy lasers, their generators, and the control systems with explosives.

A voice then came over her headset, surprising her, as it was the first positive communications from the Filipino battalion. "Apache 6, this is Do or Die 6 Romeo, over." The voice was male and definitely American.

"Do or Die 6 Romeo, this Apache 6, go."

"Roger, relaying for Do or Die 6, his organic comms are FUBAR. The plan worked and the infantry got in close before the Chinese figured out what was going on, but the mechs are way too far behind. We need them up closer for overwatch on the far side of the perimeter, especially if there's a counterattack. We will—"

A small explosion followed by a long burst of automatic gunfire interrupted the transmission. What was disconcerting was that Stacy could see the explosion and Sergeant Major Hoban diving for cover even before the acoustic sensors on her vehicle detected it. Much to her relief, she saw Hoban back up and moving a few seconds later.

"Repeat, we will need overwatch and MEDEVAC ASAP. Nine line to follow."

"Roger Do or Die 6 Romeo, acknowledged on both, recommend firing a Pigeon directly from your location as we don't have direct comms with battalion either at this time, over," Stacy responded.

Hoban did not respond, and the entire Apache company command team could see why. He had dropped the commo rig and was busy with the Carl Gustav. As they watched and then zoomed in the video, it looked like a movie. A slight Filipino soldier loaded a round into the rear of the recoilless rifle and then tapped Hoban's helmet twice. Hoban apparently yelled something, came up to one knee, and fired the 84mm high-explosive round at an enemy position barely fifty meters to their front. The round hit the mark, and an enormous secondary explosion blew dirt and debris back on Hoban and his loader, who now had a big toothy smile and was giving Hoban an enthusiastic thumbs-up sign.

A few minutes later, a ping in her helmet let her know a pigeon was inbound. Her battalion's commo section had figured out how to rig up a few man-portable Pigeon launchers for 17th's commo section, and they were proving to be invaluable. As the Pigeon flew past, it gathered her updates and continued its effort to find its "roost." With the air defense batteries down, the battalion would probably risk raising a couple relay balloons and launch a few solar relay drones.

With a little luck, we should be back to solid comms shortly, she thought as the MEDEVAC icon blinked, indicating that four Dragonflies were inbound for the "litter-urgent" patients. Three more would arrive shortly once they completed their evacuations from Mike's company and the elements of the Filipino battalion he was supporting.

Stacy turned her attention back to her combat displays. Her brow began to furrow as she became vexed with what she was seeing.

He's right…the HOMRRS and Razorbacks are falling way behind, they're of little use to the 17th as they finish up, even though it looks like they don't need it. But if Antipuesto is right and there is going to be a counterattack, it'll come quickly, and we need to be ready.

Her platoons were still not even at the edge of the park and she rapidly hologloved in new and more specific orders. As she watched, the HOMRRs and Razorbacks moved forward a bit more, to the edges of the large park, then started making much smaller repositioning movements.

Odd, she thought.

Her command screen flashed and asked her to confirm her orders prior to execution.

Huh? They are asking me if I am sure I want them to do these specific actions instead of acting under general intent? That's… super…weird, she thought as she attempted to open a private channel to both Mike and Steve. As her nearest fellow ARM units, she figured that the relay drones from at least one of their two companies would be find each other and enable direct communications. To her relief, Mike appeared in her display.

"Hey, Mike, how's it going on your end?" asked Stacy.

Mike was surprised to hear Stacy's voice but was glad to see a fellow commander and her bloodshot eyes.

"Pretty well, for the most part. Once we got around the south side of Rizal Park and your sector, the lead elements of the Philippine 21st Battalion dismounted and successfully infiltrated the area ahead of us. They fought it out with the Chinese security forces and put the stick to them. We only had to provide direct fires on a couple hard targets. It was almost like the Chinese weren't expecting us, just thirty or forty personnel. One odd thing was that the embassy complex was nearly empty, other than some heavy-duty relay equipment and broadcast gear. How about you?"

"Pretty much the same thing," she responded, "except that I'm getting some weird feedback. I was moving my units forward to provide better overwatch for the dismounts, and I got feedback from Saga that didn't make sense. Moving forward and consolidating near the far side of the 17th's troops would, to quote Saga, 'degrade the probability of mission success.' It would go down from 72 to 23 percent. Makes no sense."

Mike gave her a quizzical look then said, "Hold on." A moment later, Mike was as vexed as she was. "I'm definitely not getting the same thing here. We've already pushed past the embassy and established a solid defensive position on your right flank as we planned."

Mike paused, then asked Saga, "Why do the odds get so much worse for the Apache company move?"

"Standby," said Saga, "enemy counterattack forming."

Stacy's command screen suddenly flashed an alert warning. Both she and Mike could see the possible routes of attack and that the most likely one went through the 17th and, by extension, Apache company. Arrival could theoretically be in less than seven minutes.

"I don't like this, looks like you are in their gunsights again," Mike said with a strained smile. "What do you think we should to do?"

Stacy paused, then added, "I'm not sure."

"Me either…" said Mike.

"I have a recommendation," added Saga.

6.9

071215HOCT2033 (12:15 p.m. local time, October 7, 2033)
Corregidor Island, Manila Bay, The Philippines

The report was not good. The heavy air defense laser batteries had been destroyed, the embassy was taken, most of the airmobile infantry battalion had been frittered away, and Deng knew that they were on borrowed time.

It is only a matter of time until Allied airpower shows up, he thought before he exploded in a rage. "They are exposed and shall finally get the decisive hammer blow they deserve!" Deng shouted at the staff. "Use what's left of drones in the north to keep the pressure on and commit the reserve to Rizal Park! We will drive them into the sea! Do it now!"

The staff was momentarily confused. They knew that the decision to commit the reserve was usually held at the senior commander level—General Yu—and he was not expected to arrive on Corregidor Island and in the Malinta Tunnel for another fifteen minutes.

"But sir," the intelligence officer meekly offered, "the bulk of the enemy forces are still to the north, and we have been having great difficulty monitoring that part of the city for the past hour…"

Deng calmly put down his cigarette and walked over to her. Deng sized her up, grabbed her by the lapels, and said through gritted teeth six inches from her face, "What part of this order did you not understand? General Yu is in transit, and until he arrives, I am in charge. Are you refusing an order?"

"N-n-n-n-o, sir!" the now terrified woman responded.

"You are lucky I am a forgiving type, but if I see this behavior again, I will have you shot for insubordination during combat," Deng added in the most acrid tone humanly possible. "I am losing confidence in our precious DIYA and I think she may be wrong…too much fits too neatly up north. DIYA identified the 17th and 21st Philippine Battalions near Rizal Park, both have been working with the 1st ARM, and yet no 1st ARM in your reports? At worst we will utterly destroy a significant portion of these vermin, at best, we will catch the Americans in their deception."

Deng released the woman and returned to pick up his cigarette. With another of Deng's torrential rages brewing and without Yu's physical presence, the rest of the staff obediently issued his orders to the remaining battalion of twenty-four T100s.

He did the wise thing and repositioned the headquarters to Corregidor as I had told him. Even better that I came first. By the time he arrives here, it will be too late for him to piss away the battalion on another wasted attack like the Tarlac debacle. Best of all, they are fully armed and fueled thanks to the convoy, Deng thought smugly.

As he watched the T100s start to move from their positions and toward the exposed Filipino troops in Rizal Park and then on to the Embassy, he was genuinely excited. "A two-fer," he said softly and then thought, *The T100s may not be the brightest children on the playground, but in a pack of twenty-four with 'weapons free' will shoot at anything moving and cut an impressive swath through the Filipinos and then hopefully the Americans. Don't have to kill them all, just a lot of them.*

"And send a swarm to help them," Deng said almost as an afterthought.

He felt a burning sensation in his hand and flinched at the pain. He shook his hand vigorously and looked down at the smoldering cigarette butt now on the floor. In the euphoria of ordering the attack, the unfiltered cigarette he had been holding had smoldered down far enough to burn his finger. He licked the burn and immediately pulled out yet another cigarette.

"You, clean this up," he said to a private as he walked toward the center of the room. "And get me another ashtray. This one is full."

071228HOCT2033 (12:28 p.m. local time, October 7, 2033)
Manila, The Philippines

Even though they had the benefit of a perfect digital map of the city, the T100s struggled to pick their way through huge rubble fields as they approached the security zone and their first objective of destroying the Filipino troops in Rizal Park.

K241 came to a stop as it surveyed what was ahead and alerted its peers. "Road completely blocked. Bypass left. Rejoining in two minutes."

An entire building, approximately twenty floors high by K241's estimate, had collapsed and blocked the entire width of the street. K241's diesel electric drive roared as it backed the vehicle up. K241 rejoined the snaking column, but no longer as its lead. Acting like a group of ants seeking a route, the column made swift work of the next detours, and K241 noted that this and the other minor obstacles had delayed their arrival at their first objective by less than four minutes.

A small supporting swarm of Wasps arrived on cue and flew menacingly overhead as the T100s burst into Rizal Park, ready to wreak havoc on the Filipinos. They found nothing except a stray dog, a few T100 hulks, and a gaggle of enemy foot soldiers quickly escaping their grasp on the very far end of the park. The troops were out of machine-gun range and not worth main gun rounds. Only the dog was considered a possible threat but was assessed as nonhuman and therefore ignored. Startled by the rapidly emerging vehicles, the dog promptly ran away to continue its search for food in a more hospitable location.

The T100s moved forward and started to fan out when K241, and by extension DIYA, noted that the two lead vehicles had exploded in a shower of sparks, fragments and diesel fuel. The diesel fuel quickly ignited, and the vehicles started belching black smoke. DIYA immediately issued new commands, and the T100s surged forward into the attack.

Homer had done the improbable. With only 37 percent of his railgun ammunition remaining, he had managed to fire one sabot penetrator and kill two vehicles. It was very efficient, likely not repeatable, and had been possible only because it was predicted. It was only predicted by Saga because it was also shaped by Saga. There had been no intent of deception by Saga and Lieutenant Colonel Ruthven, the Brigade's Targeting Officer, who had approved the strike plan executed earlier that day. Ruthven had not noticed that several of the recommended targets were simply buildings that Saga needed to block very specific roads. Saga had enabled Homer, Honeybadger and their comrades to know with near certainty where the T100s would emerge during their counterattack.

Homer adjusted his recently installed thermal camouflage, which enabled him to blend in or even imitate the signature of another vehicle—like a T100 hulk—and fired quickly twice more.

Honeybadger immediately joined in and began firing as rapidly as she could. They expected to have ten to twelve seconds before the T100s and DIYA made the adaptation and began to engage them. After destroying the lead five vehicles, and almost exactly at the ten-second mark, Homer heard the first enemy round whiz by his position. His capacitors were nearly depleted, and it was time to move. He requested approval for both this move and a more controversial one, at least to his human commander. Within five seconds he received approval for both.

He ordered the two Razorback platoons forward from their hiding places in alleys and covered parking garages as he and Honeybadger pulled back and recharged their capacitors. The Razorbacks joined the attack and began engaging the T100s, but they were a poor match against the T100s and Homer noted that the kill ratio would be lopsided. At the three-minute point of the battle, three of seven Razorbacks had already been destroyed to only one additional T100 destroyed and one damaged. To Homer, the Razorbacks were cheaper and less effective than his kind, and therefore both useful and expendable distractions that bought him and Honeybadger time. Capacitors charged, Homer and Honeybadger crept from behind their respective hiding positions and reengaged the T100s.

The HOMRRs, T100s and Razorbacks were all firing desperately at each other in what was becoming a swirling melee in the park. Homer watched as a small swarm of Wasps attacked the nearest Razorback and ventilated it while a T100 scored a direct hit on another Razorback, leaving only three left. Homer felt the recoil of his railgun and saw another T100 cease to function. Another concussion from a railgun, this time off to his side, indicated that Honeybadger was still in the fight. They had killed four more of the T100s and had finished off the damaged one.

They will focus on us next, he calculated.

But then the surviving thirteen T100s did a curious thing. They ran away. Homer and Honeybadger each scored one more hit, but the fast, nimble vehicles were quickly gone and sprinting toward the northwest side of the park. It didn't fully make sense to Homer as he attempted to reposition himself and Honeybadger to cut them off. Homer quickly calculated that the speed differential was too great and that they were slipping away. Up until this point, everything had gone as the probabilities had expected: the ground troops had taken the objectives, the presence of Apache company had remained obscured, the timing for pulling the infantry back was correct, and the T100s appeared where expected.

As Homer recalculated the possibilities, he realized that the escaping T100s could swing wide and, with their superior speed, potentially pass dangerously close to the Apache Company TOC and its human occupants.

"Immediate recall. TOC defense," ordered Homer as he sent an alert to his company commander to reposition out of the likely movement route of the T100s.

Homer and Honeybadger's power plants went into high gear and began belching thick black diesel smoke as the two vehicles accelerated their lumbering mass on the most direct route to his company's TOC. The two surviving Razorbacks were already eighty meters ahead of them and moving quickly. Homer's prime directive was to defend his humans above all else, and it would take him four and a half minutes to arrive in a position to do so. Three minutes later, Homer and Honeybadger abruptly found themselves under the electronic command of the Bull Company Commander. This was normal protocol as Homer's commander had suddenly gone off-line. Homer and Honeybadger didn't care. They were machines, and couldn't.

6.10

071319HOCT2033 (1:19 p.m. local time, October 7, 2033)
1st ARM Battalion Assault Command Post, Manila, The Philippines

Buck Gammon was beyond angry, but he was not sure who he was raging at: the Chinese, as they had killed four more of his troops with drone strikes and possibly one of his best commanders who, along with her entire headquarters team, was unaccounted for and perhaps even dead; Saga, as he was not sure she had been right on a number of issues; or himself, for the same reason.

War, he reminded himself, *always results in death. Always.*

"Bull 6, get over there ASAP. It's the last-known spot of the Apache's TOC," he said as forcefully as his team had ever heard him. Touching a point on the 3D AR map that was Apache TOC's last known position, he added, "And report immediately with what you find. Medics will link up and move in as soon as you secure the area. Major Bennett, what's the status on the MEDEVACs?"

Never having heard even a hint of stress in Gammon's voice until now, she responded quickly and concisely. "Sir, five Dragonflies are working the area. Two are returning to the brigade's casualty collection point for recharge. The others are en route to other pickup sites but can be diverted if our casualties are higher priority."

Everyone knew that Dragonflies would not—and should not—be diverted for either the dead or the hopeless, a thought that settled like an enormous wet blanket on everyone listening.

"Roger," Gammon answered. The frustration in his voice was not directed at any of them and he stayed focused on the mission. "Currahee 6, chase down the T100s running loose. Get them quickly or they'll kill everything they come across," Gammon said, adding the expected routes with a number of quick flips of his hologloves. "Focus here for starters," he said, with another sweep of his hand across the 3D AR map.

Steve Hester acknowledged, and the net was suddenly quiet as subordinate commanders worked to fulfill their assigned tasks with haste.

"Okay, John, what do we have left for fire support?"

Captain John Bruchmuller, the battalion's Fire Support Officer, was the only one in the battalion TAC with some good news. "Sir, with the air defense batteries out, we'll have inbound air within ten minutes. They were anticipating success, and the Navy has four strike packages en route. The *USS Minneapolis* is also in position. It's one of those old cargo ships with a robo-nav system and a buttload of containerized ballistic missiles. We should get at least thirty for our battalion alone."

"Roger, thanks. Megan, get the last Griffon well out to the front of the battalion. We're going to finish them off. Captain Bruchmuller, I want to approve the targeting plan as soon as you have it.

Gammon turned to his left to the intel officer's station and was about to ask Captain Olive a question, then caught himself. Olive's temporary replacement, First Lieutenant Anderson, was hard at work but still getting up to speed. At this point, he was not providing anything more than Gammon was already getting from Saga himself.

This brought him to Technical Sergeant Gress. "Are we seeing any improvements after brigade put up the aerostats?"

"Roger, sir, starting to get a much better feed on remaining Chinese positions. A lot of Filipinos are pretty pissed and more than happy to respond to our blanket text request once the aerostats went up. They are, remarkably, the functional equivalent of surveillance platforms and mini cell towers."

"Good. But more importantly, was CYBERCOM able to use the information we gave them on Chien Li's loop?" he asked.

"Roger, sir, they finally broke in about twenty-four hours ago and just needed good material to exploit the breach. We can expect impact around 1700 tonight."

"Most excellent. Should be quite a show."

With orders given, and even with one of his commanders missing, Buck was still on his game and resumed flipping his hologloves like a mad conductor. He was prosecuting the fight with great precision and was quite good at it. Other than the prospect of death for him and his people, he almost enjoyed combat.

Mike reviewed the visual feeds with increasing concern. As his JLTV arrived at Stacy's last known location with a platoon of four Razorbacks as an escort, Stacy's Buffalo was nowhere in sight.

"Do you think they tried to make a run for it?" he asked his operations sergeant as his JLTV jostled over the debris in the road.

"Maybe..." he answered. "Sir! There! Over there!"

Mike quickly focused on a man in Philippine Army fatigues swinging his arms wildly to get their attention and pointing down a nearby side street.

"Spread the company out, secure the area around that street," Mike said while also thinking, *I see what you were trying to do, Stace, but they were too fast.* He had a sickening feeling in his gut. "Signal the medics as soon as it's secure and get a Shrike over there ASAP."

Mike intently watched his AR display as the platoon fanned out, but he found himself most focused on the video from the Shrike. It quickly closed the distance to the side street, turned the corner, and showed the team what had happened.

The Buffalo lay halfway inside a storefront at a forty-five-degree angle with the last four wheels still on the sidewalk. They could see several large holes and numerous smaller ones in the vehicle. Thick black smoke was pouring out of the front of it.

"Sir, the area's secure. Medics are moving in."

The entire team was suddenly silent as the Shrike showed them two bodies face down in the street, the large blood pool indicating that they were either already dead or about to be.

"Sir, the medics found two. Three are still missing. The rest are dead."

"Roger, XO, you have the con," Mike said with urgency as he transferred command authority to his XO back in the Bull Company Buffalo. As Mike grabbed his rifle and left the vehicle, he tripped and hit the ground like a sack of potatoes. He quickly stood back up and sprinted the 200 meters to the burning vehicle in the alley ahead of him. As he rounded the corner into the side street, he was already out of breath.

The young medic was doing everything he could to stop his female patient's bleeding, and when he saw Mike, he yelled out to him, "Sir! Those two are dead, and I'm categorizing this one as 3B. I've done all I can. Hold this clotting bandage on her chest for me so I can get to that one lying against the door over there and work on him."

3B…urgent-surgery category for MEDEVAC…surgical intervention required within two hours to save life…God…no! Mike thought. If the other soldier was easier to stabilize and it came down to having to make a choice, the medics would pick the man in the doorway for evacuation over Stacy.

Mike looked down at her. She was a bloody mess and had her eyes closed. With one hand he held the bandage and with the other he reached over to move her left hand. He recoiled swiftly as he realized it wasn't there—just a tourniquet on her mid-forearm. He reached for her other hand and gently held it.

"C'mon, Stacy, hang tight," he pleaded with her, almost begging.

His heart was already in his throat when he heard the high-pitched whine of the Dragonfly as it approached the makeshift landing zone.

"Only…one?"

071545HOCT2033 (3:45 p.m. local time, October 7, 2033)
Headquarters, Philippine Home Defense Command, Manila

"The good news is, Chinese resistance is collapsing faster than a punctured whoopie cushion," Brigadier

General Viale stated. General Adevoso gave him a puzzled look before Viale added, "Which is a good thing."

Viale then turned to his aide-de-camp and told him, "Tell the INDOPACOM Commander that we have agreed that we aren't going to assault the final Chinese holdouts on Corregidor, we're going to sink the island!"

The aide departed the room and both men relaxed slightly and sat down, exhausted.

"We agree, no need for more risk, been too much death already and I will need as many people as I can to get control of the city. It's going to have to be martial law, at least for a while," said General Adevoso. "But what a shame that we'll be destroying a national landmark. Destroying the Malinta Tunnel and the rest of Corregidor Island will be like someone destroying Washington's Headquarters at Valley Forge and all the encampments around it."

"I agree, sir, but with your permission," Viale said through a pained grin. Then he continued. "We have bunker busters inbound from the States. The B-21 Raiders are fast, but they still need some more time to get here."

"When will they hit?"

"Around 2100 tonight. Won't be anything left of the tunnel and the rest of the Chinese forces. We have drones up so that the Chinese won't escape. We did invite them to surrender, but some jackass by the name of Deng told us to go to hell."

"May he not live to regret his response," responded Adevoso.

071710HOCT2033 (5:10 p.m. local time, October 7, 2033) Beijing, China

Warbot 1.0

It was early evening and, as usual, both the traffic and air pollution were insufferable. With rush hour in full swing, people had nothing to do but look at their phones, the holographic billboards, and the video screens in every driverless taxi they rode in. The war had become boring, and people's attention quickly drifted back to the mundane. This was by design.

The news service hosts, often called "explainers," had nearly completely diverted the population's attention back to economic concerns caused by the blockade, the insults proffered by Western leaders, and how the Chinese Communist Party was restoring China's rightful place in the world as The Middle Kingdom.

Chien Li appeared on the news feed, once again presumably preparing to provide increasingly dull coverage of the Philippine situation, another clever attempt to inoculate the population against other views.

"This is Chien Li, reporting from Manila. Once again…" and then she paused. "Once again…" She paused again, almost as if confused. This was different, and people began to notice. The feed overrode all other programming, and the uncertainty in her demeanor began to draw attention.

Li seemed to suddenly focus and started again. "This is Chien Li, and I am NOT reporting to you from the Philippines. The government of China, and specifically the Central Military Commission with the approval of the president, conducted an aggressive and punitive campaign against the Republic of the Philippines. Their election was legitimate, and the PLA National Assistance Task Force conducted a decapitation strike against the over 2,000 members of the Philippine Government. The economic hardship we are now enduring has been caused entirely by our own doing and provocation. If you don't believe me, look at this."

A flood of digital images assaulted the minds of all who were watching, which was pretty much the entire nation. The images depicted the initial decapitation strikes, complete with families torn apart by missiles; T100s shooting Philippine soldiers, sailors, airmen and civilians; Transitional Government of the Philippines personnel meeting with Chinese leaders; and all the other offenses committed on the Philippine people by the PLA.

"If you want further proof that what I saw is true, I will prove it. I am not even real. I am a created image. Observe."

Chien Li then turned into a Panda, then a Las Vegas showgirl, and then Mao Tse Tung wearing nothing but a Speedo.

"Nice finish," said Gammon as he watched the feed.

"I thought I'd get in touch with my creative side," responded Gress.

"I need to claw my eyes out. I can never un-see that," added Bennett.

"Oh, we're only getting started," said Gress with a sinister laugh.

"All right, everyone, back on your heads," intoned Buck. "We still have three loose T100s out there and scattered elements of their Airmobile forces. The Filipinos are rounding them up pretty quickly, we just need to provide extra firepower to help convince any diehards of the error of their ways."

Buck pulled up a private channel with Major Verault. As he came into view, Verault knew what the boss wanted to know. "Iffy, sir. It was a lot of trauma, and she lost a lot of blood. I spoke to Lieutenant Colonel Hawkins a few minutes ago, she told me that the surgical team is still working on her. If they can get her stable, they can move her to the rear and the field hospital. Unfortunately, Lieutenant Dellert bled out before they could stabilize him. The only other ones to survive were Technical Sergeant Staple and Private First Class Loveless." Pausing briefly, Verault added, "Sir, also got a report from Brigade, and they positively IDed K241. Steve's team torched it about fifteen minutes ago."

"Roger, nothing further, thanks," he said as an odd thought entered Buck's mind. *If it's just a machine, why am I happy that it's dead?*

6.11

072145HOCT2033 (9:45 p.m. local time, October 7, 2033)
Headquarters, PLA National Assistance Task Force, Malinta Tunnel, Corregidor Island

In the dim light of the Malinta Tunnel, Major General Yu looked at the screen with disgust. It was over. All was lost. He coughed into his sleeve and noticed some blood, which was odd. A dark-gray boat was waiting for him at the north dock of Corregidor Island. He knew that he would not be escaping to freedom, but to judgment on the mainland.

Yu stood up, began to turn toward the door and was about to leave when a news article on one of the remaining screens caught his eye. Xi Chen, an attractive news reporter he had not seen before, was giving a somber report.

"This is Xi Chen, reporting for Xinhua News. After defying the orders of his superiors to stand down and assist the Transitional Government of the Philippines in nonmilitary ways, rogue General Yu Bai Jin aggressively defied the Central Military Commission and implemented a harsh and repressive policy against the Filipino people. This policy was never condoned by the People's Republic of China. While unfortunate, General Yu Bai Jin was killed today by American forces. The People's Republic of China looks forward to beginning armistice negotiations with the Republic of the Philippines, the United States of America, and the other members of the Pacific Alliance."

What? he thought in horror, then he caught a faint wisp of…smoke, cigarette smoke. Straightening up, he turned, knowing who would be there. Deng was at the doorway, pointing an assault rifle at Yu.

As beads of sweat appeared on his brow, Yu asked, "Why?"

"Seriously?" Deng responded in a sympathetic voice. "While you were enjoying the perks of your rank, you apparently forgot that expendability is one of them."

Yu's voice began to crack as he picked frantically at his thumb. "I did my duty, and I did it to the best of my ability for twenty-six years. It's not my fault that the supply lines were cut, that the Central Military Commission had a half-baked strategy, or that we didn't have enough troops. You know that full well!"

Yu's attention had been so fixed on the assault rifle in Deng's hands that he had not noticed Commissar Xi join them.

"Interesting," Xi said in a soothing, pragmatic voice, "probably even true, but entirely irrelevant. Unfortunately, you are now a liability, and our country must reduce its political risk exposure after this fiasco. Nothing personal, just business."

Yu's heart was pounding as fear swallowed him. "But…why?" he asked meekly.

"For the greater good," answered the Commissar. "It all goes back to timing. The Americans have barely six percent of our history, and we are playing the long game with them. Sacrifices have to be made."

"I…I don't understand… Why are you turning on me?" Yu's voice trailed off.

"Do you think your precious robots and DIYA were the only experiments during this operation?" Deng asked with his usual contemptuous voice. "Did you ever wonder why I was so much more perceptive than you? Why I could process more data, why I only needed three hours of sleep a night, why my analysis was so accurate? Are you so dull? Did you really not understand that a number of us were biologically augmented? Did you really not consider that we would be testing biological agents and other technologies as well, even on Chinese personnel deemed potential liabilities?"

Yu coughed, and more blood appeared, the salty taste growing stronger in his mouth. Xi nodded to Deng.

"I'm doing you a favor," said Deng as he fired a 6.5mm cased round into Yu's chest. Yu staggered back, wide-eyed, as Deng noted the confused look on his face.

He really hadn't been that bad for an unenhanced officer, Deng thought as he fired once more into Yu. Yu collapsed and Deng sprayed the rest of the magazine into the tunnel for spite. He dropped the rifle, fully aware that the Americans were about to turn the tunnel into a smoking hole. With the biggest loose end tied up, his mission was complete.

"Let's go," he said.

Commissar Xi, Lieutenant Colonel Hwang, Major Chiang, Major Zhiang and Captain Tsu followed him out of the tunnel and down the long path to the north dock, the same one McArthur used in 1942 to escape, which only added to the irony.

As they boarded a Chinese Navy special operations fast assault craft, they saw several anti-drones arc skyward from Topside, the highest point on the island. Less than a minute later and in darkness far overhead, they saw a single, small explosion. With the enemy now at least partially blinded, they quickly headed out to sea to make their escape.

Warbot 1.0

From high altitude during daylight, Corregidor would have looked like a large green tadpole surrounded by the dark-blue water of Manila Bay, but it was night and the B-21 Raider's pilot saw only the enhanced image in his AR helmet. After a long flight, he wasn't interested in what it might have looked like, but only in delivering his ordnance load and then putting as much distance between himself and anything that might come looking for him.

He was the only human on board, and the other two aircraft in his flight were "optionally manned." He wasn't sure why he was along for the ride, especially now that the Chinese had captured another crew after downing their first B-21 last week.

"Target acquired," he said, thinking, *It's all digital. Not sure why we even make this verbal call anymore.*

"Weapons away."

My wingmen aren't making calls like this.

He quickly turned the aircraft toward home as the other two B-21s dutifully followed, also with empty bomb bays.

"Time to get the hell out of Dodge."

A few long seconds later, he made his final call. "Good hit."

The Chinese boat travelled quickly into deeper waters, bounding over the waves and shuddering when it bottomed out in the troughs. A few minutes later and after they had put a safe distance between them and the island, Deng and a few others looked back at Corregidor as it erupted into a massive fireball. Enormous flames shot out of both ends of

Malinta Tunnel, and Topside was engulfed in flame. It took nearly ten seconds for the sound to reach them, indicating that they were only two and a half kilometers away.

"Our timing is fortuitous. If I didn't know better, I would think the Americans were trying to sink it," commented Deng.

About thirty minutes later, they scuttled the boat and boarded a Type 39A Yuan Class submarine for the trip home. It had been a long night in what might still be a long conflict, even if there was an armistice.

6.12

091400HOCT2033 (2:00 p.m. local time, October 9, 2033)
Metro Manila, The Philippines

Joseph had been only mildly impressed by President Davila's speech that described freedom, unity, peace and rebuilding. The usual political things to say. Joseph was more concerned with pragmatic matters, like finding his father and avoiding both the looters and the vigilantes.

He looked down at his phone. Coverage wasn't good, but he was still getting news. And it wasn't good. The latest clip came up on his screen, and he hit the "play" icon.

"This is Randy Galloway reporting live from Manila for Facebook News Network. Vigilantes have already begun public executions of members of the so-called People's Security Auxiliary, which was closely affiliated with the Chinese occupation forces. Reports indicate that over 1,200 people have already been executed. Police forces, which had been decimated in the opening days of the occupation, are not capable of stopping the violence. In some cases, they are also being attacked as collaborators. Widespread looting has already begun, and sources are saying that General Adevoso, commander of the Armed Forces of the Philippines, is about to declare martial law. Needless to say, it's pure pandemonium in downtown Manila."

For Joseph, this had been a statement of the obvious. The day was hot, he was sweating, and he pedaled a bike he found on the side of the road. When he arrived at the checkpoint where his father had been captured, he wasn't sure where to start looking for him, but this seemed as good a place as any.

101930HOCT2033 (7:30 p.m. local time, October 10, 2033) 1st ARM Battalion Assault Command Post, Manila, The Philippines

"Well, I have some good news and some bad news," Lieutenant Colonel Gammon said as he tried to conceal his personal disappointment in the information he was about to deliver to his assembled commanders and staff.

"Most importantly, let me remind you that we have made history. In less than thirty days, you've been part of a brigade task force that landed, advanced over 200 kilometers, fought in several major engagements—including fighting in a megacity—with new weapons, and suffered only forty-seven killed and 183 wounded. We can also be thankful that Captain Doss is in the latter category. All of this is quite a remarkable achievement by any estimation."

Gammon didn't mention the 8,700 Filipino military casualties or that the Filipino authorities were still counting civilian dead. The total was 12,700 and still rising.

"You have every right to be proud of your achievement." He paused and then dropped the hammer. "But we have to finish the job. As we all know, war is a means to a political end-state, and that has not yet been achieved. We just got new orders. We will not be home by Christmas."

It was like the air suddenly left the room. Gammon noticed the absolute silence as everyone stared at him.

"We experienced a rapid defeat of the enemy, and…well…the post-conflict planning wasn't exactly what it should have been. The Davila government is struggling, and our Psyop, Civil Affairs, Military Police, and Engineer support won't start arriving in force until the end of next week. We don't even have a good estimate of when the interagency folks will be able to get here. Until then, we're it. Plan on being here through at least January. More to follow."

It was a grievous blow to morale, and Buck knew it. As he left the room, he thought to himself, *The only thing we learn from history is that we don't learn from it.*

Epilogue

7.1

121130HOCT2033 (11:30 a.m. local time, October 12, 2033)
1st ARM Brigade Command Post, Manila, The Philippines

Colonel McClellan sat across from General Viale in the cramped work area of his command post.

"So, explain this to me again," asked Viale. "Why did the Chinese crumble so quickly in the end?"

"Sir, we—in the royal, broad alliance sense—outfought them. And one of the main reasons we were able to do that was because our AI was better than theirs."

"You're saying part of the reason we won was that Saga kicked DIYA's ass?"

"Pretty much, sir."

"Okay, explain."

"Sir, there were three major factors. First, Saga was designed from the outset as an open architecture system, almost like a smartphone that allows updates and apps. No one was allowed to use proprietary software or hardware. In the old days, we had to have a program just to get all the programs to be able to talk to each other. This new approach revolutionized the integration of sensors, intelligence, fires, effects cyber, media, and maneuver in one place."

"All right, go on."

"The second thing was that Saga made recommendations based purely on probability of success, minimizing loss of life, and maximizing efficiency. It made recommendations and, when allowed, took actions based on outcomes alone. Like when she flipped on the electronic emissions at 1st battalion's Admin Log and Ops Center as a huge decoy, and later when she set up the Filipino troops to essentially bait the T100s into entering the kill box. It was necessary to win with the smallest net loss of life."

Viale seemed uncomfortable with this. "Takes the humanity out of it. We can't outsource morality. That's the one thing AI can't figure out."

"That's correct, sir. Which is why having humans close in and controlling the chaos is still essential. Centaur teaming between man and machine is tricky. Too much 'man in the loop,' and we fail to reap the benefits of AI systems at the tactical combat level. Go too far in removing humans from the loop, and we can lose the judgment components that machines just can't do, and end up with potentially unexpected and undesired consequences. We hit it about right. The Chinese removed themselves too much from the fight and really lost control in the end."

Viale considered this for a moment. "You said there was a third factor."

"Roger sir, and this was probably the most important part. Saga was easier to train and was able to learn faster than DIYA at the macro level. We could disseminate it to the force in real time. It was almost like an app update. We still don't fully understand how machine learning works, and despite our best efforts, AI systems still have a hard time explaining how they get to their conclusions. It's still tough to check their math."

"That explains a lot."

"Every drone that was shot down, every engagement, and every scanner sweep and missile strike by the enemy was analyzed. Looking back, this explained why their strikes became less and less effective. We simply became harder to hit once Saga began to understand DIYA's targeting protocols and could issue better daily movement commands."

"But I suppose there was some trial and error with this. Not everyone was so lucky," said Viale, referring to the strike that killed his original Chief of Staff.

"True, but we have to think in terms of net loss of life. In the end, Saga was able to fool the Chinese and get them out of position. We destroyed their mobile forces with light human casualties to our force and at the cost of only thirteen Razorbacks and two HOMRRs."

"Wow…well, thank you, Colonel, nothing further."

McClellan left, intent on making a quick call to his wife, who had finally calmed down after their last discussion. *Perhaps this one will go better,* he thought as he walked out into the evening heat.

Viale was quiet. That was a lot to take in. *The pace of technological change is only accelerating. I hope I can keep up.*

7.2

090800RNOV2033 (8:00 a.m. local time, November 9, 2033) Walter Reed National Military Medical Center, Bethesda, Maryland

The America Building housed several departments, one of which was the Department of Orthopedic Surgery. Stacy slowly regained consciousness in the recovery room and, once fully awake, was wheeled to her hospital room where she would stay for two more days before being discharged, again. She looked up as she rolled past a sign that read "Amputee Care."

She felt her eyes water slightly and then shook the self-pity from her mind. *Got so much to be thankful for. This is waaaaay better than when I woke up last time in the Mobile Field Hospital,* she reminded herself. *A Traumatic Brain Injury, or TBI, a tourniquet on my arm, which hurt like a bitch, and a big poofy mass of quick-clotting foam and bandages where my left boob used to be. Worst birthday ever!*

The wheelchair moved smoothly along the floor, and she saw a few other amputees along the way to her room. She recognized one and called out, "Hey, John!"

He didn't hear her, but that wasn't his fault, she remembered. They had been in physical therapy together, and his hearing was pretty much shot. Noting his situation, she had asked him face-to-face, "What's the hardest thing now?"

As the fog of her anesthesia continued to lift, she remembered his response. "Having to learn to do everything—and I mean everything—all over again. You have to learn how to get dressed, feed yourself, drive, and go to the bathroom." Then he added with a grin, "And when it comes to the last part, I'm sure glad we've progressed from hooks."

With a slight sense of sympathy in his voice, John went on. "The biggest danger is feeling sorry for yourself. You lose some of your freedom and everything's harder. Some lose their way, totally tragic."

Stacy remembered thinking he seemed pretty upbeat for a guy with no legs—or, more correctly, not his original ones.

The orderly pushing Stacy's wheelchair turned a corner and then entered the room where her parents and brother, David, were waiting. While this had been a less exciting surgery than the first few, their presence was always reassuring. They had become regulars at the Fisher House, and Stacy always welcomed their help in what was the beginning of a long road to normalcy.

Looking at her bandaged stump, her eyes welled up again briefly as the sight hammered home, with a certain degree of finality, the permanence of the situation.

"How are you, honey?" Shelly said with the concern only mothers can transmit.

"Fine, Mom, just hurts a little. Still having phantom pains where my hand was."

John touched her on the forehead with tears in his eyes. "You're a tough chick, always have been."

David came up and, after some small talk, showed her a nice bouquet of flowers in the corner. Stacy loved flowers of all types and found that their beauty perfectly matched their transience. It was to her a reminder to always enjoy the moment.

"Thanks, Mom and Dad," she said, sounding tired.

"For what?" asked her mom.

"Those."

"Those aren't from us. They came from someone by the name of...Mitchell, Marshall, Guinness, just a second..." Shelly picked up the card and tried to act as if she was reading it for the first time. "McGinnis. Mike McGinnis. Do you know him? The name sounds familiar from somewhere. Would you like me to read it to you?"

Stacy smiled faintly at the note and her mom's clever plan to nose her way into Stacy's social life. *What harm can it do?* Stacy figured and answered, "Sure, Mom."

She had been in mostly regular contact with the battalion leadership and her friends, but an old-fashioned paper note was unusual, even if it was imaged in the Philippines and printed here.

Delighted, Shelly began to read.

"Dear Stacy,

Everyone in the battalion sends their greetings, especially Major Bennett, who took your wounding especially hard. Believe it or not, I think she actually likes you. As you probably heard, we're going to be tied up with stability operations for a while, and though we won't be home for Christmas, at least we don't have to move twice a day now. This has led to more sleep and poker for all of us, with the added benefit of some time to think.

I owe you a debt of gratitude that you may not remember, or probably even know about. When I was eleven, I was a punk with lots of attitude. My parents tried everything to temper my lack of self-control and discipline. In desperation, they finally enrolled me in jiujitsu. One day I made the silly mistake of running my mouth to a girl with a brown ponytail. I was annoyed that I had to spar with her and figured it would be over quickly. It was, but not in the way that I'd expected. Despite my utter humiliation, I was awed by your focus and tenacity. I realized I wanted that for my life. That day became a turning point, and I thank you for it.

On many days since then, I wondered what had become of you and nearly fell over when you showed up in the battalion. You were the real deal and had grown far more beautiful than I could have imagined. I was, however, greatly dismayed when I saw the engagement ring on your finger, and I figured your fiancé would have to be equally impressive…"

Stacy was lucid enough to think, *Yeah, not so much, as it turns out.*

"…and so I figured it was best to keep a low profile. Since then, a lot has changed, and now that I've finally worked up the nerve, I wanted to ask you out on a real date. The bad cup of coffee that one time at the command post didn't really count. After we redeploy, I plan to take leave and visit my parents in Annapolis and would like to invite you to dinner if you're interested.

Best regards,
Mike

P.S. The betting pool here is 5:1 against me, so if you say yes, I'll make enough money to pay for a really nice dinner.

P.P.S And a Titanium exhaust for my Ducati. No pressure, just sayin'."

7.3

170700TFEB2034 (7:00 a.m. local time, February 17, 2034)
Gammon Home, Fort Bliss, Texas

The hurricane of paper kicked up by the Gammon kids was a sight to behold. Buck had just gotten back the week before, and the family had decided to celebrate a delayed Christmas. One thing they had learned was that redeployments never came on time.

Buck and Julia watched their three kids tear through the mound of presents. Paper was everywhere, and their laughter was a fleeting reminder of the joys of family.

"Too bad they're only young once," Buck said to Julia as he reached over and handed her a thin 8x11 box. "A final present for you, my dear."

"Okay…" she responded with a slightly inquisitive tone. When she opened the box, she found inside a simple handwritten note from Buck.

> "My dearest Julia,
> It's been a tough road and you've done more for our family than I could ever have hoped or expected when we got married. It's been almost seventeen years, and for large portions of that time, you've been virtually a single mom. The frequent moves

have also prevented you from pursuing your career, which I want you to succeed in because when I retire, you can be my sugar momma."

Julia looked over at him and gave him "the look" that let him know his attempt at humor had fallen flat.

"For all those reasons, I'm going to request a staff job for my next assignment and will submit my retirement paperwork as soon as I'm eligible.
As much as I love the Army, I still love you and the kids more.

Your devoted husband,
Buck"

Julia took a deep breath, gave him a big hug and kiss, and then softly said, "Thank you."
She then went quiet for a few moments. Buck had no idea what she was thinking and decided not to ask for the time being. He just enjoyed the moment, a nice cup of real coffee, and watching the kids playing with their new toys.
Julia tapped him on the shoulder, took his hand in hers, and looked intently at him. "Buck, that wouldn't be right for us to go down that path for a lot of reasons. Look at our kids—they're happy and healthy, and by moving around and growing up in schools with a lot of other military kids from all walks of life, they're growing up color blind. The three years in Poland was a cultural experience they'll never forget.
"The friends we've made, the hard times and the good times—I wouldn't trade them for anything. Give my fellow

battle-hardened Army wives on our street a mule and forty acres, and well, we'd be called a commune. Plus, you're really good at this. You'd be utterly miserable doing anything else, and with you moping around, you'd be less fun to live with. I married you for better or worse, so let's see where this goes."

7.4

140800RMAR2034 (8:00 a.m. local time, March 14, 2033) Anniston Army Depot, Anniston, Alabama

"Pretty damn impressive."

The man was admiring the twenty-seven hand-painted rings on the HOMRR's barrel. He noticed the mismatched external parts, the paint and scorch marks, and concluded that the vehicle had been repaired several times before.

"I saw him in the tech bulletins. I think he was even in the news. Highest-scoring HOMRR so far," he added in a light Southern drawl.

A second tech, the first man's boss, spoke up. "Hey, we can admire him later. We need to get this show on the road. We have a schedule to keep."

With that, Homer started down the line of the rebuild process. In two months, he would look like he did when he first rolled off the assembly line in Lima, Ohio, except that once he was finished with the rebuild, he would have several new upgrades and, more importantly, be even smarter than when he arrived.

7.5

311500HNOV2034 (3:00 p.m. local time, March 31, 2034)
National Military Command Center, Beijing, China

"Major General Deng, do you have anything else to add to your testimony?" asked the old general, squinting at Deng through his thick glasses.

"No, sir, I have given a full and complete account of the activities of that traitor Yu and all our efforts to stop him."

The inquisitor looked at him closely. "Rather convenient that only you and your closest associates escaped."

"Fortuitous, yes. My condolences to the families of the servicemen and women on the island who died from the American biological agent after being captured."

The old general didn't seem convinced but, lacking hard evidence to the contrary, had to end the proceedings. "You are dismissed," he said curtly.

Deng wheeled about and departed the courtroom. He left the building, walked to the street corner, hailed a driverless cab, and got in. After darkening the windows, he changed out of his uniform into unremarkable civilian attire. He travelled to the far side of town, got out at a nondescript bar and walked to a booth.

It took him a moment to recognize Lieutenant Gencral Wei when he arrived, as he was also not in uniform. Wei joined him in the booth, an automated waitress soon arrived, and both ordered Yanjing beer.

"So, are the loose ends tied up?" asked Wei.

"Yes, sir, they are. All of them. The final Court of Inquiry concluded today," replied Deng.

"Very well then, we will proceed tomorrow. Good thing we are playing the long game, eh?"

"A good thing indeed."

The men clinked their bottles in a toast and each took a drink.

"Are they ready?" asked Wei.

"Almost, sir, almost."

THE END

Warbot 2.0: White Sun Rising
Coming by Summer 2023

Ten Real-Life Heroes

While the characters in this book exist only in our minds, we live in a time in which the term "hero" has often been devalued and lost its meaning. In a culture that is often self-absorbed and frequently cynical about the possibility of altruistic motives and true honor, we still occasionally see individuals who display incredible character and courage during times of extreme danger. In so doing, they leave an example to us of the better angels of our nature. The names of many of the characters in this book were drawn from these men and women, most of whom neither achieved, nor even wanted, the fame that came with their actions. Please note that no character in this book is specifically intended to represent in any way the below individuals; listing them is simply an attempt to honor them for what they have done and to encourage readers to see what true heroism looks like.

In approximate order of appearance:

Corporal (CPL) Desmond Doss, U.S. Army (USA) – Congressional Medal of Honor (CMoH), April 29–May 21, 1945, Okinawa. CPL Doss earned the CMoH for numerous actions over a three-week period, the most notable of which occurred when he personally saved seventy-five lives on Hacksaw Ridge. He also earned a Bronze Star for Valor for his heroism during the fighting on Guam. He was the first conscientious objector to earn the CMoH.

Specialist Ross A. McGinnis, USA – CMoH, Killed in Action (KIA) December 4, 2006, Adhamiyah, Northeast Baghdad, Iraq. While he was serving as an M2 .50-Caliber Machine Gunner on a HMMVWV (Humvee) during a patrol in Northeast Baghdad, an insurgent threw a grenade into the vehicle. McGinnis shouted a warning to the four other occupants and prepared to jump to safety. When he realized that the other four would not get out in time, he threw his body against the grenade to protect them. McGinnis was killed instantly, but all four other occupants survived the blast.

Staff Sergeant (SSG) Archer T. Gammon, USA – CMoH, KIA January 11, 1945, Belgium. After he single-handedly knocked out a German machine-gun nest, SSG Gammon's platoon moved forward into cover but was then suddenly attacked by German forces that included a King Tiger tank. Without regard for his personal safety, Gammon moved forward, killed six of the supporting infantry, and caused the tank to begin to withdraw. While withdrawing, the tank fired an 88mm main gun round that killed Gammon instantly.

Colonel Paul Gruninger, Swiss Police – Righteous Among the Nations (RATN), 1938, St. Gallen, Switzerland. Gruninger was the Swiss Police commander of St. Gallen, a border region between Austria and Switzerland. After the 1938 Anschluss, the Swiss government closed its border to fleeing Austrian Jews. Gruninger ignored the order, falsified papers, and allowed between 2,000 and 3,000 Jews to enter Switzerland. After his actions were discovered by Swiss authorities, he was tried, convicted, and dismissed from service with the loss of all pension benefits. He struggled to make a living for the rest of his life, but even at the end, he never regretted his actions.

Second Lieutenant (2LT) Robert M. Viale, USA – CMoH, KIA February 5, 1945, Manila, Philippines. While leading his platoon through ferocious urban fighting in Manila, 2LT Viale personally led a successful assault on three enemy pillboxes. Despite being wounded, he continued to lead the advance against another enemy emplacement. He and his troops entered a building that they found to be occupied by civilians caught up in the fighting. While attempting to throw a grenade, his wounds caused him to drop it in the room with his men. He recovered the grenade, and with no safe way to dispose of it quickly, he turned into the wall and deliberately bent over the grenade with his body to shield those around him from injury or death. He died within minutes of the blast.

Private First Class (PFC) Milton L. Olive, USA – CMoH, KIA October 22, 1965, Republic of Vietnam. While PFC Olive and four of his fellow paratroopers were pursuing Viet Cong insurgents, one of the insurgents threw a grenade into the midst of them. With only seconds to act, PFC Olive reached for the grenade, pulled it to himself, and sacrificed his body to absorb the blast. He was eighteen years old at the time of his death.

First Lieutenant (1LT) Mary Louise Hawkins, USA – Distinguished Flying Cross, September 24, 1944, Bellona Island, South Pacific. 1LT Hawkins was a flight evacuation nurse on a C-47 evacuating twenty-four wounded patients from the fighting on Palau, when their aircraft had to make a forced landing on Bellona Island. During the crash landing, a piece of a propeller ripped through the fuselage and tore open one Marine's trachea. Without adequate trauma supplies, she improvised with various items, including the inflation tube from a life preserver, and kept that Marine and all her other patients alive until help arrived nineteen hours later.

Chief Bugler Ferdinand F. Rohm, USA – Medal of Honor, August 25, 1864, Reams Station, Virginia. As his unit fell back under enemy fire, Regimental Commander Colonel Beaver was struck in the leg by a musket ball and fell from his horse. Severely wounded, he was unable to move and at imminent risk of capture by the advancing Confederate forces. Seeing the situation and with complete disregard for his personal safety, Rohm grabbed a horse and went back for Colonel Beaver. He rode under constant fire in front of the advancing Confederate forces, hoisted the colonel onto the horse, and successfully returned him to friendly lines. Colonel Beaver went on to serve as the governor of Pennsylvania.

1LT (Chaplain) Alexander D. Goode, USA – Distinguished Service Cross (DSC), KIA February 3, 1943, Labrador Sea. The German submarine *U-223* torpedoed the *USS Dorsetshire* with over 900 soldiers bound for England. In the twenty-seven minutes before the boat sank, panic ensued. Goode, a Jewish rabbi, and fellow chaplains George L. Fox, a Methodist minister, Clark V. Poling, a Reformed Church in America minister, and John P. Washington, a Catholic priest, helped organize the terrified soldiers and get them to the undamaged lifeboats. When the life jackets ran out, each of the four men gave up his own to another soldier. Once the remaining lifeboats had made it away, the men then prayed with those who could not escape. The four men were last seen standing on the deck of the sinking ship, their arms linked in prayer.

The Garbuliński Family, RATN – Father and son executed April 4, 1944, Czermna, Poland. The Garbuliński family hid and took care of a Jewish mother and her two children in their granary in occupied Poland. When the German police were tipped off by villagers, they raided the granary, killed all three Jews on the spot, and arrested Andrzej and his son, Władysław. Both were later killed in prison.

Recommended for Further Reading

1. **Ghost Fleet** by P.W. Singer and August Cole. New York, Mariner Books, 2016.
2. **China's Vision of Victory** by Jonathan D. Ward. Washington, D.C, The Atlas Publishing and Media Company LLC, 2019.
3. **War in 140 Characters** by David Patrikarakos. New York, Basic Books, 2017.
4. **On China** by Henry Kissinger. New York, Penguin Books, 2012.
5. **Wired for War** by P.W. Singer. New York, Penguin Books, 2009.
6. **Starship Troopers** by Robert A. Heinlein. New York, Ace Books, 1987.
7. **Army of None** by Paul Scharre. New York, W. W. Norton & Company, 2019.
8. **1984** by George Orwell. New York, Berkley Books, 1983.
9. **Burn In** by P.W. Singer and August Cole. New York, Houghton Mifflin Harcourt, 2020.
10. **The Art of War: The New Illustrated Edition (The Art of Wisdom)** by Sun Tsu, translated by Samuel B. Griffith. Toronto, Canada, Duncan Baird Publishers, 2012.

About the Author

Colonel Brian M. Michelson, U.S. Army, Retired

Over the course of his career, Col. Michelson has served in a number of diverse units including XVIII Airborne Corps, the 101st Airborne Division (Air Assault), the 97th Civil Affairs Battalion (Airborne), United States Special Operations Command (USSOCOM), and Joint Special Operations Command (JSOC). His military duties have taken him to numerous overseas locations including Laos, the Philippines, Indonesia, Cambodia, Bangladesh, the Maldives, Sri Lanka, the Republic of Korea, Thailand, Panama, Iraq, and Afghanistan.

Colonel Michelson holds a Bachelor of Science degree from West Point, a Master of Business Administration from Webster University, and a Master of Strategic Studies from the United States Army War College. He served as a Senior Fellow at the Atlantic Council in Washington, D.C., and retired from the Army in 2019.

Facebook: https://www.facebook.com/BrianMichelson Author
Website: https://brianmichelson.com/
Email: brian.michelson.author@gmail.com

Additional writings:

Warbot Ethics: A Framework for Autonomy and Accountability
18 May 2017; The Strategy Bridge
https://thestrategybridge.org/the-bridge/2017/5/18/warbot-ethics-a-framework-for-autonomy-and-accountability

Rapid improvements in robotic technologies are presenting both civilian policy makers and military leaders with uncomfortable ethical choices. Emerging artificial intelligence (AI) technologies offer impressive gains in military effectiveness, yet how do we balance their use with accountability for inevitable errors?

Blitzkrieg Redux: The Coming Warbot Revolution
28 February 2017; The Strategy Bridge
https://thestrategybridge.org/the-bridge/2017/2/28/blitzkrieg-redux-the-coming-warbot-revolution

Using the historical lens of the blitzkrieg and the remarkable way that the Germans integrated the common technologies of the era, two key trends can help inform our concept of future warfare and our ability to wage it: the rise of lethal warbots as primary combatants and adapting current leadership methods to a future era of manned–unmanned, or Centaur, teaming.

Strategic Landpower in the 21st Century:
A Conceptual Framework
March 2015; The Institute of Land Warfare
https://www.ausa.org/sites/default/files/LPE-15-1-Strategic-Landpower-in-the-21st-Century-A-Conceptual-Framework.pdf

About the Publisher

This book is published by War Planet Press, an imprint of the Ethan Ellenberg Literary Agency.
https://ethanellenberg.com
Email: agent@ethanellenberg.com